The Passage

A Novel

By

Steven Wilkens

Copyright© 2000 by Steven Wilkens

All rights reserved. No part of this book shall be reproduced or transmitted in any form or by any means, electronic, mechanical, magnetic, photographic including photocopying, recording or by any information storage and retrieval system, without prior written permission of the author.

No patent liability is assumed with respect to the use of the information contained herein. Although every precaution has been taken in the preparation of this book, the publisher and the author assume no responsibility for errors or omissions. Neither is any liability assumed for damages resulting from the use of the information contained herein.

This is a work of fiction. Names, characters, places, and incidents are either a product of the author's imagination or used fictitiously. Any resemblance to actual people, living or dead, places, or events is entirely coincidental.

ISBN - 9798605959113

This Book is dedicated to:

Christine Nichol and Brittany Ann
I couldn't imagine my life without these two Lovely ladies.

A special Thank you to Edna Marsh for helping me get the manuscript to this stage. And as always a special thanks to Miss Becky and my parents for their unending support.

A very special thank-you to Vincent H. Gaddis for his inspiring work "Invisible Horizons" 1965, Chilton Book Co. Radnor, Pa. His account of the OCTAVIUS (p104-108) was the inspiration for this book.

Cover Illustration: Pixabay.com
Author photo: Gordon Nash

Other titles by Steven Wilkens

TRANSPORT

ESSENCE OF COURAGE

HARVEST MOON

NANA'S WILLOW

REDEMPTION

THE LOST TRIBE

THE SWORD OF DAVID

COINCIDENTAL JOURNEY

THE TRACTOR

CHARLES' STORY

TATTOOED ANGELS

THE LONG HOT SUMMER

OPERATION PARADOX

Happy Oscar, the model A

Having My Say

"It seemed as though the genius of the place had been roused at finding that we had nearly slipped through his fingers, and had come down upon us with tenfold fury..."

Richard H. Dana Jr.
Two Years Before The Mast
Published in 1840

Chapter 1
Plymouth, England
September 1761

The afternoon sun was unusually hot for this time of year, baking the weathered, light gray planks of the dock dry. Its brilliant rays bounced off the oily water of the harbor. Christopher Jamison could feel the sweat running down his back and soaking his sleeveless shirt. Making his muscular arms glisten as he made his way along the waterfront. At eighteen he was a tall strapping young man. He was well tanned from almost seven years at sea on one ship or another. His sandy hair was plastered to his neck by the sweat. His bright blue eyes focused on the bits of flotsam bobbing in the filthy harbor. The flotsam consisted of scales and bits of fins of cleaned fish and other rubbish thrown overboard by ships either just in or preparing for sea.

Christopher felt a kinship to the rubbish, discarded and unwanted. He had gone to sea at an early age as a cabin boy. The first step in many toward becoming a sailor. For him, there had been only two choices. Working the mines as his father had done, and his father before him, or go to sea. He had chosen the sea and it had been a good choice.

He loved the sea and was proud of the fact that he was a very good Able-Bodied seaman, or AB. That, however, was before the LEAF RIVER. He had known that the LEAF RIVER was an old ship when he had signed on. Later he was to discover that she was even older than he had imagined. Despite the ship's age, the voyage was billed as only a month or two and the promise of a good wage was a strong enticement. Even the LEAF RIVER, he had thought at the time, beat working in the mines.

His stern but loving father was the Vicar of a small and very poor parish. His work for God would be rewarded in the next life. It certainly had not been in this one. Needing to support his family, his father had taken work outside of the church. Since the only work to be had in that area was in the mines, a miner he became. It was hard and dirty work, work that Christopher had wanted no part of.

Instead Christopher went to sea, and usually he truly loved being a sailor. He loved the exotic ports, the brilliant, beautiful sunrises that one could only experience at sea. He loved the feel of the deck as the ship rode the waves. Of course, sailing had its detractors as well, the bad food, the stale water, the terrifying struggle when nature went berserk.

Christopher weighed the good against the bad and the good had always won. A sailor he was and a sailor he would always be, or so he had thought. That was until fate played its hand nearly three weeks ago in the North Sea. That single event had Christopher wondering if God was trying to speak to him as his father had said God once spoke to him. The event had left Christopher scared and penniless. He was hungry, tired and dirty, and had no means by which to remedy any of those things. He could always go home and work in the 'pit', as the mine was called. The mine's owners were always hiring as the work was deadly, and always laying claim to those so employed.

That reason, as much as any other made Christopher resist going home. His only viable choice was to find another ship to sign on. Of course, if he could find one that would have him. Word of the LEAF RIVER had spread quickly. Everyone seemed to know all there was to the whole sorted affair. Most of the better ships were steering clear of anyone that had anything to do with the LEAF RIVER. That only left the older, less sound vessels to try for, and he had to do something. Not all the older ships were in as sorry a state as the LEAF RIVER had been.

The Master had been a tyrant, always screaming and ready to use the whip. That too, was not always the case, although it was indeed the case often enough. If had been only a two-month voyage up the continent, three ports of call and then back home, things would not have been so bad. In hindsight, he now realized why the Master had offered such wages, it was his only means of securing a crew. Christopher should have paid heed to the fact that only the Mate had sailed with that Master before. That alone should have said volumes about the ship, the Master, or both.

Straight off, things started to happen that changed the vessel's itinerary. Most, Christopher now realized was intentional. The Master had been a clever man, the wage was for the voyage, however long it might be. Not one shilling paid until the ship returned to her homeport. Suddenly, the great pay became a slave wage. Then, that terrible night when the savage sea laid claim to the ship. Only a handful of sailors made it off the dying ship into the longboat. Two of which were the Master and the Mate. Christopher had not been one of them. He was below deck with the off watch when the end came. Since the pinnace was too rotted to even bother lowering, the Master had lowered the longboat and allowed those on that watch to escape. Not once did he or anyone else try to raise the alarm for the others below deck.

Luckily, as the ship started to founder by the head, the doors to the cupboard in the galley swung open and discharged the entire complement of pans to the deck. The racket had most of those below deck out of their berths in seconds. The moment Christopher and the others had tried to stand, they realized that things were not right and made for the deck.

By this time the longboat had just reached the water and those in it were trying to free the falls. It was clear to those left behind what had been attempted. Many of the ones that had been left to die with the ship quickly slid down the falls or jumped into the water next to the boat. Seeing no choice in the matter, Christopher jumped overboard. Before he could swim toward the longboat in the cold water a mutiny had taken place. The Master, Mate, and the others that had been in the boat were now in the water. Most of them floating face down and drifting away in the angry sea. Few if any had the chance to drown, a knife or an oar across the head had been the retribution of those left behind.

Christopher realized that he could not survive in the water but was afraid of approaching the boat now filled with an angry mod of killers. He had nearly concluded that he would stand a better change in the water than trying for the only boat when one of those now in the boat called to him and offered him a place.

It had taken three days for them to reach land, and then another two weeks for Christopher to find a ship headed for England that would allow him to work for his passage home. Luckily, this ship was bound for Plymouth, his home port. Since the Master of the LEAF RIVER had been killed, whether rightly or wrongly, there would be no pay awaiting his return. The ship he had worked his passage on was little better than the LEAF RIVER, and the Master only a small improvement. All these things made Christopher take stock of his chosen profession. He felt a deep fear within about ever going to sea again. His meager savings and well-worn gear had gone down with the LEAF RIVER, leaving him with nothing but the clothes on his back.

Captain Richard Weegens strode confidently down the street toward the docks. His much younger and beautiful wife walked by his side, her slender arm laced in the crook of his. To her side and slightly behind them their young son followed along with a stick to hit and poke at anything that caught his fancy. The family looked the picture of British society. Seeing them, one would have thought them on their way to visit friends, family, or someone important. They were headed down to the Captain's ship. Their belongings had already been sent ahead and was at that moment being loaded onto the ship.

Captain Weegens was not one to relish having a woman aboard his ship, his wife or any other. Loose talk and rumors about his Sarah, spread by old busy bodies, who he usually wrote off as knowing little or nothing of the truth, made him reconsider. The last trip had lasted two years, during which time he knew that Sarah's father and older brothers had paid her visits, as had his own brother. Regardless, the gossipers had seen men calling on her while he was known to be at sea and the rumors went wild. Whether or not there had been other men, he didn't know and was not about to ask her. The thought had occurred to him and was at present occupying his mind as they reached the pier and turned toward the ship.

As Christopher shuffled along the dock struggling with the internal demons and watching the floating debris, he didn't notice the handsome couple turn onto the dock right in front of him. The collision wasn't hard, but it sent Mrs. Weegens toppling over a pile of lines lying on the dock and pushed the Captain into several metal buckets half filled with fish scales and guts. The buckets spilled over and coated the dock with a slippery slime that caused the Captain to lose his footing and crash down into the mess.

Christopher's heart stopped in his throat. Up and down the dock people started laughing and shouting. Mrs. Weegens had gone over the pile of lines at an awkward angle which made her roll as she went down. She landed on her backside with her feet nearly straight up in the air. Her fancy dress rained down upon her head as her petticoat legs flayed about. The Captain went face first into the slime and was just starting to turn himself over.

Christopher finally came to his senses and went first to help the lady. As he tried to lend a hand, he accidently caught hold of her petticoat and the frail under-thing ripped wide open exposing a fair-skinned and very shapely leg. He quickly let go of the petticoat and reached for the dress and tried to gently pull it down to cover her legs. The lady was struggling too hard for that to succeed and the dress also tore. Finally, her head appeared through the rent in the fabric and he was able to grab a slender hand and haul her to her feet. By this time the Captain had struggled to his feet. His dark pants and uniform jacket were covered in fish scales and blood. He brushed himself off and turned toward the young man holding his wife in her tattered clothing.

"Young man, you have done quite enough. Now, please un-hand my wife."

"I'm very sorry, Sir." Christopher stammered as he quickly let go of the woman's arm. "Please forgive me. I wasn't watching where I was going. I am very sorry."

Captain Weegens eyed him for a moment, deciding if the lad was sincere. "What's done is done. Just watch your step in the future. For your sake and the welfare of others." With that the Captain took his wife's hand and led her down the dock.

Christopher watched them go and then sat down on the pile of lines. He should be paying attention to finding a berth, not watching floating rubbish and running people over. At the moment, he didn't need any more enemies.

"Christopher!" A voice called out to him. "Christopher Jamison!" It was a voice that Christopher recognized at once. The voice belonged to his friend George Sutherland. Christopher looked up and spotted George waving and running toward him between the stacks of supplies and cargo lining the dock. George was about the same age as Christopher, tall and lean. He had hazel green eyes and bright red hair, that never appeared to have seen the effects of running a brush through it. That wild hair was now bouncing up and down as George ran toward him.

George was working one of the local fishing boats, or at least he had been the last time Christopher had seen him. He was an easy one to like, always smiling, always polite, always willing to lend a hand. In fact, the only flaw, if one could call it that, was a nervous twitch in his left eye, which made people think he was winking at them. It was something that didn't always play well in the rough and tumble pubs of the waterfront. George hailed from London, where he had grown up in an orphanage, having never known his father or mother. Christopher had always wondered where his kindly spirit had come from. Maybe the harshness of his early life had left George with a keen ability to see things for what they were and the knack for finding the good in any endeavor.

Christopher forced a smile as his friend neared and reached out his hand. "George! You sorry sight you. How have you been?"

"Great!" George took the offered hand with a broad smile. "And you? Where have you been? I heard about the LEAF RIVER foundering. You had me worried."

"It's a long story." Christopher shook his head. "And one I'd just as soon forget."

"Well," George smiled. "You looking for work?"

"They need help on the fishing boats?" Christopher hadn't really wanted to work on the fishing boats, due to the hard labor and awful smell, but it was better than nothing.

"Probably," George replied. "But that isn't what I mean. I got me a new billet. I'm signed on a Cape Horner, the OCTAVIUS. The pay isn't much for that kind of trip, but I've heard that the Master is fair and the ship sound."

Christopher was instantly interested. "You sure about that?"

"I took a look myself when I signed aboard."

"They still looking for help? Maybe they filled their billets already?"

"Maybe," George shrugged. "But it wouldn't hurt to find out" With that he turned around and started guiding Christopher back the way he had come. "You'll like this one." George was saying.

"If it is such a fine ship and Master," Christopher found a flaw in George's logic. "Why are they needing help?"

"I'm sure the usual reasons." George replied as they turned the corner and started down the long pier at the very northern end of the jetty. "These long trips are more than some care to make a second time. There she is!" George pointed to the Brig at the very end of the pier.

The OCTAVIUS was indeed a smart looking ship. Gloss black hull, well tarred masts and yards, all rigging looked taut and in top shape. As they neared the ship, Christopher could see several men working on deck and one mean looking, red-headed man standing at the top of the gangway. The redhead had been watching them come down the pier and waited until they were close in before speaking.

"George, where the bloody hell have you been?"

"Chips sent me into town for extra lines." George replied as he started up the gangway. Christopher stopped at the base of it, which caused George to spin around. "Come on, Christopher. I'll get the Master."

"Permission to come aboard?" Christopher directed his request to the red-headed man.

"What the hell for?" The redhead responded. "Is this one of your fishing buddies?" Before George could answer, the redhead asked another question. "If Chips sent you for line, where is it?"

"It's going to be delivered this afternoon," George answered. "Red, this is Christopher Jamison. Christopher, this is 'ol Red. His bark is worse than his bite. Thank heavens for that!" George was smiling.

"Watch your mouth," Red shot back. "Unless you want to take a swim in the bay."

Christopher hadn't budged from the bottom of the gangway. George motioned for him to come up, but with Red standing there,

Christopher wasn't sure he should. Red finally shrugged. "Suit yourself."

Christopher started up the gangway.

Red turned back to George. "You didn't say what he was doing here?"

"Going to sign on." George replied.

"Sign on?" Red nearly laughed. "We got a full crew. Besides, one of you stinking fishing lads is enough for one trip."

"Oh, Christopher isn't from the fishing boats." George replied. "He's a deep-sea sailor. He was on the LEAF RIVER when she went down."

"He was, was he?" Red turned from George to glare back at Christopher. "Found a way to save your own miserable hide, did you? We don't want you here."

"I do." George shot back. "He needs a billet and he's a damn good sailor!" George had taken about all of Red he could at the moment.

Red was not through yet. Christopher was nearing the top of the gangplank when Red stepped over in front of him, blocking his way to the deck. "Sorry mate, we don't need your kind here. Go look somewhere else."

"I'll be the one that decides that." A strong sounding voice said from somewhere out of Christopher's line of sight. "Send that one to my cabin."

"Aye, aye, Sir." Red sounded defeated, but the look in his eyes showed he was anything but. He moved slightly to the side, giving Christopher just enough room to pass if he turned sideways. Red turned to George. "He's your baggage, you show him to the master's cabin." Red slowly stepped to the side and allowed Christopher to pass, but not without an angry glare.

George led Christopher to the cabin. "Captain Weegens is a good and fair man," he said as he knocked.

"Enter," came the voice of the Master from within the cabin. George opened the hatch and motioned for Christopher to enter. As soon as Christopher was inside the cabin his jaw dropped. He was both stunned and embarrassed. He instantly felt his heart and hopes sink. The man seated at the head of the table was the same man he had knocked over just moments before.

Captain Weegens, a bear of a man with broad shoulders, thick neck, large hands with fat meaty fingers, was seated at the head of a sturdy oak table with a stack of papers before him. He was in shirt sleeves, well groomed and polished. His dark hair was combed straight back exposing a high forehead, dark brown eyes that were deep set under bushy, dark brows. The Captain smiled and motioned for him to come farther into the cabin. "So, we meet again, and so soon."

Barely able to find his voice, Christopher apologized again for his clumsiness. "All is forgotten," Captain Weegens smiled. "As you can see, I clean up, so no permanent harm.

To his right, another polished and proper gentleman was seated. This gentleman appeared to be taller than the Master and much thinner. His demeanor spoke of an education. This gentleman Christopher correctly guessed to be the Mate. In contrast to the master's abundant and exaggerated features, the Mate's were fine and almost sculptured. Bright, blue eyes, thin nose, in perfect proportion to the size and shape of his head.

To the Captain's left sat an older man whose features were at best a potpourri of curiosity. This man's gray hair was long, and shaggy, as was his salt and pepper colored rat's nest of a beard. His wide cheek bones made an honest attempt to straighten severely wrinkled and weathered skin covering what could be seen of the face. His shaggy eyebrows arched in Christopher's direction revealing bright, intelligent, grayish eyes. When he smiled in his direction, Christopher noticed the man had only four teeth. The center two on the bottom jaw, and the two to either side of the center ones on the top jaw. The teeth bypassed each other when he closed his jaws, making him look a bit like a walrus.

George followed Christopher into the cabin and stood at his side.

"Did you get that line?" the old man asked of George.

"Yes sir," George quickly replied. "It'll be brought out this afternoon.

"Very good, Mr. Sutherland." The Master had a gentle voice for a man of his stature. "You are dismissed."

"Aye, aye Sire," George turned and left the cabin.

The Master waited for George to leave before addressing Christopher directly. "Okay lad, what's your name?"

"Christopher Jamison, Sire," he replied.

"Tell us about yourself, Mr. Jamison," the Master asked. "What do you do when you're not bumping around on busy piers?" Christopher flushed, cleared his throat and told them as much as he thought would be of interest, such as what ships he had served on and what experience he had. They quietly listened without any indication of what they thought until he mentioned his last billet aboard the LEAF RIVER.

"Tell us about the loss of the LEAF RIVER," the Master instructed. "And please tell us everything including how you came to survive the wreck."

Christopher didn't reply for a moment. He looked from one man to the next, trying to decide just how he would do that, and if he did, what would they think of a man who took refuse in a boat with killers.

"It's okay Mr. Jamison," the Master seemed to be reading his thoughts. "We already know some of it, and what you say here will go no farther."

If that statement was to make it easier for Christopher to recount the events of that terrible night, it didn't. Sensing the inner struggle, the old man spoke up.

"Don't fret about the three of us lad, jus' say it the way it was." He then offered a chair next to himself, which Christopher slowly seated himself in.

It still took a while for him to get started. He slowly, carefully, started from the time he went off watch and recounted everything as truthfully as he could, right up to the point of his jumping into the water.

"Why wasn't the pinnace lowered?" The mate spoke for the first time.

"It was rotted through."

"Where were the officers at this time?" the Master asked.

"In the longboat along with those of the larboard watch."

"What happened then?" The Master's soft voice was encouraging.

Christopher then told them all he had seen of the struggle for control of the boat. When he finished everyone was quiet. The three men before him sat staring at him in disbelief, or maybe disgust, he wasn't sure.

"Mr. Jamison," the Master finally spoke. "I believe what you have just said. All of it. I put no blame on you, neither does the crown."

Christopher had been looking down at the table to avoid their eyes. On hearing the crown, his head bolted up.

"That's right," the Master smiled. "The LEAF RIVER's Officers and a small number of crew were recovered a couple of days later floating not far from the wreckage field. Several had clearly drowned, others had not."

Christopher sat still, not knowing what he should do. He had no part in their deaths, but he had allowed the killers to save him, and for that he had told no one about the murders.

"Your story agrees with what other survivors have said," the Master went on. "However, if I were you, I'd still give the crown a statement."

Christopher looked back up at the men sitting before him. "How do I go about doing that?" To the men sitting around the table, the lad sounded totally defeated. Captain Weegens studied the young man before him and weighed what he had heard about him. George had spoken very highly of him, as had other Captains that this lad had sailed for, ones that Captain Weegens personally knew. He tried to remember just what it was that Captain Whitwell had said of him. Something about him being a good sailor, honest, hard working, and never complaining. This lad's only flaw, according to Whitwell, was that he was always trying to live up to impossible standards. Standards the lad put upon himself to measure up to his father, a man the lad worshiped. Well, that wasn't a terrible flaw really.

"I will have the constable brought down here so he can get your statement." The Master offered. "In the meantime, you must be looking for a billet?"

"Yes Sire, I am," Christopher answered rather quietly.

"Do you have any gear?" the Mate asked

"No sir," Christopher replied. "Everything I had was lost on the LEAF RIVER."

"Okay Mr. Jamison," the Master smiled for the first time. "Are you aware of where we're going?"

"George mentioned that you were a Cape Honer," Christopher offered.

"Is this the kind of work you seek?" The Master still retained half of that smile

"I've always been interested in the stories told of such voyages," Christopher admitted. "Yes Sire, it is.

"You've got yourself a ticket. I'll see to it that you get a full set of gear. You'll be on the larboard watch, under the Second Mate." The smile was back and as broad as before.

"Aye Sire and thank you."

"You're welcome," the Master said as he rose and offered his hand. "Just sign the ship's articles.

Christopher looked down at the offered paper and noticed that all the signatures were mere marks. Not a man amongst the crew could sign his name. Well, that was about to change; he took the offered quill and penned his name below the numerous marks. Officially he was now Able-Bodied Seaman Christopher Jamison of the brigantine OCTAVIUS.

True to his word, the Master gave Christopher a voucher for a store in town to replace his gear. "It's not charity," the Master had made that clear. "This will come out of your wages." He also set up the interview with the Crown's solicitor regarding the loss of the LEAF RIVER.

It was well after sundown when Christopher finally headed for the foc'sle to find himself a berth aboard his new ship. He had crossed only half the length of the deck when two men moved out of the shadows toward him. The lighting was so poor that they were nearly upon him before he recognized one of the men as the fellow called Red. The other man was somewhat shorter than Red and appeared to be every bit the scoundrel Red was. His clothes were soiled and tattered, the face sweaty and dirty. From less than five feet away, where they finally stopped in front of him, Christopher could smell the odor of sweat and rum on both. The short one stood somewhat in front of Red and was looking Christopher over.

"This the one you told me about?"

"That be the one," Red confirmed.

"Was on the LEAF RIVER, was you?" The short one stepped closer and slowly walked around Christopher. Christopher didn't answer. "I asked you, scallywag, a question!" The short one sneered as he stepped in close to Christopher's back.

"Yes, I was."

"A lot of good men were lost," the short one commented. "And yet you managed to survive. How did that happen?"

"Just lucky I suppose," Christopher offered.

"Lucky, huh?" The short one rubbed his dirty whiskers and then grabbed Christopher's arm, pulling him close; "Well, laddie, your luck seems to have run out. You're on my ship now!

My neck won't be so easy to slit! You won't be getting my place in the boat, I can tell you that!"

"That's not the way it was." Christopher defended himself.

"Wasn't it? They found my brother with his throat slit! Floating face down, drifting with the current! But you survived! You got into the boat!" Then the short one pulled a long-bladed knife and placed it tightly against Christopher's throat. "Your neck wasn't cut, not yet anyway."

"I was pulled from the water by those in the boat," Christopher replied, trying hard not to swallow with that blade against his throat

"Well laddie, I kin assure you that no one here will do that for you this time. So just watch your step." He slowly took the knife away and released his grip on Christopher's arm. "I'm gonna be watching you, day and night. You so much as cross my path the wrong way, it'll be your last. You hear me laddie?"

"I'm hearing you." Christopher did his best to control his fear and anger. He was very careful not to appear as any sort of a threat to this scoundrel, but he would always have to watch his back .

After the two men had moved off toward the gangway, probably heading toward some pub, Christopher took a deep breath to relieve his tension, then started making his way for foc'sle.

"That Liverpool is a bad egg," a voice that sounded vaguely familiar to Christopher said out of the darkness. Christopher turned and stepped to the left of the foc'sle hatch and peered into the darkness. Sitting on an overturned wooden bucket was the man from the master's cabin when he had first come aboard. The man George had called Chips, which meant that he was probably the ship carpenter, since that was what all carpenters seemed to be called. "Jamison isn't it?" Chips asked as Christopher stepped closer.

"Yes sir, Christopher Jamison"

"Well Christopher Jamison," Chips said in a very slow manner. He was either thinking of what to say or didn't really care if he said it or not. "You got yourself a nasty little friend there, in that one."

Chips had his feet propped up on another bucket and was carving on a small piece of wood. He finally looked up at Christopher and smiled with those mangy whiskers and four measly teeth. "Have a seat my young friend," Chips offered as he lifted his feet off the second bucket.

"He's no friend of mine," Christopher shrugged like it didn't matter. "Who is he anyway? Not the Second Mate, I hope.

Chips laughed at that, "Wouldn't make sailing under him much fun would it?"

"No sir, it wouldn't." Christopher nodded. "How much of that did you catch?"

"Nearly all, I would say." Chips replied while turning the piece of wood over and making a few well-placed cuts into the wood, then blowing away the slivers.

"Would you have just watched him cut me?"

"He wouldn't have cut you," Chips smiled, while holding the wood up to the dim light to check his work.

"What makes you so sure of that?"

"Not here in port. If he wants to do you harm, he'll wait until we're well at sea. Fewer problems that way."

"I see," Christopher wasn't overly cheered by the prospects of a long voyage with this lot. "Maybe I should rethink this all."

Chips put his piece of wood down, and then looked at Christopher. "No need to do that, lad. Liverpool ain't much in the way of being a gentleman. Hell, he ain't much in the way of being human. But remember, he just learned that his brother was killed, and you were in the area. That makes you the closest thing he has to something or someone to blame. Of all the things Liverpool is, a killer is not one of them. His being sore at you is a part of his grieving, you see?"

"Maybe," Christopher still wasn't convinced. The little bastard sure seemed like a killer a few minutes ago.

"If it would make you feel any better, I'll keep an eye on him for you, what do you say?" Chips smiled as only he could.

"Yeah, sure," Christopher rose to his feet. "I'm going to get my berth. See you in the morning." Chips nodded and went back to his work.

The foc'sle is the common sailor's home, his haven from the rigors of a sailor's lot. It is located in the forepeak of the ship just below the foc'sle deck, or foredeck, as it is sometimes called, hence the name. The foc'sle is accessible from the main deck through a low hatch, that one must duck below, then down a short, steep companionway. Being in the forepeak of the ship, the foc'sle is triangular. The berths are affixed in tiers to the inside of the hull and line the sides of the foc'sle.

This brig has twenty-eight berths in the foc'sle, eliminating the need for someone to reside in steerage. Down the center of the foc'sle, mounted on either side of the foremast, that sprouted from the keel and rose up through the decks to tower high above the ship itself, were two well-worn wooden planks with slight lipped edges that served as a mess table. The only other protrusion for the men to bang against in a hard blow were two stout wooden stanchions that supported the fore deck above.

The foc'sle was dimly lit by a single whale oil lamp hanging from a hook off the forward mast. Several men were already in their berths and fast asleep. George was nearly so, until he saw Christopher come down the companionway. "Over here," George called to him. "I've saved you a berth, right above mine."

Christopher nodded his thanks and set his new gear down next to George's berth. Each berth was twenty-eight inches wide and six feet long and came with a standard straw mattress covered with a course linen cloth and two woolen blankets. Beneath the mattress was a lid that could be lifted to reveal a small storage space for personal items. Since space aboard a ship was for carrying cargo that generated revenue, personal space was very limited.

Christopher stowed his gear, while first thanking George for getting him this ticket, and then asking him what he knew of a man named Liverpool?

"Liverpool is a sour one," George said. "Even more so lately, why?"

Christopher told him of his run in with him and Red. While he was telling the story, several of the others turned to listen. One of the men, a large man with broad shoulders and thick arms and legs and an almost comically narrow waist stepped over to where Christopher was standing. George introduced him as simply Joseph, from Hamburg. The big German was probably in his mid-thirties, had a well weathered face and kind eyes.

"Ve vant nine trouble," the German spoke with a thick accent. "This Liverpool is nine goot, should not be with us. The old man is a goot one. This is a goot ship. Ve vant nine trouble. I take this berth next to you. John," he motioned to another man. "You take that berth." Pointing to the one on the other side of Christopher's. Then he directed others to certain berths. "Ve vatch you vhile you are in here. Out there," he motioned up the companionway. "Ve will try to vatch out for you too, but you must be very careful. Ve vant nine trouble on this ship."

Christopher was nearly asleep when Liverpool and Red returned to the foc'sle very drunk and very disorderly. As soon as they came down the companionway, they noticed that the others had switched berths on them. Instead of just taking the empty berths, they became belligerent. Liverpool went to the man sleeping in the berth he had once called his and tried to pull him from it. "Get the bloody hell out of my berth, you stinking swine," he spat at the startled man.

Big Joseph stepped up to the short Liverpool and grabbed him by the collar of his blouse and lifted him clean off the deck. "This is my ship," Joseph calmly stated. "I've been sailing her for ten years. So that makes me senior AB. I decide who sleeps vhere. You sleep over there." With that Joseph let the small drunk fall to the floor and pointed to the berth he should take. "Vhen you threaten vone of us, you threaten all of us. There vill be nine trouble on this ship! You understand me?"

Liverpool slowly picked himself up off the deck, nodding as he stepped across the foc'sle and threw himself into the assigned berth. Joseph turned and winked at Christopher before turning in himself. Christopher laid there on his berth staring up at the deck above, feeling much better about his prospects already.

The following morning Christopher awoke at six bells, just as they were about to be called for the morning meal. The galley was located just aft of the foc'sle in the tween deck', an area above the cargo holds and below the main deck, between the foc'sle and the officer's cabins aft. At breakfast George introduced Christopher to William Stratton, Cooky, the ship's cook. Cooky was a rotund fellow with little or no neck, a small round, nearly bald head, and a full beard. He had short heavy arms and hands, and thick short legs that tapered in at the knees as if straining under the weight. Like most of the crew Christopher had met, Cooky was one he liked instantly. He didn't say much, just smiled and nodded a lot. Big Joe, as the rest of the crew called the big German, Christopher learned that morning, told him that Cooky was a cook, dumber than spit, but a great cook.

The morning was a busy one. The balance of the cargo was brought aboard and stowed below securely. At the midday meal all that remained to be done was securing the hatches and towing the ship out into the harbor. The Second Mate, John Bonney, turned out to be a decent fellow, tall and thin like the Mate, with brown eyes and ebony hair. He walked with an air of purpose and knew well this business of sailing. He was kind when possible and a tough master when someone had to be told twice to do something. When the midday meal was called, the Second Mate came up to Christopher and properly introduced himself. "Looks like you know your stuff," he said to Christopher. "Do your job as well as you have this morning, and we'll get along handsomely." Before Christopher could reply, he was gone.

Once the cargo hatches were secured, the boats were lowered and manned. The heavily laden OCTAVIUS was pulled away from the dock ever so slowly. The men in the boats were pulling hard on their oars, first the bow was brought out and around, and then the stern line was let go. Christopher and George sat side by side, Christopher handling the third starboard oar, George the opposite number on the larboard. Red and Liverpool manned the second set of oars which put them directly behind Christopher and George.

The entire time they were pulling the ship around and out into the channel, Liverpool kept up a constant barrage of insults and lewd comments directed at Christopher. He was careful to do so quietly enough to keep the Second Mate from hearing, or so he thought. "Not as easy as slicing a man's throat, is it, preacher boy?" Liverpool jeered.

"Liverpool!" the Second Mate yelled. "If you were as good at being a sailor as you are at running your foul mouth, the brig would be halfway to the colonies now!"

A number of laughs and a couple yeah, shut up" was heard. "All of you shut up and pull!" the Second Mate admonished them. For the balance of the task they worked in silence although twice Liverpool's feet slipped off the cleats in the boats floor and slammed against Christopher's back. Christopher said nothing, biting his lip and trying to control his anger. He was reaching the limit of his patience with this bastard. "Turn the other cheek, my eye," Christopher thought to himself.

Once the brig was nearly centered in the harbor, the anchor was let go and the boats called back. Not a moment was lost. The boats were brought aboard. Securing them could wait. All hands were sent aloft to man the sails, except the six men needed to raise the anchor. As Christopher had come over the wale, he noticed a small lad and the handsome lady he had knocked over yesterday, standing next to the Master.

Within minutes men were standing at the ready on the yards waiting for the orders to loose the sails.

"Hard to starboard," the Mate called.

"Hard to starboard," the Second Mate was standing at the wheel.

"Hove in the anchor!"

"Weighing anchor!" Chips was standing charge over the windlass as the six men began forcing the capstan around.

"Anchor free!" Chips called.

"Stand by!" The Mate yelled for all to hear. Those in the rigging cast off the yardarm gaskets and bunt gaskets. At the end of each yard a man held tightly to the bunt jigger with a turn around the tye in preparation of letting go the sails.

"Already forward?" The Mate called.

"Aye, aye, all ready forward."

"Already main?"

"Aye aye, all ready the main."

"Anchor hoved in," Chips called.

"Loose the sails!" the Mate bellowed as all square sails aboard the ship were suddenly furled. Already they could feel the ship lurching forward. Most of those aloft returned to the deck to overhaul the rigging. Then the topsails and gallants went up, followed by the studding and light sails and finally the jib. In less than five minutes the full spread of sails were up and sent the brig charging out of the harbor, leaving Plymouth in her wake.

Later that day they passed off the southern tip of Ireland. As the sun slowly set before them, Christopher stood quietly on the fantail watching the last glimpse of home fade from view. It would be some time before he laid eyes upon these shores again.

Chapter 2
The Georgia Colony
Late October 1761

      Two weeks into the voyage, the fresh vegetables and fruit had either been used up or were too rotten to consume. Despite this, the spirit of the OCTAVIUS remained higher than any other ship Christopher had sailed with. This he believed was due to the quality of her Officers. Captain Weegens was seldom seen on the deck, except for the times he came out to smoke his pipe. Evidently Mrs. Weegens didn't approve of pipe smoking in the cabin. While he was on deck, the Master rarely spoke to any member of the crew, only the Mate, Second mate, and Chips. This was not that unusual, as on most ships, the Mates handled the crew.

      Mrs. Weegens and the boy were only seen once or twice in the first two weeks. Chips kept mainly to himself, always making or fixing something, like a pulley, a block, or carving on a piece of wood. As for the crew, everyone was kept busy during their watches. The decks were scrubbed, the masts and yards were tarred, lines spliced, or whatever needed doing. Cooky kept their bellies full of the best that could be offered. Each day was started with biscuits and gravy and ended with some form of bread pudding. It was a happy ship. The only exception to the harmony was between Christopher and Liverpool. Liverpool never missed a chance to torment or heckle Christopher, which Christopher never responded to. All his anger and resentment kept building to the point where for the first time in his life, Christopher truly felt hatred toward another human being.

Each of them felt it was something just between them; they were wrong. Not a single member of the crew, Officers included, were unaware of the animosity between them. The Second Mate did his best to keep them apart doing jobs on opposite sides of the ship. When all hands were called aloft, they were sent up different masts.

For her part, the OCTAVIUS was a fast ship, averaging nearly five knots, with the occasional bursts of seven or eight. Four and a half weeks out of England they were nearing the American coast. Christopher had been off watch for over an hour but not yet asleep when he heard the lookout sing out, "Land- Ho!" Everyone aboard, including the master's wife and boy rushed out on deck, peering off into the night in search of what the lookout had seen.

"Where and away?" The Mate called up the forward mast.

"Off the bow directly." The lookout called back. "Low on the horizon."

Christopher couldn't see anything from the deck, so he shot up the rigging for a better look. The night was a bright one, with a new moon and clear heavens. He was almost as high as the crow's nest before he too, spotted the dim sparkle of lights low on the horizon. They were indeed within sight of civilization. The Georgia colony, as Chips proclaimed it to be. Most stayed on deck excited about the prospect of reaching shore soon. Christopher had been at sea often enough to know that they were still three to four hours out, so he decided to return to his berth for much needed sleep. Maybe as early as tomorrow they would have to pull the ship along a pier, and then unload her. Once that was done there would be other cargo to load. Their time at the Georgia colony would be plenty busy, so now was a good time to rest.

As Christopher entered the foc'sle, he surprised Liverpool, who was doing something at Christopher's berth. As soon as Christopher cleared the companionway and shouted at Liverpool, Liverpool spun around with that knife of his banished toward Christopher. For a second no one moved, and then Liverpool advanced. Slowly swinging the knife back and forth, waiting for just the right moment to strike. Christopher slowly backed to the starboard side of the foc'sle, until his back was against the berths. To his left, Christopher noticed that someone had left a boot sitting on top of their berth. He slowly inched his way toward that berth as Liverpool closed. Suddenly in a flurry of motion Christopher went for the boot and Liverpool dove in with the knife. Christopher spun to the left, grabbing the boot and swinging out at arm's length, striking the left side of Liverpool's head. Liverpool had misjudged where Christopher would be and found himself slashing the knife through thin air.

Liverpool was stunned by the turn of events, but only for a second. That was all it took for Christopher to move behind him and slam him, face first into the berths. Liverpool tried to reach around himself and strike Christopher with his knife, but Christopher was able to grab his wrist in his right hand and bang it against the top edge of the berth, knocking the knife to the deck.

Christopher then spun Liverpool around, pinning his back against the berth with his strong left hand while punching him repeatedly with his right fist. In seconds, the fight in Liverpool faded, as did the pent-up frustration in Christopher.

Liverpool's face was covered in blood from a bleeding nose and busted lips. For a moment Christopher stood there holding him fast with his left hand, staring into his eyes.

Liverpool was totally surprised and beaten. The preacher boy had whipped him good and was now standing before him with nostrils flaring. Why he didn't just finish the job, Liverpool couldn't guess. Then Christopher leaned in close, putting his face mere inches from Liverpool's.

"I am truly sorry about the loss of your brother! I had nothing to do with it, whether you believe it or not!" With that Christopher grabbed Liverpool with both hands and bodily tossed him across the foc'-sle into a heap on the deck next to the berths lining the other side. Wiping his hands on his pants, Christopher turned to go back out on deck when he noticed Liverpool's knife lying on the deck. He reached down, picked the knife up and turned back toward Liverpool.

Liverpool's eyes showed the terror of what he thought would be his last moments on earth. Christopher jammed the blade into the wood edge of the berth next to Liverpool's head. He released his grip on the knife, reached down to Liverpool's collar with his right hand, pulling Liverpool into a sitting position. With his left index finger, Christopher pointed to the blade only inches from the side of Liverpool's bloody face. "If you ever so much as pull that thing in my presence again," Christopher's words were tense and filled with anger. "I'll see to it, that you'll be able to ask your brother personally about what really happened on the LEAF RIVER!"

Christopher released his grip on Liverpool, allowing him to slide back down to a prone position. Christopher stood, taking one last look at Liverpool before making for the companionway and the upper deck.

As Christopher emerged from the foc'sle he found the entire ship's complement, less Officers, standing around in a semi-circle, the apex of which was less than ten feet from the foc'sle hatch. It seemed that everyone but Christopher, knew what was coming. Most seemed surprised to see him emerge from the fray. They parted silently and allowed him past. As he stepped through them, he heard someone mention that he didn't have a scratch on him. Making his way aft for some space to himself, Christopher noticed the Officers, the Master and his family, watching the goings on from the quarter deck in silence. Just what they thought of this incident, Christopher thought he would find out soon enough. Out of respect, he nodded in their direction as he climbed the short companionway that led to the fantail. Curiously, they didn't say a thing, most surprising, the Master returned the nod, with a wink and a faint smile.

George soon appeared to make sure his friend was okay. So much for his being alone. "How was it," Christopher wondered out loud, hoping for an answer from George that would make sense. "That everyone seemed to know what was going to happen but me and Liverpool? I know he was surprised, by the way he jumped when he noticed me enter the foc'sle.

"We were all up on deck," George shrugged. "When ol' Red says, "oh shit!" We just turned to see what he was talking about when we noticed that Liverpool wasn't on deck and you were headed into the foc'sle. With all he's been doing lately, we just figured there would be trouble.

"They sure seemed surprised to see me walking out," Christopher noted.

"They sure were," George smiled. "Except me and Chips."

"What do you mean except you and Chips?"

George looked down at his feet, ashamed of what he was about to admit. "I personally won over a pound, and I think Chips did better than that."

"You bet on me?" He couldn't believe it. "What if I would have lost? He had a knife; I would be dead!"

"But you didn't." George beamed. "And it looks like he didn't even lay a hand on you."

"That's hardly the point!" Christopher shot back. "It's not because he didn't try! I got lucky! I came away alive, and you and Chips made a profit!"

"I'll gladly share," George was beginning to feel a little guilty

"I don't want your money/' Christopher shook his head. "I just want some time to myself, okay?"

"Sure," George patted his back, then turned and went forward again. God, Christopher thought, it was all just a side show to them!

When George got to the foc'sle, nearly everyone was in there watching Red wipe blood off poor old Liverpool; he was truly a mess. His nose wouldn't stop bleeding, both eyes nearly swollen shut, and from the way he winced when they helped him into his berth, his entire body must be bruised.

"Damn," John Tholman, one of the older AB's, said. "I sure as hell don't want to get that preacher boy cross with me!" Several of the men agreed wholeheartedly, some laughed. All drew an angry glare from Red.

"That's right, jus' make light of it," Red yelled at them. "That bastard nearly beat ol' Liverpool here to death, and its jus' a joke to you all."

"Shut up, Red," John Tholman shot back. "We know who started this. This didn't just happen, old Liverpool there has been asking for this since the boy signed on!"

"Amen to that!" Three or four of the others agreed in unison. Red started to say something, then thought better of it, instead he turned his attention back to Liverpool.

Christopher spent the next two hours sitting alone on the fantail watching the ship's wake trail off into infinity

"Not one to gloat," Chips said as he stepped up from the shadows behind Christopher, startling him and making him jump.

"Don't sneak up on me like that!" Christopher admonished him.

"I sure won't do it again," Chips promised with a sly smile. "After seeing what you are capable of. I'll be mighty careful."

"You made a nice profit out of it," Christopher said.

"The fight was gonna happen anyway," Chips shrugged indifferently. "Why not take advantage of a sure thing?"

"You couldn't have known how it would turn out."

"Nasty little men with big mouths and big knives," Chips smiled at Christopher, are as gutless as they come. Also, Liverpool isn't a smart one. I knew it was just a matter of time before you or someone else adjusted his attitude.

Just before midnight, the ship came to anchor just outside the harbor. All were sent below except a four-man anchor watch. These names were read off by the Mate. For the twelve to four watch, two of the names were Jamison and Liverpool. At the mention of Liverpool's name, Red stepped forward and offered to take the watch for him.

"Is there a reason for this?" the Mate asked with a straight face.

'He's feeling' a bit under the weather," Red replied, hoping that the others would not laugh out loud.

"Very Well," the Mate agreed.

The anchor watch consisted mainly of making sure the ship didn't slip her hook or drag it ashore. It also meant walking around the deck to insure against boarders. On one of the trips around the deck, Red and Christopher came toward each other from opposite directions. As they were about to pass, Red stepped over in front of Christopher, blocking his path. "You think it's over, do ya, preacher boy?" Red snarled, "You beat my friend nearly to death, and ya think it's over? Well, it ain't over, not by a damn sight!"

Christopher just looked into Red's eyes for a moment, and then he stepped up face to face with him. "It's over, unless you don't want it to be. I'm sure the Mate will find someone to stand your watch as well."

Do think ya kin do me like Liverpool?" Red challenged;

"You think I can't?" Christopher wasn't backing down.

Red started to have second thoughts. "You didn't need to beat him so badly."

"He came at me with his knife," Christopher was still in a sour mood. He wouldn't think twice about doing the same to Red, and Red sensed it. "I could have killed him," Christopher pointed his finger at Red's face. "And I would have been within my rights! If the shoe had been on the other foot, he would have killed me! So, don't you go telling me what I should or should not have done!"

At eight bells, four others came on watch to spell Christopher, Red and the others. In the foc'sle, most were fast asleep. Christopher walked over to where Liverpool was finally sleeping and took a close look at his handiwork. In his heart, he was truly sorry that he had done so much damage. He knew how much poor Liverpool would be hurting in the morning, so he went over to his berth and pulled a towel from underneath it. This he soaked in the water cask, and then laid it across the sleeping man's swollen face.

At first light, the ship was brought into the harbor and alongside the wharf. The balance of the day was spent in unloading the cargo that was to stay. The next day they started loading the cotton and furs that would make up part of their China bound cargo. At one point in the afternoon, both Christopher and Red were in the hold stacking and securing the cargo. To survive the rigors of the passage, Christopher knew the load would have to be stowed very tightly and secured in place. Red didn't seem to care how the goods were loaded and Christopher let him know just what he thought.

"How long have ya been sailing, preacher boy?" Red sneered.

"Over seven years," Christopher answered.

"I've been at sea over twice that," Red shot back. "I'd say I know more than you about how to load!"

"Not by the looks of it," Christopher challenged, which instantly set Red off. He took a wild swing with his right fist at Christopher's head. Christopher ducked and drove his fist into Red's unsuspecting gut. Red instantly flushed and collapsed on the hold's deck, fighting to catch his breath.

"Damn," Christopher rarely swore. "Don't you scoundrels ever learn?" Red was doubled over on his side and clutching his chest. Christopher knelt down beside him, "You okay? Why did you swing at me?"

Red couldn't answer, he was in too great of pain, so Christopher helped him to his feet and half carried, half pulled him out of the hold and into his berth in the foc'sle, next to

Liverpool. On the way across the deck, the Second Mate spotted them and asked what happened?

"I fell and busted a rib, I think." Red whispered through clenched teeth, while looking up at Christopher. The Second Mate accepted the answer without believing it.

The loading was done before sunset, but the OCTAVIUS would remain in port until the Master had conducted his business in town. The crew was given the night to enjoy town, tomorrow they would set sail for the Horn, and China.

Christopher stayed aboard and volunteered for the deck watch. Between rounds of the deck, he would check in on his two victims, as his guilt had taken to calling them, offering what comfort he could. Which for Red, was wrapping his chest tightly and keeping a cold towel on Liverpool's face. Twice he apologized for what he had done, but he also reminded them that they had asked for it. Neither man said much in return, mostly because they didn't know what to say to a man who beat the stuffing out of them, then turned around and mothered them as if he really gave a damn.

Christopher was checking the forward cable to be sure it wasn't chaffing, when he heard footsteps on the deck behind him. He quickly turned around, fist clenched, jaw set; he was ready for anything as it seemed everybody wanted a go at him lately

"We're sorry, Mr. Jamison," the Master offered, his lovely young wife's hand in his arm. "We didn't mean to startle you."

Christopher forced himself to relax, at least appear to relax. The Master had to know the happenings of late, and Christopher was sure he was about to be dressed down for his part in it.

"I understand Red fell in the hold today, hurt his ribs," the Master said with an air of concern.

"Aye Sire," Christopher lamely replied, knowing that the Master must surely know he was lying.

"How is he doing?"

"His ribs are sore," Christopher answered honestly. "But I think he'll be fine in time."

"I hope so," the Master nodded, "he's a good sailor. I signed that rascal Liverpool on, just to entice Red to sign up as well." The Master admitted, then added with an air of wonder, "hard to imagine them both down at the same time, but then odd things happen sometimes

"Aye." Was all Christopher could think of saying.

By the way the Master had said what he said, told Christopher he knew exactly what had happened.

"Oh, and by the way," the Master added. "This is my wife Sarah. Sarah, this young man, I'm sure you remember well, is Christopher Jamison. I thought it might be nice to properly introduce the two of you."

"Ma'am," Christopher nodded toward her. "I am truly sorry for my clumsiness that day in Plymouth."

"Christopher," Sarah bowed her head slightly. "We are as just to blame; we were not paying much attention to what was going on around us either."

"I was just taking Sarah to the foc'sle to look in on those two," the Master smiled, as he led his wife off toward the foc'sle hatch. Christopher wondered what those two would say, but he was pretty sure they would be smart enough to keep their mouths shut, for fear of punishment, if nothing else.

As the Master and Sarah exited the foc'sle they strolled aft along the starboard rail. Christopher was checking several lines and didn't see them until they stopped next to where he was working. "They seem to be well taken care of," the Master said. Christopher could only nod, but he did notice that they were both smiling. And boy, did Sarah Weegens have a beautiful smile!

The following morning was spent rigging pens on the deck to house the livestock being brought aboard to provide fresh meat, at least for awhile. Liverpool was doing much better that morning and joined the others in deck duties. The entire time, Liverpool kept his distance from Christopher, except when the work made a close passing necessary. Each time he passed, Christopher felt somewhat ashamed of himself, as the poor fellow looked a fright. Both eyes were still somewhat swollen and deeply blackened, not to mention the dark bruises on the jaw and cheek.

By the dogwatch, the ship was hauled away from the wharf and all readiness made for departure. Sundown would find them well at sea once again.

The next four and a half weeks were truly a blissful voyage. The weather was mild, the sun bright and hot, but the wind steady and the ship heeled well to the helm. Both Liverpool and Red recovered well from their encounter with Christopher and were doing duty as everyone else. Although, both did their best to steer clear of the one they called preacher boy.

The spirit of the ship was great. The fresh vegetables and meat had been expended over a week ago, but salt pork and dry, hard biscuits did little to dampen things. The pens were taken down and the deck cleaned.

Although there would be no more fresh meat, there was also no more foul smell, and no more extra work tending to the animals.

Christopher found himself truly enjoying this ship and this crew, even Liverpool and Red no longer bothered him. He felt blessed for having found this billet. Somewhere along the line Christopher felt the Master had taken a liking to him. Evidence of this was in the way he addressed Christopher, and the fact that he spoke to him at all. As usual, the Mate handled the crew, gave all the orders, and carried out the master's wishes. Seldom did the Master speak directly to the crew, unless it was to address them all as one body or with ship's business. But it surely seemed different with Christopher.

For the first month aboard, Christopher rarely saw the Master, when he did, they never spoke. Christopher simply did his job to the best of his ability no matter what the task. He took pride in being the first to report on deck when called and the first to go aloft when instructed. Although he enjoyed a bit of an enviable position amongst the crew, he was more agile than the older, more experienced men and more experienced and knowledgeable than the younger men.

About a week after departing the Georgia colony Christopher was standing his watch during a stunningly beautiful sunrise when the Captain appeared on deck. Christopher usually is so cheery at this time of day that he was prone to forget his place at times. He knew that to address the ship's Master without being addressed first, or without it being urgent business was frowned upon, but Christopher spoke without giving it a thought.

"Top of the morning to you Captain," Christopher smiled as he strolled past him. "Is this not a glorious morning to be alive?"

The Captain stopped for a moment and smiled at the boy. "That it is young Jamison, that it is," he said as he gazed across the black sea being painted by the blazing horizon. Then he walked on. Against protocol or not, that became a typical occurrence every other day when Christopher had the watch at dawn. They seldom said much, just a few words, but always something. Now after several months at sea the Master called him by his Christian name.

>November 12, 1761
>South Atlantic Ocean

The weather since leaving the Georgia colony had been beautiful every day. This morning dawned gray and cloudy, and rain was falling before the morning meal, but by the time six bells of the late morning watch, the sky had once again cleared, and the sun was shining through light fleecy clouds

"Sails-Ho!" The lookout shouted, bringing everyone on deck. Spotting a sail in the middle of an ocean is something both longed for and feared. The stranger could be either merchant, or a pirate. If the vessel proved to be another merchant, well, there's always safety numbers, especially against the latter.

"Where and away?" the Mate called out.

"Low on the larboard rail!" the lookout replied instantly. Which brought everyone over to the larboard rail in hopes of getting a look at the stranger.

It took several hours for the two ships, sailing on converging courses, to truly get a good look at one another. The stranger was indeed a merchant, a Spanish merchant, by the look of her. Bound from Africa, or India to some southern port, possibly Rio.

Since the two ships were heading in different directions, the Master felt it prudent to give the stranger a wide berth and had their course altered ten degrees to larboard, which had the OCTAVIUS pass well astern of the Spaniard. There was always the possibility of it being a wolf in sheep's clothing.

By the time the dogwatch was called, the stranger's sails disappeared off the starboard rail. They were once again alone on the big ocean. Life aboard had become routine, the crew constantly employed in ship maintenance. Every line was checked, and then rechecked a few days later. Caulking details were formed, and every seam that could possibly ship water was attacked with purpose. In less than a month's sail they would be upon Cape Horn, and any weakness in vessel or crew would certainly be exploited by nature there.

CHAPTER THREE
CAPE HORN

Friday, December 4,1761
South Atlantic Ocean

Black clouds thundered out of the southwest, driving rain mixed with occasional hail to torture their bodies and minds as they clawed at the canvas to reef and then furl the sails, desperate to stay alive. The fury of the wind and seas roared upon them with all malice the heavens could inflict. The small brig was tossed about like a child's toy as water crashed over its bow, sweeping across the foc'sle deck and then swelling down onto the main with a terrific roar where it swirled around the scuppers before returning to the sea.

As the OCTAVIUS battled the sea, her crew, the living soul of any ship, clutched tenaciously to anything to keep from being swept overboard and trying to keep the brig's bow to the sea. One moment the prow was pointed toward the heavens, climbing a heaving angry mountain of black water, then a moment later sliding down the back side of the wave, crashing to a sudden halt as the skip buried its bow to the jib mount into the next thundering wall of water. Each time the brig shuddered and slowly recovered with a ton of water running down her decks only to repeat the ordeal.

Once the sheets were set, trimmed and in order to the master's liking, the rest of the crew, those not on watch, were sent below. Christopher, on the larboard watch, had to endure. Envying the starboard watch as they scurried to the relative haven of their berths below in the foc'sle.

Not that the foc'sle was the best place to be now, the sounds penetrating through the hull of the battered ship were deafening. Water leaked from the foredeck at any place not properly caulked. Normally the foc'sle would be an inviting haven. The soothing warmth of the iron stove was gone. The seas had swept the chimney over the side. Water had poured through the gaping hole dousing the fire before they could get a tarp pulled across the hole to seal it off. Now there would be no warmth of a fire until a new chimney could be fashioned.

Even so, Christopher envied them, being out of the wind and spray. They were soaked the bone and shivering, but they could at least lay their tired bodies down to attempt rest. For those left on deck the trials of this storm were far from over.

With hands so cold and stiff that they barely flexed, Christopher paid out the lines, and then heaved them back in. The course lines were frozen, tearing at his hardening flesh. The cracks in his hands seeped blood that was washed away instantly by the freezing saltwater. All of things combined in tormenting him into a state of misery such as he had never known. With each new blast of near freezing water, he felt as though he was standing almost unendurable punishment

Suddenly, he heard the heart-stopping sound of surrendering canvass. Peering upward, Christopher spied the main topsail parting across the middle. As the mate called for 'all hands", Christopher was clawing his way up the rigging to rip down the useless cloth. Another could not be fitted until the fury of this storm abated.

He could not recall ever being colder. His stiff body trembled as he made his way back to the uncertain safety of the main deck. The oilskins did little to stop the icy fingers of the sea water. His trousers were soaked to their tops, clinging to his legs and lower body. His undershirt-soaked moisture up the sleeves and around the neck. With each passing moment the cold moisture soaked deeper into the cloth. He wondered how much longer it might take to soak him through.

Suddenly, through the roar of the storm, Christopher heard the friendly din the ship's bell as the starboard watch appeared on deck to spell the larboard. As he thankfully started toward the shelter of the foc'sle, across the steep incline of the climbing deck, the tilt reversed, and he nearly fell head over heels as the ship began careening down the back side of the wave. Instinctively reaching out to catch mast shrouds in his stiff, nearly frozen fingers, Christopher barely retained his precarious balance. Before he could reach the protective the foc'sle, the prow bit into a black mountain of sea, its crest collapsing upon the fore section of the hapless brig, sending a thunderous crash of swirling, pounding, freezing water across the decks.

This he couldn't escape and was swept back across the now climbing deck, gasping for breath and nearly drowning under a ton of confused sea before being slammed into the starboard wale. Christopher had his answer, he was soaked through and through. Finally, he inched his way to the foc'sle.

Entering the foc'sle wasn't all that pleasant. A dim light from the lone whale oil lamp cast long flickering shadows across the heaving cabin making the foc'sle look as cold and damp as it was. Without the modest heat from the stove, the only warmth to be had was in one's berth. He threw himself, as ably as he could in his present state, into his berth knowing that his soaking wet clothing would soon soak his bedding also, but the berth offered the only respite. The bedding was composed of wheat straw enclosed in a heavy woolen cloth to form a mat, with a course linen cloth sheet and two heavy woolen blankets to offer warmth. Having only one of the woolen blankets on himself at the time, Christopher still felt chilled to the bone, so he begrudgingly climbed from his berth.

He quickly lifted the planking beneath the mattress, revealing a small storage space for personal items, and grabbed the second woolen blanket before throwing his shivering body back into his berth and wrapping the blankets snugly around himself to trap any body heat he might be able to produce

As the ship drove herself down the backside of each wave, the mattress would slide forward until his head hit the forepart of the berth. Then, as the ship surged up the face of the next wave, the mattress would slide aft until his feet hit the foot of the berth. All the while the waves pounded the prow with such terrific force as to make the entire ship shudder, threatening to split open at the seams at any moment. Since Christopher was trying to sleep within mere feet of the very forepeak of the ship, the sounds of the gale were even more threatening. He was convinced the stem would rip open with the next blow and drown the lot of them. Maybe being on deck hadn't been so bad after all. At least there, one could see what was coming.

Christopher had only been in his berth for minutes when the hatch was thrown back and 'all hands' called. He cursed his luck, as the others did. Forcing himself against his will out of his bunk and toward the hatch, donning his oilskins as he went; for all the good they would do. Resigned, he stepped back on deck and found himself back in the thick of the storm's fury. Icy cold water swirling around his numb feet and legs as he hauled on the lines and then slowly checked them back as the necessary cloth was reefed.

After five terrifying hours, the wind started to abate. Still of gale force, but nothing compared to its earlier thrashing of the brig. The crew, however, was not to rest. The new mainsail had to be put into place, the foc'sle chimney had to be replaced and now was the best time of all to get these things done. It was hard to imagine that beyond a horizon they could not see; life went on in an orderly fashion.

Saturday December 5, 1761
In the region of Cape Horn

By the first light of dawn a heavy sea was still running directly ahead and crashing into the bow, sending spray as high as the foreyard. The brig was still at least a hard day's sail from the Cape proper, and those experienced sailors among the crew didn't expect a change in conditions until at least a day's or so sail beyond Cape horn.

According to old Chips, that could be months from now. He told of ships being held in this wicked place by strong currents and head winds for months before they were either wrecked, turned back, or able to double the Cape.

Christopher had really grown to like the old carpenter and enjoyed the time spent in his company. The stories were always entertaining to be sure, but they also had a point to them. Just listening to Chips tell a story was entertaining in and of itself. He had a low and grating voice that seemed to have trouble escaping his slovenly growth of beard, trimmed haphazardly with knife whenever the mood struck. No one was truly sure of his exact age, but some said well past his fiftieth year, tall, about 5'10" and lean and hard as they come.

On his right hand the third finger was missing. Claimed to have been lost in a pub when some cursed devil bit it off just above the knuckle. He walked with a limp because of a bum left leg, again as he told it, crushed within the hold of this very ship by of all things, a barrel of rum.

Chips was a bit of an enigma, appearing to be hard and cold, but, in fact, quite the opposite. He was careless about himself, but very proud and careful about his tools of trade. He had taken the task of shepherding the green ones under his guidance. Some would benefit from his experience, some would not. Christopher seemed to be a quick study and listened closely to all the old salt said. Chips naturally took a special interest in the boy and within a month at sea, was treating Christopher as he would his own blood. He would tell him to carefully chew his food, while he himself had only those four teeth in his whole head.

He had bull-like strength but enjoyed carving intricate sculptures of birds and ships. He was both very religious and superstitious. He was also very fond of the Master, which appeared to be mutual. All in all, Christopher both enjoyed and respected Chips and believed most of what he was told. Although old Chips tended to stretch the truth from time to time to make a point, he believed him on this matter, He had been on many long voyages to this place before with this same ship and Captain. And Chips had predicted that the sail around the Cape could take months.

The Cape Horn is the last place on earth anyone would want to spend months. Of all the bodies of water to sail on, the Cape Horn is beyond question the most feared and respected. This murderous span of sea is seldom calm, throwing storms of all sizes upon those who venture here. Even in a relatively peaceful passage, the wind can be expected to vary in intensity and direction any number of times. Regardless of the wind, the ocean swell is always mountainous. Many a ship has surrendered to the fury of the Cape. Of all the places for a ship to founder, this is the most merciless, desolate place.

Old Chips said not to fret. "She's a stout ship and well crewed. We'll survive, as we have before and will again." His words gave Christopher solace as he lent a hand to replace the lost chimney.

It was almost the end of Christopher's watch when the lookout sang out, "Land – ho!"

The ship's entire complement rushed to windward and stared across an angry sea toward two small dots on the horizon, the Falkland Islands. In a matter of hours, the Falklands disappeared astern of them. There would be but one more landmark before reaching the Cape. If they would be able to even see it, Staten Island, which came into view just about sundown at eight bells. There was no turning back now, they were in the region of the Cape. Not that they could or would have turned back before. The OCTAVlUS's owner, the Captain, was an experienced seaman and had rounded the Cape before. Each time he said he dreaded it and each time the sea tried to lay claim to him and his ship, or so it seemed. But he was a sailor, risk is part of that profession, and that was that.

By the time Staten Island could no longer be seen, Chips and Christopher had a new chimney fashioned and installed. They quickly went about striking up a fire. Within a short spell the stove started to heat and the biting dampness of the foc'sle began to retreat. This time they carefully braced the chimney and secured several stout guys so it wouldn't be carried away quite so quickly next time. Christopher had little doubt that a next time would surely come. Just as the foc'sle began to get toasty, eight bells were rung. Time to spell the starboard watch. Before going out on deck, Christopher quickly changed from his wet clothes into a set of dry clothes offered to him by his friend George, as Christopher's own extra set was soaked as well. The fact that he lent Christopher his extra set of clothes stood tribute to that winning character of his. Warm in the dry set of clothing, Christopher stepped out onto the deck with the rest of the larboard watch to spell those of the starboard. Night had set in dark and troubled. The brig was still rising and falling with the giant swells. A light snow was falling, but unless you were looking at the oil lamp affixed to the mast, you would have never known it not to be rain. It was summer in this southern purgatory. Summer indeed!

During their time on deck, the Second Mate kept them busy, which was expected, the labor allowed them to keep warm with four hours of hauling this line, bending that line, bailing more hauling, bending and bailing. With visibility down to a few feet, there was nothing to distract them. Under such conditions, they turned in a fair piece of work for those four hours and the time passed rather quickly. However, by the time the bell tolled eight, Christopher's borrowed clothes were nearly as wet as his own set. He hoped that his own had dried some, hanging in the foc'sle as near to the stove as William, the cook, would allow him to hang them.

Sabbath, December 6, 1761
Cape region

By midnight, with a fresh wind blowing out of the southwest, the royal, topmast and topgallant studding sails had been set as the OCTAVIUS tacked into the wind.

Until reaching the Cape region, the Master had always seen fit to honor the Sabbath with a short service at eight bells midday, after which the crew was allowed to rest, mend clothes, tend to cleanliness or whatever they wished until it was time for the night watch to be set. The only exceptions were those standing watch that day. A duty rotated among the crew and mates. Even the Master himself took every third Sabbath so the mate and second mate could have their turns off, something rare. Occasionally, the crew would be called aloft as the sails would need tending, but only when it was most prudent.

Until this Sabbath, all the others since their departure from England had been pleasant. Even this one was to bless them in its own way. During the night the sky cleared, giving their weary souls the one bit of beauty to be had in this tormented place, a crystal view of the Southern Cross, the brightest four stars in the heavens. These stars hung in the form of Almighty's cross and gave hope to their hearts. They could also clearly see Magellan's Clouds as well.

Magellan's Clouds are not clouds at all, only appearing to be. They are stars to be sure, three clusters of stars really. Two of the clusters are brighter with the third being only slightly dimmer. It is said that when one is directly beneath the Southern Cross and Magellan's Clouds, he is directly abeam of Cape Horn.

By daybreak (3:00am) however, this southern world had become angry once more. Suddenly the brig was ploughing sea again with her jib. Wild black waves of ice-cold water cascaded across her decks. The expected call came, "All hands ahoy! All hands aloft! Furl the sails!" The Master decided it prudent to scud (plough into a gale with bare poles, no sails set). So, the off watch quickly donned their cold, wet britches and scrambled aloft to furl all sails. The task was nearly done when a tremendous wave crashed onto the foredeck. The brig shuddered as tons of water smashed freshwater kegs and swept debris into the sea. One giant plume of sea, like the right arm of Neptune himself, plucked a hapless sailor from the foreyard, taking the sailor and the foretopmast studding sail boom back with it into the dark sea.

His short, horrified scream was heard by all, even above the deafening roar of the wind and sea. Christopher didn't know at the time who was lost, not having the time or chance to even glance in that direction. The elements were testing them all. In the next heartbeat Christopher could join him as might the lot of them. If any were to survive, they could do nothing but what they had been taught to do and do it as quickly as possible. The lives of all aboard hung in the balance. They would mourn his loss later if given the chance.

Oddly, the most affected by the loss was the master's wife. She had not experienced death at sea before, and she found the suddenness of it to be terrifying. In an instant one of their own had died making the rest of the crew hold on tighter and work more carefully, realizing it could have been any one of them.

The unrelenting sea thrashed them for hours as they struggled waist deep at times in the frigid, swirling water to secure the deck gear and re-batten the hatches. Although it was daylight, one could not tell since the sky was as dark as the sea. There seemed to be no horizon. As Christopher pounded his stiffened hands against his sides to warm them, he cursed his stupidity for signing aboard this ship and prayed that the Almighty would see fit to spare his miserable life. When the deck was finally secured, they were sent below, not to rest, but to secure the cargo that had torn loose and tossed about the hold in scattered disarray. Of course, trying to roll a cask in a dark, damp hold that is at one moment sloped, this way, and then at the next moment sloped away becomes nearly impossible. It took them several moments to learn to use the pitch of the ship to their advantage.

Christopher hated working down in the hold, blind to what was happening outside. If he could see a big wave coming, he could brace for it, but numerous times they had nearly completed their work only to have the brig take a sudden lurch just as they were lashing the cargo.

At last they finished this task, and the hold was secure, at least for the time being. A chance to rest would have to wait. The hull was shipping water, so the bilge pumps had to be manned. Each of the crew took his turn on one of the four pumps. By the time the gale had let up, Christopher realized that he had never been so wet, cold, frightened and grateful in his entire life, all at the same time. He had sailed on ships before, up and down the English coast, to Spain, and even to the colonies, but never to Satan's caldron.

He was finally able to lay himself down and seek some rest. Instead of on his usual berth, he chose instead to lie down on the planking just above the bilge at the very bottom of the ship. This spot was near where he had just finished his turn at the pump, and he didn't have the energy to go elsewhere. Although, the ship was still being tossed and rolled by the sea, the effects of it seemed less down here than anywhere else on the ship.

Soon seven bells were struck and at last it was time for breakfast. Christopher wearily himself up and made for the foc'sle knowing every meal was the same, cold salt pork, biscuits and water.

Why had he ever left his home for this, Christopher wondered. The pork was hard and tough, the biscuits even harder and tasteless, except for the occasional weevil which infested the flour, The water smelled and had a thin greenish film covering it, and due to the fresh water being in limited supply it was strictly rationed. Now they feared that there might be even less, since the storm crushed several of the casks on deck.

The balance of the morning and most of the afternoon was spent repairing rigging and replacing caulking where leaks had developed. Two rather serious leaks had developed forward near the bow just above the bilge. Old Chips was called down there to inspect the affected area and to do what could be done. Luckily, part of the cargo were crates filled with iron nails from which he fashioned a patch of sorts to hold everything together until such time as proper repairs could be made. By late afternoon the weather had quieted down some. Even with a cold, light wind from the southwest, it was the best weather they had had in the last three days.

After the evening meal, the sea chest of the lost sailor was brought out and laid open upon the main deck. Shortly thereafter the Master appeared and read off the sailor's name. Walter Cummings, a young lad of questionable origin, he had been a strong sailor, well liked and already sorely missed. The Master asked if any one among them thought that more could have been done to rescue the lost sailor. Silently shaking their heads, they knew they had done nothing to save him and yet it was all that could have been done. He had been beyond help the moment he was swept overboard.

Then, as was the custom, his belongings were auctioned off to those gathered, his final shipmates. They could buy anything they wished and have the expenditure withheld from their pay when they settled after the voyage.

Since Walter had been about his age and size, Christopher purchased his foul weather gear. The biggest surprise came when the Mate pulled from Walter's chest a quill, a vial of ink and an entire box of parchment which Christopher purchased for a fraction of its value because only the officers and he were capable of reading and writing. Exactly why and how Walter came to possess such things no one knew. While Christopher did not know him well, he had never seen him engaged in either reading or writing. And as not one piece of the parchment had been spoiled by ink, he thought Walter's motives were most likely for trading rather than using. Intending to record the entire voyage, Christopher could use the supplies. As he thought about it, Christopher felt certain Walter would approve of his purpose, since it would also record his passing.

About four bells, the sea came roaring upon them with renewed purpose. As no sails were set, they were to ride this one out below decks, they hoped. The force of the sea against the brig's hull sounded for all the world as though she had run hard aground for sure.

Monday, December 7, 1761
Region of the Cape

At eight bells (midnight), the jib boom snapped with a sound of a musket report. The heavy seas carried it backwards and deposited it in a tangled mess on the main deck. However, the more serious problem was the damage done to the shrouds and stays. Something miraculous had saved the precious chimney to the foc'sle stove. As the jib came crashing back, it sliced through the forestay and starboard fore-shrouds, leaving the foremast in danger of snapping as well.

Christopher was sent aloft to the foretop, a platform just above the foreyard, to affix new lines to replace the stays that had been carried away. He was terrified as he quickly scrambled up the larboard shrouds, worrying that the foremast, which was swaying violently by this time, would break at any moment. Six new lines had been tied around his waist, allowing him use of both hands for climbing. He took one line from his waist at a time, securing it to the foremast then signaling when his end was secure. Those on deck would then haul it taut and secure it below. With each new line, the mast felt more stable. Within minutes they had secured the six stout stays to the mast and it seemed content to stay with them a while longer.

December 8, 9,1761
Cape Horn

For three terrifying days they scudded along battling one gale after another with only slight respites to separate them. Three days of being soaked to the bone with ice water, eating salt pork and sleeping in a severally leaking foc'sle. The Master ordered the cook to serve hot tea and keep the stove hot so they could warm themselves as conditions permitted. The tea was strong and hearty and did wonders at sustaining them.

For their time on deck, they were employed almost continually at repairs. The OCTAVIUS was a strong-willed old lass that would do her part at staying afloat. Christopher found himself frightened, but proud of the ship he sailed upon. Old Chips had almost completed repairs to the jib but remounting it would have to wait until clear of the Horn.

Thursday, December 9,1761
Cape Horn

Shortly after midnight, the Master ordered the sails set and they were called aloft. They climbed the shrouds amid a nearly blinding snowstorm. The wind was moderate and the sea calmer than at any time recent. The balance of the night was spent setting and reefing the sails. Christopher believed he had gone aloft at least half a dozen times.

The brig seemed to be herself again and was running strongly into the wind. By seven bells, the sky was clearing, making the Master happy. It made getting a proper sighting, to fix their position, promising. The last sighting was four days ago, and with what they had been through, they worried that they may have been driven towards the coast with its jagged rocks and crushing surf. And they all knew, Cape Horn was the last place on earth one would want to be wrecked.

The ship had survived. She was alive and so were they. Cape Horn behind them for now, however, they would have to pass this way again on the voyage home. Although past the horn, they were still sailing in the same latitude and could therefore expect to experience weather conditions to be little improved.

CHAPTER FOUR
BECALMED

This morning Christopher had the dawn watch. As he strolled along the main deck: checking gear, the Master appeared.

"How is Christopher this gray morning?" he asked pleasantly

"The truth, Captain?" Christopher wearily replied, not thinking how it sounded.

"Aye lad, the truth," he responded with a bit of concern in his voice.

"Well," Christopher started, nervous about what he felt he had to say and how the Master might take it. "Begging the Captain's pardon sir, I'm a bit worried."

"Worried? About what? We've left the Horn astern. The worst is over."

"Fresh water, Sir. We lost six barrels of it passing Cape Horn."

"Aye, the water is a concern for me as well. Have you taken stock of it?"

"Aye Sir, I have and reported my findings to the Mate."

"Very good, Christopher. But tell me, what did you find?"

'We have half a barrel here on deck, Sir. Two in the hold, and one, half empty in galley. We use about a fifth a barrel a day, Sir.

Leaving us with about fifteen days of fresh water."

"Fifteen days of fresh water and just over two months of sailing to reach Eden," The Captain pondered. "Thank you, Christopher, for your thoughts. I shall look into the matter. "

"Thank you, Captain," was all Christopher could say as the Master started to walk, away. Then he stopped and turned back to face him. "I always enjoy these little chats, Christopher." He said before turning and walking off.

Saturday, December 11.1761
Southern Pacific Ocean

Noon sighting. Course change at last! They had been steering an almost true west course for over a week. The headwinds were unbelievable! Two days tacking into the wind only to find themselves about where they had begun! A hard, two full days of rugged sailing to just to hold their place!

The Master ordered course changed to nor' west by west. As promised, the Master had given thought to the freshwater problem. Daily rations were cut in half! Christopher and the rest suffered from constant thirst. But there was reason for hope. The Master had Chips busy joining any extra cloth that could be spared into a large tarp. With the dark rain clouds that were forming off to the southwest, it was obvious what the tarp was for. Their biggest concern was whether it would be done in time to be of help. Anyone not on watch or engaged in other duties, eagerly pitched in. Joining one cloth to the next and so on. Just before the squall was upon them the large tarp was spread out over the main deck, the four corners drawn up to create a large bowl.

This effort provided a quarter of a barrel of fresh water from this one squall alone. They had high hopes of ending the severe rationing that had left them parched.

While the rain fell, they stood with their mouths open and their hands cupped in front of faces to catch as much water as they could. Christopher positioned himself directly beneath the foresail, catching both the falling rain and the run-off from the sail!

He was able to arrest his thirst for the first time in four days. Though somewhat dehydrated, the lack of water was not yet life threatening, but when one does not have ample supplies of vital items, such as water, the mind makes it worse than it really is.

Almost as soon as it started, the rain stopped and they carefully transferred the water from the tarp into the water barrel.

Great effort was taken to avoid spilling any of the precious liquid. At best they captured a quarter of a barrel, the rationing would continue! The tarp would be stored on deck, always at the ready. Should they be blessed with rain again soon, they would be ready to capture it.

Saturday, December 25,1761
Christmas Day
South Pacific Ocean

Until reaching the Horn, this was the happiest ship Christopher had ever sailed on. Now the OCTAVIUS was a desperate ship with an equally desperate crew, and a determined master. Thirst was driving them mad! They floated upon a world of clear blue water and were dying of thirst! There had been no more rain, and as of daybreak, no wind.

They were becalmed! Becalmed in an area that the Master said was noted for its stiff breezes! He said this was the last place in the world he would figure on being becalmed. Christopher saw him talking with the Mate, then both men looking skyward before both shaking their heads.

Becalmed, Why? Dear Almighty, why? The sails hung limp from the masts. Every sheet set and reefed taut. They even drew buckets of water from the sea and doused the sails to make them hold any breath of wind, to no avail, there was nothing to catch. They knew they must reach land to reach freshwater, but they could not move without wind. There appeared nothing to do but endure.

Shortly after midday one of the crew dropped to the deck violently ill. Clearly the cause was drinking from the sea. Before sunset two more would suffer the same fate, one of which was the Second Mate. The Master had them strapped down to prevent further injury and called for all hands to assemble. He explained that the only hope for the afflicted men was large doses of fresh water. But, in doing so, would deplete the already low supplies for the rest. For his part, and on behalf of his wife and son, he would give up a portion of their water to help the sick men. From this point forward, his family's meager rations would be cut in half again.

He also explained that he did not believe that that alone would be enough to make a difference. He then asked if any among them would volunteer to do the same. At first, no one stepped forward, then old Chips did so. For reasons he didn't understand, Christopher did likewise. If a man of Chips' age could make the sacrifice, then he could do the same. When no one else stepped forward, old Chips turned and stared for a few moments at each man, then with his right index finger he slowly pointed to the deck next to himself, not one man refused. One by one they all took that step forward, making the Master smile.

"Tis the same soup we're in, Captain," Old Chips said with a sly grin.

The Master bowed, thanked them, saying how proud he was to sail with them. It made no difference that old Chips had to shame them into volunteering.

The Master's wife did what she could to comfort them, but their screams were heard continually. The Master's young son stood off, watching in wide-eyed horror as the dying men thrashed in torment.

It was nearly impossible to walk past the water cask affixed to the base of the mast, but as much as Christopher longed for a sip of its refreshing contents, he dared not go near it. For should he as much as peer into the cask, he doubted he could remain strong enough to refrain from stealing a sip of the life-sustaining liquid. Sitting on his berth writing in his journal, he heard the shuffling of leaden feet upon the deck above him. An old tar, Will, was caught that morning trying to steal from the water cast and was given thirty lashes of the leather. He now laid in his berth moaning in agony. His back was raw and blistered. It was the first stiff discipline Christopher witnessed the Master deal out. He felt for Will but realized that the vital supply of water must be protected, or they would all die.

To spare themselves the agony of adding to their thirst, most had given up eating the salt pork. How long they could go with little water and no nourishment? He knew that they would grow weaker steadily. Christopher was reminded of an old saying he once heard, "There are three types of man: the living, the dead, and those at sea!"

Some of the old hands had told him that this area of the world was usually quite pleasant. When they had sailed here before, the weather had been cool and the wind stiff. Now they found themselves with no wind and an unnatural heat. Never had they experienced this suffocating heat in these latitudes.

The stench was sickening, the burning heat of the sun fermented their filth, burning it into their being. Without the wind to carry the stench off and cool the ship, they stewed in a sweltering, malignant, hopeless prison, uttering humble prayers for deliverance through parched lips and swollen tongues. Their bodies were racked with pain and open sores. Their strength sapped to the stage of utter collapse. Their minds tortured by all of this and the dying screams of their shipmates.

When the sun finally set, Christopher had the evening watch, for which he felt grateful. At least he had the ability to walk the deck and feel some sense of being alive. He had the night and its shadows to hide his fear and foreboding in. He thought of home, wondering if he would ever see it again? His self pity was broken suddenly.

"Christopher," the voice of the Master called quietly

"Aye Captain," he croaked a response.

"You can read and write?"

"Aye, that I can Captain. My father is a Vicar, I learned from him.

"That is good," the Captain said as he leaned against the bulwark and looked across the glistening sea. "The second mate is dead," he stated flatly. "You are the best man to fill his job."

"Me?"

"Aye, Christopher, you. You will be the Second Mate. As soon as we have committed John to the deep, I want you to move your belongings aft to the Mate's cabin.

"Aye Captain thank you."

"Don't thank me, it may not be a pleasant experience. This is the damnedest situation my eyes have ever seen. There should be a fine breeze to carry us along, but we have nothing. It's the damnedest thing. Our situation is getting desperate. The crew will need a strong hand over them to maintain discipline. We could be becalmed for days. Have you ever been becalmed before?"

"Never like this, Captain. Never have I seen no air at all, not even a breath," Christopher replied honestly.

"Being becalmed is maddening enough, but when lack of fresh water threatens life itself, the crew could be driven to mutiny."

"Mutiny Sire?"

"Aye, mutiny. Our best bet at avoiding that will be to keep their minds and backs busy. Therefore, at sunrise we lower the pinnace and longboat and haul the brig in search of wind."

After the Master left Christopher to himself, he pondered what had just happened. He was now an officer. Indeed, a positive step towards his goal of being a ship s Master one day. This, however, is the one step in his chosen field that he had looked forward to the least.

Being second mate is without question the most undesired position on ship. The reason for this is simple, as Second Mate, he would no longer be a member of the regular crew and not quite a full-fledged officer. He would eat and sleep in the cabin like an officer, but not as an officer. The Master and the Mate ate together at the first setting. The Second Mate could eat what's left at the second setting, when they had finished.

He would still go aloft with the crew and handle the canvass as an ordinary seaman, yet he was no longer one of them. As Second Mate he was responsible for supplying the crew with oakum, spun yarn, tar, and anything else that they might need in their daily duties, as the

Second has charge over the boatswain's locker. A fair comparison would be that of a handmaiden for both the officers and crew

Christopher knew men who had been Second Mates for years, not a very attractive possibility. However, since both the Master and the Mate are well past their prime, over forty, that should not be the case here.

The balance of his watch went well. The calm sea and absence of wind left little for him to do, so his mind wondered. Being Christmas Day, he thought of home, his parents, and friends. He offered a silent prayer for them, hoping that they were well and enjoying this Holy day. For the poor souls aboard this ship this cherished day only brought despair, suffering, and death. How he longed to be back home, to sit by the fire and feel its warmth against his skin on a cold winter's day.

But he was not home, in fact a world away from it. Dreaming would accomplish nothing, so he shook it off. Soon the ship's bell was struck eight, the end of the watch and the end of a memorable Christmas day, if not a happy one.

Monday, December 27, 1761
Becalmed in South Pacific Ocean

From first light, all-hands were called. Water was hauled from the sea in buckets and tossed upon the canvass. A wet sail will hold more air, if there was any air to hold. Christopher prayed for even a whisper; it was not to be. After breakfast, a mere break in their labors, as not a morsel of nourishment was touched, for fear of increasing thirst. The boats were manned and lowered. He was put into the pinnace and the Mate took the longboat. The lines attached from the launches to the ship and made fast in such a way, the two boats would be able to haul directly ahead and not foul the lines.

The work was back breaking, the burning sun unmerciful. Three of the men in Christopher's charge were of little help on the oars. They had been strong and eager lads when they last saw home, now barely shadows of the men they once were, even the will to go on was past. Death seemed to be their only hope of release.

Christopher shaded his eyes from the sun's glare off the sea and gazed up the OCUVIUS, the first he had seen her from afar since joining her. He remembered what a sight she was in Plymouth harbor as he came down to sign on. Her hull so bright and freshly painted. Her canvass was pristine white then. She was indeed a smart ship, like a lovely young lass full of promise.

Now she looked like an old woman, who worked much too hard with far too little rest. Her hull was streaked and weathered. Sails patched and stained, hung limp upon the yards like an ill-fitting garment on fragile old bones. The ship's appearance seemed befitting their plight.

All around them the sea taunted them with its untouchable bounty. It glistened and sparkled in the distance, up close it blinded them with the sun's reflection. Here, they were all there was in the world, nothing else existed. Land with its trees, grass, and above all else, fresh water, was a product of their overly taxed imaginations. As the rest of the world no longer existed for them, they no longer existed to the world. Should they perish here and now, no one would be the wiser. No one would mourn their passing, never knowing they were dead. If they were not to return, their lives ended as they sailed away.

By day's end the men had barely enough strength to haul the launches back to the ship, let alone pull the OCTAVIUS. The Master saw this and called them back. His eyes were filled with sympathy as the men struggled over the bulwarks. The Master never openly showed his compassion, but it was, nevertheless, revealed in the little things he did. Unlike most of the ship's master's that Christopher had had the misfortune to sail under, this one was never a tyrant. He never unrighteously accosted any member of his crew, never raised his voice. This was the reason his crew always gave all they had for this man.

As this was his first voyage with this captain, Christopher wondered whether his having his wife and son along had anything to do with his demeanor. He was assured by members of the crew that had been with the OCTAVES for years that the Master had always been a good and fair man.

The stench of stagnant water from the bilge, mold, and the rotting flesh of the dead rats that had infested the lower holds of the ship, mixed with the suffocating oven-like heat below decks, keeping the entire crew up on the open deck. They sought out any form of shade they could find for pitiful rest. The soothing coolness of night would soon be upon them, their only respite from the torment.

Another serious threat to their well-being, second only to the shortage of fresh water, was the appearance of beriberi and scurvy. Luckily, only a couple of the crew had contracted beriberi. These poor souls could scarcely move, with lower limbs painfully swollen, suffering from nausea and listlessness.

Others suffered the just as common, but not as deadly, seaman's malady scurvy. Christopher was among these; his symptoms were just beginning to manifest themselves. His bright red gums had started to bleed. In time his teeth would probably fall out unless landfall was achieved soon. Rotten teeth or no teeth at all were sure signs of a long voyage. Beriberi and scurvy were a constant part of the sailor's life, the severity of both in direct proportion to the length of time at sea.

> Tuesday December 28,1761
> South pacific...WIND!

The Master came on deck just shortly after midnight. The stars shone brightly, giving his ruse of wanting a bearing check credibility. He spent a few moments taking his sights before wandering over to where Christopher was standing his watch.

"Mr. Jamison how are thee tonight?"

"Very well, Captain," he lied poorly, and the Master could tell. "A perfect night for getting a fix, Sire, although I doubt that they've moved much since noon."

The captain eyed him closely for that undue remark but didn't address it. "This long with empty sails could have us drifting farther than you might expect." He said with a fatherly tone, gazing across black water, so smooth it had a mirror quality to it. Then he started fumbling through his pocket for something or other before producing his treasured long-stemmed pipe. Clenching it firmly between his teeth that also now had bleeding gums, he strolled over to the oil lamp, lighting his pipe with a dried reed stick. Christopher could tell there was something he wanted to say.

"Mr. Jamison," he said, and then seemed to ponder what would come next. He rubbed his chin, now covered in a rough growth of beard, puffed intently on the pipe, leaving a swirl of smoke trailing behind him as he paced back and forth across the deck. "What course are we trying to hold?"

"Nor'west by west," Christopher responded, worried that he had somehow failed in. his watch keeping.

"Still no sign of a breeze?" He looked prayingly up into the limp canvass.

"Not a breath- sire."

"Should that change, I want you to call all hands at once."

"Aye, Captain."

"The moment the wind does return, Mr. Jamison, I want you to steer a course of nor'west by north. Is that clear?"

"Aye, Captain, nor'west by north."

"Very good, carry on." He turned and started aft with the pipe smoke swirling madly around his head.

"Captain?" Christopher called after him. Not at all sure that he should question an order from the Master.

"Yes, Christopher, what is it?" He turned so the glow of the full moon illuminated his rugged, yet gentle looking features.

Christopher stammered for a moment, his mind racing for a proper way of questioning the captain. But the new course would take them thirty degrees more to the north.

"Out with-it lad! What is troubling you?"

"I don't want to sound out of place, Sire, but would the Captain enlighten this simple sailor. Would not a course of nor'west by north take us out into the vastness of an empty ocean7"

"That it might my boy, that it might. But if I'm half the sailor I claim to be, I should be able to find one small island out there to replenish our supplies in about twenty days of good sailing."

"An Island, Sire? In twenty days?" Christopher was astounded and excited that they might find refuse far sooner than he had thought possible.

"Yes, a place called Easter Island. A small plot of land in the middle of the Southern Pacific. Discovered by the Dutch almost twenty years ago. Although I must confess, I do not know that much about it, other than the description in the journal about it. We should find it ahead somewhere along a course of nor'west by north. I'm also told that there isn't much there, and the inhabitants may or may not be friendly. We should, however, be able to refill our water barrels and get some fresh fruit of some kind to tide us over until we reach Eden. According to the location given in this journal, it should be around 30 degrees latitude."

"That's great news, sire, but..." Christopher started.

"But why not turn back toward the mainland just ten days due east?" The Captain seemed to be reading Christopher's innermost thoughts.

"Aye, Captain," he sheepishly responded.

"If we get some wind in the next day or two, we head for Easter Island. If we drift for much longer than that, then we will have no choice but to head back for the coast. In turning back, we will lose almost a month of sailing whereas Easter Island will cost no more than several days."

"Aye Captain, I'm sorry for the questions."

"That is quite all right my boy, 'tis how you'll learn to be a Mate, then a Master yourself one day." He seemed to be in no hurry to return to his cabin now, as he just leaned on the bulwark enjoying his pipe. "They call this stretch the roaring forties, did you know that, Mr. Jamison?"

"No sire, I did not."

"Yes, my boy. The roaring forties. Usually when I sail this area of sea the wind is fresh and a good ship is rather quick in these parts."

"Well sire, 'tis not exactly roaring for us now, is it?"

The Master laughed and patted Christopher's shoulder. "No lad, tis sure as God is not." He tapped his pipe clean and finally headed aft.

Almost before Christopher could believe it, a fresh breeze sprang from the south and started to fill the sails! He quickly called the new course to be steered, "Bring her to nor'west by north!" Then he ran to the hatchway and called down, "all hands ahoy!"

"On course nor'west by north!" George at the wheel called out, as the weary crew began muster from the foc'sle. Any complaints there might have been were quickly dispelled by the realization that the ship was underway again. And by the appearance of the Mate and the Master stepping out onto the deck, almost as if one.

"All hands aloft!" The Mate bellowed. "Set all the canvass we've got! Let's make up for lost time! Quickly lads, aloft I say!"

Being only the Second Mate, Christopher was soon on his way up the shrouds to reef the sails just like any other hand. One moment he was the Officer on deck, the next he was aloft in the rigging talking orders like the rest of the crew. But at least he was doing his duty in a fresh wind out of the south and he would much rather be a sailor on a running ship than an officer on a dying one.

Oh, to be alive again! Christopher thought happily to himself. To feel the ship racing along under full billowed sails. He lingered on deck a while after his watch. Resting himself on a bollard in the bow and feeling the life-giving movement of air as the brig held her new course north by northwest. After refreshing himself in the welcomed breeze, he went toward the cabin and much needed rest.

"Still on deck, Mr. Jamison?" the Master asked as Christopher was about to go below.

"Aye Captain." He smiled for the first time in a great while. "Just wanted to fill my lungs with the fresh breeze.

"So ya did lad, so ya did."

Christopher paused in the hatchway.

"Something else, Mr. Jamison?"

"Just a thought sire," he laughed. "Where do you suppose we'd be if you had told her about Easter Island earlier?"

"She does seem a bit anxious at that doesn't she?"

"Aye, that she does. She's a good ship Sire." Christopher said. "Good night, Captain."
"Good night lad, rest well."

CHAPTER FIVE
EASTER ISLAND

Wednesday, December 29, 1761
South Pacific

Wind was from astern and driving the brig with a gentle hand. The Master had the fresh water supply rechecked and was allowing each man an extra cup of water per day. For which they were very grateful. It was amazing how cherished this stale water had become. As little as an extra cup of water was, it was a true bonus for those with parched lips and those who had to sustain life on only three cups a day before. While he would still like to bury his head in a freshwater stream and drink to his heart's content, Christopher noticed that he was feeling better than he had a day ago.

The day had dawned bright with big billowy clouds of snow white, set against a sky of brilliant blue. With the brig running as a prize steed with a bit in mouth, Christopher once again took pleasure in being a sailor. In the years since he left home and went to sea, he often wondered what his life ashore would have been like had he stayed home. He most likely would have turned out to be a miner, as his father. What Christopher admired most about his father was his compassion for the people of their church. He was never too tired to visit the old and sick. And with Christopher's mother, would go and do for those who could not do for themselves. Some lads dreamed of being a prince or a knight, Christopher rather fancied himself as becoming a man like his father. That was until, he saw his first ship.

Christopher had visited the pit' with his father as a child, had stood at the gate as the shifts slowly mustered out. Their faces and clothes as black as the soft stone they pried from the earth. Christopher remembered being terrified of the 'pit'. It was the last place he wanted to be, let alone spend a lifetime. He was fortunate that his father also hated the 'pit'. His father allowed Christopher to choose something else for himself. As a lad, Christopher watched his father trudge off to a place he hated to be, then after a day of back-breaking labor he trudged back home with little to show for his efforts.

At one point in his youth, Christopher did not recall just when, he accompanied his father to Plymouth. He was taken by the sight of the tall sailing ships that lined the wharf. Christopher knew in that moment he would go to sea. He even told his father as much. His father seemed a little saddened by his son's announcement, but he also seemed to understand, and as time went on, he grew to appreciate the boy s decision.

Christopher also fondly remembered when he reached eleven, it was his father that took him back to Plymouth and helped him sign on a ship to give him a taste of the sea. Maybe deep down his father hoped that Christopher would grow homesick, and on that first trip he did have bouts of homesickness. But somewhere along the line in that year at sea, Christopher grew into a man. He learned to carry on as a real sailor.

Upon his return home Christopher told his father that he intended to continue as a sailor and that he wanted his blessing. His father had looked tired, but then he smiled and assured Christopher that if sailing was what he really wanted to do, it was all right with him. He even seemed relieved that Christopher would not have to endure what he had by working the pit.

This was a day that every sailor dreamed of, a fresh breeze to fill the canvass, calm seas to sail upon, and a bright sunny day to fix their position, scrub the deck, and tend to the business of sailing.

The Master's son came on deck just before seven bells. He was a fine young lad of about nine or ten, well behaved and polite. The sight of the lad on deck had been seldom since leaving England. Christopher heard someone say that the lad was sickly, and his health was the reason the Master brought his wife and child along. The gossip went, that the Master was afraid that if he went to sea alone and was gone for the usual year, the boy may not be alive when he returned.

This day, the boy looked to be the spirit of life itself, but then looks can be misleading. Christopher had only seen the master's wife several times during the entire voyage. She looked well but appeared troubled by the hardships suffered by the crew. He doubted whether she had recovered from the loss of poor Walter and the others. He couldn't help but feel pity towards the Master. How he must have his hands full, worrying about his ship, his crew, his life, and worst than all of these... his family! The sea is many things: mistress, temptress, nemesis, livelihood. It can be bountiful, beautiful, giver and taker of life, but of all the things it is, a place to have one's family it is not!

Christopher was standing a turn at the wheel when the master's son came up and sat on a coil of rope along the bulwark on the larboard side.

"A fine day, isn't it, Mr. Jamison?" He stated more than asked, as if they were old friends.

"Aye lad," Christopher replied, the first he had ever spoken to the boy. "A fine day it is."

"Have you been sailing long?" the boy asked.

"Aye, that I have. Almost since the time I was about your age." Christopher smiled, remembering his first voyage up the coast. "And yourself, first voyage?"

. "Naw," the boy quickly replied while squinting to protect his eyes from the sun's glare. "I have sailed with father many times before. Never on such a long trip mind you, but many times up the coast."

"I thought as much," Christopher said, playing to the boy's pride. "You look like a lad who has been to sea before." He could see the boy's eyes light up and his chin come up a little and his back suddenly became a little straighter. "You like sailing, do you?"

"Oh yes, I love to sail," the boy proudly replied. "Why, one day I will take my father's place as Master of the OCTAVlUS. And I will sail her all over the world."

"I bet you will," Christopher answered, truly believing that one day he might do just that.

"I sure will," the boy promisingly sighed. "But my father says I have much to learn about being a sailor first. Do you think that true, Mr. Jamison?"

Christopher turned and looked into his wide blue eyes, searching for the right answer. The lad seemed so sincere and looking for the truth, so he felt compelled to honesty. "Aye, we all have to start somewhere. Even your father, the great sailor that he is, had to begin learning sometime."

The lad watched and studied Christopher as he spoke. Christopher was sure the boy was judging him by his every word. In the back of his mind, Christopher guessed that the boy's father had answered the same questions before, and now the lad was judging him by the way his answers matched his father's. "I reckon that every good sailor is always learning, even your father. The secret is to remember what you have learned."

"Will you teach me, Mr. Jamison?"

"Me?"

"Yes. Oh, please teach me what you know," the lad pleaded. "My father says I could learn much from you."

"He does, does he?" Christopher asked, not masking his surprise very well.

"Aye, he says that you're a fine and smart sailor. And I could learn much from you. Will you teach me?"

Christopher pondered the thought for a moment. How could he refuse after such surprising praise? And the lad did seem to be rather likable. In fact, he reminded Christopher of William, his lost brother. That alone struck a soft spot in his heart. "Why not?" Christopher laughed. "But first I will have to know your name, a proper teacher should know who his student is, don't you think?"

The lad sprang to his feet and extended his hand. "Richard," he beamed. "My name is Richard. Richard Weegens."

Christopher took his hand and they shook on their agreement. His agreeing to be the teacher, and Richard agreeing to be the pupil. "Well Richard, why don't we begin right now by teaching you to handle the wheel."

"Do you mean it? You want me to steer?"

"Why sure lad," Christopher laughed at his enthusiasm. It made him remember his first trick at the wheel. "But be well to remember that holding a true course is serious business. The life of all aboard is in your hands. Watch the compass and keep the wheel steady, next to your father's job, being a good wheelsman is most important."

The lad took to the wheel like a gull to the air. He held the course steady on nor' west by north. He even took just pride in having the crew see him standing tall with the wheel smartly in his grip. He even managed to hold a steady course when his father came onto the quarter deck.

"What's this, Mr. Jamison?" the Master bellowed, louder than anything Christopher had ever heard him speak. He believed this to be for the lad's benefit, or the crew's

Christopher quickly straightened his stance and smartly replied, "I've been spelled by the Junior Mate, Sire.

"So, I see," the Master said as he stepped closer to the binnacle and studied the compass. "Steady on course, Mister!" He tried to sound stern, but his pride in what his son was doing was clearly evident.

Young Richard's response was quick and proper. "Steady on course! Aye, aye, Captain!"

The Master and Christopher exchanged suppressed smiles. "Carry on," he said before turning and walking away

As Christopher looked down at Young Richard, he caught his eyes peek a quick questioning look in his direction, as if to ask, "how was that?" Christopher couldn't help but laugh. "You're learning fast young Richard, you're learning fast. You'll make a fine sailor!"

Young Richard smiled with pride and did a fine job of steering for the rest of the watch. Christopher truly enjoyed himself as well. The boy's company took his mind off his troubles and the troubles besetting the ship.

After his watch, the lad followed Christopher around the ship and asked a thousand questions, taking great interest in every answer. When they finally said good night, Christopher felt that he had just found a true friend. He was not sure of who was looking forward to tomorrow more, the lad or himself. Yes, he thought, this lad was much like William would have been.

>Tuesday, December 31,1761
>South Pacific

The crew was given the day to themselves, apart from the times all hands were called aloft to reef or furl the sheets. Joseph, the big German, succumbed to beriberi before midday. His body was committed to the deep with a few soft words by the Master. The Master's wife silently cried, as it was she who tenderly took care of the gentle giant among them, to no avail. Christopher wondered how long she could endure the sadness of this horrible voyage. He felt it odd, but he thought it was nice for Joseph to have a fair woman shed tears for his passing. He sometimes wondered if sailors as a lot had become too hardened to death at sea. Never, during all the burials at sea he had been witness to, had he ever seen a tear. Sorrow, yes that was there, but never the emotional tear. It pleased him to see the master's wife cry. It was good for Joseph and probably her as well.

This morning the larboard watch had the eight to twelve watch. Shortly after three bells the Master came out on deck and slowly strolled along as if deep in thought. Christopher, near the bow inspecting the buntlines, spotted him coming on deck, but continued in his tasks. The Master slowly made his way toward the bow and acted surprised to see Christopher. The act didn't fool Christopher for a moment, he was sure the Master had known he was there all along.

They talked a bit about the weather, each expressing a hope for rain, The Master quickly figured out the watch tables and reaffirmed that Christopher would be standing the evening watch. Christopher confirmed the calculation. The Master asked him to call all hands just before midnight at eight bells. Being New Year's Eve, Christopher knew right off what he had in mind. He also informed Christopher that if the winds stayed with them, they should reach Easter Island in roughly two weeks time.

"And I want to thank you for taking an interest in my son," the Master said quietly. "He seems to really enjoy his time with you. I hope he isn't becoming bothersome."

"Not at all Captain," Christopher quickly replied, suddenly afraid the Captain might keep the lad away from him to spare him from being bothered. "I truly enjoy the lad's company."

"Truly?"

"Aye Captain. He's a smart boy and a joy to have around. I mean that sincerely, Sire. Even if he wasn't the master's son, no disrespect intended, Sire."

"None taken, Christopher, and thank you." He smiled and patted Christopher on the shoulder and walked aft.

At eight bells, noon, the starboard watch spelled Christopher's larboard and they went below. Christopher passed his free time mending his clothes, writing in his journal and thinking of home, something he rarely did. Thinking of home accomplished nothing and tended to leave him saddened and listless. Therefore, the practice was wholly unacceptable, and he tried to avoid it, but today he failed. He found that he was still prone to homesickness even after all these years away at sea, especially at the holidays. Maybe young Richard had something to do with this. He reminded Christopher so much of his younger brother William, who died of fever when he was but seven years old. Christopher suddenly realized how much he missed him and his company. He always pictured him in his mind's eye as Richard is now. Smart, bright eyed, and fun.

He could picture himself sitting with his father and mother in their home. Sitting before a crackling fire, the warmth seeping into his skin, a wisp of cedar smoke soothing his nose. The vision was as real as life, he could even taste the warm, sweet cider laced with cinnamon on his lips and feel its warmth in his mouth, down his throat, spreading in his soul as he slowly sipped from the tall mug his mother had given him.

Sadly, he became aware of the motion of the OCTAVIUS and realized that his vision of home was only a cherished memory. He wondered if they too thought fond thoughts of him, wondered about him, missed him as he did them. He knew they did but wondered just the same. It had been some time since he last laid eyes on them and would be even longer until he returned. They looked so much older each time he would return, as the harshness of their lives slowly eroded away their very being, the inevitable toll of ageing. As he sat there on the edge of his berth thinking these morbid thoughts, he realized why it was that he tried never to think of home, it could never lead to any good while one is so far out to sea.

He was slowly tucking his self-pity away for another time when he heard the bell start to chime. It was four o'clock in the afternoon and time for the daily dogwatch. The dogwatch is a means by which the two watches switch which hours they stand watch. In effect, half the crew takes the first half and the other half the second half of the watch. Thereby during a single watch, the entire crew is on deck and the hours one stood watch the day before are shifted. That is to say that if you had the eight to twelve watch one day you will have the twelve to four watch the next day. It ensures that each watch stands an equal amount of time on watch.

Young Richard was on deck as he came up. He seemed eager to begin another lesson. These lessons were a Godsend for relieving the tedium of his tasks.

"What are we to do this watch, Mr. Jamison?" Richard asked seriously as he fell in stride along his side.

"Well lad," Christopher thought a minute, trying to think of what the boy could do and what might be in most need of being done. "Let's see what the starboard watch left for us to do."

"There will be something?!" The boy seemed worried.

"Of that you can rest assured," Christopher smiled, "There's always plenty for a sailor to do at sea."

And plenty of work there was. Work to which the lad threw everything he had into. From scrubbing the deck with holystone, splicing lines, to caulking the planks with oakum. Young Richard wanted to learn and do it all, and a better worker he'd rarely seen. Of course, the mess the oakum made of his clothes caused the master's eyebrows to raise and possibly raised the mother's dander as well. But the boy did want to be a sailor.

At four bells the Mate came on deck with the starboard watch and spelled Christopher and the larboard watch. Richard followed him to the galley and took his place at Christopher's side. They split a biscuit, and each nursed their allotted cup of water. At first Richard tool short, quick swallows. Then he noticed how Christopher and the others would take half sips and swish the liquid around their dry mouths before swallowing. In seconds he was doing likewise, savoring the stale but wet liquid.

At eight bells the second half of the dogwatch ended, and it was his watch again. The galley was closed, the Mate attended to the log, and the evening watch was set. Time for the evening to come embrace them. Before going below, the Mate advised Christopher that the pressure was dropping fast, and the Master wanted all hands called for tarp duty should rain decide to appear. The watch went smoothly. Richard joined them on deck around three bells and stayed until five bells.

Within a matter of several hours the wind shifted from aft to a point off the larboard quarter with moisture ripe in the air. Christopher took the liberty of preparing the tarp just in case. They had all sails set and the ship heeled slightly but surged on her intended course. At six bells a light rain began to fall, and all hands were called. The rain lasted for less than fifteen minutes, but as they were ready for it, they gathered a fair amount of the much-needed water for their casks. After the rain had passed, the heavens cleared, and the stars shone brightly

Just before midnight the Master came on deck and asked that Christopher call all hands. After all had gathered on the deck, the Master gave thanks for the recent rain and prayed for more, "if it be Thine will." Then he had every man issued a full cup of water and toasted their health, courage, and they're being a fine lot of sailors everyone. He finished by wishing them a most joyous New Year and then bowed slightly and returned to his cabin, along with his wife and young Richard.

Before young Richard stepped into the cabin, he ran up to Christopher and shook his hand and personally wished him a happy New Year, and he responded in kind. Moments later the ship's bell began to toll eight times and the starboard watch appeared on deck. Christopher returned to the cabin to complete his journal and get some much-needed sleep.

Friday, January 1, 1762
South Pacific Ocean

The day dawned fair and warm. The wind had slackened, and they were in dire need of replacing the missing jib. Chips had the new one made and ready for placement. Replacing the jib would normally be done when the ship could ride at anchor, but that was not a practical option for them at this time. They would have liked to wait until they reached Easter Island. However, the jib would enhance their speed and speed was of the essence.

Replacing the jibboom at sea is a trying task at best, difficult if things go in one's favor, near impossible if they don't. Chips had been with the Master for many years and held his respect and complete confidence. Therefore, it came as no surprise that the task was placed totally in Chip's hands.

As with any such task, one must do the first things first. In this task, the first thing to be done was the safe removal of the OCTAVIUS's maiden figurehead. How she ever escaped being destroyed when the first jibboom was carried away Christopher didn't have a clue. Chips, true to form, was quick to point out that because they were still among the living, was due solely to the fact that the maiden was still intact and on their bow. It was a point about which he would not even argue. The very fact that the ship still rode the waves was all the proof he or anyone else, for that matter, should need.

Removing the maiden was a job in and of itself. It also proved to be a task for which young Richard was well suited, due mainly to his size. Also due to his ability to learn quickly and do as he was told. He was fitted with a rope safety harness and was light enough for several men to lower over the forepeak and hold him safely out of harm's reach. The lad worked like a man and did a fine job of the work, winning the appreciation of every sailor on board.

Once the maiden had been safely removed, the stays were attached, and the jib slowly slid out until it was affixed into its proper place. Then the martingale striker and its stays were replaced. Next came securing the inner and outer foretopmast stays and finally the maiden reaffixed. And after a full day's hard labor, much of which was done by young Richard. The jib was as good as new. They set the jib sail and the flying jib sail and once again the OCTAVIUS was whole.

Monday, January 11,1762
South Pacific Ocean

It had rained steady for almost four days! A fair wind was out of the west-southwest with occasional gusts. They were one day away from Easter Island and suddenly found themselves with ample fresh water!

The Master made it clear to Christopher that he planned their stop at Easter Island to be a short one. Just long enough to take fresh fruit and vegetables aboard before shoving off again. At one point he summoned the Mate and Christopher into his cabin to inform them of his intentions.

"Little is known of the island's inhabitants," the Master said, weighing his thoughts very carefully. "I realize that the crew is hoping for a brief holiday there. It cannot be. We must be on our way as soon as possible."

Christopher felt a bit saddened by this news but understood the master's intentions. They had lost much time in diverting to this place and it would be unwise to intentionally lose more.

The OCTAVIUS was being scrubbed and polished as if she were about to be the object of Royal review. The crew, those that could still function on swollen limbs, were in good temperament. Each looking forward to setting foot on land, even though it was land that no one aboard, not even the Master, had been to. They all felt slightly apprehensive about calling on a land they knew so little about. What would fate have in store for them there? They had no choice, so Easter Island it was.

Tuesday, January 12, 1762
Easter Island!

    To the larboard watch fell the four to eight in the morning watch. As Christopher came on deck, the night sky was black as pitch. He could smell the foul stench of land! He thought they must surely be upon the island. The Mate however, soon dispelled that notion, saying he thought them to be several hours from it yet. The wind had shifted during the last watch from off aft quarter to dead ahead. They now found themselves having to tack into it, which Christopher guessed was probably a good thing. With the night as dark as it was, they may not see the island until well upon it. With the wind coming towards them, they should be able to turn off their course in good order, should they come upon the island too quickly. The Mate was probably right in that the island was yet some distance ahead. The smell of the land was being carried far out to sea by that head wind.

    It was not the land itself that caused this pungent odor, but rather the shoreline. Where land meets sea. Where all the elements of both work against each other in a bid to conquer. It is the shoreline that creatures from both worlds find death when the two worlds collide. A land animal is helpless when swept into the sea and will soon perish as will a fish washed ashore.

Man is a curious beast; he is of both the land and the sea. He reigns over each world, never quite conquering either. He is, however, most vulnerable when attempting to go from one world to the other, like attempting to land on an island he has never been to. The OCTAVIUS had never been to Easter Island. Christopher realized that they would have to watch themselves very well indeed.

The pending sunrise was starting to paint the darkened sky with streaks of the most vivid color. Minute by minute the heavens lightened. Daylight would soon be upon them and land should be sighted soon after that.

Christopher loved the night as it allowed him time to himself, between tours of the deck of course. Tonight, he decided to bring his journal on deck and add some thoughts to it, with the aid of the ship's lantern mounted on the base of the mast about five foot off the deck.

The smell of the land had become stronger, so he kept a sharp lookout for any signs of a land mass ahead of their prow. He had twice shouted up to the nest to be sure that the lookout had not fallen asleep. Both times his calls were answered by a voice he knew to belong to James Stuart, a man with very sharp eyes. If land was to be spotted at a fair distance, James was the man to do it.

"LAND-HO!"

The voice that bellowed the call was not that of James Stuart. It had the sound of being shrill and very familiar, young Richard!

How did the lad get up the shrouds to the crow's nest? It seemed that Christopher wasn't his only teacher! The rest of the crew had taken a shine to the lad and had been showing him what they knew about sailing as well. The voice also had one undesired effect. It brought the Master out of his cabin rather quickly; he too recognized at once who the voice belonged to.

"Mr. Jamison," the Master called, as he peered up towards the darkened sky to spot the boy. As if he needed to see for himself where the lad was.

"Aye Sire?"

"Pray tell, what is my son doing aloft?"

"Experiencing life at sea, I should think, sıre," he quickly answered. Hoping to find the right words, since he personally had not given permission for the boy to be up there. Never mind the fact that as Officer on deck, he didn't even know he was there and should have.

"You think it wise for a child to climb the shrouds in the dark?" He eyed him with a doubtful stare.

"Safe enough for a lad of young Richard's ability."

Master said nothing, just looked directly through Christopher as if searching his soul for sincerity. Christopher could only hope that he would find at least a shred of it there.

"Begging the Captain's pardon," Christopher quickly added, hoping that he might have found an angle. "How old was the Captain when he first went aloft?"

The Master thought for a moment. "Never with my mother onboard." He smiled, "if she knew where he was right now, she would faint dead away."

"Sorry, Sire." Christopher quickly apologized. "I'll bear that in mind next time."

"Be sure that you do," he said with a smile. "Just where is this land?"

"Where and away?" Christopher shouted up at young Richard.

"A point off the larboard bow!" Young Richard shouted the reply, after a slight pause, which Christopher knew was to confer with James as to the proper response. "Low on the horizon!"

The Master pulled an eyeglass from his pocket and peered through it toward the spot directed by his son. "And so, it is," the Master almost whispered. "So it is."

It was the way he had said it that puzzled Christopher. He acted as if he was surprised to find the island where he thought it would lay. The Master told him a few moments later that that was indeed the case, since he had only latitude and guess work to go on. Christopher was instantly grateful that he hadn't shared this lack of knowledge with him earlier! He would have despaired long before. The fact that the Master found this place at all was a testimony to his navigational abilities.

By eight bells they thought they were closing in on the island, but the island would take longer to obtain. This was due largely to the height of its mountains rising more than a thousand feet. Upon reaching the island proper, the Master thought it prudent to sail around the island in search of a decent anchorage, which was found on the northern end of the island.

As night was falling, they came to anchor in ten fathoms of water. The ship was first set right, and then the night anchor watch was set. Just before the sun was totally set, the Master came on deck and called all hands.

"Men, we have arrived at Easter Island. We will not be going ashore this evening. Instead we will wait until first light before putting the Mate and ten men in the pinnace to scout the lay of the place. Remember, we know nothing of this land, so we must always be on our guard." Then he turned and went below. The only men on deck were those few who had to stand their watch. What a lovely night to stand watch. Christopher was thinking to himself about what would lay ahead. Suddenly, regardless of the time, young Richard paid him a visit.

"What do you think of this place, Mr. Jamison?"

"What do you mean?"

"Those figures on the side of the hills. Do you think the people are that big too?" His eyes wide in both wonder and Christopher supposed, a bit of fear. "Father says the Dutch, who found this place describes the men as being ten feet tall, painted black, and the women painted red! Do you think that possible?"

"I would not know since it is the first that I have ever been here," Christopher answered, noticing how that answer sat with Richard. He instantly knew that he had better play that down. The boy's eyes would not stand to become much larger. "I doubt that we will see people of such stature."

"I hope not," Richard sighed. "How would we fight against someone that big?"

"Why would we have to fight them?" Christopher asked.

"I don't know," Richard thought a moment. "I just thought that if someone was so big, they would not allow anyone like us to come to their land. They might think of us as stealing."

"They might also be very glad to see us."

"I suppose you're right," he smiled. "Can you wait until the morrow to set your feet upon land?"

"Reckon I can," Christopher offered. "If that's what the Master says we will do, then wait until tomorrow it is. I think it would be wise to wait until one can see where he is going."

"Yes, I know you are right of course," Richard shrugged. "But I can hardly wait until I able to walk on solid ground again."

"Tiring of the sea so quickly?" Christopher asked in jest.

"Surely not!" Richard was quick to reply. "But I look forward to being on land again just the same."

"Truth be told," Christopher laughed. "The rest of us are equally eager to do just that."

"Honestly?"

"Of course."

"What do you think the island will be like?" He asked after only moments of silence.

"No way of knowing without going there and taking a look," Christopher answered. "I would like to see one of those statues up close," he said. Pointing toward the island and the darkened shapes that could be seen from the deck of the OCTAVIUS. It made one feel a bit eerie seeing all those statues standing on the hill. What if the Dutch were right? What if the people who inhabit this island are ten feet tall? What if they were unfriendly?

"What are you thinking, Mr. Jamison?" young Richard

A moment's thought to come up with an answer he felt was suitable, Lord knows he wouldn't want to frighten the boy, "I was just thinking that it was high time we made our rounds of the deck and made sure no one had taken it to mind to try and board us."

"Do you think they might?" The boy quickly asked. Christopher knew right off that he had not done so well at choosing what to say

"No, I do not think so, but it does give us purpose to keep a sharp eye. One has to do this even in Plymouth."

As they began their stroll down the deck, Christopher took notice again of how lovely a night it was. The brig rode quietly at her cable. A light breeze was blowing in from the sea, generally from west to east. A new moon decided to make an appearance. While low in the sky. It did its job of lighting up this part of the world.

Young Richard walked and talked with Christopher most of the watch. Then about seven bells he sat down on a coil of rope. In minutes he was fast asleep. At eight bells the starboard watch came on deck and relieved them.

Since the night was so lovely, Christopher returned to the cabin just long enough to retrieve his journal. He made every effort to record his thoughts and the events of the day as soon and as completely as he could. His thoughts as to what purpose the journal would serve were this: when he became Master of his own ship, he should like to have a record of how a Master as good as Mr. Weegens handled different situations. It would also hold cherished memories for him and the next generation, should he be so fortunate as to find a mate. Christopher supposed deep down, that the latter was the primary reason for this effort.

Not wanting to leave young Richard by himself, Christopher decided to sleep this night on the deck close to him. Which proved to be a rather nice choice since the weather was so agreeable.

Wednesday, January 13, 1762
Easter Island

At eight bells, four in the morning, the larboard watch spelled the starboard. All remained quiet throughout the night. As night gave way to dawn, the early morning light against the odd stone figures on the island cast long shadows that would move ever so slightly.

Giving the impression that the figures were alive. One could not actually see the shadows move, but when next they glanced in that direction, they looked different somehow.

By seven bells the sun was well up. The Master decided to send the Mate and ten men to the island in the pinnace at this time. These preparations were underway when the lookout reported a single boat putting out from the island and heading in their direction. Christopher quickly scanned the shoreline and finally picked out the low form of a canoe with a single native in it.

Christopher was amazed at the speed with which this lone native could row his frail looking craft through the swells. Within minutes he was close enough for him to make out his brown skin. As this native was naked from the waist up, Christopher could also see the black and white paint the Dutch had written about.

Soon he was close alongside. From this distance Christopher also noticed other oddities about this strange fellow. His earlobes appeared to be much longer than any he had ever seen and pierced with large rings. Christopher had sent for the Master as soon as the lookout spotted the native putting out from shore, and the Master was standing next to him as the canoe came alongside.

Using hand signals, the Master invited the native to come aboard. The signals appeared to work rather well, as the fellow seemed to have no trouble understanding the master's meaning. Christopher watched this stranger closely as he tied his canoe to their side and deftly made his way up the Jacob's ladder, they had lowered over the side for him. As soon as he was on deck, Christopher noticed that he was of average size and height with big brown eyes and large brow. He lacked the wide nose of the other dark-skinned people Christopher had seen in the past.

The native took great interest in everything on deck. He carefully paced the length and width of the deck, studied the rigging, and took his time examining each member of the crew.

Several of the men winched as the stranger stood face to face with them. The Master told them to stand their ground and allow this to happen. Which was no easy feat, as Christopher soon learned when the native put his face in his and stared into Christopher's eyes with great intensity. Christopher could not help but wonder what it was that he was looking for? And if he found it in any of them?

Then the native noticed young Richard still asleep on the coil of rope. He quickly stepped over to the sleeping lad, stooped very low to closely examine him. What happened in the next moment seemed humorous later, but at the time nearly scared them all to death. What it was that had awakened young Richard at that moment, Christopher didn't know. When the boy opened his eyes, the first thing he saw was this dark-skinned stranger with black and white paint all over his upper body. The lad shot off that coil of rope and released such a terrifying scream that it unsettled the native so badly that he dashed for the wale and jumped into the sea. Before they could calm Richard down, the native had pulled himself aboard his canoe and was rowing for all his worth back for the shore. Not once did the native turn and look back!

For a moment they all stood stock still, not knowing what to do, and then someone started to laugh. Before long they were all laughing as hard as they ever had. Christopher believed it was the first good laugh many of these men had had in months. Poor young Richard was not laughing. Had Christopher used his head, he would not have either. Richard was ashamed and went directly to the cabin. After what seemed to be the right amount of time, the Master called everyone back to the business at hand. He also pointed out that what had just happened could either help or hurt them. Going ashore would not be something to be taken lightly. He had already lost enough good men for one voyage and didn't want to lose anymore. The muskets were brought out and given to each of the crew.

The pinnace was made ready and lowered over the side. Then the men that the Mate had chosen to go with him climbed down after it. Finally, the muskets and empty casks for food stores were lowered.

Aboard, they all watched as the pinnace reached the distant shore and the ten men quickly debarked. Several of the men ashore already had the muskets at the ready and stood guard as the others pulled the pinnace out of the surf and onto the beach.

When they had the boat secure, they quickly made off up and over a hill. The Mate chose not to leave anyone guarding the boat, as Christopher thought he would have done. Possibly the Mate's decision was the right one, time would tell. Christopher held no doubts that a lone man with one musket could do little in the way of preventing the natives from taking or wrecking their boat if they had a mind to do so anyway.

Time seemed to drag on as they waited. Ever searching for any sign of the Mate and his party ashore. After a time, the Master had them prepare their muskets and get ready. "We could be in for trouble," he said with concern clearly showing in his furrowed brow.

"Ever use one of these things, Mr. Jamison?"

Christopher felt a bit foolish but answered with the truth. "No sire, I've never had the occasion to learn its use. I went to sea before I had a chance to do any hunting and they seem of little use at sea.

"I could teach Mr. Jamison how the musket is used," the voice of young Richard offered behind.

"Would that be all right with you, Mr. Jamison?" the Master asked.

"If Master Richard would be so kind, yes that would do very nicely." Christopher replied, glad to have the chance to be with the boy. He thought after the incident with the native, his laughter might have hurt the lad's feelings, and pride. If so, Christopher thought now would be a good time to set things right. So, after the Master left them to study this musket business by themselves, he asked Richard if it was so.

"Naw," the boy shrugged. "I know I must have looked very foolish. I was a bit ashamed, that's all."

"Nothing to be ashamed about," Christopher assured him. "I would have been just as frightened. In fact scared out of my wits, if that native's face was the first thing I saw when I awoke. You were startled, nothing more."

"Yes, you're right! I was startled." He laughed, feeling, Christopher thought, quite comfortable with that answer.

In a matter of minutes, young Richard had taught Christopher how the musket was loaded and fired. Christopher could not say that it was something he cared about very much. If, however, it would save the life of any member of this crew, Christopher felt that he could and would use it.

About an hour or so later the Mate and his party appeared on the shore near their boat. With them a few natives followed along. In minutes the pinnace was once again on its way back to the brig. The only thing the Mate brought back with him was the same native that visited the ship earlier. This time things would go much smoother than before. Even young Richard would get to meet the stranger. He did so standing straight and proud.

As the native was studying young Richard's face, Christopher glanced over at the Master and noticed he appeared quite proud of the lad's performance this time. After what seemed the appropriate amount of time, the Master was able to converse in sign language to the native that they needed food. For which they were able to trade a fair amount of their own salt pork. This the native seemed to really enjoy, and a bargain was reached.

The native went off with the Mate and three men, back to the island while they readied the bartered food stores from their own staples. About an hour later they had the longboat loaded were pulling for the shore. It would be a day they would long remember. Some of the crew were able to spend a few minutes of their time walking around the island. The island's fresh water came from several large craters inland. No running water anywhere. No rivers, no streams, no springs, nothing of this sort, only the lakes formed in the craters.

Thursday, January 14, 1762
Easter Island

They were to be a bit disappointed in what the island had to offer in the way of fresh fruit and vegetables. There were a few fruits, varieties unknown to Christopher and a bit sour. But after their diet of salt pork, Christopher found that even they had a taste that one could grow use to. The only item that seemed in abundance there was yams.

These they were able to get a fair amount of. Little time this day was allowed for exploring the island. Christopher did, however, get to see several the stone statues up close. How these simple people ever erected these giants was certainly a mystery to him.

The Master had been to a place he called Eden before and had learned some of its language. He found the language of these people somewhat similar and by nightfall he was able to converse to a small degree with the natives.

Most of the crew could spend the night ashore. Of this number, young Richard and Christopher were included. They built a fire on the beach and the natives supplied enough food for a feast fit for a king.

Friday, January 15, 1762
Easter Island

As the Master wanted to be away as soon as possible, this day was spent much like the day before. They hauled items in from the ship to be offered in trade. Then hauled the traded items back to the ship. By the day's end the Master felt that they had enough fresh supplies to last until they could reach Eden. The farewells were said that evening, and all was made ready aboard the OCTAVIUS. The following morning, they would set sail. The Master wanted daylight, to be sure of avoiding shoals or low rocks that could rip the bottom out of his ship.

By the dogwatch all was shipshape and ready to shove off. The balance of the day would be spent in ways that would benefit them later. Splicing lines, tarring the masts, and general maintenance. They had twice experienced trouble with their rudder cable, so they sent a man over the side in a sling to check it out. The last repair job had held and looked strong enough to get them to Eden at the very least, possibly to Canton.

Chips was slightly worried about his patch job to the starboard side of the bow and spent most of the day going over it He had wanted to find a port suitable for careening the vessel to do proper repair, but the Master thought that impossible here, so it wasn't done.

Careening is a process by which the ship is beached during high tide and with the use of blocks and tackles, tipped over on beams end to repair the vessel's hull. Repairs that are impossible at sea can be easily carried out. As they were still more than two thousand miles from Eden, the hull would have to be sound.

Young Richard helped old Samuel work on the hull, labor for which the carpenter presented the lad with a wonderfully carved miniature of the OCTAVIUS. The small model instantly became the boy's prized possession and rightly so. Christopher would like to have such a fine and correct model of this ship himself. He had seen several the carvings Chips had done, but he thought that this model was by far the most exact one he had ever seen. It was complete with full billowed sail and many fine string lines.

As Chips handed the model over to the lad, Christopher would never forget the faces of both. The sheer pride of his handiwork showing fully in the old man's eyes and face, and the look of astonishment showing in the boy s wide eyes.

Even the master's wife had come out on deck and asked to see other examples of Chips' work after the boy showed the ship's model to her. Chips took great delight in showing off his crafts to her. By the time he had carried a dozen or so from his berth out onto the deck most of the crew had assembled as well. Many of the crew had seen a work or two while old Chips had been in the act of carving it, but few if any had ever seen a completed work, let alone so many of them at once.

The carvings were so real looking. There were a few gulls, petrels, seals, whales, dolphins, and even an albatross. But the most popular items were the ships and men of the sea. Chips had carved figures of Nelson, Drake, and even one of this Master, Captain Weegens. A very good likeness of the Master indeed, Christopher thought. The Master's wife was so taken by that piece of work that Chips offered it to her on the spot.

Saturday, January 16, 1762
Easter Island

At first light all hands were called, and the anchor weighed. A stiff breeze out of the west forced them to run south a bit before turning into it and making course for Eden. The Master figured that with a good wind they should make the island of Eden in ten to fifteen days.

It had been so good to walk on solid land again after so long at sea. It was equally good to be back at sea again. By the noon meal, Easter Island had faded into a small speck on the horizon, just visible where the light blue of the sky met the deep blue of the sea. This meal was delightful due mostly to the yams they had traded the natives for. Those members of the crew that had been suffering from beriberi and scurvy appeared to be getting slightly better already, Christopher included. Everyone was in good spirits and looking forward to their next port of call, Eden.

Christopher had never been to Eden before, but those among the crew who had, spoke very highly of it indeed. All spoke of the sheer beauty of the place and the friendliness of the natives. Even old Chips claimed it to be the exact spot of heaven on earth. When Christopher attempted to argue the point, Chips only asked him to wait until after they left Eden to finish this conversation, if there would be any need to do so.

Even the Master seemed to be in unusually high spirits. He came on deck for his usual smoke and stayed for most of the watch.

CHAPTER SIX
TROUBLE!

Sabbath, January 1751162
South Pacific Ocean

Being the Sabbath, they spent most of the day mending clothes and personal chores. Surprisingly, young Richard took great delight in learning these tasks as well. Something his mother told Christopher later, he would never have sat still long enough to learn mending from her.

The weather was bright and hot. If not for the stiff wind that carried them along, the heat would have been unbearable. A length of canvass was fixed over the well deck as a shelter from sun and most of the crew gathered there. Nearly all were taking lessons from old Chips in the art of carving. For Christopher's effort, he ended up with an odd-looking piece of wood. Regardless of his carving ability, Christopher viewed the day as very pleasing anyway

Monday, January 18, 1762
South Pacific Ocean

Rain! Less than two days out of Easter Island with their water supply nearly full, they got rain! The rain started to fall just after first light and increased in intensity all morning. Christopher had all the casks filled anyway, which was done by midmorning. Once the starboard watch had relieved his, Christopher took the opportunity the warm rain offered. He went up on the poop deck and stripped down to his shorts and enjoyed a bath. The warm rain felt and smelled wonderful after the heat of yesterday. He didn't bother drying off, instead he spread himself out on the deck and napped in the rain.

Only three hours into the starboard watch, around six bells, "all hands" was suddenly called. Christopher jumped to his feet and quickly pulled his trousers on and jumped down to the main deck to see what the matter was. He wasn't ready for what he found! The patch Chips had worried over in the forward hull just aft of the prow, had given way. The good ship was shipping seas in great quantities. Already the brig had taken on a strong list to starboard.

The ship had carried four pumps with her when she left Plymouth, now only two were in good working order. These two were put to work in quick fashion while old Chips took Christopher and another forward with planking to stem the flow of water. The Mate and another worked on the two broken pumps and after a spell were able to fashion one good pump from the two. This was soon in the fray of things doing its best at trying to keep them afloat.

To make matters worse the wind had picked up and drove the sea into large rolling waves that hammered against the already weakened hull. To a ship in strong shape these seas would not matter much at all. It was far from the seas they had seen in rounding the Cape, but in this situation, these swells were more than their ship could handle. If they were going to save her, they would have to do something to stem the flow of water into it and do it soon!

Chips and the Master came to this realization almost at the same time. They quickly came up with a plan that had a measure of hope in it. They would take the large canvass that they had used to catch rainwater and quickly turn it into a patch. The canvass was spread out and quickly smeared with oakum and tar, making sure to put it on extra thick where they thought the rent in the hull would be once the large bandage of sorts was put into place. Next, they fixed strong lines to the cloth and rushed the whole thing aft towards the stern. The stern was decided upon because they felt they would have less trouble getting the cloth around the rudder than they would have getting it around the jibboom. Once the cloth was over the end of the ship and clear of the rudder, they carefully walked it forward.

While this was being done, Chips had gone down into the hold to direct the placement of the patch from there. They encountered two problems in doing the task. The first was in the form of the weather, while the rain beat down upon them blurring their sight and making the deck beneath their feet so slippery that at any given moment, several of them were off their feet, it also made the ropes slick and hard to manage. Then one moment the waves were pushing the canvass hard against the hull, making moving it very difficult, in the next moment it would attempt to rip from their grasp. It seemed as if nature herself was battling them for the prize of their lives and their ship.

The second problem was that one could not really see where the canvass was. They missed getting the tar-covered part of the cloth over the proper spot at least three times. Each time Chips would sing out, but they had trouble hearing him, or by the time they were able to stop forward progress, they had already gone too far. Then they would have to try and slide the sticky tarred cloth backwards against the rough sides of the hull. They worked as quickly and yet carefully as they could only to find that they had missed again. All the while the sea was pouring into the hold and dragging the poor ship lower and lower into the water. Already some of the swells were washing over the bulwarks. Finally, they managed to place the cloth in the proper place and the flow of water was greatly reduced. They took their time in securing the lines to hold the cloth where it was.

With the canvass finally secured in place, Chips asked Christopher to join him in the hold. Upon entering the cargo space under the foc'sle, old Chips and Christopher waded in waist deep water while the Brig wallowed back and forth in the strong swell. With each roll the ship flexed as it must do, but with the broken timber the moans of protest from the wood made it sound as if the tired old ship was pulling herself apart.

Old Chips grabbed the lantern affixed to the stanchion, motioning for Christopher to follow. As they neared the side of the hull, Christopher didn't need Chips to explain the problem. The iron nails that had held the temporary patch Chips had fashioned when the leak first occurred near the Cape had pulled loose allowing the patch to fail completely. Every time the ship plowed into a swell, the sea would seep in through the canvass-covered rent, adding to the tons of sea water already in the hold. Christopher could only imagine what it was like before the canvass patch was in place.

By this time the water in the hold had risen to their bellies and sloshed around within the confines of the hold, keeping time with the pitch of the ship. Both men realized that with the water this deep in the forward hold, the ship itself must be by now riding well down in the sea. How long she could last before surrendering to the added weight was anyone's guess. To counter this, the rest of the crew was either bailing or taking turns at cranking the pumps.

About this time the Master came down into the hold and asked of the situation. Listened carefully to what old Chips thought and only nodded when ideas were put forth. He even lent a hand at attempting to place the planks Chips had gathered over the open hole. The attempt was a dismal failure. They had nearly made it to the hull when the sea rolled into the ship's side, forcing water into the hole and rolling the water already in the hold like a tidal wave back across the hold, away from the damage. After several such tries which netted the same results, the Master panted, "If we can't stop this flooding soon the weight will be so great as to drag the bow under!"

That statement brought desperation and somewhere in that desperation Christopher found an idea. He didn't hesitate, he quickly told both Chips and the Master to grab a handful of iron nails and their hammers, then he yelled for one of the men bailing with the buckets to drop his bucket and lend a hand.

He quickly moved over to the damaged side of the hull and braced his feet against the roll of the ship. He instructed Chips to do likewise on his left and the Master to the right. Then he told Red, the sailor who had come when called to hand him one of the planks. Christopher took the plank just as the ship was just being hit by another swell. He had noticed that as soon as ship started to ride out of the swell, part of the hole rose above the waterline, this created a sort of suction which dumped water from the hold back into the sea.

His plan was to use this natural suction. As the ship started to rise, he told both Chips and the Master to get ready to nail as fast as they could. The moment the hole started to rise above the sea, Christopher quickly put the plank in place and sure enough the force of the water held it firmly there. That only lasted for a few mere seconds, the plank would have to be nailed firmly by the time the next swell hit the ship.

It took only one try for Chips to have four nails into the plank. The Master did not fare so well, and his end of the plank pulled free as soon as the full force of a wave was upon it. Luckily Chips' side held well, and the Master got a second try. When the next wave hit, the plank was secure. Christopher called for the next plank and this time it was secured before the following wave.

Within half an hour the planks were all in place and the only water shipping into the hold was just seepage between the planks. To keep the planks from pulling out, Chips took longer planks and ran bracing down from the ceiling and from the ribs of the ship to keep enough pressure against the inside of the hull to equalize the force against it from the outside.

By nightfall they had repaired the rent in the hull enough so that now the pumps were gaining on the water within the hold. If the repair job held, they should be able to have the water removed in a day or so. Then would come the job of trying to dry out the cargo, if any of it was worth doing so. Most of the cargo in this hold was iron nails and iron flat stock. But it also contained a good store of other items as well.

Christopher was dead tired after his time in the hold, but he stood his watch. During the watch the Master came on deck with his wife and passed Christopher a steaming cup of strong tea. "Here, Mr. Jamison," Sarah offered, as she held the steaming cup of tea toward him.

"This should give support to your tired bones and sooth your weariness."

Christopher expressed his thanks and took the cup. The smell of the tea brought life back to his being. The taste of its strong bitterness brought a spark of life back to his spirit as well. It was indeed the very thing he needed.

The Master made small talk for the most part, at least until his wife retired to the cabin. Then he asked Christopher what he thought of the chances of the patch holding for the next ten to fifteen days?

"I am not too certain," Christopher offered, not knowing what else to say. "Chips has done a fair piece of work to stem the flow of water into the hold. The question is whether or not the iron nails and the bracing will be strong enough to keep the patch in place that long."

"I think it best that we check the patch during each watch," the Master said as he packed a new bowl of tobacco into his pipe. "If the seepage remains constant, we hold our breath. If it should worsen, we'll have to shore it up somehow.

"What about stopping at some of the small islands that dot this area?" Christopher inquired.

"I thought this was your first trip around the horn?" The Master seemed surprised.

"Aye sire, it is," Christopher answered. "I only heard of them through Chips and the others."

"Did they also tell you that first, there are not very many islands until we are very near Eden? And did they also tell you that cannibals inhabit most if not all of these small islands? And how would one tell which island held cannibals and which did not until it was too late?"

"No sire, they did not," Christopher sounded deflated. "I did not know of such things, I'm sorry."

"No call to be sorry," the Master smiled and laid his hand on Christopher's shoulder. "That is why I sleep in the cabin. But I'll tell you something. Should this vessel take it upon herself to start sinking again, I'll give due thought to beaching her on one of those islands. In this ocean it might be better to deal with human cannibals on land than those of the deep."

Christopher only nodded his agreement. Being anything or anyone's dinner scared the hell out of him, but at least on land, against humans, he felt they would stand a chance; he was utterly terrified of sharks. The Master puffed on his pipe for a time, content to feel the ship working the swells as she should. The ship was still a bit sluggish but considering the extra weight in the hold, she was doing quite well.

He finally turned back to Christopher and suggested that he inspect the hold. "While you're at it Christopher, check the planking in the next frames. We could have more damage than we are aware of."

Christopher made his way down into the hold and took hold of the lantern. The water within the hold was still above the knees and laced with bits of floating rubbish. As he made his way toward the forward section, the location of the patch, he was the object of more than a few curses from the men working the pumps. They cared little for his taking their lantern away.

Christopher told them that they could manage a few moments in the dark, he needed the light up close to the patch to do a proper inspection. The fact that he had been ordered to do so by the Captain never came up. He was the Second Mate and he needed the light, that should be all there was to it and he let them know that.

The Master had been right to suspect the seams in the next frames, they were indeed seeping water. The amount of seepage was small enough at the moment for the pumps to stay ahead of it. Should things get no worse they should be able to stay afloat.

After returning the lantern to its place on the stanchion, Christopher returned on deck and reported his findings to the Master. The

Master nodded and told Christopher to prepare the oakum and caulking tools for the men to use at first light. He wanted to keep her at sea and heading for Eden if possible. Should they be fortunate enough to reach Eden, they would be able to do proper repairs without being overly worried about becoming someone's dinner. Judging from the amount of work to be done, it would take some time to do the repairs properly.

>Tuesday, January 19, 1762
>South Pacific Ocean

As per the master's orders Christopher had the caulking tools and oakum ready for the crew by six bells. The job of caulking started at once. The job was dirty, sticky, and very hot. They had to force the oakum into the seams by driving it in with a wide, flat, chisel-like tool. When they felt they could force no more into the seam they would use wooden mallets to drive even more in. The work was done with little complaint, as all understood the importance of the job

It was during the caulking process that Chips first noticed the splits appearing in a few hull planks. It appeared that this whole section of hull had been battered nearly beyond any point of repair. The old carpenter quickly went to see the Master to report his findings. Both men soon appeared in the hold and started to give the entire larboard side of the hull a thorough inspection. There was some discussion on what could or should be done here and now and what if anything could wait. They decided the best thing to do for now would be to place patch planks over the damaged area and seal it in with tar and oakum.

The work lasted well into the day and wasn't fully completed until the night watch had been set. Once again young Richard showed what he was made of and did the work of a man. And what a mess he made of himself in the process! The entire crew could hear his mother scolding him for his appearance as he entered the cabin that evening. Christopher had no doubts the boy's flesh would be a bit rosy in the morning from the scrubbing it would take to clean that mess. But then, he would be the only one among them that would be truly clean, as the rest of the crew would wash a little then let time and work remove the rest of the tar.

Once again Christopher found himself with the eight to twelve watch. A watch that he truly enjoyed. The warmth of the day settles into the cool of evening. The ship tends to grow quiet except for the bantering to be heard coming from the foc'sle. Tonight, he was blessed with singing. The men in the foc'sle seemed to be in good spirits and voice. Some of the strains he hadn't heard in a long spell and found them quite pleasing.

Christopher did not have to wait until morning to see young Richard. The boy appeared on deck around two bells, spit polished and quite rosy around the ears and face. At least his attitude matched that of his appearance.

If the truth was known, it was probably the true reason Christopher held the lad in such high regard. Richard was always in good spirits no matter what the circumstances. Perhaps life wears that gentle attitude away with age and in time he would find misery as the rest of them have. For the lad's sake, Christopher hoped not.

Young Richard took a spell at the wheel and as is his way, he talked and talked. What all was said, Christopher would be hard pressed to recall anything just hours later. What the boy was saying didn't matter as much as the fact that he was offering company.

When the time came for Christopher to take his tour of the ship and inspect the hold, young Richard gladly turned the wheel over to another and joined him on his rounds. Luckily, they found that the hold seemed to be faring well, as were the seams. By now the pumps had made good headway and the water was only a foot or so deep in the hold.

As they entered the hold, young-Richard had the good sense to stay on the ladder. What would the lad's mother have thought had he reappeared in the cabin with his clean trousers soaked and dirty to the knees less than an hour after she had worked so hard to clean the boy up?

Christopher felt confident that by this time tomorrow the men would have the hold dry enough to start cleaning it. Then would come the job of cleaning and sorting the cargo. Hopefully the Master hadn't lost too much of it. Since this cargo was how the lot of them would eventually be paid.

Coming on deck after being in that musty, wet hold was very refreshing. The night was quite bright with a full moon and thousands of stars to light the darkness. Suddenly, off the larboard side they heard a noise and spun on their heels to see what the cause had been. Whales!

Young Richard's face instantly lit up, he quickly ran to the rail and pointed in the direction of the now invisible leviathans. Christopher stepped up to the rail beside him and waited.

"I saw one of them go under right about there!" Young Richard said, as he pointed to a spot about a hundred yards off their larboard beam. "Think they'll come back up?" he asked, very anxious to lay eyes upon the beasts again.

"I should think they will," Christopher replied. And then added without giving it some thought. "It may not be anytime soon. They can stay submerged for quite a spell."

Richard's eyes quickly took him in, and Christopher could tell that he had given the lad cause for concern. "But since they had just appeared on the surface, I should think they will spend some time here." He quickly assured him, hoping he was right.

Sure, as the sun rises, the whales gently glided back to the surface. "They're back!" Richard shouted with glee, drawing the master's attention. Christopher had not been aware that the Master was even on deck. Next thing he knew, he was surrounded by the entire Weegen's family

Sarah Weegens, as handsome a woman as ever, with big brown eyes and raven colored hair, in this light she was very striking. Her soft voice and manner were purely feminine and added greatly to her appeal. She took great delight in watching the whales until they vanished into the night. "I have never seen whales before," she softly said.

"Nor I," young Richard chimed in. "Weren't they wonderful? Will we see any more of them? Where do they go? Do you think they live around these parts?" of his questions went unanswered for the moment while the Master looked at Christopher with a slight smile and Sarah laughed.

"One answer at a time," Christopher smiled at his young friend. "Yes, they are truly wonderful, and it is likely that we may see more of them before this voyage is over. As to where they go, only the whales know that. Because you see, the entire sea is their home. They live here, there, all over the sea. I should think that they follow whatever it is that they eat, much like a hunter follows his prey

The Master smiled and gave Christopher a knowing wink. "Time for you to come back to the cabin Richard," Sarah spoke up. "Mr. Jamison has his work to do."

"But I help Mr. Jamison," Richard protested. "Our watch is not yet over. A good sailor stands his watch from beginning to end."

That last part, Christopher was sure was for his father's sake. And probably aimed at getting his support, which failed to work as the Master said nothing. For some reason, the three of them then turned and looked at poor Christopher. What was he to do? To side with the lad might be an affront to his mother, maybe even the father. Although Christopher doubted that it mattered one way or the other to the Master. Failing to support Richard might upset him and make him angry. Neither possibility was one Christopher wished to accept.

"Can't I stay until the end of the watch with you, Mr. Jamison?" Richard pleaded.

Helplessly Christopher looked to the Master for a hint of an out, only to meet a sly grin. The Master seemed to be taking perverse pleasure in seeing how he handled the situation, Then Christopher looked to Sarah, who was returning his glance. Her eyes seemed to say, "Tell the boy to obey his mother." Christopher didn't know what to do as he looked back at the boy.

"Son go with your mother," the Master finally rescued Christopher. "I need to discuss ship's business with Mr. Jamison."

"But father!" Richard started to protest.

"Dismissed!" Christopher sternly said. Then he bent down to whisper into the boy's ear. His eyes told Christopher that he wasn't pleased, but a nod of his head said that he understood.

"Aye Mate!" Young Richard smartly replied before turning and walking alongside his mother toward the cabin. Sarah looked back at Christopher and the Master with a slight but proud smile.

"A tricky spot eh?" The Master laughed as soon as his wife and son disappeared into the cabin.

"A bit," Christopher agreed.

"You handled it rather well," the Master said. "Caught between a lad and his mother is like swimming with sharks. If you swim hard to get away, you attract them, if you do nothing, they get you anyway. Mind if I ask you what you said to the boy?"

"When you helped me out and the lad still wanted to stay. I simply told him that a fine sailor like him should know better than to question the Master."

That drew a laugh from the Master, as he packed his pipe. "You are a smart one Christopher, a smart one indeed. Walk with me, would you?" He said rather than asked as he headed for the lantern affixed to the mast, from which he lit a reed stick to light his pipe. "How's the patch in the hold doing? Much seepage?"

"Holding quite well," Christopher replied. "If things hold together, we should be able to start swabbing the last of it out by the morning watch."

"Grand," he smiled as he exhaled a large puff of sweet-smelling smoke.

"It's the cargo I worry about sire."

"I too," he admitted. "We may have lost some already."

"Aye, the soft goods are soaked through and through. I worry about being able to save your investment. I'm just sorry I didn't spot the weak planking sooner. "

"You did a fine job Christopher," the Master said in a fatherly tone as he put his hand on Christopher's shoulder. "It was you who found a way to plug the rent, you may have saved this ship with your effort. I am proud to sail with you and thank you for thinking of my investment. However, it's the cargo we haul back to England that we must protect. That's the one that pays the bills. If we can get cost and a little more out of this cargo, well, that's all the better, put the silk and tea going back is where the money is to be made. Especially, if we can time it just right."

"What do you mean?"

"If we can arrive home when the supply of both tea and silk are low, the demand and the price will be high. I can get up to three times as much for a load than if we get home right after other ships have just arrived to fill the demand,"

"How do you know when the time is right?" Christopher asked, intrigued by this marketing strategy.

"Well," the Master relit his pipe. "I try to sail when most would consider it the off season. Usually, this would mean there would be little or nothing to load in Canton. But I have a special deal worked out with the authorities there. I don't haul things they don't want and do haul things they can't get from others. That way they always hold back enough cargo for us even after all the other ships have left for home." He puffed on his pipe a moment before continuing. "When we arrive in Canton, we will take stock of who is in port and who has recently left port for home. By judging how much cargo has already left for home and when, I will time our own departure accordingly. Hopefully we can arrive home when demand is at its highest or very near it."

"What if we get home and demand is not very high?" Christopher asked.

"Then we try again on the next trip." the Master laughed. "And the one after that, if I still have a ship."

"Won't our stopping to do repairs throw that timing off?" Christopher asked.

"Maybe," the Master turned a bit serious. "But not as much as sinking."

Christopher looked at him for a moment before they both started to laugh. The Master retired to his cabin and soon Christopher could hear the chime of seven bells. Half an hour more and his watch would be over. Having the company made the watch go so quickly. After being relieved at eight bells, Christopher went to his cabin and started writing in his journal. As he sat there thinking of what to write he could hear the men in the hold working the pumps. He would hate to stand an entire watch turning the handle on the pumps! Being Second Mate does have its benefits!

Wednesday, January 27, 1762
South Pacific

At seven bells Christopher rose from his berth and prepared himself for his watch. The night was still quite bright as he stepped out on the deck. The Mate reported that not much had changed during his watch. Christopher took a tour of the deck before heading down into the hold to inspect the work and the patch.

The smell of wet cotton and furs greeted his empty stomach unpleasantly as he descended the companionway. Less than three inches of water remained on the deck as he stepped off the companionway. One of the men informed him that they had been at that level for most of the watch. The water running back out of the cotton, linen and furs was the reason for the steady water level on the deck.

As for the patches, they seemed to be holding. When they could get the cargo out onto the deck above to dry, they would have to inspect the rest of the timbers more closely. Some of them could be seeping water as well.

As darkness slowly surrendered to dawn, the heavens changed hues every few minutes. A wonderful morning it turned out to be. The sun was rising just a point off the larboard turning the sky before them a dazzling kaleidoscope of color. To their flanks, streaks of pink, yellow and indigo. While directly ahead at a distance, the sky was a deep cobalt. Seven bells were struck, and it was time for breakfast.

After breakfast, the Master, the Mate and Christopher discussed the matter of the cargo in the hold. The water that remained would have to be swabbed out. It was time to begin bringing as much of the cargo as possible onto the open deck for drying purposes. It turned into a horribly smelly, nasty job.

To dry the linen and the furs, lines were strung between the masts and anything else that would hold them. The cotton was laid upon the deck and spread out in a manner which would promote the quickest drying. Luckily, the weather remained hot and sunny and aided the drying a great deal.

Carrying the wet cargo up out of the hold onto the deck for drying was a stinking, wet, back-breaking task. All except the Master and the Mate were involved. Christopher and the others had to gather as big of a bundle as possible of the wet, smelly cotton, pull it close to them so they could walk, and then carry it up the steep companionway. While they held it close, the stale water drained from the cotton into their shirt and pants, then ran down their legs into their boots. The odor permeated everything and burned at the nostrils. Christopher had to smile as he carried another armful onto the deck. As much as he hated the task, he was sure it was one of those things he would never forget!

By the time the night watch was set, the entire deck was in shambles. Everywhere one looked was either drying furs or linen hanging from lines running in every possible direction or stinking cotton spread out on the deck. There was scarcely enough room to do a proper job of sailing.

Thursday, January 28, 1762
South Pacific

This day was a repeat of the day before! The only difference was that they would turn the cotton every couple of hours to speed the drying process. At this rate it would be several days if not a week just getting the cotton dry. Providing of course that they weren't blessed with rain!

Young Richard was his usual self, hard working and always smiling. With God as his witness, Christopher believed the lad enjoyed the dirty work of sailing as much as sailing itself! The lad even turned a pretty good voice to the singing. Singing is one way a sailor faces his tasks at sea. The harder the task, the livelier the song, nothing takes one's mind off the task at hand better than a good song.

At five bells in the afternoon, Chips asked Christopher to lend a hand down in the hold, to inspect the before now, hidden timbers. As expected, there were several leaking seams but no broken timbers. Chips and Christopher spent the balance of the day caulking those seams. By eight bells they had yet to finish the task, the Master told Christopher to stay with the job and he would stand the watch.

By the dogwatch, the task was completed, Christopher however, was spent. He could barely lift his arms, all that hammering and beating had rendered his muscles used up. As he climbed the companionway to the main deck all he could think of was laying himself down in his berth.

Christopher slowly stepped onto the main deck where he was greeted by the Master and young Richard. The Master clearly understood how Christopher felt and again offered to stand watch. Christopher nearly accepted until he looked into the lad's face. He was sure that he imagined everything he saw there, but suddenly he felt that he had to stand his own watch, maybe as an example for the boy, and he politely declined the master's offer.

When his watch was over Christopher went straight to his cabin and without bothering to clean the tar and oakum off himself, he fell into his berth and slept as dead for the next three and half hours. Sarah must have taken pity on him, for when Christopher returned to his cabin after his next watch, he found that all his bedding had been changed. She must have taken clean bedding from her cabin. Christopher took care this time to clean himself up before using the new bedding. While he worked at removing the tar, he thought of her and found that he had grown very fond of her.

Friday, Saturday, January 29,30,1762
South Pacific Ocean

For two long and tiring days work on the cargo continued. Finally, around dusk on Saturday they finished with it. The cargo was safely back in the hold and quite dry. It may retain a light odor but that is nothing unusual. As for the iron nail and flat stock, they rubbed it down with a course cloth and fine oil. Young Richard worked the entire two days with several of the crew on the kegs of nails. Christopher thought that the nails looked better now than when they were loaded back in England.

One thing did happen that dampened the spirit of the ship. While stacking the flat stock in the bottom of the hold, John Tholman dropped his load on his foot. The iron ripped through his heavy boot and cut clear to the bone in the top of his foot. The shoe was quickly removed and the wound cleansed, then tightly wrapped to stem the flow of blood. Christopher and Red carried John to his berth.

Sabbath, January 31,1762
South Pacific Ocean

Since the beginning of this voyage Christopher had always looked forward to the Sabbath. Their day of rest. This day was to be different. Christopher awoke at three that morning with an uneasy feeling. He felt unsteady in both his stomach and head. He gathered himself up enough to relieve the Mate at the watch change. But by the time the bell tolled eight again, he was dead on his feet and bent over the bulwark vomiting. When the Mate came on deck, instead going to Christopher's aid, the Mate went for Sarah, she would know what to do and could help him to his berth.

Between John in the foc'sle with his crushed foot and Christopher in his cabin sick, Sarah spent the day running to and fro. But she tended to both and by the time the night watch was set Christopher was once again able to resume his duty. He was still weak but stood his watch just the same.

CHAPTER EIGHT
BECALMED AGAIN!

Monday, February 1, 1762
South Pacific Ocean
No Wind! Again!

At sunup the wind had slackened to the point of losing steerage, not that it would have mattered. By midday the wind had died all together. Since it had been barely a month from the last time they were becalmed, they remembered it all too well. By now many were mumbling about a cursed voyage. Never had any among them seen the likes of this trip! Four of their number had already died, becalmed where wind should be fresh, a hull that was falling apart beneath them! The heat became unbearable the moment there was not enough wind to dissipate its effects. The hotter it became the more the men cursed their luck and this trip. The fresh water supply was still good and rationing not needed unless they found themselves becalmed for an extended time.

With no sails to tend, the Master thought it wise to allow the crew to find whatever shade they could and rest. "The harder they work," he told Christopher, "the more water they will need. We'll do what needs to be done in the morning and evening and let them rest during the heat of the day. With any luck this situation will change before too long."

While Christopher rested beneath the canvass, they had rigged over the quarter deck, he found himself wanting to do some fishing. By taking a few pieces of dried pork and rigging a line and hook he went about trying to land something fresh to vary their diet. Just what Christopher would catch didn't matter. He really didn't know much about fish or fishing, if he was to catch something, he wouldn't even know what it was.

Luckily for him, the cook and old Chips did know something of fishing and were soon at his side doing likewise. It was only a matter of time before young Richard was in the act as well. For the first hour nothing much happened, the rest of the crew told them they were wasting their time and energy. Suddenly all four lines started to dance, one by one they started to pull in their lines, tossing their catch on the deck. The others quickly changed their minds and went after line and hooks. Soon the entire ship's complement was at the rails.

Every time young Richard would feel a tug on his line he would let loose with a boisterous laugh and begin fighting with his fish. The lad had never fished before and reveled in the thrill of it. There was so much excitement that the day passed quickly. The Master appeared on deck and asked the cook if he intended to prepare supper anytime soon? The cook did a wonderful job of preparing the fresh fish. The feast was fit for the Crown. What a treat! Everyone enjoyed it so thoroughly that they hoped to be becalmed tomorrow as well!

After the delightful supper, it was time to set the evening watch. Usually that meant putting away the items the crew had used during the day, this evening it meant getting everything out, as no work had yet been done, it would have to be done now.

After the watch had been set and the work done, the OCTAVIUS settled in for a quiet night. Young Richard joined Christopher on the quarterdeck. The wheel was lashed to hold it steady, since there was no wind there was no point in standing a turn at the wheel. Richard and Christopher talked about many things, but mostly about fishing, the lad wanted to know the first time he had gone fishing.

Christopher could scarcely remember the first time he had gone fishing, but could easily recall who it had been with, his father. Going to the stream to fish for trout was something nearly sacred for him and his father. It was a time for just the two of them. A time to talk, dream, and tell stories and laugh. Christopher missed those simple times and he missed his father. He couldn't help but wonder after all these years if his father still went down to the stream alone. He wanted to think that he did, he wanted to believe that when he did, he would remember their time together.

Tuesday, February 2, 1762
Pacific Ocean
Becalmed

At the first light of dawn the Master had all hands called. Work commenced at once. There were lines to be repaired, cloth to be mended, masts to be tarred, decks to be scrubbed. Plenty of work for all, so with a strong voice and a merry tune they stood into their work and did a fair day s job by eight bells at midday. At noon the Master gave the crew orders to rest until the dogwatch unless wind should appear, but with the glass reading so high, that was not likely.

They spent the day fishing but without the success of yesterday. The fish were few and far between. Many abandoned the effort after only a couple of hours. This day was to pass very slowly.

Wednesday, February 3, 1762
South Pacific Ocean
Becalmed.

A repeat of yesterday. Still no wind and not one fish was caught. The heat was nearly intolerable, but as the worst of it was spent under cover of cloth and enough water was still available, Christopher didn't feel this was yet as bad as when they were becalmed before. Even he gave up on the fishing and he doubted that he would try tomorrow as this area of sea appears quite dead.

Thursday, February 4, 1762
South Pacific Ocean
Becalmed - Still!

Shortly after the break from work around midday, Sarah came to Christopher and asked for his help. He didn't know at the time what she wanted but was soon to learn that it had to do with big John, the man who had injured his foot in the hold under the flat iron.

As Christopher entered the foc'sle he instantly smelled the stench of rotting flesh. He was appalled to learn the smell was coming from John's foot and leg. The foot had become rotten and very swollen. John himself was nearly mad with pain. Sarah had tried to explain to him that the foot would have to come off, the sooner the better. If the rot was not stopped soon, John himself would be consumed by it.

John was a proud man; he was very firm about keeping the foot right where it was and wanted nothing to do with cutting it off.

Sarah was beside herself, she had never seen such a rotten piece of meat, let alone the fact that it was still attached to a man. What weighed heaviest on her was the fact that she was the closest thing to a healer they had on board. After showing the foot to Christopher she covered it back up and motioned for him to step outside with her.

"What do you think of that, Mr. Jamison?" she asked.

A severe case of rot," Christopher replied. "The foot will have to come off very soon I should think."

"I think so too," she nodded. "But John will not hear of it. What am I to do?"

"I know so little about this kind of thing," Christopher shook his head. "Is there anything we can do to the foot before it comes off? Something to relieve the pain, maybe drain some of the poison off?"

"Maybe," Sarah was thinking. "Maybe if we opened it. Maybe then some of the poison can drain off. That might help it some, I just don't know." She looked directly into Christopher's eyes, "I just don't know, I've never seen such a state of things as this."

Christopher barely heard her words as he found himself thinking how beautiful Sarah was. He felt ashamed by the thought but couldn't seem to control it. He tried to sound reassuring and hoped she couldn't tell how he really felt. "It's worth a try." He offered lamely.

Then Sarah gently took his arm, "I'll get some strong ale from the cabin," she said. "You visit with John and try to get him to see the true nature of things."

Christopher merely nodded and returned to the foc'sle. The heat within the enclosed area was intense. John was bathed in a soaking sweat. His eyes screwed tightly shut and thin trails of blood streamed from his lower lip, caused by biting his lip to avoid screaming out in agony.

Christopher's efforts at talk with John were in vain. He either could not hear him or was in too much pain to answer. The only response Christopher did get out of him was when he mentioned something about the foot having to come off, then with incredible strength John grabbed his aim and held it tight while violently shaking his head back and forth. A. firm no!

When Sarah returned, Christopher recommended taking John out on deck, under the sail cloth where he might be a little cooler and hopefully more comfortable. Sarah said that he had not wanted to be moved out there before because he was ashamed of his condition and didn't want the others to pity him. Christopher was able to get John to agree to the move and enlisted the help of others to accomplish the job. As soon as they had John set up on deck, Sarah went to work on the foot.

The foot and leg had swollen and turned deep dark colors to a point halfway up the shin, the smell of it nearly made Christopher gag. Using a small sharpened knife, Sarah neatly cut a slit into the foot which instantly began seeping a bloody gray pus. John didn't seem to feel anything at first. But as the foot drained, the pressure against the skin and the swelling went down, this appeared to also lessen the pain John was feeling. Next Sarah poured a fair amount of ale over the cut. John screamed out for a moment then settled back down in a painless darkness.

"That doesn't change things." The Master had stepped up behind them. "If he is to live, the foot will have to come off. I've seen this kind of thing before, the rot has already gone too far.

"But how do you take a man's foot off?" Sarah sharply asked. "First, is that he doesn't wish us to. Second, is that I know nothing about doing such a thing. If it is not done right, we may as well let him die from rot."

"Aye," Christopher agreed. "How does one cut another's foot off without that man bleeding to death anyway?"

"I don't know myself," the Master admitted. "But I've a book in the cabin that tells of such things. I'd suggest, Mr. Jamison, that you spend the day reading up on how it is to be done and be ready by this time tomorrow to do the job."

Christopher was stunned. "But sire, why me?"

"Aside from myself and the Mate," the Master replied. "You are the only other who can read. I recommend that you read this book and read it aloud to my Sarah so the both of you will know what it is that's to be done for poor John here."

Christopher said nothing. What the Master said made sense, but he couldn't even bring himself to think of what it would be like to cut another's body. The Master turned and went for the book in the cabin. Sarah could sense that Christopher was stunned so she gently placed her hand on his arm. "Will you do it, Mr. Jamison? Will you read the book to me?"

Christopher seemed in a trance-like state. Deep within his mind he was seeing all the horror of what he was just asked to do.

"Will you?" she asked again, this time a little more forcibly

"Yes." Christopher slowly shook his head to clear it of all those negative thoughts. "Yes, I'll read it to you. You're certainly going to need to know what it says."

"Why do you say that Mr. Jamison?" Sarah asked.

"Because I don't think I'll be able to do the job." Christopher frowned.

"I doubt that I can do it alone either." Sarah took Christopher's arm and started leading him toward the shaded area of the deck. "But maybe together we can save John's life. Don't think of it as cutting another's leg off, think of it as saving a friend's life, because, Mr. Jamison, that is precisely what we are about to do."

Christopher nodded and offered her a slight smile. "Okay, we save John's life."

"Well then," she returned his smile. "We had best get started. I am sure that there is much to learn on this matter."

Christopher hadn't noticed but could have guessed that young Richard was close at hand. As soon as his mother went to see what was keeping the Master with that book, he stepped up behind Christopher and patted him on the back. "I will help you do the job," he offered.

Christopher looked into his soft cherub face and noticed the solemn expression. Yes, he bet the lad would help, but could he allow that. Could he allow a tender young boy to have a part in such an ugly business as this? "Thank you, Richard, but I think your mother and I can handle this."

Curiously enough, as Sarah and Christopher sat under the cloth, strung over the quarterdeck reading from the book of healing, they drew a crowd. Even old Chips seemed interested in how the task was performed. In going over the written words, Christopher would come across certain terms he had never heard before. Luckily, there were numerous drawings to help them along. After the first reading they all discussed what they had just learned. Chips offered to hone his best saw down to a fine tooth to prevent chipping the leg bone too much. The Master offered whatever linen would be needed as bandages. Even young Richard offered to help Cooky boil water and prepare for the task. Others brought up questions that required Christopher to go back through the book to find the answer. The book made it sound much simpler than Christopher knew it would be. But the fact that the entire crew seemed to be of one mind that it must be done, and all seemed ready to do what they could to assist, made Christopher feel better about it.

He had the eight to twelve watch that night and as he paced the deck, Christopher was deeply troubled by what he knew he must do in the morning. Part of him wanted to honor John's wishes and leave the leg alone, even though doing so would surely kill John.

Doesn't a man have a right to die with both of his legs?

Then the other part of him, his moral side, would speak up. It accused him of wanting to honor John's wishes just so he wouldn't have to do the cutting tomorrow. Actually, Christopher knew this to be the truth, but he couldn't help wondering, "What if I do the cutting and John still dies? How will I feel then? Will I always wonder if I should or could have done something differently? But if I do nothing and he dies, will my soul have any more peace for having done nothing to save him?"

Christopher was honestly scared, more so than at any time he could recall. His stomach was acting like a small yawl in a tempest, his hands had an uncontrollable shake to them. And he couldn't seem to concentrate on his duties. What was he going to do? Before he could weigh his options, the Master appeared on deck and stepped over to the rail beside him.

"You look troubled Christopher. Worried about that which you must do tomorrow?"

"Yes," Christopher replied. "I do not feel that it is something I can do."

. "If not you, then who?" He gently asked. "Me? With my big fat fingers? How would I tie the veins as the book says to do? The Mate? He is a good sailor, true. But tends to be a bit clumsy, and even he says so. You are the only other that can read."

"But I could read to another while they do the task."

"Would you work with confidence at a task you had never done, being told what to do by another who has never done it either? Book or no book, if a man cannot read, how is he to trust the printed word?"

"But I am worried that I will fail," Christopher admitted. "How will I live with such failure?"

"Aye, but you will certainly fail if nothing is done. No one aboard is better suited for this dirty business than you."

"What of Sarah? She has swift and caring hands."

"Was she that first recommended you for the job."

"But why?"

"You are the son of a man of God. You have always done what has been asked of you and have done whatever that was, well. You are smarter than almost any other soul aboard, probably including myself. You can think fast and are sure in actions. Should John come to before or during the cutting, I feel you are the only one strong enough to complete the job. I fear Sarah would not be able to finish should something like that happen."

"I am filled with doubt and fear just the same," Christopher said.

"That is good. I think it will make you work swift and sure. How many times have you read the book?"

"A dozen or More," Christopher replied. "I could recite it by heart and still I have doubts."

"You will do fine," the Master patted his back. "I and most of the others will be with you. If you forget anything, I will read from the book for you. The others will be on hand to restrain John should he awake, Chips says that he has the saw nearly ready. From what he tells me it should saw through the bone quickly. Then he took out his pipe, filled the bowl with tobacco and stepped over to the lantern. Sucking the bowl to life he stepped back over to the rail. "This is the damnedest trip I've ever made. I've never had an easy time of it, but never have I seen so many problems! We've had more trials and misery on this trip than all my other trips combined. There are always problems crossing the Horn, but I've been thinking that there must be a better way."

Christopher just looked at him for a moment, trying to decide what he meant He was about to ask then decided not to say anything.

"There is talk," the Master went on. "Of a passage through the north country. They call it the Northwest Passage. I wonder if one could find it any more difficult than this?"

'Aye," Christopher agreed cautiously. "This has been a very strange voyage that's for sure.

"Sorry you signed aboard?"

Christopher forced a smile. "Yes, there have been times, and tomorrow will be one of those times that I wish I had chosen to stay along the coast. But you have been very kind, and this is the best crew I have ever sailed with. I suppose I will always remember this time aboard with pleasure, at least for the most part."

"That's good," the Master laughed. "I assure you that I am damn glad you're with us. Yes sir, Mr. Jamison, I'm glad to have you along for this trip." He turned and started to walk away and then he stopped and turned back around. "Stop by my cabin before turning in."

"Tonight, sire?"

"Aye, tonight. I have something that just might help calm your jitters."

"I don't take drink, Sire."

"I think you may need this tonight, please stop by."

"Aye, Sire." Was all Christopher could say as the Master turned and walked off into the still darkness. Once again Christopher was alone with his thoughts, but somehow, he had found a bit a strength in what the Master had said. He would stop by the cabin.

At eight bells the Mate came on deck and spelled Christopher. The Mate was a tall man, standing nearly six feet tall and strong as an oak. His name was James something or other, Christopher couldn't for the life of him remember it. Having always referred to him simply as the Mate. The Mate was a kind man, soft spoken whenever there was no need for a strong voice. He spoke quietly and asked Christopher about any changes in the weather, there were none. Then he offered Christopher luck tomorrow and finished by saying that he would pray that God would grant Christopher strength.

Christopher thanked him then turned for the cabin to retire.

"If I were in John's shoes," the Mate called after him, "I'd want you to do the cutting."

Christopher stopped in his tracks, then slowly turned around. "But why?"

"Because I believe you care about the outcome more than just getting it over with. That's why you're so worried about it. I think that would make you do a handy job of it"

"Thanks," Christopher smiled weakly. "See you in four hours."

"No need," the Mate quickly replied.

"What?" Christopher asked, not sure that he had heard him right. "Why do you say that?"

"The Master wants you well rested," the Mate answered. "You are to rest until breakfast. The Junior Mate as you call him, and old Chips will stand your watch. With no wind, what difference will it make?"

"The boy?" Was all Christopher could say.

"Aye, the lad. Old Chips will keep an eye on things. If the wind comes up, the Master left orders for him or me to be called. He wants you to be sharp in the morning, as do the rest of us. Sleep well, Christopher."

"Aye, aye," Christopher replied and headed aft for the cabin.

Christopher knocked on the master's cabin door and waited until it was opened for him to enter. Sarah had come to the door in her night clothes and to Christopher she never looked more beautiful. The Master was sitting at his desk and offered him a seat with the wave of his hand. A bottle of stout ale sat opened on the desk.

Sarah closed the door behind him. "The Captain tells me you are sick with worry."

"Yes ma'am, I am a bit uneasy."

"You'll do well. Mr. Jamison. You will do quite well."

"Have told him so myself Sarah," the Master spoke. "But he is very troubled over this and rightly so. But Christopher, you must remember that you are not doing it alone. Sarah will help you and we will all be there to do what we can. Your part is most important, but we will all be doing this thing. John needs us whether he knows it or not."

"But he has stated his feelings about keeping the foot," Christopher pointed out.

"The fever has his mind," Sarah quickly discounted what John had said. "John has family back home. We must do what we can for his family, as well as for him. Could you face his wife and tell her all that was possible was done, if it was not?"

"No ma'am," Christopher nodded his understanding, she was right. What if it was his father? He would want someone to do whatever they could to save his life, even if it failed. He would want them to try, and so he would try tomorrow.

The Master poured a mug of ale and handed it to Christopher, motioning for him to drink up. Christopher downed the drink in one swallow and felt it burning all the way deep into his stomach. He had never touched drink before and now he understood why. How could a man do this to himself willingly?

By the time Christopher had downed several of the mugs he felt strangely different.

Young Richard was fast asleep in his little berth and unaware that Christopher was even there. The Master told Christopher how proud Richard was when he was told that he would stand a watch by himself. Christopher had no doubt that was true, he wished he could have been there to see it. Suddenly Christopher was feeling very tired, the drink was having the effect the Master had hoped for, at least he should sleep well tonight. After the fourth or fifth mug of ale Christopher said good night to the Master and Sarah. On the way to his cabin he was thinking what fine folks they were. He was lucky to sail on such a ship even though it was on the damnedest voyage, as the Master had called it.

Friday, February 5, 1762
South Pacific Ocean
Becalmed
The removal of John's leg

    Christopher awoke to the ding of seven bells being struck on the ship's bell. He had often seen men who had taken too much drink the morning after. Surprisingly, he felt quite fit as he rolled out of his berth and stood up. He still felt weak in the stomach, but maybe a good meal would settle that.
    After breakfast Christopher went forward to see how John was doing, the foot

looked worst than ever. He had doubts about whether he would be able to cut it off. As he was standing there watching John's chest rise and fall with every breath, Sarah came forward to rinse his face and wash the leg.

"I hope we can do this," Christopher said.

"We will do what must be done." She looked up at Christopher. "We have no choice. If you were in his place what would you want?"

"I am not sure," Christopher answered truthfully. She smiled. "I know what I would want. You don't have children yet, Mr. Jamison. If you did, you would want to do anything that would give you any chance of seeing them again. I know, I am a mother and wife."

"Yes ma'am," was all Christopher could say as he turned and headed aft to read the book of healing once more.

At eight bells they gathered on the foredeck with tools and washbasins at the ready, the hour of truth was at hand. For the first time in his life Christopher would apply steel to another's flesh, he would take from John that which he did not wish to give. Hopefully Christopher would also give something to him that he did not want to give up, his life.

Following the books direction, Christopher first took a strap of cloth and tied it around the leg several inches above the rotted area. Then with a small wooden bit which he inserted into the cloth he turned it until it had pinched the skin tightly.

With trembling hands Christopher reached for the sharply honed carving knife Chips had offered for the job. He very carefully started the cut just below the tightened cloth. At first, he drew some blood, the cloth was tightened some more, and the bleeding stopped.

The skin parted easily and was cut all the way around the leg, then up the leg in four different slices leaving the main leg bone exposed. The smell from the rotted flesh was sickening, but with Sarah's help he proceeded.

Once the bone was clearly exposed, Christopher took the retooled saw that Chips had prepared and began to saw through the bone. Just before laying the blade against the bone he looked up at Sarah first, then the Master. Standing around the plank they used as the operating table was the entire balance of the crew, everyone seemed to nod in unison, and Sarah offered a sweet smile.

Taking the flesh that would remain attached to John's body and laying it back against the tied cloth, Sarah held it out of his way. The purpose of the four slits was to allow him to cut the bone high enough to be able to then wrap the strips of flesh around it and protect the remaining stub of bone.

The actual cutting of the bone reminded Christopher of dressing chickens back home. Chips had done a wonderful job with the knives and saw. Everything was sharp and the work went quickly and smoothly. Once Christopher made it through the bone, the rotten leg fell off the plank and landed atop his right foot. The thought of it nearly did him in. Quickly the Master reached down, took the leg and threw it over the side. Instantly the air smelled better.

Next, Christopher took a bottle of strong ale, pouring it over the severed leg and thread he was about to use to sew John back up. The first step to closing the wound was the tying of the major blood vessels. These were a bluish-red, and very hard to hold. The job was trying at best. Christopher would have to grab the vessels and attempt to sew them tightly closed. Luckily, they had a little stretch to them and after a couple of failures, he got the knack of it and did a fine job of sewing. The next step was searing the smaller ones, this he accomplished by placing a knife over flame until the blade glowed red. Then touching the blade to the smaller vessels, the searing heat sealed the vessels.

Finally, taking the straps of meat, Christopher carefully wrapped them back over the stub and tightly stitched them into place. After which Sarah carefully wrapped the stub leg in clean linen cloth and washed John's face and chest.

It was over. Christopher said a silent prayer, looked up towards heaven and took a deep breath of relief. He believed that he had done his best. It was now in God's hands.

The Master patted him on the back and asked several of the men to wash the deck to remove the blood. Sarah was busy tending to John and only offered that sweet smile of hers as Christopher thanked her for her help. All the while praying that he'd never be put in that position ever again.

The rest of the day went on as before. They rested during the heat of the day under their makeshift tents on deck. However, this time they returned to their fishing. They caught nothing and almost no one spoke. No matter, it was good for the soul.

Young Richard went to visit Christopher before his watch. He was quiet for the most part but did say that he was proud of what Christopher had done that day. Somehow that alone lifted Christopher's spirits. Christopher was now beginning to feel as though he had done the right thing. Then the lad's questions turned to ones Christopher couldn't answer.

"Some of the men are talking of Eden," he started. "They speak of the food, the drink, but most of all they speak of the women. Why do men want to spend time with women anyway?"

Christopher said nothing. What could he say to a lad of his years?

"Then I heard one of the men say," he continued, "That he wanted to feel a woman's naked body against his. Why?"

Christopher shrugged, "I don't know that answer."

"You think that maybe he's been drinking from the sea?"

"Why do you say that?"

"I think maybe he's mad, like the others that had taken water from the sea. Maybe he's mad and doesn't know what he is saying. Do you think it possible?"

Christopher didn't know what he should say at this point, so he tried to remain neutral. "Could be. I will watch this fellow carefully. Which man was it?"

"James Stuart," the lad replied. "You know, the one with the red trousers."

"Aye, I know the one. I will watch him more closely. You can be sure of it." What he did not tell the boy was what he really would do is have a talk with the men involved about how they conduct themselves around the lad:

At last the night watch was set. Christopher had the eight to twelve watch, one of his favorites. He had just begun his rounds when James Stuart crossed the deck in front of him. Stuart didn't much care for the talk they had but did agree in the end to be more watchful of what he and the others said in the presence of the boy.

The watch went without a whisper of wind. Christopher prayed for some change; anything would almost certainly be better than drifting with any current that happened along. He went forward and checked on John. He was still sleeping. Christopher was half afraid of the moment he would wake up. Then on the other hand he was also worried that John would never wake up. John did appear to be resting more comfortably, but Christopher could not be sure of hat.

About four bells Sarah came on deck and hung some clothes up to dry on lines they had strung across the aft deck for that purpose. Christopher was at the time on his way aft from checking on John. By the time he reached the quarter-deck she had finished her task and was starting forward with a lantern and some fresh bandages for John. "How is he doing this evening?" she asked.

"I cannot tell for certain," Christopher replied. "I think he may be more comfortable."

"That is good," she smiled. "I took the liberty of washing some of your things when I did the Captain's and Richard's."

"You shouldn't trouble yourself over my things." Christopher responded, but glad that she did. He hated to wash his clothes and would go as long between washes as possible.

"No bother at all," she smiled before turning and heading forward.

Seven bells the Mate was on deck and checking for change in conditions. Christopher inquired why he was on deck so soon and was told that he couldn't sleep. The cabin was unbearable. Christopher found that to be true, so he just grabbed his journal and pillow, then returned to the deck to sleep.

Saturday, February 6, 1762
South Pacific Ocean
Wind!

Christopher was nearing the end of the four to eight watch when the Master came on deck and informed him that they would not spend another day waiting for the wind to find them. After breakfast the boats were to be launched and they would haul before the ship in search of wind.

Christopher believed the men took this news as relief, as they too wanted to be on their way toward the paradise they spoke of; Eden.

Christopher had charge of the pinnace and the Mate the longboat. As soon as the lines were taut, they began to haul the ship in search of wind. It was back-breaking work. The sun was merciless. Each man was allowed one leather flask of water and was told that he should ration it as it would be all he would get until the dogwatch was called.

Most of the men did just that. One or two had the misfortune to drink their water up too soon, leaving nothing to quench their thirst during the worst heat of the day. Christopher pitied those men but could do nothing to help. They had done it to themselves and would have to pay the price.

The day was nearly spent, when out of the northeast, a stiff breeze suddenly sprang up and the OCTAVIUS leaped into it. They barely had time to haul themselves back to her sides before she ran away from her own boats. If not for the lines, Christopher felt she would have done just that. As it was, they were barely able to close her sides and haul themselves over the wale. The boats were brought aboard after they once again had control of the ship.

The sheets were run out and the lines set, the boats hauled aboard and the proper watch in place. It was then Sarah came up to Christopher and said that John wanted to speak with him.

"He's awake?" Christopher was surprised.

"Yes, thanks to you."

Christopher went forward and found John sitting up on his cot looking the worst for wear. His face was flush and drawn, his body covered in sweat. His lips parted into a smile when he saw Christopher coming up the companionway to the foredeck.

"Mr. Jamison," he called to him. "I am told that this is your handiwork." He nodded with his head toward the bandaged stub seeping blood through the cloth.

"Yes," Christopher replied, not knowing what he might say next and fearing the worst.

"You did a fine job. Saved my miserable life I am told. For that I thank you."

"I did what I could."

"Aye, that you did. I did not think our Second Mate a healer. I was wrong."

"The Master's wife did much to save your life."

"So, I'm told. But it was you that did the job."

"Yes."

"You did a fine job."

"Thank you." Christopher didn't know what else to say, he hadn't considered this reaction to John losing his leg.

"I do have one question for ya," John looked him in the eyes.

"What is that John?"

"What am I to do now? How can I climb the shrouds and set the sails with only one leg? Should I return home and try my hand at the soil? How well do you think I should do hopping along with a hoe? How can I tend to my wife and family?"

Christopher was taken by surprise and didn't know what he should or could say to that.

"You did save my life," John said. "But at the same time, you condemned my wife and family to a life of poverty. The Master would give her my pay for this trip and sadly announce that I was lost. My Mary is a handsome woman, she would weep a time then get on with life, at least for the sake of the children. She would find another man who could provide for her better than I will be able to now. Yes, Mr. Jamison, you did save my life, but I ask you for what?"

Christopher stood stock still. He could clearly see John's point. "I'm sorry." he stammered. "I didn't think of those things."

"Of course, you didn't." John cursed him and his stupidity.

"That's enough of that talk!" The booming voice of the Master was heard behind them. "Do you think that a man without one of his legs is really that useless?"

"Yes Sire," John answered. "I certainly do."

"Well, it just isn't true." The Master quickly replied. "There is much to running a ship. Especially, one in the shape of this one. As soon as your stub has healed properly,

Chips will have a wooden one made for you. It will be a problem to get used to I'm sure, but I know that you are up to it. Furthermore, once you have gotten use to that new leg, you will begin training under Chips as a ship's carpenter. What say you to that?"

At first John didn't say anything. He simply looked at the Master as if the old man had said nothing. Then slowly his face took on a new look entirely, his snarled lips turned into a big smile. "Do you mean it, Sire?"

"Aye."

"That is good news."

"Then I should think that you will want to readdress Mr. Jamison here."

"Aye Sire," John replied, before turning to Christopher. "I am truly sorry for the harsh words and want to truly thank you this time for my life, Mr. Jamison."

"You are most welcome." Christopher replied before taking his leave and heading aft, away from the Master and John. Christopher was so confused at that moment he did not know what to think of it all. He was most grateful that the Master happened along when he did. He also hoped that John would continue to heal and that he would enjoy his new line of work.

The OCTAVIUS ran well before the wind which was coming in off their starboard quarter. The clothes upon the strung lines were whipping around in the breeze and would not take long to be dry. The canvass covering on the quarterdeck was taken in, as it would no longer be needed. One doesn't have to hide under cover when on a living, running ship. There is enough draft created by open hatches to keep the heat off the body, even in one's berth.

As night set in, the evening watch was set and those not on watch could retire to their berths for some refreshing sleep. Christopher admitted to himself that when on land, becalmed, or at anchor, he tended to be a bit restless. The rocking motion and the constant melody of creaks and groans of a working ship was the perfect remedy for listlessness.

CHAPTER NINE
EDEN

Sabbath, February7, 1762
South Pacific Ocean

Sarah had cleaned and mended Christopher's clothes better than he could have ever done, so he went to the cabin and thanked her again. Then he went forward to visit with John a few moments during his tour of the foredeck. He seemed to be in higher spirits and looking forward to his new position on the ship.

Monday, February 8, 1762
South Pacific Ocean

Being the first day after the Sabbath, after being becalmed, there was much to do. The masts and spars were treated to a fresh coat of tar and each item was checked and repaired if needed. As before, young Richard worked like a man and if the truth be told did more than his share.

He had developed a real talent for climbing up the rigging and being very hard to keep up with. They also found that with his light weight, they could easily swing him around the rigging in the bosun chair, and few could tar as quickly as he.

The caulking in the hull on the forward starboard side was found to be leaking here and there. Most of the worst spots were taken care of, the rest would wait until tomorrow.

Tuesday, February 9, 1762
South Pacific Ocean
Land!

Land came into view around mid-watch of the morning watch and was spotted off both the larboard and starboard side of the bow. The Master told Christopher that these were not islands to be stopped at. So far as he knew, no white man had ever stopped there, and he did not intend to be the first. But he did add that they were good to see, as it meant that Eden was only one day away if everything went smoothly.

They passed between the islands around midday. They didn't look like much really, only land, and land of any sort looks inviting after so long at sea.

A very odd thing happens when one first passes so close to land. The first thing to happen is that you smell the land. It really doesn't matter what land it is; it reminds you of someplace else. Home for most, some exotic port for others. Then you notice the foul odors coming from the ship you sail on, next comes the realization that a goodly share of those odors is permeating from your very being.

Christopher suddenly realized that he too was looking forward to reaching this Southern Ocean paradise he had heard so much about. That realization took him by surprise, and he would not admit it to anyone on board, especially not young Richard, but he looked forward to being around the fairer sex. Maybe Sarah's presence had awakened something within him. He prayed that he would have the courage and would not sin before the almighty, but a part of him wished for that which James Stuart had spoken of, that which was overheard by young Richard. The thought of it made Christopher anxious, what would his aging parents think if they knew that? Thank Heaven a man's thoughts are his own!

Wednesday. February 10, 1762
Eden

At last they reached that worshiped jewel of the Pacific. It came into view just before nightfall. The Master had them close on the shore a bit, then he dropped the hook. The entire night watch stood toward the bow and stared off in the direction of that dark hole in the night. Before the island, the sea sparkled from the moonlight and stars, above and behind it the sky was well lit. Christopher couldn't wait to see what the first light of day would bring.

At first light the Master had the hook brought up and they sailed along the island in search of a sandy beach upon which to gently beach their tired old ship. They had not long to search for their haven, it came into sight at a most perfect time, as it was high tide. They gently brought the ship as near the shore as possible without going to ground. Then with the ship broadside to the beach they dropped both the starboard and aft hooks. With the pinnace and longboat, they took the ship in tow. Christopher in the pinnace at the bow and the Mate in the longboat at the stern.

Together they towed in unison as the cable was let out on the hooks. In this way they worked the ship toward the shore until they had her well-grounded. At this point the larboard hook was hauled out and placed well onto the beach. Then another aft hook was rigged likewise. It took them well into the morning to get the ship secured into her safe haven. It would take a swell of unusual proportions to cause them any concern.

Christopher was a bit surprised by the fact that the guns had been gotten out of the locker and issued to the men on deck. He would find out very soon that it had been only a precaution.

After the ship was secure, they broke for a very late breakfast. When next Christopher came onto the deck, he could see some of the natives cowering in the tree line.

"What are they afraid of?" he asked no one in particular.

"Don't be too hasty to have them come closer," the Master replied. "So long as they feel unsure, we are safe. I have stopped here before and found the natives to be most pleasant. But time and the unknown changes men, even simple natives. I warn you young Jamison, always watch your back , but be most gracious. My experience with these people is that they are proud, if nothing else. Take what they offer and give fair value in return."

"What could they have that I would know or understand the value of?"

"You will get the feel for it as you go along. Just remember, it is what value they place on it that counts. If you want to keep something, keep it hidden in your berth. Otherwise all else is fair game for barter."

"Yes Sire," Christopher replied. Not thinking of anything other than his journal that he would not care to barter for something he might find of interest.

"I will issue a number of iron nails to each of the crew for bartering." The Master added, "these are fancied by the natives. You must be very careful; the natives are prone to stealing whatever they can get away with."

"Aye, aye Captain," Christopher answered, wondering whether he would fare well against an accomplished thief.

The natives must have smelled their breakfast cooking in the galley as they seemed to gain sudden courage. A fair number of them, Christopher guessed it to be around two to three hundred, slowly emerged from the tree line and started closing in on their anchored ship.

In the middle of the throng, carried upon the shoulders of four other native males was an older, fatter man, whom he assumed was their King. The Master recognized this man and gestured for the King to come aboard, which he did at once. The Master then walked the King around the main deck of the OCTAVIUS, presenting the King with gifts as they went. After the tour of the deck, the King was given a place at the master's table and breakfast was served.

Much to Christopher's surprise, the Master asked him to join them. Christopher was shocked to find the native King made no effort at all to feed himself. He had two servants who supplied him with both food and drink. He didn't even bother to wipe his own mouth. It was surprising that he found-the energy to chew for himself.

After the King had left their deck, the Master called them all together and told them to behave themselves and watch their tails. "Those of you that have not been here before will find certain customs of the natives unusual. You will conduct yourselves in a manner befitting gentleman."

Christopher couldn't help but wonder which customs he was speaking of. Although he knew in time, he would no doubt find out.

Shortly after breakfast several them were sent ashore with Chips to search out the trees that would be needed to repair the ship. Also, tents were set up on shore to serve as workstations. Before night fell, lines would be affixed to several stout trees with which they could haul the ship over on her starboard side to begin the work of repairing her larboard hull. Several of the men had already dug out the sawing pit, and three good sized trees were cut down and hauled to the beach.

The moment Christopher went ashore with Chips, he discovered what the Master meant by certain customs. No sooner had they stepped into the jungle, not a hundred yards from the ship, than they spotted a young couple of natives entwined together in passionate lovemaking. They were thrashing about on the ground just off the path, in open daylight for all to see. The circle of natives around the white men just stepped around the couple and appeared to think nothing of it.

Christopher was appalled and stimulated at the same time. Amongst the native crowd about them were a dozen youthful beauties with lightly tanned skin, large soft brown eyes and raven silky hair. Each wore flowers tucked into their hair and little, so very little, covering their loins. Nothing whatsoever covered their upper torsos. Christopher suddenly doubted that, and he and Chips would ever need to finish their discussion on whether this was Heaven on earth. This exotic island was everything the men had claimed it to be. All around them were coconut trees, breadfruit trees, flowers of many varieties and freshwater streams. Before this day's work was done, they would see at least half a dozen more couples engaged in lovemaking out in the open.

Christopher could see that the men were going to enjoy this haven a great deal. He also wondered how he would conduct himself. That was somewhat worrisome at the moment. He had never been with a woman before and had never thought of the first time being with anyone less than the woman he would die with. Now he was not so sure, he supposed he would take things as they happened.

By nightfall much had been accomplished. Watches aboard the OCTAVIUS amounted to little more than guard duty. Of

Christopher's larboard watch, only three men armed with rifles and himself kept the watch. He paced the deck, keeping a sharp eye for boarders, remembering the master's caution about the natives being good at stealing. He suddenly became aware that young Richard was at his side, talking as usual.

"Did you see those lasses?" he was asking. "Did you notice that they wore nothing over their chests?"

Before Christopher could answer, he found himself smiling at a single thought, he was glad the lad hadn't gone ashore with them earlier. What would he have thought of that?

"Why are you smiling?" he asked.

"Oh, I was just thinking, that dressed as they are, it must be a hindrance when climbing trees," Christopher lied.

"What?"

"Pay it no mind," Christopher laughed. "It is indeed a strange land. What do you make of it, Master Richard?"

"I swear, I don't know," he answered truthfully.

Friday, February 12, 1762
Eden

At dawn's first light the Master had them all hard at work. A dozen of the men led by Chips and Christopher were dispatched into the jungle in search of just the right trees. Trees that would lend themselves suitable for the timbers they needed to repair the ship.

Their job was to select the trees, bring them down, and then haul them to the beach. A job made much easier by the willingness of the large number of natives that went along to help. Among the natives were a dozen or so of the female variety. Behaving like English gentlemen, as the Master had put it, would not be the easiest of tasks to accomplish, especially considering the natives' views toward sex, anywhere, anytime, with anyone!

By eight bells, midday, they had felled a dozen good-sized trees. These were in the stages of having all branches removed from the trunk when they decided to break for a meal of coconut and breadfruit. All of which was generously supplied by the natives

Several of the men mysteriously disappeared as did an equal number of the native lasses. Christopher chose not to notice. One of the native girls did not disappear, she was of heavenly design. Long legs of silky-smooth umber skin that glistened in the afternoon sun. Her torso widened at the hips then tapered back in to form a narrow waist before tapering back out over the rib cage. Her breasts, while smaller than some, were perfect in form and heaved slightly with each breath. Her face was angelic with full red lips, big dark brown eyes that sparkled with life. Raven hair that shimmered in the sun as it fell across her shoulders.

Christopher had noticed this particular beauty watching him since yesterday, her attention filled him with both hope and concern. She was without a doubt one of the most attractive creatures he had ever laid eyes upon. The only disfigurement, if one could call it that, was in the form of some sort of tattoo engraved across her buttocks. Since all the native girls appeared to have the same type of markings, Christopher believed them to be some sort of ritual.

As Christopher ate the delicious meal of coconut and breadfruit, the beauty watched. Nothing was said, not that they could have understood each other. Christopher tried not to notice her but was unsuccessful. He suddenly felt himself wanting to be with her, to touch her, to feel her tender softness, to taste her full sweet lips.

Finally, it was time to return to work. Christopher called for the missing men as he forced his own desires from his mind. The missing men reappeared in a matter of minutes. From their appearances, Christopher had no doubt what they had been up to. By dusk they had a stockpile of trees lying on the beach numbering nearly thirty fine logs.

After the evening meal, Christopher decided to walk off his frustrations by taking a stroll down the beach. A couple of hundred yards from the ship he came upon a small lagoon. It was a soothingly warm night, illuminated by a heaven full of sparkling stars with a gentle breeze blowing in from the sea. The ocean swell was greatly retarded by the ring of coral that formed the lagoon. The only human sounds to be heard came from the direction of the OCTAVIUS. The rustle of palm fronds and the roll of the light surf were nature's only chorus.

Being alone, Christopher stripped down to his shorts and ran out into the warm sparkling water of the lagoon, he swam for an hour before tiring and wadding ashore.

On the sand, sitting next to his clothes was the same beauty from the jungle that afternoon. She had been watching him in the water. As he stepped closer, she made no effort to speak. Her big brown eyes looked black in this light, but the sparkle was brighter than ever. As he drew near her, he noticed she no longer wore the covering around her loins.

Christopher stopped dead in his tracks, having no experience in these matters, he was confused as what to do. She smiled sweetly, slowly laying back on the sand exposing her beauty before him and heaven. Getting no reaction from him, she must have thought that he did not understand her meaning. She reached for him with her right hand while caressing herself with the left.

This was more than poor Christopher could stand, he stepped up to her and gently rubbed the back of his right hand across her smooth cheek, then just as gently cupped her chin. He smiled at her, then bent down, grabbed clothes and made off for the OCTAVIUS. What her reaction to this was, he didn't know, as he never looked back.

His reasons for doing what he did played through his mind as he walked toward the ship. First, he was not sure he could do something like that with someone he didn't know. Secondly, what if young Richard had set out to find him, only to do so with her in his embrace. All of which made the third reason even more sound. He would not make love to a woman for the first or last time for that matter, out in the open for all the world to see.

If he hurt the native beauty's feelings, then he was truly sorry, but he saw no other way. He felt he had no choice but to walk away. Still, he found himself wishing it could have been otherwise.

CHAPTER TEN
PRINCESS OTERIA

Saturday, February 13, 1762
Eden

This day Christopher worked in the sawing pit. The pit was dug to the depth of six feet with a width of four feet. Each log was placed over the pit and sawn into boards using a two-man saw. One man would work in the pit while the other worked topside. This arrangement worked very well and in a good day they could plank out four or five trees.

While the sawing was going on in the pit, the broken hull planking was slowly removed from the OCTAVIUS, exposing her ribs to the hot tropical sun. Since the ship was lying prone near the water's edge, her entire length was carefully inspected for any signs of worms or fractures.

Around midday they broke from their work for the midday meal. As Christopher climbed from the pit, he noticed that the same beauty was there watching him. Once again, she had the meek covering over her loins.

Christopher took his food and walked over to the shade of the palms. Sitting with his back to the trees he could view the entire beach area before him. His heart nearly leaped from his chest as he watched the beauty rise from where she had been sitting and walk toward him. With each step her hips flowed in a natural motion, beckoning for him to partake of their fruit.

She sat close by his side but slightly behind him. Reaching out, she gently rubbed the sweat from his bare back. The softness of her hand set a shiver up his spine, at which she giggled. All around him seemed to hang in a haze. All he was conscious of was her touch, a touch he wanted to return, a tenderness he longed to surrender to, a warmth he longed to possess.

He decided right there and then that he would have to find a way to communicate with this lovely creature. From what he had seen around him, here on the island, it was clear that mating held a somewhat different meaning than he had been reared to believe. The guilt and shame of sexual variety did not appear to exist in this place. From his observations, making love held little more meaning here than an ordinary handshake back home. That was not to say that he could turn his back on his morals and beliefs. Morals that he doubted this lass could understand, but then she did seem a bit apart from the others somehow. She had chosen to stay with him, even without the physical tie.

Maybe she would understand, if he could find a way to convey his thoughts to her.

He slowly turned to face her. At first, she appeared a bit apprehensive and pulled back. Christopher gently reached out with an open hand and took her hand in his. It felt so soft and tender. She was now showing no reluctance to his efforts. Encouraged, Christopher then pointed to himself and slowly and carefully said, "Christopher. I am Christopher."

"Tri...Tri...fe," she stammered at the name.

"Yes, yes," Christopher was delighted that she even attempted the name. "That's right! Christopher. My name is Christopher." Again, he pointed to himself and repeated the name. "Christopher."

"Tris...ta...fe, Tris...ta...fe, Tristafe!" She beamed in her delight. Then pointing at him she said, "Trisofe."

He was so happy at her success that he gently squeezed her hand, and then lightly kissed it which made her giggle at first. Then she took her hand and held it with the backside, the part he had kissed, to her cheek.

And you are?" he asked, pointing to her.

"Yoo..,,ar...e?" She tried the words.

"Your name," Christopher pointed to her, then pointed back at himself and repeating his name before pointing back at her.

She slowly caught his meaning and pointed back at herself. "Oteria.

"You are Oteria?" Christopher asked to be sure.

She beamed her pleasure in hearing him say her name. "Oteria," she said pointing back at herself. Then turning her finger and pointing at him, "Tristofe."

They smiled and laughed together at this simple pleasure of being able to communicate in the crudest sense. Seeing the other men returning to the task of turning rough logs into workable lumber, Christopher rose to his feet. In seeing him do so, she also stood up.

"Oteria taio no Tristofe?" she asked as he started to walk back to the saw pit. Christopher turned back toward her and smiled, he didn't know what she was saying, only that she had used her name and his in the same breath. He thought that it probably meant something good, so he nodded, which she did in response.

The Master had been near enough to where Oteria and Christopher had been sitting that he overheard what she had said. He walked back to the pit with Christopher and tried to translate she had meant. "Oteria taio no Tristofe," means something like Oteria friend of Christopher." He smiled. "I believe you have found a friend in that young one. You're a lucky man Christopher, she's the pick of the litter.

"She is charming," Christopher admitted.

"Aye, that she is," he agreed before turning a bit more serious. "You know that she is the King's daughter?"

"No. No I didn't know this."

"Aye, that she is." The Master sighed. "Be careful not to offend her if you can help it. We need the old King to be kind to us so we can make our ship fit as soon as possible. Do a bit of trading, then be on our way. And none too soon mind you. With the sights Sarah has already seen, I believe she thinks none too highly of this paradise."

"I intend to behave properly, Sire."

"I'm sure you do Christopher, I'm sure you do. But here in this place, that just may or may not be the way to be. As you can see around you, they feel quite differently about sex than we. Your attempt at being proper might be an offense to their way of thinking. Unpolite like."

"What am I to do?"

Master stopped and turned back to glance at the girl, then at Christopher. "On that subject my young friend, I haven't a clue. But I do hope you find the appropriate thing to do. Whatever that might be."

That day the work passed so quickly. Oteria sat at the edge of the saw pit and watched Christopher work. Chips came by to inspect the work and made comment of the girl's presence. Every time Christopher looked up; there she was. Always smiling, always looking right at him with those big soft brown eyes.

The day was nearly done when young Richard came by the pit and checked on Christopher. "How are you doing, Mr. Jamison?" Richard called down to him.

"I'm doing very well thank you," Christopher hollered back, as he pulled and shoved the saw blade back and forth through the wood.

"Mind if I spell you for a bit of water?" he asked.

"Not in the least my young friend, not in the least." Before Christopher saw him jump, young Richard was in the pit and standing at his elbow. Then Richard noticed the native maiden sitting at the edge of the pit staring down at them.

"Have you noticed her?" he asked, nodding in Oteria's direction. Christopher nodded that he had.

"What does she want?"

"Why, she wants your friend Jamison there!" Red, the man on the topside end of the saw laughed in response.

"Is that so?" Richard seemed shocked or disgusted, Christopher was not sure which.

"Aye, it be the truth." Red quickly added. "I think it be a case of love at first sight. That beauty hasn't taken her eyes off ol' Jamison here for two full days."

"You'll do well to put your energy into your work and not your mouth," Christopher tried quiet Red.

"What'd I tell ya lad?" Red laughed, while putting a bit more force into the saw. "He's already defending her. A sure sign of love, if you'd ask me."

"Pay that fool no mind," Christopher told Richard as the lad took the saw handle and offered a flask of water in return. "She's the King's daughter. I was just teaching her some English. Nothing to it really." Christopher wasn't too sure that he believed that himself, but he hoped the lad did.

"She's pretty enough Richard admitted between heaves on the saw as he tried to handle it as a man would. "But she's female, and what good is a female anyway?"

"What good is a female?!'" Red lost his grip on the saw for a moment. "Indeed? What good is a female?"

"Never you mind the question Red!" Christopher sternly tried to shut Red up. He got the point and didn't offer an answer.

"Your mother is a female," Christopher reminded Richard.

"So?"

"Females are not a bad thing." Christopher was hoping for a concession, be it ever so small. Something that he could use to reason with the lad.

"I suppose not, young Richard replied, giving him what he thought to be a small victory. But the lad dashed that prayer in an instant. "But they're quite useless on a ship. And if a ship doesn't need them, why does a sailor?"

"And how does thee answer that, Mr. English teacher?" Red was taking delight in the conversation.

"A good woman is a fine thing to behold, my young friend. Take Oteria there, certainly one of God's finest creatures. Did you know that God made woman last? As is so often the case, the finest comes last, after much practice.

"Good lord!" Red laughed.

"Do you believe that to be true?" Young Richard did not seem convinced.

"Why not?" Christopher smiled. "Look into her eyes, behold her beauty." The boy was looking. "Now look at Red there and tell me if you think I am wrong."

The smile faded from Red's face, not that it was a handsome smile to begin with. In fact, Red was downright homely himself, with a very ruddy complexion, unruly red hair, rotten teeth, and a body covered in scars that bore witness to his wild, devil-may-care lifestyle.

"She may be prettier than Red," the lad finally replied. "But on my ship, I would much rather have Red than her. He can sail, what good is she beyond being pleasing to the eye?"

"A fine woman is one's just reward for growing into manhood." Red surprised Christopher with that remark and was rewarded by a wink from him.

"You mean," Richard did not seem overly sure. "That when I become a man, I will have to take a woman?"

"Not at all," Chips was at the mouth of the pit again. "I've been a man for ages, and you don't see me with one of those!" The old carpenter pointed in Oteria's direction. When he noticed the disappointed look on Christopher's face he quickly added, "Although a woman of this beauty might be good for my old bones."

Christopher doubted very much whether they had convinced young Richard of anything. He acted rather indifferent toward Oteria but did agree to join Christopher and her that night after supper.

After the night watch was set, the three of them went for a stroll along the beach. They must have walked for over a mile before Richard sat down and took his shoes off.

Christopher thought the idea had merit, so he too removed his heavy boots. They continued down the beach letting the warm surf lap at their feet. They rounded a bend that offered a wide-open beach that surrounded a small inlet. Both Richard and Christopher sat at the water's edge, letting the water roll over their toes. Oteria moved around in front of them and sat in the water.

Christopher pointed to Richard. "Richard taio no Christopher," Pointing back to himself. "Christopher taio no Oteria. Richard taio no Oteria." Pointing from Richard to her.

She smiled and reached out and touched Richard's arm, "Ri...sL.ide taio no Tristafe-Oteria taio no Tristafe, Oteria taio no Rishide."

"What did she say?" Richard was instantly excited. "What did she say?"

"She said that you are a friend of mine, she is a friend of mine, she is a friend of yours as well."

They worked on many other words that night. Oteria showed great interest in their words, far more than she showed in teaching them hers. So, Richard and Christopher proceeded to teach her English.

In all they taught her quite a few words. She was very sharp and picked up the words quickly and appeared to forget very little of what she had learned. It was great fun for all, as she would touch something, and Christopher or

Richard would sing out the English name for what she had touched. She touched the water, they said water. She touched the sand, they said sand. She would keep touching the item until she could say the English name rather well. Then came her leg and arm. All this Richard really enjoyed, he would sing out each word and laugh with delight as she said each word correctly. But when she grabbed both her breasts in her hands, he laughed so hard that he rolled over in the wet sand.

At first Oteria did not understand Richard's reaction, but Christopher told her breasts and she quickly repeated the word several times. Each time she said the word, Richard laughed harder and harder until he could laugh no more. By this time Oteria and Christopher were laughing as well, and no ill feelings came of it.

After bidding Oteria good night, Christopher and Richard walked back to the ship. The lad kept going on about the beasts and laughing. He did manage to say that he was surprised by how smart she appeared to be. Christopher then asked him if he had had a good time.

"Oh, my yes," the lad beamed. "I never thought a woman could be so much fun."

"Your mother is a woman."

"My point exactly." Came the surprising answer. "She takes the fun out of most things. Always telling me to wash, comb my hair and the like."

"All things she feels are good for you."

"But Mr. Jamison, you don't go doing those things all the time," he was quick to point out.

"In my mother's presence I do," Christopher smiled.

Sabbath, February 14, 1762
Eden

As was the master's way, all work was suspended for this day. He conducted service on the beach before the careened ship and a multitude of natives, Oteria and her father included.

After their service, the sailors were delighted with a special native service. Christopher learned later from Oteria that the native Vicars are called Arioi, and the service was called a Reiuas. The Heiuas was not a typical religious service as the white men knew them. It was more of a pageant with singing, dancing, play acting and even a form of wrestling, or warlike games, after which there was much laughing and rejoicing.

By late afternoon the natives had built a large fire and had dug several small pits. From the fire they took large amounts of red-hot embers and placed them into the small pits. Then some small grass eating dogs were laid in the pits on beds of fronds, covered with another layer of fronds, then another layer of embers, then covered with soil.

For the next two hours the natives sang songs and danced with such gaiety. After the proper amount of time the roasted dogs were removed from the pits and served.

Christopher had noticed two very interesting customs among the natives. The first was that they bathed three times a day. Morning, noon and again in the evening. On top of that they always washed their hands and face before eating; why this was necessary, he couldn't figure. He had not witnessed much of any labor amongst the natives, and therefore, could not imagine how they felt they had gotten dirty.

The second custom was just as peculiar. At no time did the women eat with the men. It was okay to make love in front of God and everyone, but not eat together. When he asked Oteria about this, she said that it was very taboo, a word he took to mean bad or forbidden.

Never had Christopher even thought of eating a dog but was surprised by how delicious it was. As they had done the night before, Oteria, Richard, and Christopher walked along the beach. This time they did not stop to rest. Oteria would run up to everything she could find and seek its English name. To Christopher she seemed so full of life, so eager to learn, so eager to please. All she wanted in return was a smile, or a soft touch. He found her totally fascinating and the object of his constant thoughts.

Monday, February 15, 1752
Eden

Work on the OCTAVIUS resumed this morning in earnest. The job would have been easier had the cargo been removed first, but this was not going to happen. With the natives very adept at stealing, the Master felt that they would lose most if not all the cargo should they place it before them. If nothing else, it would serve to inflate their prices for supplies, which at the moment was very favorable to the English. A twenty-pound pig usually went for a single ten penny nail.

One could almost make an entire cargo of these types of deals and turn a profit back home. However, many of the pigs accustomed to the weather in the tropics would probably die once exposed to the harshness of the weather around the horn.

Since the cargo was not to be unloaded, they had to carefully stack it as far to the one side of the hold as possible. Since the cargo hold was full before, it was long and tiring work just to free barely enough space between cargo and hull for the work to progress.

John was finally up, stiffly walking around on his wooden leg. Chips had done a marvelous job of crafting it. The foot looked like a real foot, the lower leg like a real lower leg. The rotten leg had been severed halfway up the shin. Chips' design was crafted of oak and attached to the real part of the leg with leather straps. Where the real and artificial legs met was a soft leather cushion made of tanned shark skin

The most ingenious part was the ankle. The lower leg tapered down to a round thick peg. The peg was then inserted into a hollow in the rear, top portion of the foot, the two pieces were then connected with an iron pin which allowed the foot to move up and down much like a real foot would do in the process of walking.

Because of Chips' expert craftsmanship and ingenious design, John was able to walk quite well on his first day of trying. John was so impressed with Chips' work that from that day forward, he nearly worshiped the old carpenter. Since Chips was now to be John's teacher, he couldn't have a more attentive student. John also started to learn the craft of carving miniatures and was progressing very well.

As Christopher had done on Saturday, he was to spend this day in the saw pit. As before, Oteria was there from the beginning to the end. She spent the day practicing his name and could now say it as well as he could. She was still having a little trouble with Richard's.

After the evening meal, the three went walking again. The trio had gone farther than any previous walk and found themselves nearing a clump of bushes when they heard strange noises coming from the bushes. Christopher quickly stepped ahead to investigate. As soon as he stepped around the bushes, he spotted a member of their crew engaged in passionate lovemaking with a native girl. Quickly turning around, Christopher tried and failed to stop the other two from seeing what was happening. Oteria had already seen them and Richard wouldn't retreat until he had seen all there was to see.

Luckily, it was dark, and Christopher doubted that Richard could see that much, but he would no doubt ask a lot of questions. Innocently, Oteria pointed in the couple's direction and asked what the English called that?

Sex!" Richard instantly replied matter of factly. "It's also called making love." He turned to Christopher and saw the surprise in his face. "I'm not a baby, you know Mr. Jamison. I know about these things."

Christopher didn't know what to say, so he simply shrugged. Oteria was busy working the sounds together until she could say the English terms. Then without ado, she turned to Christopher. "Oteria, Christopher make love?"

Christopher instantly turned beet red. Thank God for it being dark, he thought. He could feel the tips of his ears heating up as they always did when he was embarrassed. Richard didn't need to see his friend's face clearly to know that he was wholly embarrassed. The lad roared with laughter, which caught the attention of the passionate couple. After some choice words that Christopher hoped he would not have to explain to Oteria, the couple moved off. All this only made Richard laugh harder. Oteria didn't understand any of this, her innocence protected her from both guilt and shame.

"Since when do you know of such things?" Christopher asked Richard, remembering the incident on the ship when he thought the men were drinking from the sea.

"I suppose I've always known, deep within me," he sounded so serious. "But yesterday, when I spotted several of the men so engaged, I knew right away what it was all about. I still think it silly, mind you."

"Does your father know of this?"

"I think so." Richard shrugged.

"Why do you think so?"

"He took the eyeglass from me when he saw what I was watching," Richard replied softly. It was his turn to be embarrassed. Then he quickly turned the conversation around. "How are you going to answer Oteria's question?"

"I am not sure," Christopher thought about it for a moment. "I truly don't know."

"What do you mean? Do you like this lovemaking?" Richard seemed surprised, but at his age Christopher supposed he would have been too.

"I wouldn't know," Christopher answered truthfully. I've never done it. But that isn't my meaning here. What I mean is that I must try to tell her no in a way that she will understand."

The telling proved to be more difficult than Christopher could have imagined. There are so many words in one language that one must command in order to convey feelings. Oteria didn't seem to understand when Christopher told her that he would have to truly love someone before he could make love to her. All she understood of love was that it was part of lovemaking. She failed to comprehend the emotional side of it, and Christopher was failing miserably to bring that understanding to her. "Some teacher I am," he thought sourly.

All would have been lost if not for the creative genius of young Richard. It was he that came up with the idea of hugging. Christopher was thrilled to see how much the hugging did to convey the emotional part of love to Oteria, then maybe she just liked hugging. Christopher wished so much to understand what was going on inside her mind.

When they arrived back at the ship, Christopher took the opportunity to lightly kiss her lips, he instantly knew that he would remember that kiss a lifetime. Oteria must have thought it pleasant as well, for she returned the kiss but with far more passion. Then she tightly hugged Christopher and in proper English bid him a good night. She then turned to young Richard and hugged him as well. They watched her make her way into the jungle, then disappear.

"You know Mr. Jamison," the lad smiled. "I think she does understand something about love.

"And why, pray tell, is that?"

"She only hugged me, but both hugged and kissed you."

Christopher laughed. That this boy is wise beyond his years, he didn't say.

Tuesday, February 16, 1762
Eden
Tragedy

How quickly a small thing can lead to terrible trouble. How quickly peace and serenity can become turmoil. Since he did not have to stand guard duty, Christopher stayed up late and wrote in his journal, finally retiring to his berth and within minutes was sleeping deeply. As had been the case more than not lately, he was dreaming of Qteria.

He dreamed of taking her with him, back to England. Suddenly his dreams were shattered by the sounds of muskets. It didn't truly wake him, but it didn't mesh with his dreams either. He remembered later, feeling puzzled by the sounds. Then another musket report and he started to waken, then another musket shot and the sounds of running feet and sharp voices.

Christopher bolted from his berth and ran out onto the deck to investigate the trouble. Their neat stockpile of boards on the shore were toppled and scattered. Two of their crew, those standing guard over the lumber, were lamely retreating toward the ship. Christopher could make out many natives moving in closer from the jungle's edge. His eyes were taking it all in and yet he had not the slightest clue of what was transpiring.

The two men had nearly made it back to the ship when the natives rushed forward, hurling rocks and shouting some eerie chant as they advanced. Christopher noticed that a few the crew along the ship's canted bulwark had muskets at the ready. Upon seeing the two men's plight, the Master shouted to aim over the native's heads, then shouted, "Fire!"

Christopher was stunned, he couldn't believe that this simple paradise had erupted into a war zone in a matter of hours. The cracking of muskets and the flash of fire from their muzzles had the desired effect of startling the natives enough that they backed off and halted their stone throwing attack.

No one would venture to guess how long it would take for the natives to realize that no one had been hurt and venture back out. The men were brought aboard and taken below. They had suffered cuts and bruises but appeared still fit. The Master called the Mate and Christopher below with the men. Sarah instantly appeared and started to dress the wounds. As she worked, the two men began telling their story.

They had been taking turns walking around the pile of poles and boards when one of them noticed that several of the boards had been moved. Just how the natives were able to even get to the pile without being heard or seen could not be explained. But the fact that they had started to steal the lumber was even more of a surprise.

Once the attempted theft had been spotted the guards brought a torch over to that side of lumber and noticed two young native girls standing near the tree line enticing them to come nearer. Since things had been so peaceful, the men laughed it off and began to restack the lumber.

That's when the first stone attack happened. Luckily, neither of the men were seriously hurt and were able to reach their muskets and get a shot off into the air, sounding the alarm, before retreating toward the ship. From that point, Christopher had seen the rest.

The Master, Mate, and Christopher returned on deck and found things to be unchanged. The natives, if they were still out there, were staying well within the trees and therefore unseen by those on the ship.

"Well mates," the Master finally said to his officers. "We have ourselves in a spot. We can ill afford to lose that lumber, yet, do we take lives in order to protect it?"

"Surely Sire, we won't need to kill for it!" Christopher hadn't even thought of shooting at the natives.

"We can't afford the time it will take to go and cut more," the Mate said.

"But it has taken so little time to get what we have," Christopher argued. "What difference would a day or two more make?"

"Quite," the Master replied. "But how much of that will be stolen before we can use it? Then we must go and cut more, some of which will also be stolen. One or two days can easily become a week or more. And the lumber is the least of it."

"What do you mean, the least of it?" Christopher asked. "What else is there of value for them to steal?"

"The tools," the Mate answered for the Master. "If we lose the tools, we are stuck here. We have only one set of most of those tools.

"That's right," The Master agreed. "We have to keep them from touching those tools."

"Even if it means that we have to kill to protect them?" Christopher was astounded.

"Yes," the Master replied. "Even if."

Christopher didn't know what else to say. How could they have prevented this? How could they stop it now? Then he had an idea. "Are all the tools in boxes?" he asked.

"Yes," The Mate answered. "There's three big wooden boxes in the north end of the pit. All of the tools are stored in them."

"Pray tell," the Master started. "Are thee giving thought to going out there and getting the tools?"

"I have a mind to," Christopher admitted.

"You'd most likely get yourself killed." The Mate shook his head.

"Maybe, maybe not," Christopher said. "But if I can get the tools out of the pit and back here, there will be no reason to actually kill anybody. The lumber isn't worth it, even if it takes a week to replace. Remember, it is their lumber in the first place."

"Mr. Jamison has a good case," the Master nodded. "But I don't like the idea of risking lives to retrieve those tools." He rubbed his hands together, and then started pacing the small amount of tilted deck not occupied by other men. Every so often he would steal a glance in the direction of the jungle and try to second guess what the natives might be thinking at that moment.

It all came down to him and he knew it. If he gave the okay to go for the tools and someone from his crew was killed, it would be his fault as surely as if the idea had been his from the start. If the idea worked then maybe, just maybe, this little incident could be worked out in the morning. He kept pacing, stopping now and then to peer into the jungle or scratch his head. Who would he send? How would he protect them? Slowly the answers came to him, there were no guarantees, but it stood as good a chance as not doing it. He rubbed his neck, took one last glance at the jungle, and then returned to where the Mate and Christopher stood.

"However," he started, as if the discussion had never ended, "On the other hand, how long can we hold them off? We don't have enough powder and balls to hold out forever if they take it to mind to do war with us. Okay Mr. Jamison, take twelve men with you to get those tools. Six men armed with muskets to keep the natives at bay and six men to carry the tool chests. Mr. Peters, you lead the men with the muskets."

"Aye, aye," the Mate replied. At last Christopher knew the mate's family name.

"I will lend a hand with the tools," Chips stepped up and offered. Chips always managed to know what was going on and what every man was doing aboard ship. Christopher thought that Chips must have his nose in every goings-on aboard ship.

"As will I," young Richard chimed in.

"No, you will not," Christopher quickly said, trying to put the lad off. He would have enough to do, worrying about his own skin. He did not want Richard out there to worry over as well. "The tools are too heavy for you. I am sorry lad, but this is truly a man's job."

"And how do you suppose the tools got from the ship to the pit in the first place, Mr. Jamison?" The lad was not about to surrender.

"He's got you there," Chips laughed. "The lad and I carried them there ourselves, didn't we?"

"We sure did." Richard jutted his chin out in defiance. "And I am just as able to tote them now."

The Master quickly put an end to the matter by ordering Richard to stand back. He then proceeded to arrange the party of twelve and explain how they would go about the task.

Those that would be doing the fetching and those guarding them gathered aft near the quarterdeck and hid in the shadows. They would now wait for a signal from the Master that all was in readiness. He was arranging the remaining crew into squads, since not one amongst them could fire a musket more than twice in a minute, even those familiar with the rifles. The Master decided that with squads he would be able to offer a steady volley of fire should there be a need for it.

In the center of the beach before the careened ship they had built a large fire. As the two guards had just fed the fire with scraps from the saw pit before this incident started, it was burning brightly. The fire literally danced with sparks of orange, yellow, and red flames casting shadows that seemed to move where movement was not. The shadows had the effect of making the darkened edge of the jungle seem alive with natives. Whether or not a single native was at the jungle's edge, Christopher couldn't tell. But if they were to error, they wanted to be sure it was on the side of caution.

All seemed so quiet. Christopher could hear the crackling and popping of the fire, the swaying of palm fronds, the slapping of the surf against the sand. The loudest thing of all was his own heart hammering within his chest. His idea of retrieving the tools had seemed like a good one at the time, now he wasn't so sure.

From where he stood the sawing pit looked so far away. It was slightly farther away from this point than it was from where the Master and the others stood. The advantage from this point was that the fire would hide them until they were nearly on top of it. From the fire to the sawing pit would be the dangerous part, as they would be exposed out in the open. But if they started from the forward part of the ship, they would be exposed the entire way. It was better to run farther partially hidden than a shorter distance exposed.

The signal from the Master seemed to take an eternity. The longer it took, the more time Christopher and the others had to think about what they were about to do and grow more nervous. Suddenly, there it was, time to go! They bolted from the ship, keeping as low as they could and yet run. They made directly for the fire. Once they obtained the fire they turned without hesitation and made for the sawing pit. The moment they cleared the fire and were out in the open they met a wall of flying stones. Christopher was running for all he was worth, expecting at any moment to be hit by a stone. Behind them a sudden loud report of musket fire erupted from the ship.

Instantly the shower of stones stopped. Christopher later found out that that volley had also been directed over their heads.

The natives were curious of this noise and the sounds of the bullets ripping through the canopy of palm fronds over their heads. The falling bark mixed with bits and chunks of fronds made them cautious. Again, it didn't take long for them to discover that they had not been hurt, which brought about a stronger barrage of stones than before.

Christopher finally reached the pit and threw himself into it as did the others, as they too reached the safety the pit offered. Several of the ones with rifles took up station around the piles of lumber. The man that was to help Christopher carry one of the tool chests had been hit and was currently trying to drag himself toward the pit.

The natives figured that the English had come for the lumber they wanted and started to advance on the pit. Christopher took a chance and peeked over the sandy lip of the pit long enough to witness the effects of the next volley from the ship. He witnessed the horror of the iron musket balls tearing into the flesh of the nearly naked natives, throwing them backwards. The line of natives continued to advance until they noticed that several of their number had fallen. Their screams replaced the eerie chant, but the stones kept falling.

Christopher glanced back toward the ship, surprised to see some daring fool running straight from the ship toward the fallen man. He then noticed that the fool was smaller than a man! Richard! Dodging musket balls from one side and deadly stones from the other, the boy ran directly for the injured man, helped him to his feet, and then to the safety of the pit. How the young fool kept from being hit was a miracle.

Christopher didn't have the mind or the time to tell his young friend what he thought of his daring plight. The lad's parents would set him straight if they got back to the ship. Another volley from the ship, then another in quick succession had the desired effect of turning the tide. A dozen natives lay dead or wounded on the beach before the others retreated to the cover of the jungle.

Young Richard took hold of one end of Christopher's tool chest and did a remarkable job of running under the stress of the load. The injured man was assisted back to the ship by two of the men with rifles. In quick order they made the ship and relative safety. As Christopher and his party reached the ship, another party was dispatched, their mission was one of mercy. They were to bring back any and all natives that showed any signs of life. Just how they expected to recover the injured natives without a struggle was beyond reason to Christopher's way of thinking.

As Richard and Christopher carried the chest aboard, they passed the Master. Christopher glanced at him as they went by and could not be sure of what he saw in the man's eyes, relief mostly Christopher thought, but pride as well. What a courageous fellow his son is turning out to be, and he is still only a lad. With the tools properly stowed, Christopher returned to the master's side.

"I'm sorry" Christopher offered quietly. "My great plan failed, we still had to kill natives."

"Would you have wished us to hold our fire?" the Master asked.

"No, that was not my meaning," Christopher replied. "I am thankful that you saved our skins out there, I am only sorry the natives pressed their attack."

"Don't blame yourself. I made the decision, and I thought there was little choice. Sooner or later they would have found the tools anyway, and we would have fired to protect them then. The result would have been the same later as well as now. It was they that brought this upon themselves." With that, he turned and followed the first set of men, carrying a wounded native, into his cabin.

Standing alone, Christopher noticed how quiet it had suddenly become, he could see along the jungle's edge, feeling sure the natives were there, but couldn't detect them. The brilliance of the fire with its dancing shadows, mixed with the inky darkness of the jungle, offered excellent cover. Still, he was glad for the fire, for he doubted that visibility into the jungle would be any better, probably worse without the fire. The fire did light up the open area rather well, and that alone probably filled the natives with caution.

Only three of the natives were found to show any signs of life. They were collected and returned to the ship without incident. That fact, in and of itself puzzled Christopher. He doubted that his side would have allowed the natives to collect wounded English if they could prevent it. Although, he doubted that the natives could prevent it, and they probably realized that too. It was likely the reason the recovery was carried out without conflict.

Within a few moments Richard came to collect Christopher. "Father wishes to see you in the cabin post-haste." Christopher complied instantly, knowing full well why it was that he was summoned. To do the work of a healer. Which proved to be the case.

As Christopher entered, he noticed an unusual odor about the cabin. Three lanterns were lit and suspended from the rafters overhead, providing a fair amount of light, but hardly enough, thought Christopher, if he would have to work on one of these poor souls.

One of the natives had a shoulder wound. One had a stomach wound, which Christopher noticed was the source of the odor. The third was wounded in the thigh directly between the knee and the hip. The Master instructed Sarah and Christopher, before he left the cabin, to do as much as they could for them; he wanted them alive if possible. Before the other sailors left the cabin, they made sure the natives were bound with strong rope to ensure that they could do no harm.

Christopher had already begun to examine each of three natives, the stomach wound was by far the most serious. They found him near death and beyond anything they would be able to do. They did remove the bonds to allow him to die with dignity.

This fellow was awake but very weak and fading quickly. Sarah washed his face and wetted his lips with the cloth. He seemed to thank her with his eyes. To Christopher there seemed to be so little difference between the natives and the English when death was close.

The second fellow had taken a ball through the shoulder. "Luckily for both him and me." Christopher thought, the ball had passed clean through. They took some time to carefully clean the wound and dress it. It was all they could do and hopefully it would be enough.

The third fellow was awake and wide-eyed. He became very agitated as they moved in his direction. Although he had yet to utter a sound, this was soon to change. On examining his thigh, Christopher noticed that the ball had passed through the meat of the thigh about three-fourths of the way. The most likely resting place for the ball was several inches under the skin on the inner side of the thigh. Christopher asked Sarah for her thoughts on the subject. She looked the situation over, thought on it for a moment, and then agreed that they should have a go at removing the ball.

Christopher went out on deck to summon some help for the procedure. The first order of business was to get this fellow on the table. As soon as the sailors took hold of him and started to lift him the poor fellow began screaming in a most shrill and terrifying voice. He barely stopped enough to catch a breath. All this commotion soon brought the Master into the cabin, "You must quell that screaming, he'll bring the entire island down around our heads!" He shouted to be heard over the native's screams.

This was accomplished by taking a wide leather strap and carefully but forcefully placing it into his mouth over his tongue. This did quiet him and would provide him with something to bite into when they started to remove the ball.

As soon as they had him secured to the table, they set to work. The sailors that had come to Christopher's assistance now asked to leave, as they didn't have the stomach for watching what was about to take place. Christopher consented, but instructed them to find someone else that could handle the sight and still be of service.

No sooner than those two men departed the cabin, than two more entered. Young Richard and John Tholman. "Was there nothing that bothered this boy?" Christopher thought but didn't say.

"Thought I should see my healer in action," John smiled as he moved to the far side of the table. "You're in good hands lad!" he said to the gagged native. John's deep voice did little in calming the poor fellow.

The first thing Christopher did was get one of the lights from the ceiling and a bottle of stout ale. He poured the bottle's contents over the wound's entry point, and then had Sarah hold the light close so he could examine how best to attack the ball. It was clear from all the wiggling and shaking this fellow was doing, it would be more than John and Richard could do to hold him down. Christopher instructed Richard to get the ropes that had been removed from the dying native and use them in securing this fellow to the table. While Christopher readied the tools for the task, John and Richard checked on the other two.

Christopher could see by Richard's reaction to their wounds that the boy could feel their pain. This boy would be a great man one day; he was strong, brave and yet gentle when the need arose.

At last Christopher was ready. Richard stood at the end of the table holding the leg to be worked on as best he could. John took up station across the table from Christopher, holding the other leg and waist. The upper chest was secured by the ropes. Sarah, the kindly soul that she was, stood with her back to the men, blocking the native's view of what was happening below the waist. Instead of seeing white men with knives he had her pretty face with its sweet smile and understanding eyes to look at instead. All the while Christopher worked, she kept rinsing the sweat off this fellow's face and gently rubbing his forehead. It was her way of stilling the fear in him, and Christopher thought it did wonders.

To get at the ball with the least amount of digging, Christopher decided to try and locate the exact resting place of the projectile. He first tried to do this by simply feeling of the thigh. This proved unsatisfactory due to the strong muscular build of this fellow's thighs. Having failed to clearly prove that the ball had stopped where he thought it had, Christopher next used a long thin metal shaft. He carefully pushed the shaft into the entry hole and followed the track of the damage until he felt the shaft hit something solid. It had to be either bone or the ball. Christopher placed his thumb and index finger tightly on the shaft to mark the depth of the obstruction then slowly removed the shaft. He then placed the shaft next to the thigh which proved that the obstruction was beyond where the bone would have been. His crude measuring stick also told him just how deep the ball was.

The ball was, as he expected, was closer to the inside of the thigh than the outside. He figured that he would have a go at removing it from the point closest to the skin. To do this the legs would have to be held apart and very still. Even with Sarah's efforts at calming him, the native never gave up the struggle. As soon as Christopher put blade to skin, he jerked his leg upwards forced the knife deeper than Christopher had intended. This was not all bad, as it did expose part of the ball and Christopher had little trouble in carefully picking around the rest of it until it simply fell to the table.

Christopher then washed the leg with a mixture of ale and water before wrapping it tightly in cloth. When he was finished, he took the ball close to the native's face to show him what was removed from his body. Smiling,

Christopher then gently rubbed his forehead as he seen Sarah doing. The native seemed to calm down and the look of terror slowly faded from his eyes.

Sarah had already gone to check on the other two. She called Christopher to her side as she knelt next to the stomach wound. This poor soul's breathing had become rapid and labored. Sarah held his hand lovingly, which caused him to look into her face. With her free hand she washed the sweat from his brow. He knew his death was near, and that they had caused it, yet he showed no signs of malice. Within minutes he passed quietly. Christopher noticed that his chest just quit rising and falling, his eyes remained fixed on Sarah, his pain finally over.

It was daybreak when John, Richard and Christopher stepped from the cabin. Sarah remained to look after the two survivors. The heavens had become much brighter, the sun would most likely rise within half an hour. As to what would happen next no one knew.

The Master had been giving their situation thought and had decided on a course of action. Most of the crew were scattered about the deck sleeping or at least trying to sleep. A small number of men with rifles had taken station along the gunwale, keeping a close watch on the jungle's edge.

"How are our guests doing?" the Master asked as Christopher stepped to his side.

"Two are doing as well as possible," he replied. "The stomach wound just died."

"That's a pity, I would have liked to have saved them all. It would have shown the natives that we didn't want to kill them, just protect our lumber and tools."

"It doesn't seem like something worth killing for," Christopher sadly shook his head.

First the Master said nothing, just looked at Christopher. Weighing his words maybe, Christopher couldn't tell. Then he looked out across the beach and the still dark shapes of the fallen natives, rubbed his chin then turned back towards Christopher. "It doesn't seem something worth dying for either does it?"

Christopher knew his meaning and understood that in their situation, he was right. The natives had welcomed them, not only allowing the cutting of the trees into lumber but helping do so. Why then had they changed their minds? Why had they decided to attack? Why did what they gave so freely suddenly become something worth dying for?

"I suggest that you try to get some sleep, Christopher," the Master said. "We will wait until the full light of day is upon us before we make our next move."

"May I ask of what we will do then?"

"Yes, you may," the Master forced a smile. "We will go to the lumber and bring it back to the ship. We will continue to do repairs. We have no other avenue open to us. Hopefully, we have enough trees there to complete the job. I would hate to have to go back into the jungle for more."

"They may make life difficult."

"Aye, they might at that, but we will do the same for them if they attempt to stop us. Although, that will make securing the balance of our cargo difficult." He fell silent for a moment, then continued. "Should they see fit to just allow us to do our repairs and leave in peace, without trade, we will do so. If they fight, we must do likewise. I pray for peace."

"As do I," Christopher agreed.

When Christopher awoke, it had become day. The sun was midway up into the sky. No sign of the natives amongst the tree line, the crew was being assembled along the gunwale. The time had come to make a go for the lumber. They would tempt fate yet again. Rifles were being issued and all readiness being made. The plan was a simple one, two rows of armed sailors would march up the beach toward the lumber. Should they reach there unmolested, the second row would then set their loaded and primed rifles down within the first's reach and begin ferrying the lumber back to the ship.

If the natives also advanced and started throwing stones again, the first row of sailors would open fire then fall behind the next row to reload. The second row would advance and fire and so on.

At last all was in readiness. Christopher was chosen as part of the first row, as was the Mate. The Master stood in the lead and started marching directly up the beach toward the sawing pit and the lumber. Christopher could feel the sweat running down his face, his heart pounding in his chest. He held his rifle at the ready, his fingers opening and closing around the stock. What if they did charge? Could he shoot?

They made the distance from the ship to the lumber without spotting any sign of the natives. With their backs to the sea, they surveyed the jungle before them. Each had a span of jungle to search, these spans overlapped so that if one missed something in his area, maybe the next man would not.

Having met no resistance, those of the second row placed their weapons at the feet of the first row and started moving the lumber. Each would carry as much lumber as possible per trip and run back for the next load. In less than twenty minutes all the lumber had been removed to the side of the ship.

The entire time the lumber was being moved, the Master stood out in front of his men. Christopher thought it symbolic. To the natives, if they had been watching, and he believed this to be the case, would have thought him unarmed and quite brave. In fact, under his dress blue coat were a pair of pistols, which he no doubt would have brought to bear if the situation had called for it.

Luckily the move was successful, and they slowly started to reverse course, returning to the ship. At no time did they turn their backs. They simply marched backwards, weapons always at the ready.

The balance of the morning was put to good use in continuing the repairs to the ship. Christopher took several minutes to check on the condition of the two wounded natives in the cabin. Both were doing well. They were awake, alert, and rather comfortable considering their predicament.

Around midday the guards posted around the ship sounded the alarm. All ran to the gunwale and witnessed a regal pageant of natives slowly making their way toward the ship. Oteria's father was being held aloft by four strong fellows and looked very majestic in his royal garb.

The natives advanced to within twenty yards of the ship before halting. The King raised his hand and spoke in slow steady sentences. Christopher glanced over at the Master who was trying to translate what the King was saying.

For the next few moments nothing happened, no one moved or said anything. Suddenly out of the edge of the jungle came a dozen or more native men carrying stolen lumber, which was placed neatly on the stack next to the ship. The natives then bowed before slowly turning away and stepping behind those gathered around their King. Next came a group of beautiful young maidens, Oteria among them, carrying small pigs, fruit, and flowers which were also laid upon the ground before the ship. Christopher noticed Oteria looking for, and then finding him amongst his shipmates, but he could not see in her eyes what she felt.

The next gesture came from the Master, who sent Christopher to the cabin to retrieve the two wounded natives. As he brought them forth, he was then told to escort them to the beach before the King. Both were weak from their ordeal but proudly held their heads high as they were led off the ship. The gathered natives appeared in shock as the two were led to them.

Christopher was terrified of what might come next, there he was, standing between the two opposing forces. He had to force himself not to run but walk in a dignified manner back to his ship. As soon as he was aboard, the Master stepped off the gangplank and strolled half the distance from ship, to the natives and stopped. It took several moments for anything to happen, but the King finally said something to those holding him. He was slowly lowered to the ground, and then just as slowly he walked up to the Master and bowed before him laying his necklace at the master's feet.

Upon seeing that the King stayed in this position, the Master reached down and lifted the King to his feet. The Master then bowed slightly to the King before removing his dress coat and wrapping it around the King's shoulders and then offering his hand in friendship, which the King accepted.

Christopher understood so little of this, yet it seemed so natural; the war had ended. Both sides had forgiven the other. Work on the ship would not continue this day. The balance of the day was spent in renewing friendships and feasting on the bounty being offered by the natives. Oteria found Christopher amongst the crew and remained within sight but beyond speaking distance the entire day.

As dusk settled in around them, Christopher took his leave of the gaiety, returning to his cabin to bring his journal up to date. So much had happened this day that he didn't want to forget or leave anything out. A war had started unpredictably and ended just as suddenly, all within the cycle of one day. Ten lives had been lost over a stack of lumber, but then most wars were started over something insignificant. It was a shame however, that most wars could not be settled so soon and with so little loss of life.

Wednesday, February 17, 1762
Eden

At first light, work resumed on the OCTAVIUS, Chips and John were hard at work making tree nails to hold it all together. Tree nails are hardwood pegs cut round and tapered to look like spikes. As the planks are laid against the ribs, holes are drilled into the planks and partly into the ribs. The tree nails, which are slightly larger than the holes are then driven into the holes until rib, plank, and nail are as one.

They were yet some time from the point of laying on the new planking. The Master had decided to shore up the already sturdy framing of the ship with extra bracing and heavier frames. Near the bow and out to the knuckle, the ribs and frames were strengthened to the point of beings twice as stout as they had been before. He had to be planning on rough weather before them. Being exceptionally tired, Christopher didn't go looking for Oteria this day and retired to his cabin at work's end.

Thursday, February l18, 1762
Eden

Extra sleep did wonders at rejuvenating Christopher, he awoke the next morning well rested and feeling fit. He spent most of this day in the sawing pit and not once did Oteria make an appearance. Christopher feared that his leaving her last night had given the wrong message.

The job of reframing and bolstering the ribs was proving to be most arduous. Most of the fault was with the cargo. How can one replace a section of framing that is surrounded by furs, linen, cotton, ginseng and flat iron under that?

The Master, aware of these problems, was giving some thought to the solution. Just before retiring, he told Christopher of his plan to build a stockade ashore to house the cargo so they could get on with the repairs unhampered.

Friday, February 19, 1762
Eden

After the morning meal, they went back into the jungle in search of more trees. These trees did not have to measure up to the standards of the first ones, as they would be used only as poles for the stockade. As before, a dozen male natives went along and helped with the cutting and hauling of the poles back to the beach.

Oteria followed them into the jungle and watched all they did, never venturing close enough for Christopher to speak. He could not understand what she must be thinking and wished it otherwise. She seemed afraid of the sailors, himself in particular, part of him understood that.

They had managed to kill ten of her fellow natives without them getting close enough to do serious damage. If he was in her place, Christopher believed that he would give the sailors a wide berth as well.

By day's end the strenuous task of dragging the poles out of the jungle was complete. The stockade itself was not a stockade at all, but rather a large tent-like structure. The poles made up the support, sailcloth the sides and roof. Before the sun had set, it was completed. They would begin transferring cargo tomorrow.

Christopher had the guard watch that night and was surprised by the Master who appeared around four bells in the morning. He instructed Christopher to call all hands at once. The cargo was going to be moved tonight.

By the time the sun began to paint the heavens in brilliant hues, about an hour before it rose, the moving of cargo was halted. They had displaced a little more than half of it in one night. The Master called them all together and instructed them to not mention one word of cargo to any native, no matter how close they had become. They were then dismissed to catch what rest they could.

Saturday, February 20, 1762
Eden

By late morning, most of the crew had awakened and work on the ship continued. The room created just by transferring half the cargo made work within the hold so much easier. The day was spent in earnest, rebuilding weakened frames and sawing more planks. Work was called off early, and most, knowing that a full night of labor was in store, retired.

Sabbath, February 21, 1762
Eden

The balance of the cargo was moved throughout the night. By six bells the cargo hold was empty, except for a small amount of flat stock which would stay. A small rest was taken before the morning meal, and then an early worship service was held on the quarterdeck. By late morning Christopher found himself with the balance of the day to himself. He decided that he should go in search of Oteria and set things right. The first order of business though, would have to be a bath. He set off with a fresh set of clothes and some soap in search of a secluded spot in which to bathe. He found the spot he was looking for near a tight bend in a freshwater stream. The spot was well secluded with much foliage and undergrowth. It would hide him well should someone happen along while he was bathing.

Nearly done bathing, Christopher was about to go ashore and towel off, when several young native men wandered onto his spot. Two of the natives dove into the water and swam like fish toward him. They took hold of Christopher's arms and gently but forcefully led him ashore pulled him from the water, without a stitch of clothing for cover, or a weapon to protect himself. Worst of all was not being able to decipher their intent. Christopher found himself standing before them, still held by the two that had pulled him from the water. The situation filled Christopher with a fair amount of apprehension.

The natives seemed most interested in features of his anatomy and the fact that although a different color than they, he had all the same parts. One of them even had the Gaul to fondle and tug at him to ensure that the parts were attached. They laughed and appeared to be making jokes while pointing at him, which really had Christopher feeling naked. Then, as quickly as they had come, the natives turned and walked away. Why all of this was done, Christopher didn't have a clue, but he did hear one of them, he didn't know which, say Oteria's name. He quickly gathered up his clothes and made for the ship, taking the fastest and most direct route. Once safely aboard, he entertained thoughts of never leaving it again.

As evening fell, the fire was stocked, and guards posted around the stockade. Christopher headed for his cabin early and found Richard coming from it.

"The Master wishes to see you, Mr. Jamison," the lad smiled. "I had been looking for you myself. I thought it would be fun to go find our friend Oteria."

"You didn't look very hard for me," Christopher returned the boy's smile. "I was on watch on the deck."

"Oh," Richard shrugged. "I didn't think you had the watch, so I didn't bother looking for you on deck. What about finding Oteria."

"I had thought of doing that myself," Christopher admitted. "So, what did you do instead?"

"Spent time with Chips and John. They are teaching me to carve. Ever wonder how old Chips sees that stuff in the wood beforehand?"

"What are you talking about?"

"Chips told me that he can see what the carving will become simply by looking at the block of wood," Richard tried to explain. "He says all he does is cut the excess wood away to free whatever is trapped in there."

Christopher thought a moment then nodded. "A good trade that would be, maybe I should try to learn it as well."

"Chips says that he carves every Sabbath," Richard said. "Why don't you and I join them next Sabbath."

"Sounds interesting." Christopher smiled and patted Richard on the shoulder. "Where might the Master be?"

"In the cabin," Richard said as he pointed in its direction then turned and headed aft.

Christopher found the Master studying drawings of the ship and making marks here and there. The markings indicated places he felt the ship would need strengthening.

"You sent for me, Sire?"

"Ah, yes Christopher, I did. Please come take a walk with me," he smiled as he rose from his desk and led Christopher towards the door. "I wanted to speak with you in private, if you don't mind?"

"Not at all, Sire," Christopher replied, following him from the cabin. The Master stopped by the lantern and lit his pipe before stepping off the ship onto the beach. They walked in silence for some time. Christopher thought the Master must be thinking of how he would say what he wanted to say. He was aware that the Master had a long visit with the King that day.

"Have you been seeing that native girl, the King's daughter," he suddenly asked.

"Not since the battle," Christopher replied.

"May I ask why not?"

"I haven't been able to find her."

"But she has found you, has she not?"

"In a manner of speaking," Christopher replied. "I have seen her at a distance while I work, but she hasn't dared come close enough for me to speak to her. Then she was not to be found after our labor was finished. Might I inquire why the interest in this manner, Sire?"

"Yes, yes, of course." The Master seemed a bit uncomfortable dealing in Christopher's affairs. "I dined with the King today. He was most interested in my sons."

"Your sons?"

"Yes, that was what he said. He thinks you and Richard are brothers."

"I never made such a claim," Christopher defended himself. "Nor have I done anything that should lead Oteria toward thinking like that."

"Oh, it's quite all right," he smiled as he put his hand on Christopher's shoulder. "I don't mind the error, in fact I said nothing to correct it. As far as the King is concerned, which means Oteria too, you are my eldest son. That won't create a problem will it?"

"No, no problem I can think of. But to what end is this ruse?"

"If the King believes you are my eldest son, you will be accorded the same respect as his son would be given, if he had a son."

"Oteria is an only child?"

"Yes." He still seemed ill at ease. Christopher could tell that there was meaning to this conversation, but its true purpose he could not fathom.

"Oteria is his only child, and I doubt that she is indeed his. You see, I think the King is unable to sire offspring. Oteria's mother may well have been pregnant when the King took her for his first wife."

"First wife7"

"Yes, he has several. None of which have been able to bear him any offspring, especially an heir. As it stands now, whomever marries Oteria will become King the moment he marries her."

"Are you suggesting that I marry her?"

"Not at all." He laughed for a moment. "But don't be too righteous either. She has strong feelings for you, the King said so himself."

"Then why does she fear me?"

"Why do you think that?" the Master asked.

"I can see it in her eyes, her every move shows me that she no longer feels safe with me alone."

"She doesn't fear you," the Master said in a fatherly tone. "She thinks you have shunned her; she told her father that you would not make love to her."

"That's true," Christopher sheepishly replied, more than a little embarrassed to talk about this with the Master and not knowing which way to proceed. "Making love to any woman, even one of such beauty as young Oteria, that I am not married to, feels wrong to me. However, doing what feels right seems to be the wrong thing to do in this place, for the sake of my ship and my friends."

"You have to do what's right for you, Christopher," the Master replied. "I don't have any easy answers either. But there may be a way out."

"What do you mean, a way out?"

"I am to dine with the King tomorrow evening at his home. I promised that I would bring my son with me. That means you Christopher. Oteria will be there as well. I know much more of this language than you do, so I was thinking that maybe I could help you explain your position, whatever that position maybe."

Christopher could tell that the Master really wanted to know how he felt but was too proper to come right out and ask. He decided to make it easier for him. "To tell the truth, I also have strong feelings toward Oteria, she possesses the beauty dreams are made of. Even young Richard says that she is pretty and fun to be with, smart too. But I have always thought of love as something to be savored and shared over a lifetime. I can't truly say that I love her. Nor should I. What would become of it? As soon as the OCTAVIUS is repaired, we shall sail away, I may never see this fair maiden again."

The Master was silent for a time, puffing on his pipe until its bowl glowed red hot and smoke swirled around the both of them. "Christopher, you are a very special friend, I want you to know that. When the King thought of you as my son, he was not the first. You see, Sarah and I had a son much older than Richard. He was lost at sea ten years ago. He would have been about your age. We both feel that you fill that void somehow, not that you are any replacement for our Jonathan, but you have so much in common with him. That may be the reason you and Richard get along so handsomely."

"I am sorry, I didn't know about your Jonathan, but I do thank you for your kind words." Christopher didn't tell him about his lost brother whom Richard reminded him of.

"The reason I tell you all of this," the Master stopped walking and looked Christopher in the eye. "Is so that you know that I would support you in any kind of decision you should make. Together, we could find a way of making any situation work out. Do you understand my meaning?"

"I think so," Christopher lied. The meaning of whatever the Master was trying to tell him was completely lost.

"Good," he smiled and slapped Christopher on the back as he turned them around and started back for the ship. "I feel so much better. I was worried you know, about how this little talk of ours would go."

"You can say what you wish to me, Sire."

"Yes, yes, I can see that now. Christopher, you are indeed much like our Jonathan was, I am truly glad you signed on with us."

"Thank you." Christopher felt a tad embarrassed by all this talk about how special he was. The Master did seem like a father figure to him as well. "Did the King say anything else to you about Oteria and I?"

"Well, yes, he did ask something else, but it was nonsense. Nothing to concern yourself about."

"What, may I ask. Was it?"

"Well," the Master thought for several minutes, trying to sort the words in his mind. "It was of a personal nature."

"Personal nature?" Christopher asked, not sure he had heard correctly.

"Yes," the Master nodded.

"Would you enlighten me?" Christopher now had to know what was said but wasn't too sure he would like it.

"Well," the Master started again. "He asked if your penis worked."

"If my •••" Christopher stopped in mid stride. "He asked if my… if it worked?"

"Aye," the Master replied quietly. He was either uncomfortable talking about this, or fighting to not burst out laughing, Christopher could not tell which.

"Why would he ask such a thing?"

"He could not understand why you showed no desire around his daughter, he thought that maybe you simply couldn't, well you know."

Then Christopher remembered the incident out by the stream, it explained a lot. He related what had happened to the Master. He could hold it no longer, the Master broke out in a hearty laugh, which soon had Christopher laughing as well. Then Christopher had a thought, "My God, they all think I'm not a man."

"What surprises me," the Master added. "They must talk of such things in public as if it were the weather."

"Whether or not, you mean," Christopher said flatly. Which only made the Master laugh again.

Monday, February 22, 1762
Eden

At sun rise, work began anew on the ship's starboard side. Christopher puzzled over what the Master was planning as he directed the strengthening of all the frames and beams. By the looks of it, one would think they were turning the brig OCTAVIUS into a battering ram. Christopher doubted that any ship-of-the-line could stand up to a collision with them when finished. He thought of all the ships he had sailed on since he first went to sea, and not one had such stout framing. He could only wonder at the purpose for it all.

By day's end, they had but three more logs to plank out. Those would not take all of the morrow to accomplish. Christopher inspected the work on the ship itself; he found that all forward frames were nearly completed as well. Each was nearly twice the size they started out to be.

The purpose of such improvement would not be discussed by the Master as he and

Christopher walked together to the King's residence. Having never been there before, Christopher was taken by the sheer size of the structure. It measured more than three hundred feet in length and nearly forty feet in width. The building had a simple thatch-type roof and open sides. It was more a shelter than a home, at least a home as Christopher knew them.

Upon their arrival, the Master and Christopher were treated with much ado and respect. Nearly a hundred people were gathered around the structure for this feast. Both the Master and Christopher entertained the same thought, although neither voiced it to the other. "The purpose of this great gathering may be to show us that the King has far more subjects than we have men. He may be reminding us that by sheer numbers he could overpower us at any moment, should he have a mind to.

The meal was served by numerous maidens. As before, Christopher noticed that no female ate with the men. Again, the King had two servants feeding him and supplying drink to his lips. This custom bothered Christopher the most, it was so unnatural.

After the long drawn out affair, the King sent all but Oteria, the Master and Christopher away. He motioned to Oteria and she obediently went to his side and quietly sat down. Then the servants brought forth a rich wine of sorts that the natives make from the pepper. It was quite strong and made Christopher feel strangely warm and flushed.

The King waited until the servants had moved away to begin the conversation. He was either saying something or asking something. Christopher waited for the Master to translate. "My friend, what does your son feel for my daughter?"

Christopher couldn't think of what to say, the wrong answer might start another war or get him married! The Master leaned over to offer advice in hushed whispers. Together they worked out an answer that seemed truthful yet somewhat neutral. "My son," the Master began in the native tongue, "Is very fond of Oteria. He says that he has met no other like her.

The King spoke to Oteria a few moments, also in hushed tones, before turning back to them. "If this is so, why does your son not love Oteria?"

"You've got to give the old boy his due," the Master whispered. "He is to the point." They discussed possible replies, discarding them as soon as they came up with another. Finally, the King seemed to be growing impatient, the Master felt that they had to offer a reply at once. They settled on a reply that should be free of offense to both Oteria and her father, at least Christopher hoped and prayed that it would be so.

"My son says that he would very much like to love Oteria." As the Master said the words, Christopher was watching the King's and Oteria's faces for their reactions, so far both seemed plenty pleased. "But he cannot at this time," the Master continued. The faces across the room dropped instantly. The Master noticed this too and quickly continued. "Since he is the son of the Captain, he is restricted by obligation to the ship and crew that he serves. His station demands that he conduct himself differently from the common sailor."

The King and Oteria looked at each other with faces Christopher couldn't read. The King then looked back in their direction saying nothing, only looking. As if trying to read the sincerity of the statement. Then he turned back to his daughter and they conversed in whispers. At first Oteria seemed to be dejected, but the King kept saying something over and over until Oteria shrugged and nodded. The King's smile returned. "Tell your son that my daughter and I understand and respect his obligation and honor. We too, have such obligations. As royal blood, Oteria must be very selective of who she loves as well. Only those of equal or near equal blood can love one another."

Both the Master and Christopher nodded. Then Christopher had another idea, he turned to the Master and asked if he would convey some additional thoughts. "Would

Oteria be able to spend time with me, even though I could not make love to her?"

Oteria's face lit up into a warm and inviting smile. She answered that question for herself, which didn't please the old King. Obviously, he was to do all the talking. The Master smiled and turned to Christopher with the reply. "She would enjoy that very much! It would seem young man, that we saved our hides, the peace, and your friendship at the same time."

Then the King started talking with much emotion and gestures, the Master became very serious which instantly worried Christopher. But Oteria didn't seem to change from her warm and pleased look which puzzled him even more. "He says," the Master waited until the King had quieted down. "If it would please me and my son, he would offer Oteria to you for marriage." He stopped for a moment to hear what the King was saying. "Should you accept this offer, you would become King, as would your offspring. All of this place would be yours."

Christopher was totally stunned, he had many times dreamed of being a ship's master one day, maybe even a ship's owner. But never, ever in his wildest dreams had he ever pictured himself as a King. Even if the Kingdom was a small island in paradise, with a queen like

Oteria, what would he know of being a King? Through the Master Christopher replied.

"The King has made a very great and generous offer. Just to have Oteria would be a dream in life, but as a Captain's son, I have an obligation to honor, I must take my father's place when the time comes."

The King understood this immediately and bowed toward Christopher, which he returned likewise. Christopher could not tell what Oteria thought of this as she seemed to be keeping her emotions well in check. They enjoyed more drink, then thanking the King and Oteria for a lovely dinner, they took their leave and returned to the ship.

On the way back to the ship the Master asked Christopher to give some thought to the King's offer. "It may be the best opportunity that comes your way in a lifetime." He was quick to point out. "Not everyone has the chance to become a King and have such a beautiful queen to boot."

Christopher told him that it couldn't be. "All of this," Christopher said waving his arms around in a circle. "All of this is a fairy tale land. This is not what's real for men like you and me. I look forward to the sea again. Going home to see my parents, my home."

The Master seemed to agree as he nodded with each point. But he did advise Christopher not to be too hasty. There would be no point in being firm with any reply until such time as they were ready to depart. "Matters of this significance require diligent thought," he said.

Deep down Christopher knew that the Master had his best interests at heart, but he also wondered if stringing the King along in hopes of landing a son in law, might help the cause by keeping the King friendly.

Tuesday, February 23, 1762
Eden

At sunrise Christopher found himself back in the pit, Oteria was there as well. Her face seemed to glow more beautiful than before. The Master was right, she would be hard to leave behind.

The day wore on like a toothache. Christopher longed for dusk to come so he could spend time with Oteria, she was learning so much. All day she would try to repeat words she heard them saying. Christopher was surprised how much she had gained on the language; she was able to learn and say words so much faster than even several days before. Red's hands slipped off his end of the saw causing him to stumble to the ground, he came up cursing a streak, which in moments Oteria was aping.

"Damn it to hell," Oteria innocently repeated, which caused all within the sound of her voice to burst into laughter, even Red stopped his swearing and started laughing as well. Oteria seemed to take delight in making the men laugh and soon was repeating anything they said to her, most of which embarrassed and angered Christopher.

It didn't take long for Christopher to have his fill of their foul tongues and quickly chastised them for it. At first his effort seemed to have little or no impact on the men and only puzzled Oteria. However, the words being offered the men did become more decent.

That evening, when they had a chance to walk along the beach, Richard and Christopher tried to explain what many of the words and phrases she had learned that day meant. The ones that Richard didn't know; Christopher didn't want to teach either of them. The beautiful night was capped off with a friendly hug for Richard and a hug and passionate kiss for Christopher.

Sabbath, February 28, 1762
Eden

The Master led the worship service, which for this lot usually consisted of singing hymns the men knew and his reading from the Bible. The entire ship only had two bibles, the master's and one belonging to Christopher. Not that it mattered, of the entire ship's complement only the officers and Richard could read. Christopher longed for a hymnal, so he could teach the men new songs. He was getting tired of singing the same seven hymns every week. This week the Master read Psalms 140 from the good book.

Christopher took both the meaning and the purpose of his choosing this scripture as a reminder of how quickly the natives had turned on them before. They would have to maintain vigilance and exercise caution in all things.

The balance of the day thereafter was theirs to spend as they wished, and Christopher wished to spend it with Oteria. They had decided last night that they would spend the day hiking up the mountains. Richard wanted to stay behind and practice his carving with Chips and John.

Christopher dressed in light-colored trousers and a white blouse. Oteria was never more beautiful, her raven hair silky smooth and shiny, a tender white flower tucked in over her right ear, and a reddish colored cloth wrapped about her hips. Coconut oil gave her light brown skin a sweet scent and a shimmering glow.

It was late in the morning when they set out with a light westerly breeze blowing in from sea. The temperature was already warm and promising to get warmer. For an hour they walked and talked, by this time the terrain was getting rougher and steeper. Although the going was more difficult the trees did offer shade which kept the sun off them.

After marching up thin, winding footpaths through dense, humid jungle, they decided to rest when they came to a wide, flat area with a bubbling stream. The water was fresh and cold, perfect to quench their thirst, but far too cold for swimming. That, however, is just what Oteria did. She dropped her wrap and dove into the cold water, breaking the surface laughing, splashing, and inviting Christopher to join her.

He wanted no part of it, that water was frigid, he was quite comfortable where he was on the grassy, lush bank. Oteria just laughed, swimming back and forth, diving beneath the surface then bobbing back on top. Finally, the temptation was more than Christopher could stand, he stripped down to his shorts, took a deep breath and dove in after her.

The cold water against his hot skin forced the air from his lungs as he burst to the surface screaming in shock. He quickly planted his feet on the rocky bottom of the stream and found the water only shoulder deep. Oteria laughed at his reaction and swam over to him. She lovingly wrapped her slender arms around his neck, soothing the chill with the warmth of her heavenly body pressed against his. As she hungrily kissed his mouth, Christopher suddenly forgot all about the cold water.

The words of caution from that morning's worship service were quickly forgotten. Christopher held the object of his dreams in his arms and tasted of her delicious lips. Her soft warm breasts pressed against his bare chest was something he had never known. How could something so tender, so lovely, so much the embodiment of all that is good in life be wrong? He felt excited, so full of anticipation and passion, so weak against the temptations of the sins of the flesh.

All of which he knew Oteria was doing her level best to insure. How and why it happened, he would never figure out. One moment he was living a dream with the most tender gift of heaven, in the next, his mind's eye flashed a vision of his mother. The fire of passion died a sudden death. It was his overly righteous conscience telling him to stop long enough for a breath of air, a chance for his soul to regain control over his passion. Whatever it was, it succeeded in waking his moral senses.

He gently kissed her one time more, and then moved toward the bank. This time he didn't insult Oteria with his beliefs, he held her hand and glided her back to the shore with him. Saying something to the effect that if they were to reach the mountain proper, they would have to continue. Oteria only giggled with innocence and delight, as only she could do. In his heart Christopher was grateful that she could not know how close she came to over-powering him:

They walked along hand in hand, silently Christopher thought about what had just transpired and the significance of it. It was not just a contest of wills between two people, if it were that and nothing more, she would have won handily, for he would gladly surrender. No, it was more than that, it was a collision of two beliefs. Her belief in a simple love, the love between a man and a woman, a love that governs all else. A simple love, a love that he wished he could surrender to.

Whereas his belief was more complicated, more exact, more demanding, he believed in God's love and God's law. He could not take this woman who so tenderly offered her love. He must live up to - he suddenly wondered what it was that he must live up to. Jesus Christ was the son of God, but he was also from the line of David, God's chosen line. David, a man of God, had many women and yet God forgave him. Suddenly Christopher realized that it was his father, his saintly father that he felt he had to live up to.

His father would not have surrendered to the sweetness of a moment's pleasure in the arms of another woman, how could he?

Christopher glanced over at the pleasure and torment of his life, Oteria. He realized that if he truly wanted her, he could marry her, but what then? Could he surrender all? Forsake the very being he had always attempted to live up to? Never go back to sea with the OCTAVIUS? Could he live and love in this paradise? He supposed for a time it would be heaven on earth, but what of the time when he grew tired of it, and longed for his home, his family, his life? Would he love Oteria then as he thought he did now? Or would he grow to resent her for loving him as she does now?

Could she forsake her father? Could she leave this island home and venture out across worlds unknown to her, all for the sake of love? Would she grow tired of that life as well? Would she also grow to resent him for making her do so? Could he bare that resentment?

Before Christopher could find any definitive answers, they had reached a place of exquisite beauty, a plateau about three-fourths the way up the mountain. Even the knee-deep grass was perfect in texture and in its deep, rich green color. Looking out over the jungle they could see the sea stretching out as far as the eye could see. The only break in the distant, deep teal-colored sea was the lush green dots of the neighboring islands.

This beauty was most intoxicating to Christopher. Everywhere he looked he beheld the finest examples of the Almighty's handiwork. The women were breathtaking, the island and surrounding sea, all that the true Eden could have been. No wonder the Master called this Eden after the biblical paradise. It was a name well suited.

This spot was perfect, it was here that Christopher and Oteria enjoyed their picnic lunch. Oteria had never been on a picnic before and enjoyed it greatly, although she did her eating at a distance. She too had beliefs that would not surrender to love, she would eat when Christopher ate, but not with him.

This day it was enough simply to be together. Christopher realized that here in this place he truly felt as a lad, not that his age had reversed. It had more to do with the absence of the struggles and strife of day-to-day survival aboard ship. He also realized that one day soon he would sail out of the sparkling blue bay below them and sail away from this paradise and this beautiful woman. The more he allowed himself to become attached the harder that parting would be. Be that as it may, he could not pull away from her. He Longed continually to be near her, to hold her, to feel her presence, to smell her hair and touch her soft skin.

The march down the mountain was physically easier than going up, but spiritually the trek was more difficult. On the way up they had the day to be together, now the day was spent, separation awaited them at the beach.

Luckily, when they reached the beach there wasn't time for a long parting. Christopher was due to go on watch and had to hurry back to the ship. An embrace, a light kiss, and then duty called. To Christopher fell guard duty in the stockade, he grabbed his journal and a musket and barely made it to station as the bell started tolling eight bells.

Monday, March 1, 1762
Eden

At sunup they began placing the new planks against the exposed starboard ribs, the ship was nearly half done. Once a plank was in position, several men held it in place while two others attacked it using a brace and bit. Christopher was one of the drillers. Directly behind him, Red came along with a mallet, driving tree nails into the hole. All the work was closely supervised by Chips and John.

Each rib received two holes and tree nails per plank. As soon as Christopher reached the end of his plank another was brought in and put into place. When they had a good head start, another group started caulking. By midday, three rows of planking were in place and two caulked.

After the day's work was finished, Christopher threw himself face down into his berth, he was dead tired after working all day and standing duty last night. A full day of working the brace and bit was something his body was not used to, and it was reminding him of that. Within minutes sleep overcame him.

Not finding him seeking her out, Oteria went in search of Christopher. She was led to his cabin, and when her soft knocking went unanswered, she let herself in. Trying not to wake him, she began to message his tired back and shoulders. The feeling was heavenly as Christopher slowly awoke. When he suddenly realized that he was awake and someone was in his cabin, he spun around on his berth, scaring the poor lass out of her wits.

Since this was her first time aboard his ship, he gave her the grand tour. The tour concluded with a stop by the master's cabin. Sarah opened the door and invited them in. Christopher had now known Sarah for nearly seven months and had never seen her act and look the way she did for the time Oteria, and he was there. She was polite to be sure, but something was quite different. Christopher couldn't put his finger on it, but something was coldly different.

Christopher was intrigued when he noticed that when the two women were close together, they could almost have been sisters.

They both had raven hair and built nearly the same size. The biggest difference was the color of their skin. Oteria didn't seem to go out of her way to be overly kind to Sarah either. Christopher realized that there was so little he understood of women.

The Master offered tea to his guests, which Christopher gladly accepted on their behalf. Oteria had never had tea before and found the drink to her liking. Young Richard bolted through the cabin door carrying one of his newly finished wood carvings, this one a whale. Oteria took great interest in it, and Richard quite proudly told her all about carving it. Oddly, Sarah didn't take great interest, which Christopher knew she usually did. He thought maybe she was uncomfortable with Richard standing so close to a fully blossomed woman with bare breast. If so, she had nothing to be concerned about, Richard paid it no mind.

Christopher walked Oteria home as soon as it was polite to excuse themselves from the Weegens. The King invited him to spend the night. Christopher, however, wanted to complete his journal and remembering yesterday's Bible reading, thought he had better go. He thanked the King, and then informed him that his place was aboard his father's ship. Of all things, the King seemed to understand and appreciate one's obligation to duty.

Thursday, March 4, 1762
Eden

The last of the starboard planking was affixed to the ribs that day. Caulking should follow tomorrow morning. Oteria invited Christopher to her father's home for supper, which he gladly accepted. The meal was very pleasant except for the King's way of eating. The entire time, the King kept trying to convince Christopher to marry Oteria. What words he could not say in English, Oteria translated. Ones she could not translate, he said in his native tongue, accompanied with hand and facial gestures that helped Christopher understand most of his meaning. After the meal, Oteria came to Christopher's side and sat so close he could feel her breath on his arm.

She asked of his homeland, this England. Christopher tried to paint as vivid a picture of his home as possible, always keeping in mind to take care not to reveal that the Master was not his father. He told of the rolling hills, the morning fog rising off the river and lakes, the wet dew that soaked his feet on cool autumn mornings, their homes, and the castles of his King. He told of the large number of ships like the OCTAVIUS riding at cable in the harbors, and he told them of the coal mines.

Of all the things he told them, two things seemed to be of great interest, to Oteria and her father, the castles of his King, and the mines. They could not believe or understand, how a hundred or more men could dig a hole into the earth in search of a soft stone that burned.

All the time he spoke, he had to keep his mind in focus. Directly to his left and slightly behind him, a very young boy and girl of about equal age were attempting to make love, a greater distraction he could hardly imagine. No one made any effort to discourage them, in fact maybe the opposite was true. It occurred to Christopher that they not only allowed such things, but possibly taught the children. If this were true, they must truly think of him as strange indeed.

After a time, he took his leave and headed back to the ship to record his thoughts and get a full night's sleep.

Saturday, March 6, 1762
Eden

When they finished with the caulking, it was too late to catch the high tide. This they needed to turn the ship about so it could be careened over to expose her larboard side. With no other choice, they had to wait until this morning to accomplish the job.

They did however, set the ship right and had everything in readiness as soon as high tide was upon them. Christopher took control of the pinnace, the Mate had charge over the longboat. They would have much to do in a very short time. The pinnace was secured to the stern by a long lead. The longboat did likewise at the bow. The moment the OCTAVIUS was free of the beach they would have to haul for all they were worth to bring her out into the bay far enough to haul her around. Then before the tide ebbed, they would have to carefully tow her back to the beach and ground her again.

Knowing exactly what is to be done is itself half the battle. However, there was one thing that could cause them concern, something they had little or no control over. That obstacle materialized in the form of nearly a hundred native canoes. These canoes were interesting craft, being of varying design and length. Some were as small as fifteen feet long while others exceeded one hundred feet in length. All had outriggers affixed to their beams to enhance stability and all had high post fore and aft.

These numerous native canoes were milling all around them as they prepared to do a difficult task. Should these canoes interfere with the job before them, they may fail in getting it done.

At last there was some motion from the OCTAVIUS, she was not yet free of the beach that held her, but the signs were a signal that she was not as fast as she once was. The Mate and Christopher brought their boats out into position, keeping the lines between them and the ship taut. Should the ship slip free of the beach they would have to be alert and take her in hand at once.

For the time being, the natives seemed to sense the urgency of their task and were content to stand off. The Master stood tall on the quarterdeck ready to direct the turning of his ship, Chips was at the ship's side, he was constantly running along the hull checking and rechecking the situation. Suddenly, he shouted as the ship slipped free of the sand's hold on her.

"Pull hardy boys!!" Christopher charged as he held the tiller toward the middle of the bay. The men leaned into their oars and pulled in unison, and the ship came off the beach clean. They towed her out about a hundred yards before the Mate turned his boat back toward the beach, around and under the bow. His job was to swing the bow around, Christopher's job was to hold the ship back if possible, then swing the stern the opposite way. The trick was to get the ship turned completely one hundred and eighty degrees before the tide took her and grounded her back on the sand.

To assist them in turning her, the Master had the rudder put hard over. The lines from the bow to the longboat became taut once more as the bow slowly started tucking back in towards the beach. This was where Christopher's job was most critical, he had to hold the ship against current and the pull from the longboat, and yet turn the stern around. Since the tide was running in, this task was all but impossible. The best they could hope for would be retarding the inevitable glide back to the beach long enough for the bow to have been brought about.

It was beginning to appear that they would fail, as the ship seemed to be pulling them instead of the other way around. Then almost imperceptible at first, the bow started to turn. The men in the longboat were straining with all they had, as Christopher's men were doing.

Less than an hour from the time she had floated free of the sand, the OCTAVIUS had been turned completely around and slowly allowed to drift under control back toward her resting place. The seaward anchors were lowered and slowly paid out. Then as soon as Chips gave the signal that she was back in her resting place, the balance of securing lines were affixed and secured.

By nightfall the ship was once again rigged with blocks and tackle in preparation to careen her back over. Oteria was on hand as work suspended for the evening. They spent several hours together by the fire talking. The time passed so quickly, as it always did with her at hand.

Sabbath, March 7, 1762
Eden

As before, this day began with the worship service. Instead of going off by themselves, Oteria and Christopher joined Chips, John, and Richard in an attempt at carving. Oteria was amazed at the intricacy of the miniatures. Chips had been working on a bust of her father, which he completed that day and presented to her as a gift, she took great delight in it and ran home to show her father.

About an hour later the King appeared, as before, on the shoulders of four young, strong native males, the carving of his likeness was clenched tightly in his right hand. As soon as he was lowered to the ground, Oteria led him over to Chips and told her father that this was the man was responsible.

The King stood before Chips and bowed, and then he held his right hand out and gestured at the bust. Chips looked at the King, hesitating, he was not sure if the King was pleased or angered by the work. Every eye aboard the ship was fixed on the two men, all, uneasy about what would happen next. Chips finally nodded in the affirmative that he had indeed carved the sculpture.

The King bowed again and took Chips by the shoulder and led him away. They walked down the beach to where several native canoes were beached. Then with a simple gesture King awarded the richest of the lot to Chips. Poor old Chips did not know what to do. He turned back toward the ship with a look of total bewilderment.

"Accept the gift graciously'" Christopher shouted, which he did. Now when they sail, they will be taking an artifact of this place with them. Chips was hoping that this matter would sit all right with the Master.

Monday, March 8, 1762
Eden

Work began at sunrise, the larboard planking was carefully removed and sorted. The planks showing no signs of wear would be reinstalled, the ones with cracks or other signs of fatigue would be cut into smaller planks to serve as patches or whatever they might need while at sea. The severely damaged or rotted sections were stacked into neat piles to be loaded just before departure for use in the galley stove. By the end of the day nearly half of the larboard side was laid open and exposed to the frames.

Tuesday, March 9, 1762
Eden

This day the balance of the larboard planks was removed. Removing the planks was practically as difficult as installing them in the first place. The old tree nails were drilled out using the brace and bit. First a small bit was used, and then a larger one until the tree nail was only a hollow shell.

In doing this the planks and frames were spared from the wear and tear that prying them off would cause. Once the planks were off and the frames exposed, they went to work reinforcing this side as had been done on the other. As before, each rib and frame were nearly doubled in size and strength. Christopher wasn't the only one wondering what they would need so much brute strength for.

About midday Christopher was summoned by the Master to his cabin. He wanted Christopher to take five or six men into the jungle and begin cutting firewood. Instructing him to cut enough to fill the outer sides of the tween deck, which Christopher knew would be enough firewood to last eight to twelve months in a very cold climate, far more than ever taken aboard before. He found this very unusual and inquired of the Master why so much was needed?

"I am keeping my options open," he replied without the slightest hint of emotion. "The firewood, if you please, Mr. Jamison.

'Aye, Sire," Christopher said as he turned and left the cabin. Just before being dismissed he had noticed the ship's plans spread out across the master's desk. Even more intriguing was the comer of a map sticking out from under the ship's plans. All he could see of the map was a patch of ocean, a yellow piece of land that curved inward as it went down, then a long thin finger of land jutted out from the main land mass for a short ways then turned and ran parallel until finishing in a fine point. This land was unknown to Christopher yet somehow familiar.

For the five men, Christopher chose Red, Liverpool, George, Thames Wally, and the Swede, Eric. They gathered up the tools needed and headed for the jungle. Oteria and several fine young maidens joined up with them and kept them in splendid company

After cutting a large stack of firewood, Christopher allowed for everyone to take a ten-minute breather, at which time they enjoyed the water and coconut juice offered by the maidens. While they sat under the shade of the jungle, Christopher asked Red if he had ever seen a piece of land like the one, he spied in the master's cabin. Although he didn't tell Red why he was asking or where he had seen this land. When Red couldn't quite picture what the land looked like from the description, Christopher drew it out in the sandy dirt with a stick.

"Where'd you see this piece of land?" Red asked, still studying the rendering.

"Just something I saw once," Christopher lied lamely

"Is that so?" Red studied the crude drawing then reached over and took Christopher's stick, adding items to the drawing, giving it depth and clearer features. In a matter of minutes, the drawing really seemed to resemble something, Christopher just wasn't sure what.

"I believe if that's what you saw part of," Red rubbed the left side of his face with his handkerchief. "What you were looking at is part of California. Spanish territory."

He was right, it did indeed look like maps Christopher had seen of the place called California, but if it was indeed California, why would the Master be looking at a map of it? Was he planning on going to California?

"What's the weather like in California?" Christopher asked Red.

"About the same as here, I should think. Most of the year anyway." Red smiled, "only been there once, aboard a Spanish ship, was plenty hot there then. Hot the whole time we were there, which amounted to little more than three months. Why do you ask? Think maybe the old man has a mind to go to California?"

"Naw, just asking

"Sure, you were."

It was time to get back to work. For the balance of the day Christopher couldn't think of much else. Why would the Master be studying a map of California? And at the same time request that he go fetch two or three times as much firewood as they would ever use even in rounding the Cape?

As the day was nearing its end, they bundled up the wood and began their difficult journey back to the ship. Oteria kept in step at Christopher's side and surprised him with her silence. He asked her if she felt all right? To which she smiled, then pointed at the ship. She stumbled with the words, but asked if the ship would soon be ready for sea again? He told her that he thought it should be ready in a week or two.

No sooner had he answered her question than he realized that she was all too aware of what that would mean. "Christopher will leave then?" she asked.

"I believe so, yes," he calmly replied

"I want Christopher to stay," she said.

He stopped for a moment, allowing the others to pass them by. He dropped his load and turned to her. It was such a difficult task to look her in those sad brown eyes and behold her lovely face, her full red lips, and tell her that he must do the last thing that he wished to do at this moment.

When tears appeared in her eyes, Christopher nearly surrendered, how could he hurt such a wonderful, delightful woman as this? He held her for a time and lightly kissed her cheek. Christopher could tell that she wanted more, wanted to demand more, but deep within her, she understood.

They parted there, at the edge of the jungle, she to her home and Christopher to his, the brig OCTAVIUS.

Saturday, March 13, 1762
Eden

Most of the larboard hull planks were in place, the rest will wait until next week. The Master seemed to be most cheerful, although he had told not a soul why the ship was reinforced so, and why all the firewood was cut. Several of the men have been trying to speculate the purpose, but Christopher doubted they came very close.

The hardest part of the last four days was that Oteria was not seen at all. Christopher had guard duty that night, but after service tomorrow he vowed to find her.

Sabbath, March 14, 1762
Eden

After the service, which he had always enjoyed in the past, but today longed to be elsewhere, he went in search of Oteria. His first stop was her father's house, she had been there early that morning. As to her whereabouts at present, the King did not know.

Christopher stood outside her house and thought of where he would go if he were her, the only place he could think of was the plateau up on the mountain. He set off at once, reasoning that she could go there and see almost the entire island and yet be alone.

The farther one got from the beach, the more the island changed in character, the palms gave way to hardwood trees of the birch family. The wide-open paths and walkways of the native settlement became narrow, slippery, and barely visible ribbons of dark earth that ran off into numerous directions. He remembered the path up the mountain went straight ahead, at no time during their outing together, did they venture off the main path, if this could be called a path

Christopher didn't remember the climb being so difficult, possibly because Oteria was then at his side. Maybe today he was too anxious to obtain his goal. Christopher wanted to reach the plateau as quickly as possible, the sooner he found her, the more time they would have together. If she desired that as well, which he admitted to himself, was in question at the moment.

After struggling up the path for over an hour he heard laughing and shouting and the sounds of splashing water. He instantly picked up his pace, the stream that they had swam in must be just ahead. Momentarily, he came upon the large flat area where the stream was located. The area was roughly five to ten acres in size, the stream itself widened by tenfold its size at this place. Here the stream was nearly wide enough to be called a lake. The swift current down the mountain ran along the far side of the stream while a much calmer and slower current gently glided along the near shore. The water remained fresh and cold because of its rapid turnover rate,

The entire area around the stream was heavily over- grown in trees and shrubs of all sizes, except for a small area of tall grass near a lazy bend in the stream. The closer he got to the stream the more he could see of those enjoying the water. There were no men from his crew, but Christopher could see a dozen or more natives, broken into two basic groups. The ones who were loving and caressing on the bank and those engaged in blissful play within the stream.

Christopher hesitated at the jungle's edge, wondering if he should proceed past this area within sight of the playful natives or secretly find his way around them in the thick jungle. The path led straight to the stream before continuing up the mountain. Suddenly, his heart stopped, there in the stream playing with one of the native men was Oteria; she had other interests! Christopher felt hurt, shunned, alone and without hope, all of which was no one's fault but his own.

Why should Oteria not enjoy the company of someone she could make plans with? Someone who would be there in the future? Someone who could love her. Nevertheless, Christopher felt heartbroken, he took one last look and saw her kiss her young friend. Christopher wished he had not seen that, but deep down he was happy for her too. He could now leave this place with his ship and his duties without guilt. He had gotten to know her, hold her, kiss her, and for that he should be eternally grateful. Now, he simply did not feel grateful.

He turned and was about to leave when suddenly one of those small wild dogs that the natives eat, bolted from the thicket and ran toward the stream before darting back into the jungle. It was enough to cause those at the stream to look in his direction, and Christopher was not very well hidden. Oteria saw him, they locked eyes for a moment. At first neither of them moved, only stared into each other's eyes over a hundred feet or so. She started to move toward the bank, she called his name, which spurred him into action. He quickly turned about and headed back down the path at nearly a full run.

He could hear her calling after him, but he couldn't stop. Whether it was shame for having spied on her or feeling hurt, having seen what he had, he could not say. He just couldn't stop. The farther he made it down the mountain the less he could hear of her voice calling his name,

Christopher lost his footing and stumbled three or four times, which brought him cuts, bruises and more pain, but he would jump back to his feet and continue the trek back to the ship.

If anyone saw him and wondered about his appearance as he came aboard, they did not say a word. Christopher wanted to be alone, to put his embarrassment and pain into perspective.

He spent the next few hours staring at the ceiling of his cabin, justifying his actions, her actions, and planning what would come next. The more he thought of it, the more it made simple sense that she should do what she had done. She was doing what was best for her and her future. He would do the same in her place. His actions under the circumstances were also understandable; if he had stayed to talk with her at the stream, what could he have said? If this is the end of it, and in his mind, he thought so, all was for the best, but his heart was not so sure.

As evening fell, Christopher found himself wishing for guard duty, something that would occupy his mind. He found the Mate on deck and discovered that he had the watch for the night. Christopher offered to take it for him, reminding him that he owed him that for the night he was sick. The Mate accepted and quickly went ashore. If he had a native girl himself, no one had noticed, but he did seem pleased to be able to go ashore once more.

After several hours on watch, the night had finally settled in, crew and natives alike were bedded down and asleep. Only Christopher and the men at the stockade appeared to be still awake. It was a beautiful night, warm breezes blowing in from the sea, a full moon lighting up the heavens, the gentle sounds of a light surf, the swaying of palm fronds, and the light aroma of smoke from the fire drifting in every once in a while when there was a break in the breeze. Christopher could also smell the tar of the caulking, the mildew of the upper deck, canvass, and the rigging, the sweet smell of tobacco. Tobacco? The Master must be about. Sure enough, leaning against the hatch, amidships, stood the Master puffing on his pipe.

"So, you took the watch for yourself?" he said, rather than asked, as Christopher drew near.

"Aye, couldn't sleep anyway*"

"Troubles?"

"None that really matter."

"Ah, troubles of the heart then?" The Master asked with the raise of an eyebrow. "You're wrong, you know. They are what matter most. Only that which we cherish has any real value to us."

Christopher simply shrugged.

"Oteria?"

"Aye."

"Grown tired with the morals of a vicar's son, has she?"

"I suppose."

"Do not worry my young friend, one day you will meet the woman you will want for the rest of your life. I realize that it doesn't do much to ease the pain you are feeling now, but in time you will get over this one. You will never forget her, but the pain will pass."

"Aye." Christopher wasn't much in the mood for talking.

"Christopher?" It was Oteria's voice calling faintly out of the darkness.

"I'll be turning in," the Master smiled as he tapped his pipe out. "Looks like you've got company."

"I did not ask her to come."

"But she is here. It does not matter." He winked before starting for the cabin. Then the Master stopped and turned back around. "Just keep your eyes open and stay on deck. Remember you are on watch."

"Aye, Sire."

"Christopher?" Oteria called out again, this time sounding farther away.

"Here," he called out to her, "Oteria, I am here."

She followed the sound of his voice and came around the hull to where the gangplank was located. As she drew near, Christopher stepped down the plank to help her aboard. She looked so beautiful with the moonlight sparkling in her eyes and off her hair.

"I speak to you?" she asked. She had learned so much in these past weeks. In talking with her, Christopher nearly forgot that until they landed, she had never spoken a word of English. Now her command of the language was better than some of his own crew!

"Aye," Christopher replied. "I suppose we should. I'm sorry about today. I really am. Remembering the master's words, he led her up the quarterdeck, which offered the best overall view of the ship. Oteria stepped over to the rail, which was a bit difficult with the ship careened at such an angle. Christopher sat on the edge of the upper rail which allowed him a view of the beach as well as the ship. "What did you want to say?"

"Why you run away?"

Christopher shrugged, "I didn't know what else to do."

"You afraid of Oteri?"

"No, not afraid. No, I think I was confused, surprised, hurt maybe."

"Hurt?" She came closer. Christopher could see that the word held only one meaning to her.

"Not hurt in body," Christopher tried to used gestures to convey that he wasn't physically hurt, he put his hand over his heart. "Hurt in heart, hurt by love."

Her eyes instantly went wide when he said the word. "Christopher love Oteria?"

Well, fine, there is was, out in the open. Christopher had carelessly spoken the word, but did he mean it? He thought he might, but having so little experience in this area, he could not be certain.

"Christopher love Oteria?" She asked again as she moved so close to him and looked into his eyes, he wondered what she saw in them. She suddenly laughed and cried at the same time, wrapping her arms around him and holding him so tight he could hardly breathe.

The fact that he had yet to confirm or deny his love for her did not matter, he realized that he had just lost a measure of control over this relationship by default.

He tried to think of something to say something to convey to her how he did feel, but how could he convey feelings that he himself was unsure of. "Oteria," he took hold of her arms and held her in front of him. "I have never known love before; therefore, I cannot be sure of what love is. Do you understand any of this?"

She simply looked at him with those big, bright, tender brown eyes. From what he could detect in her eyes, he might as well have been reading from the Bible. "You love Oteria?" she faintly asked in a voice that appeared very near tears.

"I think the world of you," Christopher truly meant that, at no time did he say or do anything to or for her that was not a truthful representation of his feelings for her. He would rather lose her here and now, regardless of how much pain that might cause, than lead her on with falsehoods. "I think of you every day and night. You are the most beautiful, kind, and loving woman I have ever known.

"Christopher not know love?"

"Christopher does not know love," he admitted. God, he wished his feelings and beliefs were as simple as hers, something either was or it wasn't, black or white.

"Oteria love Christopher, Oteria show Christopher love." She stepped closer, reached out with her hand and pulled his lips down to hers. Her lips were sweet, tender and so eager. He was lost in a tidal wave of emotions; he was weakening to that which he longed to surrender. Suddenly he felt her other hand against him. It surprised him, he stood back holding her at arm's length, things were moving too fast.

"Christopher afraid?" She was equally surprised by his actions.

"Oteria." It was Sarah's voice now calling out from the shadows of the rigging. Dear Lord, Christopher thought, had she been watching? What had she seen? He felt ashamed of his actions, he was to be keeping a sharp eye, instead he was being taught love!

"Oteria, could I see you?" Sarah asked as she stepped into the dim light of the lantern affixed to the main mast. Sarah held her arm out to Oteria, beckoning her to join her. Christopher nodded that she should go with Sarah, for what, he didn't know, but he trusted Sarah, and knew she would do right.

The two women stepped off the ship and walked out into the darkness along the shore. They did not return for nearly two hours. What they discussed, he had not a clue, but

Oteria was quite a different woman when next he saw her.

Upon their return to the ship, Sarah retired to her cabin, Oteria and Christopher spent the balance of the night discussing what life at sea was like. How one managed to find his way across a vast ocean. How one managed to bathe while at sea, and finally the conversation turned toward Christopher's God. Why he believed in God, and what being a Christian meant.

What of their conversation Oteria really understood was in question, she was such a good listener, always asking so many questions. As night gave way to dawn, she kissed him lightly on the cheek and took her leave.

Christopher stood there watching her slowly walk away from the ship, he was thinking that maybe he did love her. As if their thoughts were one, she spun around and shouted for all the world to hear, "Oteria love Christopher!"

Christopher bowed toward her, which made her smile. She turned and soon disappeared into the darkness of the jungle. He was glad of the early hour, no one was about to witness this.

"Red love Christopher too," Red laughed as he stepped from the shadows.

"Mate, that lass has a bad case of itch. You are out of your mind, not taking care of business."

"That's enough out of you," Christopher shot back.

"Well, if you decide she's not your type, just let me how. I won't put her off."

"How long have you been bending your ear?"

"Long enough to know that you're a fool." Red shook his head. Maybe Red was right.

Monday, March 15. 1762
Eden

The final planks were installed that day, the caulking would take another day or two to complete. Their stay in paradise was ending, by this time next week they should be well at sea again. After a day of hard labor planking the ship's larboard side, Christopher went for a swim in the lagoon with Oteria. They embraced and kissed passionately and for once she seemed content to leave it at that. It made Christopher wonder what her and Sarah had talked about last night.

Thursday. March 18, 1762
Eden

Repairs to the hull of the OCTAVIUS were completed. The Master then deemed it prudent to overhaul the steering, Chips estimated that to do the job properly would take another week. The huge rudder would be removed in the morning as well as the entire steering mechanism, then inspected and replaced where needed. That was all right with Christopher, as it meant another week with Oteria. He did have a chance in the morning to speak with Sarah about her talk with Oteria, to which she just smiled. "We just had a woman talk."

"Oh," Christopher had hoped for a little more than she was offering.

"We simply discussed the differences between British men and women."

"Which is?"

"Pride mainly" Sarah replied with that steady smile that seemed to be hiding more than it revealed. "You men take such pride in silly notions. If a woman throws herself at you, you run. You do not want anything easy. You have to feel like you've earned it. Oh, you say things like doing what's right, being proper, and all that, but if you want something you can't have, you'll walk through fire for it."

"Forgive me, Mr. Jamison," Sarah continued. "I think very highly of you, and you know that, but you are one stubborn mule. I can see how badly you want Oteria, and how badly she wants you. But before either of you can be happy, it must be on your terms, and your terms alone. Have you ever stopped for even an instant to consider what you are doing to Oteria?"

"Her beliefs are guiding her, as yours do you. Yet you discount her beliefs as meaningless. You discard her feelings and needs for those of your own. You love that girl and she you, you are just too blind to see that. Why, I think you wouldn't know true love if it were a shark that came up and took your bottom off!" With that she turned away from Christopher and left him to think over her words.

Christopher was surprised, that was a side to quiet Sarah he had never suspected. He gave careful thought to her words for some time and had to confess to being a fool. He still did not know what she said to Oteria, nor what she was trying to tell him.

Friday, March 19, 1762
Eden

The rudder was removed with much difficulty. To handle it, they had to set poles deep into the sand to form a tripod, from which they rigged lines with block and tackle to slowly raise rudder up so it could be disconnected. Once the rudder was free, they slowly hauled it down.

The next step was to remove the iron and brass braces from it so the wood could be carefully inspected. The inspection proved that the repairs were much needed. During their troubling time crossing the horn, several fractures were incurred that would have probably split and left them without a viable means of steerage.

Sabbath, March 21, 1762
Eden

After the worship service Oteria and Christopher joined a dozen or so of the natives in a canoe outing, going about a mile out into the ocean. Christopher was impressed in how stable the tiny craft were, the sea was running with about a three to four-foot swell and not one of the canoes ever seemed in peril of capsizing.

What this little outing was all about, he was not to learn, until they were well out from shore. It seems that the natives take great delight in doing battle with one of nature's most deadly beast, the shark. Some of the natives had taken the nails they had been trading for, and turned them in to hooks, the hooks were baited with bloody meat of the island's small wild dog.

In due time they succeeded in attracting the attention of several hungry sharks which set about getting the meat posthaste. Most of the nail hooks quickly bent and were lost, but when one did finally hold, a terrific fight between man and beast ensued, to the great delight of the natives.

Christopher had never fished for shark before and was fascinated by the great struggle, admiring both man and beast. Of four sharks hooked, two were landed. These were worn down by the struggle and pulled close enough to the canoes for another native to either club the beast to death or chop it to death with an axe fashioned out of stone.

After the natives grew tired of the hunt, the bounty was delivered ashore amongst much cheer and gaiety. The two sharks, of medium size, were cleaned and butchered. Both yielding fine steaks of quite tender meat which became the main fare at a feast held that evening. The fins were removed and hung to on posts with dozens of others.

Monday, March 22, 1762
Eden

    For most of them, this day's sunrise came all too early. The festivities of last night left more than half the crew very tired and sluggish. Because of this, work on the steering progressed quite slowly until around midday. After the midday meal most were once again fit, and the pace of their work became brisk once more. While Chips began the task of restoring the rudder, the Master directed the work on the balance of the gear. Worn sprockets and pulleys were found to be the cause of their previous problems with the steering gear.

    The pulleys were disassembled, and new sheaves carved out of blocks of hardwood. All through the ship men were checking and rechecking every bit of gear, anything found to be lacking was taken down and laid in a heap on the quarterdeck. Every piece of equipment imaginable was included, Deadeyes, triple fiddle blocks, running blocks, standing blocks, sheet leads, scored bullseye fair leads, even belaying pins.

    Christopher doubted the Master had any idea how close the crew would scrutinize every piece, it stood to reason, that for every piece of equipment that needed repair, a certain amount of time would be added to their stay. None of this seemed to trouble the Master, for purposes known only to him, he wanted his ship to be in top condition when they finally did depart from this paradise.

Tuesday, March 23, 1762
Eden - Sabotage

Work resumed this morning on the ship's steering and rigging gear, it was nearly midday when Chips noticed that the iron used to hold the rudder and stern post together, the pintle straps, and the gudgeon straps respectively, were missing. How and when someone could have taken them was a mystery.

The Master quickly summoned Liverpool and Thames Wally, since it was, they who stood watch last night. Both men were questioned in depth about all that transpired during their watch, neither man heard nor saw anything. Christopher instantly thought of their troubles from before, neither of those guards had heard or witnessed anything until it was too late.

A search was called for immediately. Christopher was sent by the Master to the King's residence to appeal for his people to aid them in finding who took the iron straps and returning them.

The King was most helpful, but nothing was to turn up and luckily no bloodshed came of it. The natives themselves began assisting them in searching for the missing straps. Several natives began diving into the lagoon around the ship. Thinking that the tide could have carried them off, which was highly unlikely due to their weight.

Unencumbered with logic, one of the native men was diving some distance from the ship out in the lagoon when he happened upon the missing straps. It was painfully clear that one of their own men had heaved the straps out into the lagoon in hopes of delaying the ship's departure from this place.

After much interrogation it was discovered that the guilty party had been Liverpool. In a most humane way, the Master offered the guilty man his choice of punishment, housed aboard ship for the duration of their stay or twenty lashes from the cat-o-nine-tails. Liverpool chose the latter and was taken at once to the edge of the careened ship, his hands were bound about the rail, his shirt was then stripped off and the twenty lashes administered by the Mate.

The natives instantly began crying and pleading with the Master to forgive poor Liverpool, the Master would not hear of it and the punishment was doled out.

Christopher would find out later that poor old Liverpool was the center of attention amongst the native maidens that night, and

Liverpool found their tender mercy most to his liking. The Master also noted this and warned both the Mate and Christopher to keep a close eye on the balance of the crew, he wanted to ensure that they didn't do something to merit the twenty lashes.

Wednesday, March 24, 1762
Eden

The pile of worn parts was beginning to slowly decline as Chips had a dozen men constantly busy carving new parts out of wooden block. As each new part was finished and fitted back into its block, Christopher was busy with two others putting the parts back into the rigging.

The rudder was finally completed just before sundown and would be installed the next day. The rest of the steering was nearing completion as well. The tallow coating of the newly finished hull was finally completed as well and gave the OCTAVIUS a fresh clean look.

Thursday, March 25, 1762
Eden

Installing the rudder proved to be a monumental task, it was all that was completed that day. All worked from sunrise to dusk getting it into place and secured. The next day would be spent connecting the rest of the gear.

Oteria has been very playful and Christopher found himself so drawn to her. She controlled his thoughts both day and night.

Friday, March 26, 1762
Eden

The Master was up well before sunrise, Christopher had the watch just as day was beginning to break. He came onto the quarterdeck, slanted as it was and stepped to the starboard rail, together they watched the impending sunrise paint the heavens.

The sea just beyond their careened ship was a dark grayish-black. Looking forward, the sea grew in darkness until it faded to total black, with the sky just slightly lighter so they could tell where one started and the other left off. Looking aft, the sea grew lighter each length of cable it ran, until in the distant horizon it glowed as bright a red as the sky.

There they could not tell where the sky rose from the sea, the bright red glow of the horizon melted each one into the other, and the sun had yet to make an appearance. As the eyes followed the sky back towards the ship, it cooled in color rapidly, from the hot glow of red to yellow, to purple, to indigo, to slate, to grayish-black.

The slight breeze was still blowing in from the sea as it had done for nearly the entire time they had been here. The smell of the sea was upon them. The ship seemed to sense that her resurrection was at hand. The Master was smoking a most delightful smelling tobacco in his pipe that mixed with the sweet smell of Cooky starting the breakfast of biscuits and fresh pork, everything blending so harmoniously.

This place was indeed Eden, a paradise Christopher would never have believed to hear about from someone else. There would be no continuation of his argument, with Chips. The sights, sounds, and smells were of the type one would remember until death, and yet a part of Christopher wanted to get on with it, hoist sails and make for their next port, Canton, China, the mystical orient.

As the sun finally made its appearance, Christopher went to the hatch and called, "All hands Ahoy!" which was soon followed by the muster of men. When not at sea, breakfast was the first order of the day and was quite enjoyable. Not practical at sea, here it seemed so fitting with this place.

After breakfast was concluded, work began anew on the ship. The balance of the steering gear was reinstalled and much of the rigging was completed by the midday break. Young Richard was swinging in the bosun's chair tarring masts and spars, something Christopher thought he was defter at than any he had seen, he could also imagine the scrubbing Sarah would be giving the boy that evening.

Oteria wandered down to the beach just as Christopher was stepping off the gangplank for his midday break. As he usually did, he planned on enjoying his coconut and breadfruit meal under the shade of the palms. Once they had left this place, Lord knows it would be a while until he would get to do so again. Oteria sat off to his side and talked of many things while he ate. Once he had finished all that he intended to eat, she brought up the subject to what was really on her mind.

"Your ship almost finished?" she asked.

"Aye, very well near it," Christopher replied, again without thinking of her feelings. "Should finish on her today."

"You leave today?"

"No, no… heavens no." It suddenly hit him. "Dear sweet Oteria, I would not leave you in this manner, I will tell you as soon as I know when we will leave."

"You leave soon?"

"Yes, I am afraid that it is not far off."

"I want you to not go."

"I know, and I wish there was another way." Christopher could see her pain so clearly and felt his own as well. He reached out and held her hand and lightly kissed it. She smiled at this, and then held the back of her hand to her cheek.

"Oteria love Christopher.

"Christopher love Oteria." There, he said it, but did he truly mean it? He could only think that he did. The reaction from Oteria was spontaneous, she leaped onto him, which sent him sprawling onto the hot sand, embracing him so tightly he thought that he should not draw another breath of life.

The ship's bell rang out, it was time to return to his duties. The work lasted until just after sundown. They stayed with the task until the last block was set, the last line hauled taut, and the last belaying pin in place. The Master walked around the entire ship with Chips at his side, proud as a new papa of his OCTAVIUS.

Saturday. March 27, 1762
Eden

The only task done this day was the righting of the ship. The block and tackle were slowly paid out and the seaward anchor hauled in a bit. One degree at a time until the OCTAVIUS was once again standing tall as a ship of her stature should. As soon as the tide was upon them, they slowly hauled in the seaward anchor again and pulled the ship off the beach into deep enough water to allow them to reload her without danger of her grounding again. Then they stood back and admired her from the beach. She once again looked like the proud lass Christopher had signed aboard back in England.

The natives knew the end was near and had gathered on the beach to watch them work as they brought the ship upright and hauled her out into the lagoon. As they returned to the beach all gaiety set in and further work would not do. The King had several of the wild dogs roasted in the frond pits and supplied a great quantity of their pepper-root wine. Also served was coconut milk, breadfruit, and a very tender white fish served wrapped in a green leaf of some kind.

Then they supplied them with entertaining dance, a play act battle of some sort, and much fellowship. Christopher truly felt that when they did depart these people would truly miss them. He knew that he would certainly miss one of them. Again, the King made his offer of Oteria to Christopher. Christopher had to wonder if he would be doing so, if he knew that he had been entertaining thoughts of asking her to come with him, providing of course that the Master gave his consent. He had said that together they could work anything out. Christopher wondered if he had dared to think of working something like this out.

Taking a bride aboard ship would create problems to be sure. If he did so, others would want to do the same, and what would their wives think when they arrived back home? No, the situation would not work, therefore Christopher would not ask.

The feast lasted well into the night. Since tomorrow was the Sabbath, no one was concerned about being called to. Christopher had partaken of the pepper wine and was feeling lazy and warm from its effects, he did however, have the presence of mind to keep his tongue in check. He should not want to say anything in this state that he would regret later.

Sabbath, March 28, 1762
Eden

Oteria and Christopher awoke the next morning in each other's arms. They had fallen asleep together on the beach, as did quite several others. At first Christopher was startled, this was indeed an experience new to him, but as Oteria gently stirred and then opened her eyes, he became aware of how special this moment was. Yes, he truly believed that he loved this delightful creature. Her body so tender, so warm, so smooth to the touch; he also realized how badly he wanted to love her.

Then the aroma of Cooky's stove, alive with a hot fire, heaped with fresh pork and.

Biscuits brought his desires back in line. Oteria joined them for breakfast, sitting slightly behind them on the deck. She also stayed for the worship service. Today the Master chose to read from the first chapter of James. This, Christopher believed was for his sake, and something for which his father would have smiled upon, especially verses fourteen and fifteen.

"But every man is tempted, when he is drawn away of his own lust, and enticed."

"Then when lust hath conceived, it bringeth forth sin: and sin, when it is finished, bringeth forth death."

Oteria listened very carefully to all that was read and sung, afterwards asking so many questions of Christopher's religion that he had to retrieve his Bible from the cabin to find her answers. The entire day was spent on a bluff overlooking the crashing surf below, reading from the Bible and discussing its meaning, and what some of the words meant.

Monday, March 29, 1762
Eden

With the ship finally refitted and ready for sea, it was time to begin reloading the cargo. The flat iron stock was the first to come aboard and proved to be a difficult task to accomplish. The iron stock was too long for either the long boat or the pinnace, it had to be laid upon the wales, lengthwise, and strapped or held down by hand. Once it was alongside the ship the task became easier, there a block and tackle were employed, and the iron hoisted over the rail and into the hold.

It would take the entire day just to load and stow the flat iron stock, and since this portion of their cargo was the smallest percentage, they soon discovered that it would take nearly a week to reload all the cargo.

After work had been suspended for the evening, Oteria was brought out to the ship by Red. "Found this one on the beach looking for you, Mate," he smiled. "Thought I'd be polite like bring her across."

"Thank you, Red." Christopher smiled at Oteria's excited face. Oteria turned and bowed to Red, then ran up to Christopher with a warm and tender embrace. She asked him why he hadn't come ashore after work had stopped? He explained that he could not when he had the watch.

Then she began asking about what it was like to sail on this ship? Christopher didn't really know where to begin.

"There are times," he started, "when the ship feels as a living thing, a part of the living sea beneath her. One can feel her breath as she rides the waves, she speaks through the moans and squeaks of her timbers, rigging, and cloth.

When she is happy, she flies across the water as a bird, when she is not so happy, she plows deep into troubled seas, straining all about her. Her smile is the curve of her canvass billowing full of wind, her tears are the wash and spray flying from her bow and raining upon her decks. We, her crew are as her children, we answer her call, and tend to her demands."

"If we behave well and do what is asked, she rewards us with a safe passage and delivers us to distant shores. The OCTAVIUS is many things to us, her crew. She is our home, our work, pleasure, and our pride, she is a good and worthy ship."

"Christopher speaks with love," Oteria noticed.

"Aye, I do at that." How does this simple maiden see things so clearly? She was as wise as she was beautiful.

When the Mate came on deck to relieve Christopher, he offered to row Oteria ashore. She only smiled, kissed his lips, then turned and dove off the starboard side and swam back to shore. Christopher and the Mate watched her as she glided through the water as a fish. Upon reaching the shore she sprang from the water naked, having lost her wrapping, and waved to them before turning and disappearing into the darkness of the jungle.

Tuesday, March 30, 1762
Eden - Trouble

As they began to haul the linen from the stockade toward the waiting boats, the natives took great interest in the cloth. Since they had unloaded it at night, and had it hidden under guard ever since, the natives had not seen it. Now they made much ado over it and began crowding around the sailors and trying to take the cloth.

The scene soon took an ugly turn. Whether one of his men or a native started it, Christopher didn't know. Soon however, they found themselves in an all-out fist fight. Christopher was not overly experienced in this type of activity, nor was he a virgin. Sooner or later if one sails, one will find trouble about himself and must fight. It happened once, in London, when Christopher was serving on a coal barge, and once again in Plymouth, when he thought about it, it was on that same barge. Other than with Liverpool and Red, those were the only times he had a purpose to fight, it could be that the company one keeps is more of a factor.

Be that as it may, this fight, this day was nothing less than a brawl. There were twelve sailors against twenty to thirty strong natives. Christopher believed that the idea of fist fighting was not a natural thing for the natives, so the sailors showed well of themselves. But numbers have a way of neutralizing any advantage and they soon found themselves trying to hold their skin, they had already lost possession of the linen.

Christopher had just taken a direct blow to his left eye and found himself thrown backwards into an angry mob of natives that began to beat his face and body.

Suddenly, he heard Oteria's voice screaming in her native tongue, the punches and kicks instantly stopped. In the next instant he heard the sharp crack of musket fire. Since no one near him fell, Christopher could only guess that the volley was directed over their heads.

Christopher had started to pick himself up when Oteria knelt at his side. She was looking at him but yelling something in her language at her people. Surprisingly, the natives started to move back, one even came over and helped Christopher to a sitting position. About this time, six armed men from the ship appeared with the Master. Tears were streaming down Oteria's face, as she gently cupped Christopher's already swollen face in her hands. "My Christopher, my Christopher." He forced a smile to let her know he would live; his pride was hurt more than his body.

Suddenly, Oteria jumped to her feet, as Christopher got to his as well. Her facial expression had instantly turned from a loving, caring face to one of cold anger. Again, she was shouting in her native tongue. Exactly what she was saying, he did not know, but the crowd of natives before her began to hang their heads, several even began to openly weep. He took from her actions and their reactions that she was chastising them for this incursion. The Master stepped to Christopher's side and asked if he was all right, then did a quick job of translating as much of Oteria's tirade as he could decipher.

"She's telling them how wrong they had been. How could they have done such a thing after all we had done for them."

"What have we done for them?" Christopher asked.

"Shut up," was the master's quick reply. "Now she's telling them to return the goods and make their wrong up to us."

"How will they do that?" Christopher was curious.

"Shut up." He gave Christopher a stern glance this time. "She suggests that instead of stealing, they give us something. I think she said to give us something of themselves.

"I bet she did."

"Mr. Jamison, if you please!"

They watched Oteria and the crowd of natives to see what would come next. Christopher felt so proud of her, it must have taken great courage for her to step into the fray. More than that, he was astounded at her power over the crowd before them. For them to act as they were now, she must command incredible respect.

When nothing happened, Oteria walked over to one of the largest and strongest of the native men. She spoke in a level tone, but it was clear that she was informing this man what she expected to happen. He bowed to her, then she to him. He turned and went off into the jungle. For the next ten minutes nothing more happened.

Oteria had returned to where Christopher was standing. He believed she was too troubled to think of the proper English words, for she spoke very quickly in her native tongue to the Master. He in turn translated to those of his crew around him. "She has demanded that the goods be returned to us. It will be done.

Oteria spoke some more, but the tone was different somehow.

"She is now asking why we had hidden the fine cloth from them, and why it was not offered for trade?"

"What are you going to tell her?" the Mate asked.

"Truth." Oteria quickly replied. The Mate had forgotten that Christopher had been teaching her English, for his poor memory, he felt the fool.

"Oteria," Christopher softly said, getting her to look at him, he hoped that he would have some greater chance at making her understand their position. "The cloth you speak of is not ours to trade. It belongs to the people we are going to see. They will not give us what our people back home need if we do not deliver these goods to them."

"This truth my Christopher?"

"Yes. We must give these goods to the people of China; it is all they will accept." He reached out and took her hand. "We have traded freely with all that is ours to trade, you know that I would freely give to you all that is mine."

"You speak the truth." It was a statement, not a question. Oteria turned back to her people and began to tell them what he had just said.

"If you mean what you say." Red was quietly laughing. "She just may get your honor yet."

"You shut up too," the Master turned on Red, but the look in his eyes when he glanced back at Christopher showed that he might just agree with Red.

Finally, several native women slowly emerged from the jungle's edge carrying their lost linen, the English formed a line at which the linen was laid at their feet. With a bow, the ones that had brought it slowly backed away. The Master had his men quickly scoop it up and beat it the boats. When they returned from the ship for the next load the beach was deserted, the guards posted at the stockade reported no troubles in their absence, although the Master had seen fit to leave the armed men there.

They were able to haul about half of the cargo off to the ship during the balance of the day. Extra guards were posted at the stockade to watch over the balance of their cargo during the night.

Finished with his duties, Christopher called upon Oteria at her father's house, she was glad to see him and made a fuss over his ever-darkening left eye. He told her how much he appreciated what she had done and how impressed he was with her courage; her reply was something to the effect that she too had a duty to uphold honor.

Before taking his leave, he presented her with his best white blouse. Her face lit up as if he had awarded her the crown jewels. She allowed him to help her put it on. Since its cut was long, even for him, it looked very much like a white dress on her. Christopher thought that she looked quite striking in it. Then he presented her with a bright red ribbon given to him by Sarah. This she allowed him to tie in her hair. Even the King seemed well pleased with these gifts. Christopher believed red holds special meaning for these people.

Tuesday, April 1, 1762
Eden

Loading of the cargo was completed this day, this included all the shark fins and a huge quantity of bird nests. What these were for, Christopher didn't have a clue, for these items the Master traded iron nails and two bolts of linen. He claimed that the Chinese wanted the nest far more than the linen, thereby not making Christopher out to be a liar. The next order of business was the construction of pig pens on the main deck to hold the wild pigs that they hoped to obtain through barter. The voyage from Eden to Canton, according to the Mate was roughly three to four weeks. Their plan was to try and obtain enough pigs, coconuts and breadfruit to make that time more enjoyable with fresh provisions.

They found that the red ribbon was the item the natives wanted the most. Since Sarah had little of it left, they decided to cut it into strips whereas each ribbon produced three. Then by cutting it into lengths of about one inch long they were able to turn one red ribbon into thirty. These thirty pieces of ribbon were easily bartered into thirty of the wild pigs. The natives wanted to trade the more plentiful wild dogs, but the sailors held out for the pigs.

The coconuts and breadfruit were plentiful and therefore held no value, thus they gave them to the sailors as gifts. The most difficult remaining problem was that of fresh water, not only would they have to carry enough fresh water for their own usage for three to four weeks, but enough for the animals as well. Chips, as usual, solved the problem with a plan-to construct several wooden tubs. Each of the tubs would be constructed in such a way as to have an inner layer of wood coated on the outside with tar, then an outer layer of wood.

Saturday, April 3, 1762
Eden

The building of the tubs was far more exacting than Christopher would have thought, each plank was carefully notched and fitted together, these were then held in place with tree nails. Each tub, more of a vat, would hold the same amount of water as four of their regular freshwater casks. The tarring of the outside of the inner layer was just as exacting. Each was caulked in much the same manner as the ship's planks were. Then the outer layer of wood was constructed as precise as the inner.

Christopher had no doubts that the vats would indeed hold water. The balance of this day was spent in ferrying water from the stream to the boats, then hauled out to the ship and dumped into the vats. It took many trips, but as Christopher labored in the task, he thought of how glad he would be at not having to ration water once at sea.

Finally, just before sundown, the work was complete. The good ship OCTAVIUS once again fully ready for sea. The Master called all hands to assemble.

"You have done admirably," he stated. "The OCTAVIUS is once again a fine and worthy ship. Never in all my years of sailing have, I had the honor to command such a fine lot of men. Tomorrow we will rejoice in our good fortune and bid our heartfelt thanks to these proud and fine people. At first light on Monday, we set sail for China. We will not be coming back this way until our next voyage. So, say goodbye to your friends, as it will be a year or two before we return."

"Might I inquire of the Captain?" Red spoke up. "Why we will not be coming back this way?"

"Yes, you may ask," the Master smiled. "As those of you who have sailed with me before are quite aware, we are already hopelessly late for the prime trading season. Hopefully, we can still land a return cargo without having to spend the season in China. Also, we do not make stops on the return voyage, the cargo will be silk and tea mainly. Items that bring a fine price if they are delivered in a timely manner. Once we obtain our return cargo, we will make all haste in returning to England." He looked about those gathered before him. No one questioned him further, although he did not offer any clues as to why the ship was so reinforced. "That's all. Have a good time during your last two nights here, just be aboard by dark tomorrow evening. The Mate will post the duty roster."

As luck would have it, Christopher had the watch this night and could not go ashore with the others. He had wanted so much to spend these final few hours with Oteria, but duty is duty, his personal desires would have to wait.

Christopher was surprised about an hour later when the Mate returned to the ship and asked if he wanted company? Christopher replied that while it was kind of him to offer, he should spend his time ashore.

"I assure you that that is exactly what I intend to do," the Mate smiled as Oteria stepped from behind him.

Sabbath, April 4, 1762
Eden-Final Day

Worship service this day was one of thanksgiving. The bible reading came from Psalms 107. With the emphasis on verses 23 through 30.

"They that go down to the sea in ships, that do business in great waters:"

"These see the works of the Lord, and his wonders in the deep.

"For he commanded, and raised the stormy wind, which lifted up the waves thereof."

"They mount up to the heaven, they go down again to the depths: their soul is melted because of trouble."

"They reel to and fro, and stagger like a drunken man, and are at their wits' end."

"Then they cry onto the Lord in their trouble, and he bringeth them out of their distresses."

"He maketh the storm calm, so that the waves thereof are still."

"Then are they glad because they be quiet; so, he bringeth them unto their desire heaven."

Christopher was always impressed with how well the Master knew his bible, thinking him nearly as wise to its contents as his father. All the worship services had a poignant point to bring out at a very appropriate point in their travels and troubles.

When in times of great tribulation, these services had given hope to their hearts, at times of laxity the words served to remind them of who and where they were.

As soon as the service was concluded, all scattered to the winds, each having his agenda. With less than a full day to say and do all the things they wanted to be remembered for in the hearts of these people. For himself, Christopher wanted to spend this day in the arms of his beloved Oteria.

Christopher ran into Chips as he was heading for the longboat, which was ferrying men ashore.

"You are planning on spending the day with Miss Oteria?" Chips asked.

"Yes sir," Christopher replied, stepping over the gunwale and easing himself down the Jacob's ladder.

"I'm off to see her as well," he beamed, following Christopher down the ladder. He had something wrapped up in an old piece of cloth.

"You don't say?" Christopher thought he was trying to get his goat.

"Aye, have a little present for her," Chips said, retaining that smile of his. "She asked me for something only I could provide, sorry Mate."

Christopher would not give him the satisfaction of an argument. He could see Oteria standing near the water's edge, dressed in the white blouse he had given her. As soon as she spotted him looking her way, she waved. Christopher did not think for one moment that she was waiting for old Chips and was not about to let the old carpenter get him going.

The boat was well overloaded as most of the crew was bent on going ashore. They laid into the oars and made off from the ship. In no time at all they had the boat ground on the beach. Oteria, just as Christopher thought she would do, ran up to him and wrapped her arms around his neck and kissed him. Christopher was smiling, old Chips was the farthest thing from her mind.

"Ah, there you are my dear." Chips stepped up and offered the rag-covered gift to Oteria. "Just as you requested."

"You have done my want?" she excitedly asked.

"Aye, just as you requested." Chips nearly laughed.

Oteria carefully took the offered gift and slowly unwrapped it. Her eyes opened wide as she beheld the handiwork, kissing it, then Chips. Christopher nearly dropped from embarrassment. The gift was a miniature of him! Nude! Complete in every detail, although

Chips had to have guessed at certain parts of his anatomy.

"Hey Mate," Red took an interest in the carving, "that's you! At least most of it is you. But I think old Chips here, was a wee bit generous in areas." That drew a roaring laugh from all gathered around, at Christopher's expense.

"I had to guess a bit at some things," Chips admitted. "Since Mr. Jamison here tends to be a tad modest."

"That's enough," Christopher tried to sound forceful, but it came out far too timid.

"That's more than enough I'd bet," Red laughed.

"Oteria much happy," she said as she embraced old Chips and kissed him on his whisker stubbled cheek. "Thank you much."

"Aye, you're very welcome my dear," Chips replied as he hugged her and returned the kiss on her cheek.

"I have nothing to give for this," she suddenly seemed concerned.

"No need my dear," Chips bowed slightly. "Your just reward for helping us out of that mess the other day."

Christopher was finally able to lead Oteria away from the others. Her carving held firmly in her grasp, she turned and waved her thanks one more time to Chips, which he returned.

Their day was planned; Christopher wanted to return to the plateau that overlooked the bay. He wanted this day to be one he would remember for the rest of his life, and a day she would remember just as vividly.

When they reached the plateau, Christopher spread the blanket he had brought along, across the emerald green grass. The light breeze that always seemed to be in presence, was so again. As it came in from the sea it mixed all the sweet smells of this place into a fragrance Christopher knew he would never forget. The sun was bright and warm, the mountains rose up behind them with patches of deep green and lighter greens mixed with gray and brown. The vivid blue sky behind the mountains with fleecy white clouds. To their sides and front, the bluish-green of the sea with its white-tipped breakers continually rolling toward the shore. All in all, this was the most breath-taking place on all the earth. And to be here with such a warm and beautiful woman was the true epitome of heaven on earth.

They enjoyed a picnic of coconut and breadfruit topped off with a flask of pepper wine he had managed to obtain for the cost of three iron nails. For the first time in her life, Qteria sat next to a man and ate with him, this was no simple thing, and the meaning of this gesture was not lost on Christopher.

Then they laid next to one another on the blanket watching the clouds gliding past. She asked if the clouds looked the same in England, he replied that they did, although he personally believed everything to look much more beautiful here.

Suddenly, Oteria sat up and rested herself on one aim and gazed down upon Christopher. Her face and expression were so sweet and innocent, Christopher reached up and pulled her lips to his. The fiery passion that flowed from one to the other was the combination of their love for each other and the knowledge that this time together would be their last. Here, in this time and place they would make a memory that would last to the end of time.

Christopher was no longer refusing her advances, he encouraged them. Flesh to flesh they discovered each other's love. What he had held for the woman he would love for a lifetime, he surrendered to the woman he knew he would always love. The softness of her flesh, the warmth and tenderness of her body, there was nothing else in the world. Just Oteria and Christopher, they were of one mind, one body' one spirit, one soul.

The joy and passion of being as one, their bodies joined, their hearts beating in unison, their entire being consumed by the fires within. Christopher closed his eyes and yet witnessed the sparkle of St. Elmo's fire that slowly built into a bolt of thunder. Time stood still, the more they had of each the more they hungered for. When all the energy and passion had been spent, they were left with such tenderness and desire to be together forever. Although neither spoke of such things, as both knew it could not be.

They laid in each other's arms silently until the sun's rays were settling low on the horizon, their time together was nearly over. It was time for Christopher to report back to the ship. Hand in hand they walked down the path toward the beach. When they arrived at the beach the sun had already set, the western heavens were ablaze in a fire red glow, the promise of a good day for sailing in the morning. Somehow Christopher doubted that he would have a good day tomorrow without Oteria.

Several others were gathered at the beach as well, waiting for the boat to return from the ship to take them off. While they waited, Oteria and Christopher sat close together. The evening breeze felt cool for the first time, the sand still radiated the warmth it had absorbed from the day's sun. They held each other close, still wanting to feel each other's warmth, each other's love.

Christopher longed to hear her tell him how much she loved him, but how would that change the outcome of their circumstance? It would not. He refrained from making idle talk, he wanted to tell her how badly he was hurting inside, how he longed to take her with him, but that could not be, so it would serve no purpose to utter.

He could see the launch putting out from the side of OCTAVIUS, it would be upon them in a matter of moments. In it he would return to his ship, never again to touch this fair maiden's hair, kiss her tender lips, feel her soft skin, stare into those big brown eyes.

He felt like doing something, telling her that he would return in one or two short years, telling her that he would take her off to his home, or stay here with her, none of which he could promise. Two years is such a long time, would he feel the same then? Would she? No, he would not make promises he could not keep. He may be back in two years, he may not.

The launch was nearing the beach. Christopher rose to his feet and helped Oteria to hers. With the fading sun's brilliant colors behind the island and casting the mountains in a fiery glow, Christopher stared into those beautiful, big brown eyes for the last time. "I love you Oteria, I always will."

Wet tears began to form at the corners of her eyes. "Oteria always love Christopher, Oteria wants Christopher to stay, not go!"

"It pains me greatly, but I must go." Christopher tried to sound soothing, but his voice began to crack, the agony of this parting was cracking his tough exterior. "I will always think of you and picture you as you stand here now.

The launch's bow sliced into the sand of the beach. "All right mates, let's get aboard. The old man wants you all aboard the OCTAVIUS by dark. Let's go." Liverpool sang out as he stepped from the boat, holding the painter line.

Christopher and Oteria embraced tightly, both wanting to remember this sensation, wanting to remember exactly how the other felt, how they smelled. They dearly wanted to remember each other.

"Come on Mate," Liverpool called.

Slowly Christopher started to lessen his grip of Oteria, she started doing likewise. "I love you," Christopher whispered as he stepped backward away from her.

"Oteria loves Christopher." She was crying now, which was breaking Christopher's heart. He turned around and made for the launch. He had made it to the boat's side when she called out him, screaming out his name. Christopher spun around to see her running towards him with open arms and tears flowing down her cheeks, she was begging him to stay, he was dying inside. The moment she reached him she fell into his arms, crying and shaking so terribly hard that he couldn't just push her away and get into the launch, but he must.

He slowly took hold of her forearms and gently but forcefully held her out in front of him. "Oteria, I love you so dearly, but now I must go, it is not a matter of choice. Please understand that I do love you so very much, but my duty is aboard that ship out there."

She nodded her understanding and slowly stepped back. Christopher tossed his blanket into the boat and was about to board when he decided that if this was his last opportunity, it was not to be lost, he ran over to her and tasted of her lips one long last time.

"Come on Mate!" Liverpool begged in the background.

"Goodbye my love." Christopher turned and ran back to the launch and boarded.

"About bloody well time!" Liverpool seemed put off by having to wait. "If the old man gets hot about this, it's your fault, you remember that."

"Shut up and row," Christopher shot back. "'I'll explain to the Captain, if there's need."

"Damn right you will." Liverpool had to get the last word in.

Oteria remained on the beach where he had left her, already the distance between them made her features hard to see. He closed his eyes and tried to picture her as she stood before him only seconds ago. For an instant he couldn't see her face. His eyes bolted open, there she was, so far off he couldn't swear that it was really her, but he could see her in his mind's eye. But would he be able to see her when he closed his eyes a year from now? Afraid that he might not, he decided right there and then that he would ask of Chips what Oteria had, a miniature of his sweet Oteria. Every time he should look upon it, he would remember this place and her sweet love.

Monday, April 5, 1762
Leaving Eden

As of midnight, the ship was back to sea watches. Christopher had the four-to-eight watch and was delighted by the most splendid sunrise of all.

The Master had come on deck just before the sun made its appearance. "How are thee this fine morning, Mr. Jamison?"

"Very fit," Christopher replied.

"Leaving here is always so difficult," the Master said as he brought his pipe to life. "Seems harder to do so each time. I wonder why I even stop here in the first place."

"I am glad you did, Sire."

"Aye, I'll bet you are, but I wonder, were you so glad last night when you had to say goodbye?"

"No sire, I was not," Christopher admitted, while the Master extended his eyeglass and peered towards the shore.

"I'll be damned."

"What is it?"

"Look for yourself," the Master replied, handing the eyeglass over.

What Christopher saw broke his heart. Oteria was asleep on the beach where he had left her last night. "She must have been there all night."

"That would be my guess," the Master agreed. "You are a lucky man to have held her heart for even a moment. Years from now, she will only be a smile that no one else will understand. Yes, Mr. Jamison, you are indeed very lucky. You have obtained a very fine memory, when one gets old that's how one judges his life, if you have many fine memories like that one, you will indeed be a rich man. Wealth and property are possessions one must share, memories are truly personal, never to be taken, and never truly shared."

"Oteria and I will share the same memory of this visit."

"Alike, yes. But the same, not at all." The sweet-smelling smoke of his pipe lightly swirled around them both. "You will remember it from your perspective, and she from hers. No two memories are the same."

"Aye, I can see that to be true, Sire. Still I shall remember always."

"I am sure you will, Christopher, I am sure you will. Now if you would call the hands. The sun is upon us, time for breakfast, then we will go."

"Aye, aye," Christopher replied as he turned for the foc'sle hatch. "All hands ahoy! Time for breakfast!"

Six bells were struck, and all hands turned out for the morning meal. At seven bells all hands were again called, this time to prepare to get under way. All the lines were checked and found to be in order the boats properly stowed, the galley was closed, pots and pans secured. Tubs and casks were double checked for loose lids, the pens with the small wild pigs was inspected and all seemed in order when the Mate called the hands aloft.

Within minutes men were climbing the rigging and standing by to furl the sails. All but the seaward bow anchor was weighed.

"Hard to starboard," the Mate called.

"Hard to starboard," young Richard sang out as he stood proudly at the wheel.

"Hove in the anchor."

"Anchor hoved in."."

"Standby to loose the sails!" called the Mate.

They cast off the yardarm gaskets and bunt gaskets. At the end of each yard one of them remained keeping the bunt jigger in hand with a turn round the tye, all ready to let go.

"All ready forward?" called the Mate.

"Aye, aye, all ready forward," came the reply.

"All ready the main?" the Mate called to those on the maim mast yards.

"Aye, aye, all ready, on the main," Christopher sang out.

"All set and ready Sire," the Mate reported to the Master.

"Loose the sails," the Master ordered.

"Loose the sails!" the Mate shouted as all square sails aboard the ship were suddenly furled. It must have been a sight for Oteria and those watching from the shore; one moment the ship lies at anchor with bare poles, and then full sails and under way in the next.

The crew then descended upon the deck, save one man in each mast, to overhaul the rigging. Next the fore topsail went up, then the main topsail, all of which was taking place in seconds of each other. The yards were then trimmed to catch the wind and the final seaward bow anchor, which they had nearly run over was weighed.

At once they were fully under way. The studding and light sails were then set as was the jib. Before they had cleared the lagoon, that had been their home for little more than seven weeks, all cloth was furled and set.

As the OCTAVIUS charged from the lagoon, Christopher made his way aft for one last glimpse at the land of Oteria, his love. He didn't have to ask; the Master offered his eyeglass.

"Take a look, Christopher. It will be a while before you lay eyes on Eden again."

"Thank you, Sire," Christopher quickly took the eyeglass and extended it out fully. He instantly spotted the small and growing smaller figure of Oteria standing on the sandy beach and waving farewell. It hurt to be leaving her, although he knew he must. He could not help but wonder if he should ever see her again?

As soon as Eden disappeared off the fantail the Mate called out, "Go below the watch." Since it was Christopher's watch to go below, he quickly did just that.

CHAPTER ELEVEN
CHINA

Sabbath, April 11, 1762
Pacific Ocean

It had been nearly a week since they left Eden. Christopher felt listless, he pained for Oteria. He asked Chips for the carving of her and was told that it would take time. Christopher now sat in his cabin, writing in his journal for the first time that week, he just couldn't seem to find the words to express the way he felt. He hoped that Chips would start the carving soon, before either of them forgot what Oteria looked like.

All the men had been quiet, Christopher was not alone in leaving someone tender behind. The exceptions to this appeared to be the Master, Richard, Sarah, and old Chips.

As for the ship, she appeared to be quite fit and the wind had been blessing them with a strong, steady blow. The sea was mild to medium, the weather balmy, all in all, the most perfect sailing conditions. Christopher knew he should rejoice in their fortune but could not.

Young Richard had made the week gone by tolerable; he had constantly spoken of China. The boy believed this to be the highlight of his voyage with his father, prior to seeing Oteria, Christopher too had thought the same.

Monday, April 19 OR 20, 1762
Pacific Ocean
International Dateline

    Christopher had the night watch which was something he truly enjoyed while at sea. He had just taken a tour of the deck and was heading aft when he noticed the Master standing on deck enjoying his pipe
    "Welcome to tomorrow," he smiled as Christopher came up to him.
    "Pardon Sire?"
    "I said welcome to tomorrow."
    "Aye is it midnight already?"
    "Not midnight, but the international dateline, we are coming to it sometime about now. As we sail across the invisible line, we sail into the next day no matter what the time is."
    "How can you be sure of where it is?"
    "The same way one find's any other location on a map. By the stars, my boy, by the stars. We should be well upon it anytime now."
    "So, we lose a day of our lives?"
    "Going this way, we do," the Master smiled. "But going the other way we gain a day, so we're even."

During the daylight watches there was much to do. Besides the usual work involved in running a fine square sail ship, they had the pigs to look after. This involved cleaning the pens, watering and feeding the animals. Each day there would become one or two fewer of the beasts to care for as they were used for fresh meat.

The butchering of the pigs was done on the main deck, when weather permitted. A well Patched sailcloth was first spread upon the deck, the unlucky animal caught, a rope looped a hind leg, then hoisted from a yard. Cooky quickly slit the animals throat allowing it to bleed out properly. Next the animal was skinned and cut into pieces. Once Cooky had removed all the meat to the galley, the cloth was rolled up and the deck cleaned. This butchering was usually done during the dogwatch so that there was always plenty of help to get the job done quickly and everything cleaned.

Wednesday, April 21, 1762
Pacific Ocean

Once again Christopher found himself on night watch, this the twelve-to-four, the reason he loved having the watch at night was the solitude. By midnight the watch below had retired, no singing, no storytelling, no human sounds at all. The only sounds to keep him company were the sounds of the ship herself, the creaking of the timbers, the smacking of the wind into the canvass, the tension popping noise ropes make when they are stretched taut and then some. The slapping of the ocean swells against the hull, the solitary footsteps of a sailor on watch, walking the deserted deck alone, his footsteps.

All these sounds were music to him, a whole concert of natural sounds that unless one listens closely will pass unnoticed. These sounds soothed his soul and gave him solace. These sounds were what sailing was all about, what life at sea truly was. These sounds were one of the many reasons he could not stay at Eden, sooner or later he would have longed to hear them again.

There was another part of standing a night watch that Christopher found fascinating. It was the blackened heavens on a dark night, the sailing through a total absence of light, save for the lonely mast light. It was almost mystic to travel over a world one could not see, a world that teamed with life and yet remained invisible.

On a night of a fall moon, the moonbeams dance upon ebony water, no matter where one sails on a night such as this, the moon is in a direct line to one's vessel. This line is illuminated by a shaft of shimmering silver from the moon to the vessel directly. Then on special moments, when one is least expecting, a whale or a dolphin broaches the surface within this silver line of light.

Yes, this was the best possible watch to stand, when one could feel a part of the world around himself and yet totally alone. This was a wondrous feeling that unless one has experienced it, it could not be appreciated. Christopher sailed for this simple pleasure more than any other.

By the time the Mate came on to relieve Christopher, the sky had begun to cloud over. The wind had increased, but was still out of the south. The gentle swell of the sea was picking up as well. This was something he judged by how far the shadows from the mast light traveled back and forth.

Christopher went over everything he felt the Mate should know before turning the deck over to him, this time also allowed the Mate's eyes to become accustomed to the darkness

Thursday, April 22, 1762
Pacific Ocean

The day dawned gray and dark, an angry heaven hung over them, threatening to lash out should they give it the slightest reason. The sea was running westerly, or in direction with them, the waves were mild at dawn and grew with the passing hours. By the time the dogwatch was called, the rain was beating down upon them and the sea was beginning to chum

Every man was clad in his southeaster and it was increasingly difficult to determine who was before you unless you could clearly see his face, which was seldom. As the storm grew in intensity, they had to work the rigging more and more. By the time the dogwatch was over it was Christopher's watch that was sent below, and glad of it.

Quickly stripped out of his southeaster rain gear and removed his wet clothes underneath. He then fully dressed again and put everything in order, he expected to get called from his berth if things kicked up too much.

Christopher didn't have long to wait, the wind shifted halfway around the compass in little more than an hour, all hands were called to man the sails. When this was done and all rigging secured and set, they were once again sent below, only to be called in less than half an hour when the main sail tore.

They struggled it down and out of its rigging and quickly hauled its replacement up into its place. Remembering the broken jibboom at the Horn, the jib was furled and secured. As the ship beat down an angry sea, Christopher was glad they had taken the extra time in Eden to rebuild the steering gear and much of the tackle.

The OCTAVIUS was conducting herself well and a well-mannered ship is far easier to handle in these conditions. Christopher was called to the larboard side to help haul on one of the lines. He worked behind a fellow in full southeaster rain gear, not knowing who it was before him. He was quite surprised to find John hauling the lines and doing a fine job of getting around on his wood leg.

When Christopher had the opportunity to speak to John later, he mentioned how surprised he was to see that he was doing so well with the lines so soon.

"It's a hell of a lot easier than I thought it would be," John replied. "I do watch my step better, so I tend to fall less now than I did."

"Does it hurt to fall with that leg?"

"Naw," John laughed. "But the damn thing comes off, and in a blow like that," he motioned toward the deck outside. "I have a devilish time finding it."

The storm bore down upon them with much the same fury as earlier storms, but, the wind and rain were warm and the ship itself handled far better. All the rigging was in prime condition which made hauling them that much easier. In earlier storms the lines themselves became iced and hard to handle, none of those problems were to bother them now.

During this blow all hands were called no more than six or seven times, and since this storm was to last for nearly twelve hours, that was not intolerable.

Sabbath, April 25, 1762
Pacific Ocean

Christopher had the four-to-eight watch this morning and was blessed with another beautiful sunrise astern of them. The air was so warm at night that many of the crew had taken to sleeping out on the open deck. This became a problem when he made rounds. He had to be careful not to step on someone sleeping in the shadows. Once, he nearly did so, the ship lurched just as he was passing some of the men, he had been trying to be so careful that he nearly lost his balance, luckily, all he did was brush against someone's back, which caused him to stir, but thankfully not wake up.

As the sun started to rise it painted the sea around them a bright pinkish yellow, the dolphins had come to life and were doing their playful water dance across and through their bow wake. Christopher loved watching these magnificent creatures. If only he could sail as fast as they swim, a voyage that usually takes two years could be completed in less than one.

As Christopher looked into the sails, the lower one third of cloth was painted a deep red by the sun. It lightened to a rosy pink, lightening as it rose through the cloth until it was a brilliant gold at the top. It made Christopher aware of the Almighty's presence, sailing was like that, some could see the Lord in everything around them. Others felt that the open expanse of emptiness, the loneliness was proof that there was no higher meaning. Should they die here, they became fish food, should they live long enough to reach home and die there, they became food for the worms. That's all there was to life, you lived it, then you died, nothing more.

That was the religion of so many sailors. Christopher however, could not stand on the deck of this ship, or any ship, watching the sun rise or set, watching the whales glide to the surface and blow their mighty spray or watch dolphins speed through the swells at incredible speeds and not believe in the being and power of the Almighty.

Midday the heat was becoming unbearable, two fights broke out among the crew. The first fight was little more than a tussle, the second however, took six men to pull them apart. Neither man would stop attacking the other, even when the Master ordered it. As a result, a general assembly was called.

As the entire crew drew together on the quarter-deck, the Master stepped before them. He carefully looked from man to man. "We are nearing the Equator, possibly one of the hottest places on the face of the earth, the only thing that makes it tolerable is the wind. However, the nearer we draw to the equator the more likely it is that we should be becalmed.

Working in this heat is difficult enough without undo tension, I hereby order each of you to hold your tongue against your shipmates, any more fighting will be handled with the cat-o-nine-tails. I repeat, I will not tolerate any more of this foolishness, you could get hurt and we can ill afford to lose any of you. Do I make myself clear?"

They all nodded and looked, for the most part, at the deck beneath them. They were dismissed, except for the two who had been fighting, they were attended to by Sarah. The balance of the day went along calmly, neither of the two fighters spoke a word to the other, but at least they were not fighting either.

Monday, April 26, 1762
Pacific Ocean

They crossed the equator exactly at midnight, luckily, wind has held. Since Eden, young Richard has been occupied in wood carving, and had become quite good at the trade, and his carving of the OCTAVIUS was very realistic, one look and Christopher knew that it was this ship. He admired the boy's interest in carving but missed their visits. Richard had been spending most of his time with Chips and John.

Lately however, Christopher thought the boy was getting bored with it, he had been coming around more and for longer periods of time. Today Richard came on deck shortly after the watch started and stayed for the entire watch and talked of many things. Their talk eventually turned to Oteria, which Christopher knew it would at some point, he could tell the boy missed her too. Maybe his parents had told him not to bring her up. That may also explain why the lad had not been around since they left the island.

Christopher himself had been trying to avoid the subject but found to his surprise that it helped to talk about her.

"Do you love her?"

"Yes, I believe that I do."

"What is it like this love? "

Christopher thought on that for a moment, if he could describe it, then maybe he could know for sure what it was. "Love is like a toothache you enjoy."

"A what?" Richard nearly laughed.

"It is a delightful pain, something that is nearly impossible to explain, yet almost everyone will experience it some time in a lifetime."

"Do you think that you can experience love more than once?"

"For my sake, I certainly hope so."

Richard thought on that for a while, "What will you do if we stop at Eden on the next voyage and Oteria has been married? The King seemed like he wanted that to happen, you know?"

"Yes, he did seem purposeful at that." Christopher hadn't considered this, young Richard never ceased to amaze him with the deep thoughts he was capable of. If Christopher had thought of how he would feel, he had ignored those thoughts, he guessed deep down he wanted to believe for now, at least, that she would be there waiting. It was a selfish thought for sure, but one that did allow him to go on.

"I don't know how I would feel," Christopher finally answered. "But I know how I should feel."

"And how is that?"

"I should be glad for her."

"Would you be?"

"Part of me would be, yes, the part of me that understands things for what they are. I could no more give up all I have known for the uncertainty of a future in her world. How do you suppose she would do in ours?"

"She's as smart as a whip," Richard smiled. "I bet she would do just fine.

"Maybe, maybe not," Christopher conceded a bit. "But what if she couldn't adjust, what if life in our world became misery to her. What if she longed for her home, her people?"

"I suppose you're right, but I thought you were going to bring her along, even my father thought so."

There it was the master's meaning that night. That night that seemed like a lifetime ago. Christopher could have brought her along, the Master would have allowed that, maybe he should have asked. He quickly shook that thought aside. He knew that it was his longing for her that was speaking. He had just reasons for not asking, reasons that still made a good deal of sense.

Christopher changed the subject; he could not deal with this issue just yet. They talked of Richard's carvings, the condition of the ship, the future; China.

Friday. April 30, 1762
Pacific Ocean
Land Sighted

Twenty-five days out of Eden, they had good sailing conditions with moderate weather. Rain had blessed them twelve times, giving them plenty of fresh water. The stock of island pigs was now gone, few coconuts remained. Their diet was once again salt pork and biscuits, they longed for China.

Christopher had the midday, twelve-to-four watch, the sun was intense and the wind light. They were making less than three knots. The sea was nearly flat calm and sparkled so brightly in the sun it nearly blinded them. Without the wind to temperate the sun's heat, they baked under it as surely as if they were pigs in a spit.

"Land-Ho!" the lookout suddenly shouted.

"Where and away?" Christopher shouted back.

"A point off the larboard bow!"

The crew came running from every corner of the ship. Having been at sea for so long after Eden's sweet respite, all were eager to lay eyes upon another piece of land.

"Formosa," the Master offered. "We should pass fairly close to the main island."

"How far from here is Canton?" Christopher asked.

"Only two or three days, Mr. Jamison." He smiled, "only two or three days to Canton."

"Sounds grand."

"What is our course?"

"What course, Junior Mate?" Christopher quickly passed on to young Richard, who was doing his trick at the wheel.

"Steady on nor'west, Sir." Came Richard's quick and steady reply. Christopher caught the gleam of pride in the master's eye.

"Very good," the Master smiled to Christopher, "steady on course."

"Steady on course."

The Master stood near the rail and looked upon Formosa Island through his eyeglass, "If I had my way, I would never sail below this latitude again."

Both Richard and Christopher looked at each other, then at the Master. "Forgive me, Sire," Christopher said, "but if we did not sail south, how would we ever get home? We have to sail south around the Cape?"

The Master turned back toward them, thought a moment then surprised them both. "Not at all, there is another way."

"Another way?"

He only smiled and nodded. Christopher remembered the map in his cabin, the one with the coastline that Red thought could be California. But how could they get home by way of California? Unless that passage, he, had spoken of months before was somewhere near California?

"Does the Captain speak of a route near California?" Christopher questioned.

Master turned back around to face him; his solemn face hid any hint of his true feelings. "Why do you speak of California, Mr. Jamison?"

"I saw a bit of a map sticking out beneath the plans for the OCTAVIUS when I was in your cabin while we were at Eden, Sire. I thought I recognized the bit of coast-line as that of California." He did not tell him that Red was the one to recognize the coastline.

"So, you did?" The Master stood silent for a time, and then looked Christopher square in the eyes. "Why would you pay mind to a bit of a map and remember it so long my young friend?"

His calm voice and use of words were all that belayed Christopher's fear for being so forward with the Master. "I just remember you saying something about a passage." Christopher tried to think of when it was that he had spoken of that passage but could not. "I do not remember when Sire, but you did mention a passage of some sort to me one night while we sailed the southern sea."

He thought on that for a moment. "Pray tell, why would you connect something I said about a passage and the notice of a map of California together?"

"The frames, Sire."

"The frames?"

"Aye, the frames."

And what of the frames Mr. Jamison?"

"When you ordered their strength nearly doubled, it was then that I recalled something being said about a passage. It was soon after that I noticed the map. In truth, Sire, I noticed the map the same morning you sent me into the jungle to begin cutting our large cargo of firewood. It was none of the things alone, rather the sum of all these that led me to wonder. I am sorry for my improper conduct and all the questions, Sire."

His stern look slowly melted before he let out a hearty laugh. "Improper my eye!" He laughed. "Any seaman worth his salt is naturally curious, always wanting to know what lays ahead, just beyond the next horizon. Nothing improper about it, Mr. Jamison. No sir, nothing improper about it." He stepped closer to Christopher and glanced around his shoulder to be certain young Richard was listening. Christopher was quite sure the lad was, but since he was behind him, he couldn't be sure. "Curiosity," the Master said, "is how I found my way here on the first trip. It also led me to Eden, to Formosa, and to every other place I have dared to find. Yes, there is another way home, but it is not to be found in California. It is located somewhere much farther to the north. I admit that I do not know much about it, no one does. But it stands to reason that it would indeed be a much shorter route home, this passage that people have taken to calling the Northwest Passage."

Christopher stole a quick glance at young Richard, his face was alit with wonder. It was as if his father had just spoken of a mystical place.

"Has anyone ever sailed this Northwest Passage before?" Christopher asked.

"That's the beauty of it, you see," the Master became a bit animated. "No one has ever had the courage to look for it. If we only dare to look, we could find a way in which to be home by Christmas,"

"They might even name this passage after you, father, should we find it," young Richard piped up.

"I can't speak of naming it, but I can assure you that much honor would befall anyone who could indeed find a shorter route home, not to mention an easier one at that. Why, what the crown wouldn't give to avoid the battles of the Horn."

Sabbath, May 2, 1762
Sea of China
Mainland Sighted

The mainland of China was sighted about an hour before sunrise. The starboard watch was standing watch, so Christopher was fast asleep in his berth when he was awakened by the call "Land - Ho!" Having been sleeping in his shorts, he didn't bother with trousers when he heard the call. He was completely embarrassed when he sprung onto the deck right in front of Sarah.

He beat a hasty retreat and soon reappeared on deck dressed as a Second Mate should. A morning fog was hanging over the lower coastline, but through the gray morning, Christopher could see mountains and the higher ground of China. Much cheer instantly gripped the ship and all aboard. Christopher's embarrassment soon forgotten, he joined in the signing and the dancing on deck. It had taken nine months, but China now lay before them.

Since it would take them several hours yet to obtain the river that would lead them eighty miles into the mainland to Canton, Christopher returned to his berth for much needed sleep before being called to breakfast. But sleep was not to be had. He would soon get to set foot on Chinese soil, that thought made him feel like a true salt, like the ones he heard telling stories of this mystical place in the pubs back home. In truth, it was those stories, and the want of a job that made him eager to sign aboard this ship.

Shortly after breakfast, they overhauled the river and turned into it. The Master had knowledge of this river and its every turn and channel. A few very strange-looking craft were plying the river as well, some heading toward Canton, others working their way toward the sea. The master explained that these strange craft were called junks by their Chinese owners. The junks serve as both workplace and permanent home as they were usually crewed by family.

The trip up the Pearl River to Canton would take seventeen-and-a-half hours to complete, but not a moment was wasted. The day had dawned fair and bright and all effort was made preparing the OCTAVIUS in all readiness for her arrival. The masts and spars were tarred, the lines were run out and checked, finally the decks were holy stoned to a crisp whiteness, the ship was indeed ready to arrive.

They did not truly arrive at Canton proper until well past sundown. They could clearly see all the lights of the city sparkling across the black water before them. They had finally made Canton, China, their destination from England over half a world and nine months away.

They did not go ashore, opting instead to drop hook in the river and wait for daylight. Also, the Master would have to go ashore in the morning to secure a berth at the British quay

Monday, May 3, 1762
Canton, China

Although they had now reached their destination, no one could sit back and relax, there was much to be done. The ship had to be made ready to off load the cargo. The hatches were opened, which also allowed the stuffy holds with the precious cargo to air out.

At seven bells they stopped in their labors for the morning meal. Throughout the meal, Cooky was promising better rations come evening. At eight bells Christopher and young Richard were summoned by the Master to accompany him ashore. Numerous large warehouses lined the river's edge, above each a different national banner was fluttering in the morning breeze. That of Britain was slightly to the left, with Spain, Portugal, France, and Holland to the right.

They arrived at the jetty in due course and quickly disembarked, being met there by a proper English gent by the name of Sir Sidney Whittington. He was the agent who managed the British warehouse.

"Where have you been?" were the first words out of Sir Whittington's mouth. "We'd given the lot of you up for dead. The local Viceroy seemed pretty upset that you didn't show during the trading season. I dare say that I'm none too sure what good your showing up now will do, everybody has returned home. Doubt that I'll be able to put much of a cargo together for you."

Finally, the Master had a chance to speak. "And how is his Excellency the Viceroy? Well, I trust?"

"Well enough."

"Be sure to see to it that my regards are sent to him this morning, will you?"

"I'll see to it," Sir Whittington nodded.

"Also be sure to mention that I was nearly wrecked but have kept my bargain." The Master smiled. "Discreetly let him know of your problems with landing me a cargo, he'll be of help, I'm sure."

"For you Captain, I'm sure he'll do what can be done. Just don't hold your breath for miracles."

"Just do what you can. I can ask for no more."

Whittington nodded. "What have you brought me this time, my dear Captain?" he asked after looking out into the river toward the OCTAVIUS.

"The same as last time Sidney," the Master replied with an easy, friendly manner.

"Linen, cotton, and steel is it?"

"Aye, that be the lot."

"Not much demand for those items, you know?"

"Demand enough I should hope."

"I'll do my best," Sir Whittington smiled and motioned for them to follow him with a wave of his hand. The Master stood in stride with Whittington, while Richard and Christopher followed closely behind.

"You know," Whittington said. "I could make you a rich man if only you'd relent and transport a cargo that is truly in demand."

"We've talked of this before," the Master turned slightly toward Whittington. "I'll not damn my ship and name to be any part of that trade. To kill a man outright is a shameful thing, but to kill his soul and leave the body to rot alive is a mortal sin, Mr. Whittington."

"I think you overly state your case my friend, we are businessmen. We supply our clients with what they seek, to get that which we want. Free and simple trade is what it is, nothing more. Besides it is not us who decides what cargoes to ship, their demand does that for us. We merely comply to their wishes as they do ours, what can be the harm in that?"

The Master said nothing for a moment, Christopher thought that maybe he was deciding if this line of conversation was in his best interest. "It is I who decides what cargo goes into the OCTAVIUS. No one else."

"But you barely make enough off these cargoes of linen, cotton, and steel to meet your expenses, my dear friend."

"Money enough." The Master ended the conversation of a more lucrative cargo right there. "When can we come alongside to begin unloading?"

"As soon as you please," Sir Whittington smiled. "Although the labor to unload you will take some time and only a small portion of a return cargo is available."

The unloading we can handle ourselves," the Master stated, seemingly a bit irritated. "How long before enough goods are present for us to fill our hold?"

"I doubt that I can obtain enough for several months."

"Why so blasted long?"

"The KITTY VIRGINIA just cleared the harbor for home not four weeks ago, I had just enough cargo on hand for her. But I'll do what I can to expedite the acquisition of another cargo. "

"The KITTY VIRGINIA, you don't say?" the Master asked in a manner that clearly showed his interest in this other ship.

"Yes, the KTTTY VIRGINIA."

"Left four weeks ago?"

"That she did," Whittington replied, bored with the conversation, he hid a yawn with his right cupped hand.

"She too was late this year," the Master noted. "Had some trouble in Calcutta, did she? Where is she bound?"

"London, I believe the Captain said. He was surprised that you hadn't arrived yet, said that you had departed England before him with a cargo, while he had to go to India for his, he likes to make money with his ship."

"He did, did he?" The Master was clearly not taking the other Captain's remarks too well. "If we hadn't run afoul of the sea around the Horn, we would have beat him for sure. That, you can count on Mr. Whittington! We had to seek shelter and repair our ship, and if that heady Captain thinks he can out sail the OCTAVIUS, then he's got another think a coming! Just be sure you get me a cargo with all due haste." With that the Master bid Sir Whittington a good day and turned on his heels with Richard and Christopher in tow.

Upon returning to the ship, the Master went directly to work to bring them along the jetty. The hooks were weighed and with only the spanker sail hoisted. The OCTAVIUS was brought in close to the shore then hauled about using her boats and eased in against the jetty. It took less than an hour to bring the ship in and secure her to her berth.

Not a moment was lost in rigging the gangplank. The Master went ashore to inspect the warehouse and make sure of where the cargo was to be placed. Unloading of the cargo was gotten underway at once. The Mate took charge over this, with Christopher becoming one of the crew again

The cotton was the first to come off. They carried as much as their arms would lift from the hold to a strange looking cart. Red explained that the cart was known as a Chinese wheelbarrow. This wheelbarrow differs from those Christopher was used to, in-so-much as it was built with the wheel located in the middle of the cart. Large flat platforms were built outside of the wheel on either side. Red claimed the Chinese have a saying that goes something like "let nature do most of the work." This odd cart was able to carry large amounts of their cargo per trip and was much easier to operate, once you got the balance of the thing worked out. Unlike the wheelbarrows back home that featured a wheel at the very front, thereby making sure that one's arms carry a percentage of the load. With the Chinese cart, all the operator had to do was take care in loading, being sure to keep everything balanced, then simply push or pull it wherever you wanted it to go. There was no weight being carried by the operator at all.

The warehouse was about two hundred yards up the well-worn path from the river. It took them the balance of the day to off load the cotton and the linen. The kegs of iron nails and the flat stock would wait until the morning. As for the shark fins, and the bird nests, the Master said those were to stay aboard.

Christopher was surprised by how few Chinese he had seen that day, less than two dozen. He did however meet Sir Whittington's son, Sidney the third. Sid, as he liked to be called, was about Christopher's age; he also lent a hand in the off loading and was right off, a very likeable fellow. He asked so many questions of home that Christopher thought him to be homesick, he found out later that that wasn't the case.

When work was suspended for the evening, Sid invited Christopher to his house for supper, which Christopher accepted at once. Glad to be away from the ship, and for something other than shipboard tack to eat.

"Mind if I bring a friend along? Master Richard?"

"Not at all," Sid laughed. "He is the Captain s son is he not?"

"That he is," Christopher answered.

"Then he will probably be coming anyway. My father has already insisted that your Captain attend with his family. I understand that he has his wife aboard."

"Aye, Sarah. She's a fine woman."

"Must be, a ship at sea is not the place for most women. My mother stayed in England to avoid the trip."

"You must miss her."

"A bit, but I like it here," Sid replied.

The Whittington house was large, by the standards of the other houses around it. Built of lumber and plaster, the house sat squarely on a small knoll that overlooked the river and the row of warehouses

The meal consisted of steamed rice and fresh fish topped off with a sweet rice wine. Christopher thought it was the most enjoyable meal since their departure from Eden. The Master, Sarah, and young Richard also attended the meal as guests of Sir Whittington. Sir Whittington took great interest and delight in Sarah's company. Christopher wrote this off to the lack of English women in China and the fact that his own wife had decided to stay behind

On the way back to the OCTAVIUS, Christopher was still puzzled by the earlier remark of Sir Whittington. "Sire, what did Sir Whittington mean by a cargo more in demand?" he asked of the Master. By his reaction, which was not even a break in his stride, Christopher thought that he had not heard him. He was about to put the question to him again, when the Master turned slightly to address him.

"You have the eight-to-twelve watch, Mr. Jamison?"

"Aye, Sire I do."

"We shall speak of this matter then." It was clear by his demeanor that it was a subject not to be addressed at this time, so Christopher held his curiosity in check. Of course, his failing to render a reply to a simple question made Christopher wonder at its answer even more.

Later, as he strolled across the deck during his watch, Christopher noticed the familiar scent of sweet pipe tobacco, it was often the first indication he had of the master's presence. He quickly turned about and found the Master emerging from the shadow of the main mast.

"Good evening, Sire," he called to him.

"And a fine evening it is," the Master offered as he strolled past Christopher to the rail of the starboard side, the side against the wharf. "A gentle berth this is. I can only pray that our time here is short."

"The KITTY VIRGINIA?" Christopher asked.

"Aye, that bloody bugger Fanington. He's the devil's own child, that one is. He sails only for riches. Flogs his crew, drives his ships to ground. Protected by Satan himself, he always manages, he does. Twice he has lost almost an entire crew when a ship of his has foundered under him, did he care about them I ask you? Did he?"

His eyes were afire with anger. Christopher didn't know what to say. He had never known this fellow Farrington, so he could not answer.

"I'll tell you what that bugger cares about, I will. He cares only for his own miserable hide, he does. Only his own miserable hide, next to himself, he cares only for riches, rum and whores. Did you know that both times he lost his ships, he let them go under with more than a crew still aboard?"

Christopher could only shake his head to the negative.

"And what do you suppose was in the boats then if not crew?"

Again, Christopher shook his head.

"Cargo! That's what the bloody hell was in the boats! Bloody cargo, Mr. Jamison, and just enough men to be able to handle the boats so his royal rottenness would not have to lay a finger on the hard task of the oars.

"What you sow, so shall you reap." Christopher quoted the bible.

"So, one would think, not so in this bugger's case. He uses up ships and men without regard."

"How did he get that crew to stay aboard a sinking ship?" Christopher couldn't help but wonder why any man would be so foolish as to be left on a dying ship. Mutiny is a serious matter, but not so serious as certain death.

"Oh, they didn't know the ship was doomed, only that it was taking on water. Farrington told the poor souls that he was lightening the load, giving them a better chance and all. They were to try and reach port, then send help back for him and the boats. Only he knew that the timbers were rotten through and through."

"How did he know that?"

"He knew because he never spent a day's time or a shilling on repair, he drove the ship until it could go no farther. Then he took only those he needed to man the boats, his precious cargo, and condemned those poor souls remaining aboard to death. The fewer sailors to pay off you see. He's a sly one, he is. The devil himself has more mercy." In the background Christopher could hear the strike of seven bells.

"Your watch will soon be over," the Master stated, finally a bit more settled. Christopher nodded. "Would you like to see what his cargo to China is? And what the purpose of it is?"

Again, Christopher could only nod before he went on.

"He was one of the first to begin shipping it, but he is not alone in blame. Whittington's hands have just as much blood on them. It's greed it is, every manager has had the same problem and found it easier to solve in the same way."

"I'm not familiar with any of this," Christopher confessed.

"What I speak of my young friend, is that which you asked coming home tonight." He replied in a fatherly tone, repacking his pipe and taking his time to bring the bowl back to life.

"The cargo that is more in demand?"

Aye that," he frowned. "That is indeed the root of the problem. You see, we want the fine teas and silk of this land, but we want it in trade for goods from our land, a good and simple business proposition, right? Just like Whittington said." He nearly mocked Sir Whittington's statement from this morning.

Christopher nodded.

"The problem here is that the Chinese are so efficient and self reliant that we can offer nothing that they cannot produce themselves, cheaper. So how does one get goods if not in equal barter? One must pay for those goods, in this case the Chinese wanted silver. Well, we could not afford to ship all our silver to China in trade for items that we would soon use up. You see, we English had taken quite a fancy to their tea and silk, so we had to find something for which the Chinese would have an equal demand for. And what Mr. Jamison, do you suppose that item was?"

"I do not know."

"Well, it sure was not something the Chinese had known they wanted, we had to create that need. It took the cunning of the likes of Farrington to ship the cargo here, and the likes of Whittington to see to it that the Chinese would demand more of it. That cargo my friend, was opium from India."

"How did they manage to get the Chinese to buy it?" Christopher had heard of opium and what it could do to a man that used it.

"They gave the first couple of shipments away," the Master sadly shook his head. "They just gave those first bloody shipments away. Samples, so to speak. Even showed the buggers how to use the stuff. From that point on there has always been a strong demand for opium. The price for shipping it is good, much better in fact than what we have shipped. And that, Mr. Jamison, is exactly why that devil Farrington hauls it every trip. In a couple of trips, he has enough profit to outfit another ship. So, what does he care if the one he has now is rotting?"

The ship's bell was almost ready to strike eight bells when the Mate appeared and began to relieve Christopher on watch. The Master then asked Christopher to accompany him ashore as soon as the deck was in the Mate's care. Christopher had no doubt what the Master intended for him to see.

It was a place, the likes of which Christopher would never forget, an opium pit he called it. There were a dozen Chinese within the darkly lit hole of a place. The stench of urine and vomit could be smelled as well as the sweet yet bitter smell of burning opium. As they passed through the shadows of this place Christopher experienced a strange fear that he had never known. In the dank darkness he nearly stumbled over a Chinese man who was sitting on the dirty, damp floor with his back against the wall. The feet spread out in front of him, the arms hanging limp at his sides with the hands laying palms up and the curled fingers pointing upwards.

Christopher caught himself just before falling on top of this troubled soul, not that he would have known. Instead Christopher fell in front of the man, just missing the legs. Christopher quickly picked himself up and bent over to apologize for his clumsiness when he instantly realized that he was facing a man in a death-like stupor. His eyes were blood red instead of white, he didn't blink once as Christopher stared into the vacant eyes. From the lack of reaction, he was sure that the man was totally unaware of his presence. The front of this fellow's tunic was covered in a foul-smelling vomit that still dripped from an agape mouth.

Christopher didn't spend a second longer with this fellow, jumping to his feet and following the Master. He felt as though he was passing through a chamber of living death. Tasting the bile in the back of his throat, Christopher ran for the safety and freshness of the muddy street outside.

The Master followed him out and patted Christopher on the back. "That is the cargo Whittington spoke of," he quickly said. "Remember what you saw here, it is why I will not ship the horrid stuff."

Tuesday, May 4, 1762
Canton, China

The balance of the cargo was off loaded, including the nests and shark fins. These were taken under the close eye of the Master and stowed carefully in the warehouse. Then they were covered carefully with a sailcloth. Before leaving, the Master had two armed men stationed there with this strange cargo.

Once this was completed, the ship was sealed and smoked out to rid it of vermin. As Christopher did his work, the look of that poor bugger at the opium pit kept invading his mind. How could anyone do that to themselves?

With little of their return cargo on hand at the warehouse, they would wait until more was there to begin loading. If the cargo took too long to appear, they would have to smoke the ship again, something that would probably do it well anyway

Wednesday. May 5, 1762
Canton, China

With little to do, Christopher obtained permission from the Master to accompany Sid on a visit to a tea plantation. He was thrilled with all he saw, having always enjoyed fine Chinese tea, he was to learn what made it so good and how it was prepared.

Christopher had never given thought to what the tea plant would look like and was surprised to find that it looked for all the world like a three- to five-foot shrub of the willow family, with long leathery leaves.

As Sid walked him through the rows upon rows of the tea shrubs, Christopher noticed that the plantation was divided into many smaller parts, each of these parts contained shrubs of varying height. This, explained Sid, was due to the plant's age. The shrubs are planted close together in rows when the plant is barely half a foot tall. It takes two to three years before the shrubs begin to flower with pink and white blossoms. A good crop of tea leaves is not produced until the plant is five years old. When older plants begin to lose production, they are weeded out and saplings are planted in their place.

In this manner, the plantation owners are assured of a constant and abundant crop. Christopher also found it of interest that most of the labor was being done by women. Sid assured him that that was the custom here. He even joked about this being a good land for a man to live, as the women do nearly all the work.

The women picking the tea leaves were encumbered with large woven baskets affixed to their backs, into which the leaves were placed. When the basket was filled, the leaves were taken to a large square building filled with row upon row of multi-level flat racks made of bamboo. Here the leaves were dried until they wilted. The wilted leaves were then placed on flat stones and crushed with round wooden rolling pins.

Next, the crushed leaves were once again placed on the bamboo racks and left until they turned black. Sid explained that a fermenting process was taking place, which is why the leaves took on the black color. Once the crushed leaves had turned black, they were quickly placed in a huge oven and baked. This was to stop the fermenting process. The next step was to roll the dried leaves and bake them once more before cutting them into even sized pieces and sorted for quality and then packed into shipping crates. What is known as green tea was done in much the same manner except that it was not allowed to ferment. Christopher was also surprised to learn that tea contains a mild poison.

Sid explained that so long as one didn't boil the tea in the kettle, the poison was not released into the water. If it is, one can taste a bitterness to it.

Being late in the season, the trading season ended in March, there was only two other European ships in Canton. Those two ships were not going anywhere anytime soon. From the looks of them, they had been rotting in this filthy river for many seasons. The dilapidated ships appeared to have joined the ranks of hundreds of smaller junks and various other craft as a floating part of the city. It was aboard these craft that the poorest of the poor lived. The human waste was simply tossed over the rail to float or sink. Then, moments later, Christopher spotted someone from that same boat drawing water from the river in nearly the same spot as the waste had been thrown.

Saturday, May 8, 1762
Canton, China

About noon they received an official-looking Chinese visitor. This visitor was surrounded by at least a dozen male servants, all dressed in brightly colored silk waist coats, hats, and silk trousers. Their shoes appeared to be little more than light house slippers. To a man, they seemed bored and above it all.

The visitor was directed straight to the master's cabin, where he and the Master remained for nearly an hour. While their master was in the cabin, the twelve colorful Chinese guards, if that was what they were, stood in two very straight rows, backs ramrod straight and eyes always straight ahead. Christopher couldn't help but wonder how they were feeling as the heat of the day was upon them.

He took the ladle off the hook on the mast, dipping it into the water cask, and then offering it to the first guard nearest the mast. At first nothing happened, and then the lad's eyes darted at Christopher, then a quick glance toward the rest of his companions.

"Here," Christopher offered the ladle to the lad. "Quench your thirst a bit." When the lad didn't budge, Christopher took a quick sip of water to show his meaning. Once again, the lad glanced up the row of guards. Finally, the guard on the end of the first row nodded ever so slightly. That was all it took, the first guard quickly took the ladle and emptied its cool contents, bowing slightly to Christopher, then returned to the stone figure he was before.

Christopher and Richard in turns offered the same to all the other fellows. They, like the first, took the water, bowed their thanks, and then stood back in line.

After a time, the Master came out of the cabin with this important Chinese fellow. The two of them went off the ship with twelve guards in close tow, heading directly up the shore to the warehouse.

An hour or more passed before the Master came back to the ship; he didn't appear to be in the best of spirits. As soon as he was on deck, he called all hands to inform them that they would be bringing the shark fins, ginseng, and nests back aboard at once.

By sunset, those items were once again stowed away in the hold. What the purpose of this move was, only the Master seemed to know.

Tuesday. May 25, 1762
China

More than two weeks had gone by since Christopher even bothered to write in his journal, there was nothing to write about. The sun baked down upon them in this stinking hole called Canton. Christopher was told that during the regular trading season the place is full of action, not now.

The Pearl River is anything but, it stunk to high heaven with all the waste being dumped into it. Christopher couldn't believe that people still drew their drinking water from it. He would rather die of thirst than drink from this river.

The Master had said little about the incident with the Chinese, and the returning of the odd cargo to the ship. As is usual, the gossip is far worse than the real story, whatever that may be. Some of the men were saying that there was no cargo to be had until season. That would leave two choices, neither of which was very attractive. One, they could take what's available then and go home. The Master would lose his shirt, so that wouldn't happen. The second was to wait there until the start of the season some six to seven months away!

Monday, June 21, 1762
Canton, China

They were still stuck in this stinking cesspool of a place. Nothing had happened until this morning, When Sir Whittington came aboard before noon with that important Chinese official. They were escorted to the master's cabin and conducted business in there for over an hour. When they did come out, all appeared to be happy with whatever they had agreed upon, as smiles were all around.

Wednesday June 30. 1762
Canton, China

The deal worked out by the Master was just what they had been hoping for, a full cargo! According to the Master, this was his richest cargo yet! It included tea from the Viceroy's own stock, the very finest. Silk, hand-painted wallpaper, china, and hand-crafted furniture covered with intricate carvings and paintings.
The portion of their cargo that had been returned to the ship was once again off loaded to the warehouse. Each trip Christopher made to the warehouse, he noticed that more and more of their return cargo was arriving.
Once they had the ship cleared out, they sealed her up again and smoked it out. Hopefully this would make life uncomfortable enough for the rats and other vermin aboard that they would choose to disembark. Of course, if Christopher was to be given the choice of a smoke-filled hold or Canton to stay, he would choose the hold!

Thursday, July 1, 1762,

Canton, China

Started taking on the return cargo, Chips and Christopher spent the entire day in the hold carefully stowing everything into its place. The tighter the load, the better the ship will handle in foul weather.

Friday, July 9, 1762
Last Night in Canton, China
Finally!

The last of the cargo came aboard yesterday. Today they took aboard a full load of provisions, including many goats, pigs, and several cattle. The water casks were topped off with water hauled in from a well in town and all about the ship made ready.

Several fresh men also signed on to work for their passage back to England. One of these men was a tall blonde Swede, one German, and two Brits. All told, the number of souls aboard the OCTAVIUS was thirty-one men, the Mate, Christopher, Richard, Sarah, and the Master.

An hour before sunset they were once again ready for the sea. They slipped their lines and stood out into the river's channel before dropping their hook to wait for dawn. Once the ship was set for the night, the Master called all hands. As they stood silently and waited for him to appear, many were guessing about what he wanted. In the back of Christopher 's mind, he thought he knew, but these thoughts he kept to himself.

When the Master did appear, he had many charts and maps clenched in his big right hand. He led the men over to the hatch cover and spread the charts out before them.

"Men," he started in a deep loud voice. "You are the finest lot of men I have ever had the pleasure of sailing with, the most capable as well. Therefore, I have decided to propose to you a different way home, a difficult way I'm sure, but if you recall our trip here, how much worse could it be?"

That drew more than a few laughs.

"A way" he continued "that promises to be much shorter and faster. If all goes well, we might even be home by Christmas. If not, and we get iced in, or must turn back, we will have lost valuable time, that's why I'm bringing the decision to you. I feel that we must decide this thing together. If most of you want to go for it, and only one or two of you do not, those that don't can be put ashore here in Canton. But if more than three don't want to give it a go, we'll have to head for the Horn, because more than three and we'll not have enough crew. What say ye?"

"What way are you speaking of?" the new man, the German named Peter asked.

"It's called the Northwest Passage," the Master said evenly, but just the name of the place sounded magical.

"It is somewhere about here," he added as he pointed to an area on the charts. All were well aware of how poorly the information on those charts was, no one had ever been there and back, much less charted the region.

"I've heard tell," Ian, a big Irish man spoke up. "That once yer in ther' ain't no way fer ya to git back out, what makes ya figure we'd be able to git through it?"

"Why this ship and you, of course." The Master expertly replied. "It hasn't been done, because we haven't tried it. However, since it will be a bit more risky, I'll leave it up to the lot of you. If you don't want to try it, okay, well head for the Cape. We are all familiar with that place. But I'll tell you what, if you are willing to go for the Passage, I will put up whatever profit is left from this cargo after we've all been paid off. We'll split it evenly amongst the lot of you, everyone. And remember the extra strength we built into her at Eden? Well, this is exactly why that was done, should we get iced in, the timbers should be strong enough to hold." The Master paused a moment to let them think it over. "What say ye then?"

"I say we go for it," the Mate spoke up and was soon joined by most, if not all the rest.

If any amongst them was against the idea of this venture, they didn't voice their objection. They were probably more afraid of having to stay in Canton than anything they might find out there.

"That's it then," the Master smiled. "In the morning we set sail for the Northwest passage." With that he rolled up his charts and departed for his cabin.

Saturday, July 10, 1762
Pearl River, Canton, China

Breakfast was finished before the anchors were weighed and they began their journey down river. The Master's sharing the profits with the men had a great effect on all. They now held an interest in everything they did, a smarter looking and acting crew the Mate had never seen.

Every man, even the ones usually slowest, were up the ratlines and on the yards in no time at all. Every command was smartly carried out and the sheets expertly trimmed. By nightfall they had made the China Sea.

Sabbath, July 11, 1762
China Sea

A short service at the midday, giving thanks for their precious cargo and the safe journey thus far. To a man, they also prayed for guidance in the journey that lay ahead.

Friday, July 16, 1762
Pacific Ocean

They had been tacking into a fair southeast wind, their course has been steady on east-southeast, weather has been very mild, the ship was making just under six knots. Christopher had just come off watch when he ran into Chips just before entering his cabin. The old carpenter had something in his hand and a smile on his face.

"Here you go Mate," Chips smiled. "Would have had it sooner for you but my arm and hand have been giving me trouble lately." He held the sculpture out for Christopher to take. Christopher's heart skipped a beat, it was Oteria! Christopher was stunned. It was in his opinion, the best work Chips had ever done, and he told him so. As he stood there holding the delicate sculpture, a tidal wave of emotion swept over him, it looked every bit like her. For an instant he could see her face, with the light sea breeze of Eden lazily blowing a strand or two of her raven hair around. He could almost hear her voice, feel her soft skin, smell the sweet coconut oil she always wore. Old Chips just stood there seeing the emotion in Christopher's eyes. He had done a lot of carvings in the past, most highly appreciated, but none, he knew would be loved as much as this one.

Christopher suddenly felt alone; it would be some time until he could lay eyes on his Oteria again. He felt a terrible weight in his heart, a powerful yearning to return to Eden. Christopher slowly looked up into old Chips' face. The carpenter could see the beginnings of tears forming at the corners of Christopher's eyes. He knew the young man was having trouble saying how much he appreciated the gift. "Christopher, even if you hadn't asked me to do it, I would have done it for you. I know how much this means to you, and you are very welcome."

Christopher now had tears starting to run down his cheeks, he nodded then put an arm around old Chips and gave him a hug before turning around and entering his cabin to be alone with his memories of Oteria. The old carpenter stood there for several moments; he had never been hugged by a man before and found it a strange sensation. "You're welcome lad," he shook his head and headed aft to check on the steering gear.

CHAPTER TWELVE
PIRATES

Sails Sighted!

As Christopher sat on his berth staring into the eyes of his sculpture, he suddenly heard the lookouts shout "Sails Ahoy!" All aboard instantly ran for the deck. Out here this does not come as a welcome cheer; the sails could belong to any number of honest vessels, but they likely belonged to pirates!

All hands crowded to the ratlines to get a better view, as the sails could not be seen from the deck proper. Christopher quickly went aloft and joined the lookout. He pointed the direction of the sails out as Christopher quickly brought the eyeglass to bear upon them.

The stranger's sails were quite distant and low upon the water. He may or may not have seen theirs by this time. The Master quickly asked for details, which Christopher supplied. The Master then ordered all sails set as he took charge on the quarterdeck, the wheelsman stood sharp and carried out each command the instant it was given. Since there were no heavy guns on deck, the OCTAVIUS was an easy target should that prove to be a pirate.

Losing to a pirate out here would mean only one thing, the lucky victims are left dead. The rest would be enslaved and tortured, the prospects of what would happen to Sarah were beyond thought.

The log line was slowly fed out along the larboard flank of the ship, it showed the OCTAVIUS to be doing about eight-and-a-half knots and gaining speed. To accomplish this feat, most of the crew had to stay on the yards to handle the sails as the Master expertly tacked first to windward then to leeward.

For three hours they raced along hoping that the stranger had not seen their sails or that he was a merchant as they were, but for all that time his sails stayed visible to them. It stood to reason that if they could see him, then he could also see them; hopefully he would turn off and avoid a closer meeting. If this stranger did decide to come after them, it would end the debate on what he was. As no other merchant would venture upon another for the very reason, they were trying to outrun this one.

Sometime over the next two hours they lost sight of the stranger's sails; all were greatly relieved. The Master kept the pace up for another hour after that to put additional space between the two ships, then he turned the deck over to Christopher and went to his cabin. For the next two hours they tacked along the south-southeasterly course. Then just before sundown the lookout spotted the stranger's sails again; there was little doubt about this fellow's intentions.

At once the Master was back on deck and full canvass was once again put to the wind. For the next hour they watched in fearful fascination as the stranger slowly gained on them. It would be sometime around midnight when he would overhaul them. When that happened, most likely their fates would be met. As darkness slowly settled upon them, all light was extinguished except for the stern post lamp. Why the Master wanted that to remain lit was troubling to Christopher and several others.

Once darkness was upon them properly, the mystery of the stern light was solved. The Master and Chips held a private, short conference in the master's cabin. When they emerged, both wore serious expressions and went to work on the problem before them. Chips had several of the men help him bring the native canoe from where it was lashed to the main hatch, up to the quarterdeck. Once there it was placed into the falls of the longboat and swung out. Next, a long spar was affixed into the canoe's stern. While this was being done, the Master sent Christopher aft to retrieve the stern light. "Be sure to hold it at nearly the same height all the time. Also hold it out away from yourself as far as possible," the Master instructed. "Walk very slowly, hesitate between steps, I don't want that bugger out there to sense that the light is being moved."

Christopher did as he was told. As he was about to take hold of the lamp, he peered out into the darkness of the night, he thought he might have seen something but couldn't be sure, maybe his imagination was taking over. By the time Christopher had the light at the rail alongside the Master, they had already lowered the canoe into the water and was holding it with a pair of lines. The light was fixed to the spar sticking high off the canoe's stern, then the canoe set adrift.

The Master instantly altered course to the north-northeast. They were now running for their lives and hoping that the pirate would fall for their ruse and chase down the empty canoe. All night they sailed for all they were worth in the hopes that daylight would bless them with an empty ocean.

The total absence of light this night would work in their favor. The only speck of light to be seen all around the compass was the little bright glow of the canoe's lantern. It would be sometime before midnight that the canoe should be overhauled by the pirate, especially since the ocean currents were flowing from east to west. Those currents would take the canoe right to the pirate instead of away from him. Their greatest hope lay in which way the pirate would think they went. Being a merchantman, Christopher would in his place, bet on their turning south. In the direction of Cape Horn and the trip home. But, on the other hand, by turning north they did get the extra boost of having the wind from astern of them. This would aid in their escape but also it would make the pirate think to head north for the same reason.

Saturday, July 17, 1762
Pacific Ocean-Pirates

All night they held their breath for fear of what the dawn would bring. If the pirates had figured out their scheme and given chase, they would most likely all be dead before this day was over.

Having the four-to-eight watch, Christopher nervously paced the deck and peered off into the darkness. What he did this for, he couldn't say, there was nothing for him to see. Even if the pirate was a cable's length astern, he would not be able to see him. At half past five came the false dawn. Christopher had a second lookout posted at once in hopes of answering the lingering question that had plagued them all night. As Christopher, and everyone else aboard waited for the first light of day, he felt as if a great weight was upon him, constricting his chest nearly to the point of making breathing difficult. He had no idea of what they would do if the pirate was upon them. With what rifles they had, they could scarcely put up a fight. They would have to take whatever the pirate doled out as meekly as sheep being led to slaughter, which was no doubt what would happen.

It wasn't until five bells, or six-thirty that the world had enough light to show them what did or didn't exist around them. There was not a patch of sail to be seen at any point of the compass! They were alone!

The great amount of relief that that afforded them was beyond belief. Christopher could once again breathe easily. The world once again looked so beautiful, so wonderful, the sky with its bright crimson streaks that stretched across the heavens from the glowing orange ball in the east, that was only half above the horizon. Christopher wondered if he would have noticed the splendor of this day had the pirate been waiting.

At seven bells they had a most delightful breakfast, not that the food was anything more than normal, shipboard tac, but everyone was in a jovial mood. Thanks to the Master and Chips, they had cheated death and that in and of itself tasted so sweet.

After breakfast, life went on as before, the mundane duties of a sailor. There were lines to be spliced, tarring to be done, the foc'sle hatch needed proper caulking. These tasks and many more were attacked with vigor and joy.

Around six bells in the forenoon watch, Christopher had finished writing in his journal and was fast asleep when he heard the lookout's dreaded shout of "Sails Ahoy!" Christopher was on his feet before he had become fully awake. He ran to the deck and made it up the lines to the lookout's nest. There it was! Snug between the deep blue of the ocean and the lighter blue of the sky, just a small patch of white.

Once again, they were in the rigging, setting every bit of canvass they carried. When all was done that could be done, most of the crew aloft returned to the deck. A few were told to stand by on the yards in case there was need to quickly alter the rigging. Before going down, Christopher stole a quick glance astern, the sails could be seen a little more easily now, the pirate had a swift ship and was gaining on the OCTAVIUS. How long they had to run was in question, the wind had suddenly shifted from dead astern to a point off the larboard quarter.

Three bells, the noon watch. As this was Christopher's watch, he stood rooted on the quarter-deck. He would look into the billowed sails above him, praying for more speed, he would then look astern at the ever-closing pirate. The log line had been fed out and was now showing their speed at six knots, the pirate must surely be making seven or eight, with each passing hour he came nearer. At his current rate of closure, Christopher figured that the pirate would be upon them just after sundown. The wind shifted again, it was now abeam directly, or what is called a soldier's wind.

The dogwatch, the pirate had closed enough to allow them to see his lines clearly through the eyeglass. He was a smart looking ship with a blood red hull and gilded fret work. Two rows of gun ports lined his flanks. There was no doubt about the outcome should this fellow overhaul them, which indeed was happening.

Wind has continued to shift and was now full and by. As the minutes passed Christopher noticed that the pirate didn't seem to be gaining as quickly as he had, there was a chance that in head wind the OCTAVIUS may be as quick as he. Should this prove to be the case, how long would this horror of running before certain death continue? Not that they should want it to end, if they were running, they were alive.

Eight bells, the night watch, the wind was now dead ahead, the sails are close hauled. Once again, the pirate seemed to be gaining on them. Far to the north, dark clouds were gathering, there may be hope yet. If they can have a night as dark as last night, brought on earlier than usual by a storm, so much the better. True, a storm would have them lessening the cloth aloft, but the pirate must do so as well. The only hope lay in their being difficult to follow in the darkness, but even should night befall them early, it was still several hours away at best, although Christopher doubted that the pirate would be upon them before that.

Sunset; the squall was upon them, wind suddenly gusting to gale force, all hands were called, furled or reefed all but main sail. Tacking was close hauled; they gained some ground on the pirate before he too got his ship in order. The sea remained relatively calm, only the wind and rain were aware of the storm.

Christopher was able to still see the pirate in the dim light astern. He prayed that God would grant them an hour or two of safe running. The longer they were able to run, the harder it would be for their enemy to find them.

Total darkness had now encased them. The bad news was the lightening, brilliant flashes splintered across the sky every few seconds, illuminating the pirate for them, and they for him. The Master was at Christopher s side checking the rigging one second, then looking aft in hopes of spying the pirate.

"Pray for an end to this lightening," he yelled to Christopher. "Our only hope is to disappear into the void of night. If he gets close enough to fire upon us, he'll light us up. There will be no hope then.

Christopher could only look upon the pirate and pray for that total darkness, their chances were fleeing by the second. If no change soon, they could not hope to last another hour.

Miraculously, about an hour after the total darkness of night had set in, the lightening diminished. The Master and Mate passed amongst the crew and ordered everyone to maintain absolute silence. They would soon be turning about to put the wind behind them. They all knew what was expected of them and what their jobs were. Therefore, the Master expected everything to be carried out without the slightest need for verbal commands from the deck.

Knowing that the report of the wind filling their sails once the turn had been executed would be easy to hear if the pirate was close enough, Christopher knew the turn would have to be made very shortly.

Sure enough, no sooner had they attained their positions in the yards, they could feel the ship heel over to starboard, the Master had put the helm hard over. Without any oral commands or foul oaths, as was usually the case in bringing the rigging about, something usually goes afoul, but not this time, everything went off without a hitch. Even the expected popping noise of the wind catching the sails once the ship had turned was absent.

The OCTAVIUS seemed to sense that her very existence was at stake. As soon as her sails had once again filled with fresh wind from astern, she quickened her pace and ran like a prize steed before the wind.

They collectively held their breath as they silently glided past the pirate, starboard rail to starboard rail. In the ink blackness of the night the hunter and hunted passed close aboard heading in different directions. The only way they knew they were passing alongside the pirate was the loud shouting and curses of strange voices. They had no sooner made it past the pirate when someone in their company let loose a loud yell; it was someone up in the foremast. All became silent once more, including Christopher's heart as he worried that the pirate must have surely heard that! But as the OCTAVIUS ran the balance of the night before the wind and not once laid eyes or ears on the dubious fellow, he must have surely missed it, or heard it and thought it to be one of his own.

As soon as they were once again on deck, they all set about finding out who it was that had yelled and why he had done it. Christopher had his suspicions as to why it was done. No one admitted to being the guilty party, each claiming that it had come from his right or his left, in that absolute darkness, who could tell for sure?

Sabbath, July 18, 1762
Pacific Ocean
Traitor Among Them

Christopher was afforded several hours of sleep, which he took out in the open deck, as did most of the off watch. They knew that should they be needed, they wanted to be close at hand, as their very lives depended upon it.

At seven bells Christopher awoke to the chime of the bell, he instantly bolted to his feet, awake and ready for action. After a night of hard running hull down in dead silence, the sound of the bell had not only startled him but everyone else as well. Once on his feet, he instantly climbed up the shrouds for a better view of all around them. Nothing! Turning slowly to view all directions, he could see nothing that even remotely resembled a sail. Their little trick last night had worked. They had once again put some distance between themselves and that pirate, but for how long? How long would it take for the pirate to realize that he had been hoodwinked again?

How long had they charged into the teeth of that northern wind to realize that their prey couldn't have outrun them? How long before they put about?

Those questions would have to wait for now, it was time for a well-deserved breakfast.

Being the Second Mate, Christopher's turn would come as soon as the Master and the Mate had finished. Someone had to stand at the ready, all were at breakfast except the wheelsman and Christopher.

There was usually a bit of rousing and banter to be heard coming from the foc'sle during meals and this morning's meal was no exception. Christopher glanced back at the wheelsman to be sure he was paying proper heed to his course. Then Christopher checked the compass, still on east by southeast. Cooky appeared with two piping hot mugs of coffee, just what the doctor ordered.

It was about time for the Mate to appear and relieve Christopher for breakfast when he heard such a commotion coming from the foc'sle that Christopher at once ran forward to investigate. He had nearly made the hatch when Cooky leaped from the hatch.

"You've got to stop them Mate, they're wrecking havoc in there, they are!" Without stopping for details Christopher jumped down the short companionway into the foc'sle proper. Before him was a mass of bodies struggling to and fro in a test of might. What had started this mess, he didn't know. Not knowing what else to do, Christopher yelled at the top of his lungs for everyone to fall back, much to his surprise they did just that!

"Now what in heaven's name is going on here?"

"We think that maybe there's a pirate amongst us," Red offered boldly

"And why would you think that?"

"How did the pirates even know we were in this area in the first place? Wasn't the regular trading season well over? Had no reason for staying around if you'd ask me," Red stated sourly, "Else wise he'd be well clear of here, probably in Calcutta or somewhere like that."

"You think maybe someone told him we were still in Canton?" Liverpool asked.

"Would be my guess." Red nodded.

"And how do you suppose that could have been accomplished?" Christopher asked.

"There's always ways of doing, if one has a mind to," Red shot back.

"And just who do you say this spy is?"

"There can be no doubt about it Mate! It's one of them new ones," Red jerked his outstretched thumb toward the four men standing a bit apart from the others. The ones joined up in Canton.

Several of the others gathered about, everyone that had signed on in England seemed to agree with Red on this point. So, having little choice, Christopher told them to settle down and he would bring the matter up with the Master at once. For their safety, Christopher asked the four new crew members to follow him.

As Christopher entered the master's cabin to report the disturbance, he found him setting at his desk, hands folded in his lap and head bowed.

"Excuse me, Sire," Christopher felt as though he was interrupting something.

"Yes Christopher, what is on your mind?"

He listened to Christopher's report quietly, barely even beating an eyelash. After Christopher had finished, he sat very still for a full minute before rising to his feet and stepping to the windows affixed in the very stern of the ship. Christopher thought that he might be checking if the pirate was once again trailing us. "What they say is quite possible. Not likely, but still very possible." He rubbed his stubbled chin, looking at Christopher for several moments, then returned to the stern windows, watching the wake of their passing, trailing off behind them. "Ask Chips to take the deck, then bring the Mate and yourself back here."

"Aye Sire," Christopher replied, turning on his heels and making for the door. As soon as he returned with the Mate, Christopher was instructed to bring the first man in. The first was Leff, the Swede. As Christopher was about to return to the deck, the Master told him to take the third seat at the larboard side of his desk.

Leff appeared a bit nervous and the Master was taking his time in asking what he wanted to know.

"How did you happen to be in Canton so late in the year?" the Master asked.

"I was paid off there in March. Could not find another berth until you came along."

"What was the name of your ship? And why were you paid off?"

"The ship was the BRISTOL QUEEN, I asked to be paid off."

"Why?"

"Her Master and Mate were very cruel men."

"Who is her Master?"

"A man named Leonard Church."

"What other ships have you sailed on?" The Master went right on with the questions, never once taking his eyes off the man before him, and not once bothering to take notes of any kind. "And pray tell, how long were you on them, when, and who the Master was?"

"I was on the SEA QUEEN out of Bristol a little more than a year ago. You see t took a year off to go home to visit my family. Her Captain was Nelson Hawkin. I sailed her for two years. Then before her I sailed out of London on a ship named JOSHUA, this I did for three years. Her Captain was Robert Turner."

"I see," the Master gave no clues to his inner most thoughts. "Where were you born and where do you now call home?"

"I live in Lund, lower, eastern Sweden. It was there that I was born.

"You say you still have family there?"

"Yes Sire, my elderly parents live there, and three brothers and one sister."

"Very well then," the Master nodded with a slight smile. "You can go, and if you'd be so kind as to send in the next man.

Each man in turn came in and answered the same questions. Then without further ado, the Master sent them away. After the last man had left, he turned to the Mate and Christopher to inquire about their thoughts on the matter. Luckily for Christopher, the Mate spoke up first. "I think that if any of them are pirates, I would think Leff would be my first guess, with Alfred a close second."

"And why is that?" The Master asked.

"Leff's answer as to why he was in Canton, is an easy thing to claim, a cruel Master. I think that maybe I don't believe him, but I have heard of the SEA QUEEN."

The Master nodded in thought.

"Alfred would be my second guess," the Mate continued. "The bloke has no home or family, and I'd wager a shilling or two that he has had his scrapes with authority. Then there's the ships he's sailed on, I've never heard of any of them and there was quite a number at that. Why does he keep moving about?"

"I see," the Master replied. "And you Christopher, what say you on this matter?"

"Well Sire," Christopher swallowed hard and quickly collected his thoughts. "This matter is a very serious one. One that has dire consequences. I cannot say that I didn't believe any of them. I think I would rather believe that the run in with the pirate was one of pure chance. We did not run onto him in our usual course, which would have been to the south-southeast. I don't believe that I could honestly label any of them a pirate from what I've heard."

"Yes, well put," the Master said as he rose from his desk and walked over to the aft bulkhead. Again, watching the ship's wake stream out behind them. "This is indeed very serious business, but the consequences are greatest if we turn a blind eye to what might be, rather than what we truly know." He turned toward Christopher with a fatherly smile. "We Christopher, are not a court of law. We must act accordingly, to our conscience and our gut, there are many other lives at stake here."

"I agree with Mr. Peters," the Master said. "That Alfred is probably our pirate. You see I know of the ships Leff has sailed on, and I know this Captain Church, he is every bit as cruel as Leff said he was. Now Alfred, I am also aware of the ships he spoke of, several of them anyway. You see they went missing several years back. No trace."

"I'd also wager that Alfred is not what he claims to be." The Master scratched his chin. "You see, he was also the only one of the four that was in the forward mast when we turned back against the pirate last night. The only one of the four that could have made the sound, that might or might not have been an attempt to alert the pirate that we had turned."

"That's right," Christopher felt a shiver go up his spine. "If he is indeed a pirate, what will we do with him?"

"We'll do nothing. Nothing at all."

"But if we know him to be a pirate," the Mate quickly but calmly said. "Why don't we just drop him over the rail?"

"What if we're wrong?" the Master replied. "No, we'll do nothing for now. In fact, we will even downplay the whole idea of a pirate amongst us, but we will keep a sharp eye on that one, that Alfred, won't we?"

The worship service at midday was from Matthew verse seven; judge not, that ye be not judged." As always, the Master has chosen another perfect scripture, the sermon fit the situation perfectly. As he closed the service, he told them that he had full and complete faith in every man aboard. That the contact with the pirate was pure chance. Idle talk of a traitor amongst them, was in his view, foolish and based on false assumptions.

The next four hours were Christopher's to spend as he wished. He had time to bring his journal up to date, and time to stare lovingly at the figurine of Oteria. He still couldn't believe what a wonderful job Chips had done, she looked like she could spring to life at any moment. He missed her terribly and longed to be with her again. Christopher had just recently decided that he would tell his parents of Oteria. Whether he would marry her and live with her in her world, or she in his no longer mattered. What really mattered was that he should be with her.

The four hours of off time flew by and it was time for the dogwatch. All went better than Christopher had any right to expect, several of the men were quite cool to one another, but no fights or other acts of vengeance took place.

Wind was full and by, having shifted back to the north-northwest, course was altered to the south-southeast to push them before the wind. They trailed the log line, nine knots!

By the time the evening watch was set, the wind had swung back to a true west wind. Taking full benefit of this favorable wind, the Master had course changed to a due east heading. Log was fed out again, and again a nine-knot reading! At this rate of speed, they could reach the California coast, which the Master believed to be about three thousand miles off, in about twelve to fourteen days.

By sunset, they had yet to see any sign of the pirate and for the first time since spotting him, Christopher began to feel relaxed. The crew also seemed to be back to their old selves, although the new ones still stood off a bit.

CHAPTER THIRTEEN
IN SEARCH OF THE PASSAGE

Tuesday. July 27, 1762
Pacific Ocean
Death pays a Visit

Weather has been near perfect for sailing, wind has remained steady and favorable, the ship held an incredible speed of seven to nine knots for nine days. The days have been hot, but not unbearably so. The evenings were warm and clear.

All seemed to be going along so well until this morning. At seven bells it was time for breakfast. As usual, the crew gathered for the morning meal, all that is, except for Chips, and since this was his favorite meal of the day, he was missed. Worried about the old carpenter, Red went below to Chip's berth, which was situated in the 'tween deck space. A few minutes later Red appeared on deck looking confused and flushed in the face.

"Not sleep well?" Christopher called out to him, noticing how pale he looked, and unaware of what he had been doing, at first Red acted as though he hadn't heard, then he looked around himself before coming over to Christopher's side.

"Mate," Red said in hushed tones, with a voice on the verge of cracking. "He's dead."

Christopher wasn't sure he had heard him right, and then he suddenly feared that Red might have done something to one of the new men that he had accused of being a pirate. "Who's dead?"

"Chips. He's dead."

Christopher could only look at him for a few seconds, it took that long for what he had said to sink in. "Chips?"

"Aye," Red looked back toward the hatchway. "He didn't show up for breakfast. he always liked his breakfast. I thought he might be sick or something, so I went to check on him. He was cold and stiff. Like he died early in the night."

"Who have you told?"

"Just you Mate, I came here straight away. No one else knows, for now.

"Take the wheel and hold her close. I'll go see to Chips.

With that, Christopher took his leave and went directly to Chip's berth, finding him laying as if in slumber, the cabin smelled of death. Although Christopher was sure that what he smelled was the usual odor of a ship at sea, the mildew, the scent of stale bilge water, the smell of the damp wooden hull mixed with the smells of human sweat and body odor. All these mixed together, and knowing that a man laid here dead, Christopher knew that was what he took for the smell of death.

Christopher stepped slowly over to the edge of the berth. Chips was laying on his side with his face turned away from him. Christopher stood looking upon him and could have sworn that he noticed his sides expand as if inhaling breath. He slowly reached out and touched the shoulder, the body was indeed quite stiff and clammy to the touch, which made him quickly withdraw his hand. Christopher called his name several times, each time louder than the time before, to no avail. He realized sadly that Red was right, Chips was dead.

The next course of action was to inform the Master, this would be no easy task, as the two of them had been together for many years and were as close as brothers.

Christopher interrupted the master's morning meal; the Mate had already finished and was just finishing his coffee as Christopher entered. Sarah and young Richard were also in attendance.

"You have something to report?" The Master was curt and to the point.

"If I could have a moment of your time in private, yes Sire, I do."

"Sarah, would you be so kind as to retire to the cabin for a moment or two with Richard?" The Master smiled at his wife and son.

"Of course," Sarah nodded and took Richard by the hand and led him away. Christopher could see in Richard's eyes that he didn't want to go but would obey since he sensed this report was of a very serious nature.

"Now then," the Master said as soon as his family was out of the cabin.

"Chips is dead," Christopher quickly said, afraid that if he tried to be kind, he would screw it up. So, he came right to the point. "Red found him this morning, when he failed to show for breakfast, must have died in his sleep. I'm truly sorry Sire, I know how close the two of you were.

For the longest time the Master said nothing. Only looked as though he was going to be ill. Then he slowly lowered his head, said a silent prayer, before dismissing both the Mate and Christopher.

By the time the Master emerged from Chips' berth, the entire crew was aware of the carpenter's passing. He was very well liked by all and would be sorely missed. The Master did the honors of sewing up his friend, the last stitch was, as always, placed through the departed one's nose to ensure that he was truly dead. Then the Mate and Christopher carried the old carpenter from his cabin and placed him on a sturdy plank amidships, starboard side.

By this time, it was well near midday. All hands gathered around their friend to pay their final respects. The Master had dressed in his Sabbath best as did Sarah and Richard, the rest of them felt a bit ashamed of themselves for not making the effort. Although for many of them, this was their watch and they were still on duty.

The Master stood solemnly over the canvass wrappings on his long and dear friend, his words were spoken in strong but even tones, finishing with the traditional three verses from the book of Revelations 20:12,13,14;

"And I saw the dead, small and great stand before God; and the books were opened: and another book was opened, which is the book of life: and the dead were judged out of those things which were written in the books, according to their works."

"And the sea gave up the dead which were in it; and death and hell delivered up the dead which were in them; and they were judged every man according to their works."

"And death and hell were cast into the lake of fire. This is the second death."

With a trace of tears edging around his eyes, the Master looked toward heaven. "In the sure and certain promise of the resurrection we commit our friend and Mate Samuel Wilson to the deep embrace of your sea. May you have pity on his soul." With a slight nod from the Master, the plank was raised to allow the body to slide off, but nothing happened. John and Liverpool were the two men raising the plank, they looked at each other, then started to lightly shake the plank to get the body to slid off; it would not. Seeing what was happening, the Master stepped over to the plank, laid his hand on the corpse and said, "Cradle our friend, dear Lord, in the security of your ocean depths for the day when the sea shall give up her dead." He then pushed the body to get it moving. Without any further mishaps the body of their dear friend Chips slid off the end of the plank and splashed into the waiting embrace of the deep.

The balance of the day went by slowly and quietly, with most of the crew left with treasured memories of their friend and shipmate. Toward the end of the dogwatch, the Master had Chips' belongings brought out on deck. As is the custom, the items were auctioned off to his last shipmates. Christopher bought a small detailed carving of an Eden canoe, much like the one Chips' had been given by the King. Christopher placed the canoe next to his most prized possession, the sculpture of Oteria.

In his final duty of the day, the Master announced that John was now the ship's carpenter. It seemed that providence had seen fit to make John an apprentice to Chips at a most opportune time. Because of John's accident and subsequent retraining, the ship would not be without a capable carpenter.

Tuesday, August 3, 1762
Land!

Close on midday the lookout shouted the joyous news, "Land Ho!" All rushed to the rail but could not yet see it. However, within an hour land was indeed visible on the eastern horizon, now the difficult part of the journey would begin. No one among them had any idea of where this Northwest Passage was to be found. To find it they would have to keep a sharp eye to the land and explore every inlet and bay. Although they fully expected that the entrance to this passage would be rather large, it could appear from the sea as nothing more than a river's mouth. All of which would take time, and time was something that as the Master clearly pointed out, would be in short supply, since they were sailing into northern latitudes and could fully expect foul weather to be upon them in several months.

With any luck they would find the entrance to the passage and be well into it before the northern winter set in. At least then, they should be well protected from the winter storms that wreak havoc on ships at sea. Icing would no doubt be their biggest worry then, and that worry was precisely why the Master had the frames reinforced.

Saturday August 7, 1762
Large Bay

Having sailed north along the land for nearly four straight days without spotting so much as a river that should offer promise, they came upon a large bay during the dogwatch. This looked quite promising and course was set to take them between the headlands, which was accomplished just before sundown.

They reached a safe anchorage inside the bay and spotted numerous small islands. The Master decided to drop the hook and wait until daylight so they could see what was about them. The biggest concern this evening would be making sure they didn't drag their hook, and drift onto unseen rocks.

Keeping an anchor watch was serious business, the safety of the ship and all souls aboard depended on the watch making sure the ship wasn't drifting in the darkness. To accomplish this, they took clear sightings on six different points, these points were land formations that they would be able to spot even in the darkest part of the night. They carefully recorded each sighting and its relative bearing with their ship, then on every strike of the ship's bell, these sightings were once again checked and rechecked to be sure they hadn't changed. If everything was as it should be, the ship was holding still against a solid hook.

Sabbath, August 8, 1762
Large Bay

The service this day was about the people of Israel wandering about in the wilderness and how God showed them the way. Certainly, this was something they all prayed for here as well.

After the service the hook was weighed, and they set sail for the southern area of this large bay. Every hand stayed on deck all day and kept a constant eye for any sign of an opening to the passage; it was not to be spotted.

Wednesday, August 11, 1762
Southern end of bay

Reached what appeared to be the southern end of the bay shortly after the morning meal; here they found the mouths of two large rivers. It was decided to explore those with the boats in hopes that one of them would prove to be the elusive passage.

Each boat was prepared with enough stores for six men to be gone three to four days.

Should either of the rivers prove to have enough promise of travel further than the boats could make in that time, the boats were to return, and the ship would take to that river. The Master took the longboat, the Mate was assigned the pinnace. Christopher was to stand charge over the ship itself. For now, there would be no exploring for him.

Boats were away just after the midday meal, disappearing about forty minutes later. Christopher found Sarah and Richard standing near the bow of the ship looking after the direction that the master's boat had gone.

"He'll do all right," Christopher offered.

"Do you think so?" Sarah seemed worried.

Sure." Christopher didn't think there would be much danger in what they were doing. "They're just scouting ahead to see if either of these rivers offers hope of being the passage we seek."

"What about natives?" Richard asked.

"I do not know," Christopher lamely replied. "I am sure that the natives, whomever they may be, will offer no problems. Even if they do, the men are armed with rifles, they'll be all right."

"But there is only six of them, they could be outnumbered!" Richard added to his mother's worries.

"The rifles will even the odds," Christopher reassured them.

Balance of the day passed slowly. A constant lookout was posted in the mast top in hopes of eyeing the return of one of the boats. Sundown, neither of the boats had been spotted. Since the Master and the Mate were off the ship, and an anchor watch had to be maintained, Christopher put Red in charge of the starboard watch.

During the night, as Christopher paced the deck, he couldn't help wondering about the men in the boats and how they were faring. Had they continued, or had they made camp for the night. What if the rivers forked off into several directions? What if they became lost? "What would he do if the boats did not return? Could he sail this ship back to England? Or should he head back to Canton or maybe to Eden?

When Red came on to relieve him, Christopher nearly brought the subject up with him, his console would have been a comfort, but Christopher was afraid of appearing too self-doubting. If he would have to take command of this ship, he would have to command each man's respect as well. He kept his concerns to himself.

Thursday, August 12, 1762
Southern end of large bay

Eight bells Christopher relieved Red, the false dawn was yet an hour-and-a-half away but already the heavens were starting to lighten. He could make out the lay of the land, but barely see the mouths of both rivers, and so far, no sign of either boat.

As dawn came upon them, Christopher looked through the eyeglass in hopes of any sign of the boats, nothing. Sarah came on deck shortly after sunup, paced around for a spell, asked if they had seen anything, then sadly shrugged at their reply and returned to her cabin.

Thus, the entire day passed slowly, as they waited and waited. To keep their minds off the wait, Christopher had the crew busy doing maintenance and repairs. The deck was scrubbed down, the masts tarred, lines spliced, and sails mended. When the Master does return, he will find his ship in good order.

Instead of retiring to the foc'sle, the off watch sat out on the foredeck playing cards and telling stories, waiting for the boats.

Friday, August 13, 1762
Friday the 13TH
Still at Anchor

    Christopher doubted that a man exists that is more superstitious than a sailor. More than once during the day he heard men saying that if the boats came back today claiming to have found the passage, they wouldn't go. Finding it on Friday the 13th would lead to no good. He tried a couple of times to explain that if the boats did come back today, they would have probably found the passage yesterday, since it would take them a day or so to return to the ship. This explanation was logical but did little or nothing to quell the talk.
    Just before sundown the lookout sang out that a boat had just emerged from the river to starboard, the Mate's boat. It took them almost an hour to reach the ship, by which time the sun had already set. The news was disappointing, no passage that way, maybe the Master would have better luck.

Saturday, August 14, 1762
Waiting for the master's Return

    The Mate told them of seeing some natives, but none too close, which was just fine with him. He thought they looked rather sophisticated, and even a touch regal in their costumes, but others of his party thought they looked completely terrifying.

At least now, if the Master shouldn't return, the Mate was an able seaman and capable of getting them back home. Talk started around breakfast that the Master should have returned by now, something must have happened. This, Christopher discussed with the Mate, away from others, especially Sarah and Richard. His reply was that if the other boat did not return in a day or two, they would send another out to find them. they would winter here if need be!

Sabbath, August 15, 1762
First Sermon

In the absence of the Master, the Mate assigned Christopher the job of leading the morning service, since his father was a Vicar and all. It proved to be a pleasant task, and everybody seemed to be in a praying mood. Knowing that patience was growing thin, Christopher chose his passage of the bible from Romans 15:1-5.

"We then that are strong ought to bear the infirmities of the weak, and not to please ourselves. Let everyone of us please his neighbor for his good to edification. For even Christ pleased not himself; but as it is written, the reproaches of them that reproached thee fell on me. For whatsoever things were written afore time were written for our learning, that we through patience and comfort of the scriptures might have hope. Now the God of patience and consolation grant you to be likeminded one toward another according to Christ Jesus.

After the service most of the crew went back to the foredeck to wait and hope, with patience; at least they appeared more settled. Sarah was the one amongst them that didn't seem to find comfort in the service. She paced the deck the entire day. Christopher and the Mate were worried that if the Master didn't appear soon, the poor soul would suffer a fit of anxiety.

Christopher had the evening watch, and a more peaceful night at anchor he could not imagine. The ship rocked gently in a light but steady swell, caused he believed by a tide action. The night grew quite dark, by six bells the mouth of the river the master's boat would have to come from could no longer be seen.

At eight bells, the Mate was standing ready to relieve Christopher on watch when they heard a familiar voice hailing them from out of the darkness. The Master's boat had come from the river out of the darkness and closed on the ship without anyone on deck being the wiser. What if the boat drawing near had been someone other than their own? They might likely have had their throats cut before they were the wiser, and the Master pointed that out first thing.

The river he tried was promising for a great distance, but it could not be the passage. During his trip upriver, the Master remembered something he had read somewhere, saying that the entrance of the passage was much farther north. Around a cold and dangerous land with tall standing ice and titanic mountain ranges. Why he had not remembered this piece of information before, he could not say, but for some reason it came back to him just as he was about to go to sleep their last night camped on the river's bank.

Monday, August 16. 1762
Sailing North Again

Weighed anchor at sunup and sailed to the north again. About midday they came upon the numerous islands within the bay proper and decided to skirt around them and the mainland. Men with leads stood in the bow calling out depths, to this point they were not in any danger of running aground, but the progress was slow and very tiring.

Friday August 20, 1762
Another river sighted

Having sailed into a wide passage that runs north by northwest. Shortly thereafter the lookout sighted a large river, a point off the starboard bow. The Master was informed and decided on trying the river first, as it was surrounded by mountains and could be the passage they were looking for. Course was altered to north by northeast. Then to almost due east to bring them in line with the middle channel of the river.

Spirits among the crew remained high and hopeful. To navigate this river, they had to sail against a strong current and feel their way along. Once again, the men were stationed in the head; heaving lead lines, sounding the bottom. So far, they had plenty of draft, but in a river, that can change in a moment. One must always be diligent.

Monday, August 23, 1762
Four Wasted Days

They had reached a point where they now realized that they could go no farther, they would have to return to the sea; what a disappointment. The river had been fighting them all the way, now they must use the boats to turn themselves back around. Hopefully, they would make better time in returning, as the current would be aiding them along.

One positive thing about their trip upriver was the amazing beauty of the place. At times the banks of the river were sheer rock walls, canyon-like, formed by many different layers and hues. At other points the land ran out from the river flat and lush. The most delightful part of this was that it teemed with salmon, one could almost lower a bare hook and land a large healthy specimen whose flesh was heavenly to eat. They had the aft deck covered with salted salmon drying in makeshift racks.

The Master's talents at ship handling never ceased to amaze Christopher. He turned the ship around without lowering the boats at all. This was done by lowering a stern anchor and allowing the bow to swing around with the current. Once they had turned, it proved all they could do just to retrieve the hook. As soon as the hook was weighed, the Master had the sheets lowered, using the current to propel them along. With canvass set, the ship had charged down the river too quickly. They were anxious to get back to the sea but wished to do so in one piece.

Friday, October 1, 1762
Following Coast North

    Sailed north along an inside passage. A large island passed off their larboard beam during the night. Just before going off watch, Christopher spotted land in the distance before their bow. The weather was much cooler than before, but still rather pleasant. If they were to search every nook and bay along this route, Christopher thought, they would be at it until the end of their days. The scenery about them was breathtaking. Whales were to be seen nearly every day. Christopher thought of the first time Richard and Sarah had seen those whales in the South pacific, the boy was still fascinated by the mild giants, but not to the degree as before. Seeing so many of them had taken the novelty of that first sighting away.

    Having just come off watch, Christopher threw himself into his berth and fell asleep at once. He had been asleep only moments when Richard came barging in filled with such excitement. Christopher had no choice, he had to comply and return on deck with the lad, and little wonder.

    To starboard was the most beautiful sight he had ever laid eyes upon. The rocky precipice appeared to be made up of a dark gray rock, mostly covered in dark green moss and ferns of numerous types. Above all these the craggy mountain ran upward toward peaks thousands of feet above them. The peaks, blanketed in a permanent snow cover, were partially hidden by a light bluish-gray mist. The most spectacular part of this all was a dozen or more waterfalls that cascaded down the face of the mountain, falling hundreds of feet per step to beat against a lower step. Which in turn created a fine mist that reflected the low sun and bathed the entire scene in prismatic colors of numerous rainbows.

Although Christopher was in much need of sleep, he found himself transfixed by this rugged splendor and unable to leave the ship's rail. A moment later he heard someone shout, "There she blows!" He ran to the larboard rail and spotted a large pod of killer whales transiting abeam of them in a north to south direction.

The entire region lay enshrouded in this light gray mist, nearly a fog. One could see perhaps a mile in all directions. As they sailed northward the shroud parted before them and closed after their passing. Christopher could only imagine at the beauty of this land, wishing he could for just a moment view it all.

Just before eight bells, the dogwatch, a large fjord appeared about a point off their starboard bow. Straight ahead a land mass, then a larger fjord or a small bay to their larboard, the larboard direction seemed to hold the most promise. The helm was ordered over to a course of west by northwest which brought them along the back side of the island that had been off their larboard beam.

With large land masses passing off both rails they proceeded slowly. As darkness fell, only topsails were set in hopes of checking back their already slow pace. All night they kept this slower pace, posted extra lookouts, and hoped and prayed that they didn't miss anything or run her aground before the light of day returned.

Saturday, October 2, 1762
Unknown Straight

At midnight there was just enough light for them to discover that they had come to a crossroads of sorts. It appeared that the straight they had been sailing emptied into another, this second straight ran on a truer north-south course. Since it was still believed that the direction in which they must surely find the passage was to the north, they opted for that direction.

Daylight found them with another land mass off their larboard beam, the heavy mist off the starboard rail prevented them from seeing anything in that direction. If the opening to the passage laid to starboard, they would certainly miss it. The land to larboard was for the most part, also shrouded in this mist, they were able to glimpse only parts of it at times. It appeared to be heavily forested and lush, although in places it too had rugged terrain.

Shortly after ten that morning they had to once again decide on which way to go. The course to starboard looked to offer the most hope, as the course ahead was blocked by a small island, so they turned on a new heading of east by northeast.

Due to the grandeur of this place, most of the off-watch crew remained on deck, everyone wanted to witness everything, never had they seen so much beauty in one place. Day after day, hour after hour, the abundance of it all was staggering. There were whales of all sizes and types, seals, birds of numerous descriptions, forests, glaciers, mountains, bears, moose, deer, wolves, goats, and so much more to be seen on the land masses as they slowly passed. No one, Richard and Sarah included dared to turn away, afraid of missing what might come next. Occasionally, they even spotted a native settlement or two, none paid them the slightest mind.

All this amazing scenery kept them at the rails nearly all the time, which in turn caused the Master concern. If they didn't rest when they had the opportunity, how long could they continue before mistakes started to be made. Mistakes that could land them on the beach, which in turn could easily mean forever. Although breathtakingly beautiful, there was no doubt about the harshness of survival here. Therefore, the Master issued orders for every man to take to his berth for no less than six hours per day.

By the dogwatch, course was once again altered to north by northwest. And then again at midnight to west by northwest.

Sabbath, October 3, 1762
Unknown Sound

By breakfast, course was altered to south by southwest, a large land mass off starboard beam. This land mass, like the others before it, was mountainous and beyond belief. Here for the first time since they entered this region the mist burned off during the day. Offering them their first glimpse of the total area around them.

The angry, gnarled land rose up in steep angles, falling away again the next instant. All of which was forested or at least moss covered, giving it an emerald coat. This beautiful coat was heavily wrinkled in many places, giving sharp contrast between shadows and brightly lit areas.

In certain areas the land leveled off and gently sloped down to the water's edge. In these areas there was almost always a small cove or inlet, where the crystal water lay calm as glass, reflecting the picturesque surroundings like a quality painting.

A long and clear straight appeared off the starboard bow at noon, helm was brought to almost north. Barely following master's orders, Christopher found himself exhausted and retired to his berth.

> Monday, October 4,1762
> Still in Wonderful Maze

At six bells the straight forked once more, Christopher had been entertaining the idea that this wondrous place would go on for all eternity. It was some sort of wonderful, beautiful maze, a labyrinth like those of old. His watch came on deck at midnight and found things unchanged. The Master was on deck at that time and Christopher wondered if he had been there all day?

Shortly after his eyes were accustomed to the darkness well enough for him to spell the mate, the Master came over to him.

"Our bloody luck can't hold forever." He took a few moments to spy through the eyeglass, only to find things unchanged. "If we keep running around in this place, well put her ashore for sure."

Christopher said nothing.

"Christopher, keep a sharp lookout, a couple of men in the masts, two more in the bow. First sign of an opening to the west, take it."

"To the west, Sire?"

"Aye, to the west, lad," the Master said. "Best to be out of here, I say. I have had a belly full of it, I want to get back to the sea and try our luck out there.

With that he left Christopher to retire to his cabin. No such opening appeared until six bells; ahead of them the channel narrowed a bit, but to the larboard it remained wide and ran northwest by north. Following his directions, Christopher had the helm put over to follow the straight on the larboard side.

This new course was followed until two bells of the morning watch, which was Christopher's watch again. As he came out on deck, the Master was there to greet him with the Mate. Christopher knew after he said it, that he shouldn't have, but he asked the Master if he had gotten any rest himself.

"I'll get plenty of rest if we put this old gal ashore." He replied sharply, then in a lower, more kindly voice. "You needn't worry about me, Mr. Jamison. I'll do right nicely, thank you."

Around nine that morning they came upon a fjord off their starboard that defied words. The water appeared glass-like, studded with white diamonds of ice. A heavy gray mist enshrouded most of it from their eyes, but they could clearly see titanic glaciers just beyond. The only break in the mirror-like surface water was caused by another pod of orcas having a feast on the fat bodies of unfortunate seals.

Then to larboard, the channel they had been following turned sharply to the west. For the next six hours they sailed nearly due west until once again they felt the swell of the Pacific Ocean under their keel. Back on the ocean, they followed the coastline northwest by north.

Of all the wonder this region had offered so far, this was more awe-inspiring than any. Here they could see into the past for thousands of years, back in time to the age of ice. Christopher found himself comparing this place to Cape Horn. There were differences to be sure, but similarities all the same. This place appeared calm, at least for them now. Where the Cape Horn was always hard with strong wind and seas. Both places are desolate and completely inhospitable to man.

They slowly sailed past a scene that brought all to the rail to stare in awe-struck wonder. It appeared to be a small cove or bay, the water leading into it black as coal, dotted with various size chunks of floating ice. In the middle of the cove was a huge hump of black rock, the top of which was hidden in mist, they could only see up to a point where the wind whipped the permanent snow covering around in eddies. Patches of snow and ice lay encrusted to the sides and hollows of this massive black rock, giving it the appearance of a mammoth humpback whale, the white snow taking the part of barnacles that cling to the whale.

To either side of this rock were valleys filled with frozen glacial ice. This ice was imbedded with bits and pieces of this black rock, giving the whole thing the illusion of movement from its texture. Everything worked in unison to make the black rock appear as a whale coming toward them, with the frozen rivers to either side looking like the roll of a surfaced whale's nose wake.

At other places along this area, the glacier ice was a thousand feet high or more. They were passing one such area when they heard this terrific roar and turned to see the entire face of an ice cliff fall away and crash into the sea. The wake from this calving action nearly rocked the OCTAVIUS over on her beams end. The slabs of ice shot deep into the sea before shooting back the surface as if shot from a gun. The danger was obvious, as one nearly wrecked them. It shot to the surface just astern of them and luckily, its wake shoved the small ship forward and out of harm's way.

For the balance of the day they stood out a little farther from shore. Doing so limited their view of this magnificent place, but it also afforded them a little more assurance that they wouldn't fall victim to the whims of nature. Extra lookouts were also posted to keep a sharp eye for bergs, as this place was literally a hatchery for icebergs.

Thursday. October 7, 1762
Exploring a large Bay

Shortly after two bells of the morning watch, they came upon a couple of islands on either side of the bow. These served as a gateway of sorts to a large bay that looked quite promising to the Master, so they altered course and passed between them to enter the bay proper.

By three in the afternoon, they found themselves turning to the north by northwest again to run along the shoreline, hoping against hope that another opening northward could be found. This place was also extremely beautiful but harsh.

Nearly six more hours passed before they concluded that this was nothing more than a large bay and that they would have to return to the sea.

Saturday, October 9, 1762
Another Promising Northward Passage

    Half the way through the dogwatch, a very wide-open passage appeared off the starboard bow. Always afraid of passing the true opening to the passage, they could ill afford to not attempt this one. Course was set to bring them into this passage.

Sabbath, October 10, 1762
Another Failure

    By four bells, middle of the dogwatch, they found that this was not a true passage, they came about and once again headed back for the sea. Just before they came about, in the far distance, they spotted the largest mountain any had ever seen, its peak was beyond the clouds, and this was a clear day!
    Since he was a child, Christopher had always heard people tell of something that was called the northern lights. He was to see them himself in this region, they looked as though they were translucent wisps of illuminated gases, these wisps of colorful lights danced and blazed across the heavens.
    As the sun set this evening, it painted the white-topped mountain ranges in the most

splendid shades of pink and lavender. Christopher thought if he should not live to see another day, he had seen all the beauty the world had to offer. This place nearly made him forget Oteria, which was a statement indeed.

Tuesday October 12, 1762
Following in Drake's Footsteps?

Entered another scenic straight. To the larboard a land mass they believed to be another island, this island appeared little different than all the others. Ruggedly handsome and heavily forested. While to starboard, the mainland was just the opposite. It was of volcanic rock, towering, rugged mountains with white, snow capped peaks. At sea, the climate was chilly but still mild. From what Christopher could see of those mountains the conditions were anything but, the snow was constantly whipped by strong winds from one peak to another.

The crew seemed to be getting used to the grandeur of this place, most have once again taken to the routine of ship life, they stood their watches then retired to their berths.

Friday, October 15, 1762
Fog

Christopher came on watch at four in the morning. He could not believe the world he stepped into. The fog was so thick as to make the mast lantern a yellow haze that he had to slowly walk toward in order to find. The Mate and he discussed the matter and decided to alert the Master.

In short order the Master appeared on deck and instantly called for all hands, they were to drop the anchor.

"Get a line to the bottom, Mr. Jamison," he called out of the soup.

"Already have," Christopher replied smartly. "Fathoms twelve and a half, Sire."

"Very well, reef the sails. Keep sounding the bottom. The moment you have eight fathoms or less drop the hook."

"Aye, aye." Christopher shot back and went forward to stand by the bits in order to be ready to drop the hook as soon as shallow enough water was obtained. They had enough cable to anchor here, but the chances of dragging their hook was much greater than in shallow water.

Half-an-hour went by as they drifted with the current, all sails reefed. The leads were swung out and hauled back in, carefully counting the knots to check their depth. It was the only thing a sailor could do in this fog as well as on a fine day

Suddenly, one of the leadsmen sang out "Fathoms Seven!" They dropped the hook and prayed for it to take a strong bite and hold them fast. Once they were at anchor the starboard watch went below, the only task for Christopher and his watch was to try and keep a proper anchor watch. In this fog that was easier said than done. How could he be sure that they weren't drifting when he couldn't even see the opposite beam?

The only solution Christopher could come up with, and a poor one at that, was to lower the lead lines off both rails, angle them out a bit, so that if the ship was swinging about, sooner or later one of the lead lines would be under the hull. In this fashion they attempted to keep a proper anchor watch.

The problem with this simple system was that the lead weights on the bottom could be washed around by strong currents, although Christopher doubted that would happen at seven fathoms deep. As a precaution, he ordered for absolute silence on deck. He wanted all ears to be piercing the darkness for any sounds of surf or other dangers that could befall them. At seven bells Christopher could smell the smoke from Cooky's stove but could not see it. As soon as the smoke left the chimney it blended in with the thick blanket of gray fog. The fog seeped into their being as well as their clothes. By the time Christopher had finished his watch and was spelled by the Mate, his clothes were thoroughly damp.

Master, Sarah, and Richard were sitting at the table when Christopher finally sat down for his breakfast. The Master asked of the watch and was told what had been done to ensure the hook was holding.

"See there, Richard," the Master beamed. "That's a smart sailor for you, always finding a way to do the impossible."

Christopher could feel himself blushing. "I have my doubts as to the certainty of such devices."

"We're not on the rocks, are we?" the Master was quick to point out. "Then I'd say that it is working quite well. Yes, well indeed. Any signs of the fog lifting yet, Mr. Jamison?"

"Not in the least, Sire."

The Master and Sarah left Christopher to his breakfast; Richard decided to stay. His mother, thinking that Christopher might wish to eat in peace, asked Richard to come along. Christopher interceded and asked that the lad be allowed to stay, he did truly enjoy the lad's company. He loved to just listen to the boy ramble on about all that he had seen and what he thought of such things. Christopher believed this allowed him a moment to once again see the world through the innocent eyes of a child, although he would not dare say such a thing to Richard.

The fog stayed with them all day, thick, wet, and heavy. It was impossible to see through, which made it heavy on their spirits as well. When one cannot see more than ten paces in front of one's own face, the imagination takes over, imagining all sorts of dangers. Christopher silently walked to the very bow of the ship to stand and listen, what he hoped to hear or not hear was anything other than the sounds of the current flowing around the ship's hull.

They had been at anchor the entire day. As night was beginning to close around them, Christopher thought it queer that the color of the fog was the only way they could judge what time of day it was. The light gray fog was slowly changing to charcoal, the mast light was found and brought to life. Only in his cabin was Christopher's world normal. For reasons he couldn't explain, he placed the carving of Oteria on his pillow next to him as he slept, it brought him comfort. This simple thing represented two very special beings in his life. The one he would surely miss. The other he hoped to see again.

Saturday, October 16, 1762
Still anchored in Fog

Christopher came on watch at midnight. No change in the weather, fog, fog, fog. It neither got warmer or colder, no breeze to dissipate this curtain of blinding mist that entombed them. Christopher stepped over to the binnacle and checked their heading - unchanged - good. Then he went in search of the Mate, he was where Christopher had expected, with the leadsmen.

The Mate asked if his eyes were accustomed to the dark yet. Not that it would make much difference, Christopher thought, amused. It was, however, what one asked when being spelled at night, and since that was what was happening, it was the proper question. Christopher replied to the positive.

Someone had taken the liberty of turning up the mast light in the hopes of burning through the fog, to no avail. It only served to burn more precious whale oil, so Christopher turned it down.

This watch was as the one before, and the one before that, to pass without change. At eight bells the Mate appeared and in due course spelled Christopher of the watch so he could return to his berth, back into a world of relative safety and calm. Christopher admitted to himself, that the fog out there was beginning to spook him, and a fair share of the others as well, he should imagine.

Seven bells Christopher returned to the deck to spell the Mate for Breakfast. Daylight had come, the fog was once again a light gray.

Still thick and blinding, just lighter in color. Around eight bells the Mate came back and allowed Christopher time for the morning meal, and then it was back to duty for him.

Sabbath, October 17, 1762
Fog Finally Lifts

This morning's service was held down in the 'tween deck, as it was the only place all could gather and yet see one another. This day's message was of Saul who was blinded by sin, then whose sight was restored through faith. Christopher could think only of his time with Oteria as a sin bad enough to warrant punishment in this manner. However, he could not say with any certainty that he felt any repentance, but he did pray for a break in the weather. He had faith in there being a day, hopefully soon, when they could once again see far enough ahead to raise their hook and be on their way.

That break finally came about midday, the sun and a light southwest wind worked together to sweep the heavy gray veil away. To their great fortune, broad on the starboard bow a wide pass between two of the many islands that ran out to the southwest in a never-ending chain.

They quickly called all hands and went to work hoisting sails and weighing anchor. In quick order they were once again making headway and swung their bow over to make for the pass. Once through the pass they found themselves in what they believed to be the Pacific Ocean again. The shoreline behind them faded from sight within several hours, as their course was northwest by north. No other land was visible in any direction. Wind was southwest and pushing them along at a fine rate.

Wednesday, October 20, 1762
Crossing 60 Degrees North

Weather had remained mild with a firm breeze to speed them along, holding course for northwest by north. Before noon the Master was able to get a good sighting and proclaimed them over sixty degrees north, they were now entering the extreme north. Anytime now they could expect the weather to sour and become more like they had experienced along the Cape. Another sure sign of where they were. The days were growing incredibly short as the sun barely rose above the horizon. Christopher had heard stories of how this place is in perpetual night for six months a year. He hoped that they would be turning east soon, before they truly reached the place of perpetual darkness.

Thursday. October 21, 1762

63 Degrees North, 169 Degrees West
The Northern Region

Have reacquired the shoreline of the mainland off their starboard beam. Most of the lushness of this place has been replaced by stark harshness. They were sailing northeast by north, about a mile off the land. Weather had stayed on their side, but time had not. The further north they went, the later in the season it was. Sooner or later, probably sooner, those two elements would collide. When they did, Christopher worried about their welfare, in some respects they deserved whatever befell them. They had come here in violation of nature ill prepared. Christopher thought sourly. Everyone knew what this region held for weather and when. Yet here they were, very late in the season sailing north with little or no proper gear for such an undertaking, he shouldn't wonder if they all froze to death in this place.

A large bay appeared to starboard just before midday and looked promising. Christopher overheard some of the men grumbling over their fix. They seemed to forget that they too decided to come here, all they could do was find fault with the Master, at least until Christopher restored their memory. Then they probably still grumbled, just not in front of Christopher.

Friday, October 22, 1762
No Passage, Back to the Sea

It had suddenly grown very cold, the wind cut through the inadequate fabric of their clothing as if they were naked. The wind was a fresh northern wind, which they had to beat against for every foot of sea they conquered.

It was frightening how quickly things had turned on them. They had been following the coast in a west by northwest direction, when they came to a point where the coast turned sharply northward, exposing them to the frigid north wind. They now sorely missed being in the lee of the land, they were wholly unprepared for the sudden and complete change in climate.

Shortly after the midday watch change, they were able to fix their position as about 64 degrees north, 168 degrees west. The sea was kicking up and driving hard against their bow with sheets of spray being thrown high into the air only to freeze before falling back down, pelting their already nearly frozen faces.

Snow started to fall just as the dogwatch began, and snow it did, for the next six hours without let up. It came down so hard during most of that time, they found themselves in white out conditions. All the while the wind was whistling through their rigging. The sea was pounding an angry fist against the bow, spray was still freezing in mid-air and striking them painfully. All of which was causing the men, Christopher included, to curse themselves for coming here.

The worst part of all was that the snow had to be removed from the deck before it froze there. It was too late for some of it, but the bulk of the snow they were able to discard over the rail. Every shovelful was wet and heavy, hence the reason it had to be dumped as soon as possible.

They had no sooner finished with the snow removal than the waves increased, and they found themselves with icy green water running across the deck. They could have saved themselves the bother, the sea would have removed the snow.

A miserable darkness had come over the ship. The wind screeched through the rigging, the timbers moaned under the strain, at least the snow had subsided. Not so the freezing spray, that had grown worse. Suddenly out of the maelstrom came a terrified scream, a man overboard!

They rushed to the larboard rail to do what they could; nothing could be done. Another crash of freezing water crossed their deck at near-knee height. One of them at the rail was nearly swept off his feet into the sea. There was no doubt what the scream had meant, but who?

Christopher divided the men up and they went about the deck to check on each man; Red was missing! Christopher quickly ran to the forward hatch and dropped down into the foc'sle, hoping that Red might have dropped below for dry clothes, that was not the case. Christopher was sick at heart, it had been Red, his friend, gone.

He reported the loss to the Master, who had not even heard the scream over the roar of the storm. He took the news rather badly, "Why didn't we heave to? Could a boat have been lowered in a rescue attempt?" Both things he knew to be impossible. Christopher thought that maybe the Master had just reached the point of being unwilling to lose anyone else. To lose anyone on a voyage is difficult at best, but this voyage had cost numerous lives in the thirteen months they had been gone from England.

Saturday, October 23, 1762
68 Degrees North, 167 Degrees West

A bitter cold morning, at least Christopher thought it was morning. The sun was only a bright distant glow on the horizon, never reaching enough zenith to cast light their way. The position was fixed off the North Star. The wind was fresh and still out of the north. Since they had altered course to northeast by north, the wind howled through their rigging on a northwest to southeast heading. The sea had calmed a great deal, making the rest of this much more tolerable. The deck was still heaving in a deep rolling swell, but the freezing spray was not strong enough to rise above the wale.

Near midday the Master called all hands to the quarterdeck, the formality of asking if all had been done that could have been done? Liverpool grumbled a bit; Red was his best friend. The Master heard him and asked for him to speak clearly so all could hear.

"I said nothing," Liverpool replied sourly.

"I heard you speak something, now speak your mind and be done with it. We've got to handle this matter here and now. Be quick about it, will you?"

"All I said Guv'nor, was that we didn't raise a bloody finger to save ol Red. How's it that we can stand here and speak of doin' all we could hav' don' fer the bloke?"

"And what says thee that should have been done?" The Master seemed sharp with old Liverpool.

"We could hav'lowered the bloody boat. Tis' the least we could've don' fer a mate,

I'd say. Had it at least appear as though we tried, but we just let 'im drop over the rail while we sailed on. Why we'd not laid a hand on a fall fer, me mate ol Red." Liverpool shook his head. "No, I can't say that we did what we could hav' done fer' me mate. I'd not sleep should I say that."

"And if a boat had been launched, most likely to be swamped and drown the lot of mates in it, do you think that maybe we could have saved Red?" The Master was clearly not taking kindly to Liverpool's accusations.

"No guv'nor, I doubt it very much. It wouldn't have made the least bit of difference fer ol' Red, I'd say." Liverpool suddenly seemed very depressed. He too now realized that although nothing was done, it was all that could have been done.

Red's belongings were sold off to his final shipmates. The clothes were the items of most desire and brought high prices. Christopher could not bring himself to bid on anything belonging to Red since it was he, who had done nothing to save him. The fact that there was nothing he could have done made no difference. He was not going to profit from his loss even though he could surely make use of extra clothing.

After everything was sold off, including Red's trunk, which Liverpool bought, the matter was finished. Another one of their number was gone from them. Christopher hoped that Chips, Big Joseph and the others keep him in good company in that special place reserved for fine sailors.

Land was sighted straight before them. It appeared to run from northwest to southeast. Meaning that their best hope lay in turning to the northwest. No wonder the storm had abated so quickly. They had fallen under the lee of the land again. This would be short lived once they cleared the land and came under the full force of the northern wind.

They cleared the Land's End at about six bells of the evening watch. Once again, as expected, they came under the storm's full fury. It was no longer snowing, but the fury of the wind whipped freezing spray around, making their time on deck utter misery. With each passing moment they prayed for relief of some kind. Most of those on deck sought shelter in any form from the wind; they took station on the lee side of the mast, the foredeck, anything that would block out the wind even a bit.

At midnight the Master decided to run closer to the shore in hopes of finding any form of a sheltered bay or inlet in which to seek protection. They would have to get much closer to see any such place if one truly existed at all. Course was set north by northeast.

Sabbath, October 24, 762
73 Degrees North, I67 degrees West

    The storm started to abate around eight bells, four in the morning. By seven bells of the morning watch they were riding a deep but gentle swell. The wind had reduced to the point of not washing spray beyond the foredeck. The temperature was still bitterly cold and none among them expected a change for some time.

    They spread more canvass to the wind and brought the helm over to a heading of northeast by east. Christopher pitied the poor soul doing lookout duty. The wind, although less than gale force, was still plenty strong, worst was the biting coldness to it. To keep a man from freezing to death, they rotated lookouts every fifteen minutes. When one's time aloft was over, his limbs were so nearly frozen that he could barely descend to the deck.

    By two bells of the forenoon watch, they crossed the line of 70 degrees north. Pack ice and icebergs could be seen in any direction. Numerous times they had to alter course to clear either or both hazards.

Monday, October 25, 1762
Trapped in Ice!

The Mate came on deck at fifteen minutes to midnight and held small talk while his eyes adjusted to the darkness, also allowing his body to adjust to the arctic conditions of the open deck. Christopher mentioned to him that the ship did not heel as she had earlier, in fact she was riding quite steady. He had thought that the Mate would take this as good news. Instead he rushed over to the larboard rail and peered over. Then, just as quickly, he ran over to the starboard rail and did the same thing. What on earth he was doing, Christopher didn't have a clue until he turned back to him.

"Go call the Master."

"Aye, aye," Christopher replied, totally puzzled by what was going on, as he knocked on the master's cabin door.

"What is it?" came from inside a moment or two later.

"The Mate requests your presence on deck Sire."

"I'll be right along.

Christopher didn't wait until he came from the cabin to return on deck. The Mate was still peering over the starboard rail as Christopher came up along his side. "What's the problem, Mr. Peters?"

"Ice.

"Ice?"

"Aye, ice is forming along our flanks, and a fair amount at that. There is your reason for steadiness!" the Mate shot back.

The Master suddenly appeared at their side and knew instantly what the matter was. "How long has this been happening?"

"For some time," Christopher admitted. "I didn't realize it until the Mate pointed it out to me during the watch change."

"Well, we'll have to get right after it, I'd say," the Master said. "There'll not be more light than right now in these parts. Best get some lines run and some tools."

It was pitch dark out and Christopher couldn't believe they were about to put men over the sides to rid themselves of the unwanted ice built up along their hull. But that precisely what they were about to do. Two men had lines fastened around their waists and through their legs for lifelines, they were swung out over the rail while the others held the lines taut.

The task was nearly impossible from the start, already the ice had built up to six feet thick in areas. As quickly as the men would chop an opening in one spot and start on another, the first would begin to freeze over once more. By the time the second opening was finished, the first had shut again. The middle of the dogwatch all further efforts to clean their sides was halted. It had been a grueling effort doomed to failure from the start.

By eight bells, traditionally the start of the night watch, they had acquired quite a large field of ice around themselves. Then suddenly, near midnight, a slight jar was felt which brought the Master and the Mate on deck as one, they were now trapped in the ice.

The Master returned to his cabin and quickly donned heavy foul-weather gear. Upon his return on deck, he instructed them to lower him over the side down to the pack ice around them.

He made several trips around the hull before hailing them to haul him back up. He had no sooner landed on deck, than he instructed them to have all hands turn in for eight hours rest. In the morning they would start to make plans for saving the ship and their lives.

Tuesday, October 26, 1762
Trapped. Day One

At breakfast, the first in which Christopher ate with both the Mate and the Master, the Master explained what it was that they must do. The ship was now a part of a large ice pack. The weakest part of this pack was the point in which the ship was pinned, it was the ship itself. In time the ice will grind and crowd against itself until it crushes the ship. Therefore, it is imperative that they set about getting the ship out of the water and onto the ice. Only then, can they be reasonably sure that the shifting ice wouldn't crush them.

The first order of business was to take a survey around the ship. This included drilling numerous holes thru the ice to test its depth. Then at the most opportune place, they would begin to carve from the ice a slip. After that was completed, they would use block and tackle to winch the ship onto the ice. In order to do this, they would most likely have to unload their entire cargo onto the ice to lighten the ship. The plan seemed simple and straight forward. In truth it was anything but.

A gangplank was rigged to reach the ice below the rail, all hands were turned out and the surveying began. Due to the bitter wind and extremely low arctic temperatures, they found that they could stand the elements for only an hour before having to retreat to the warmth and safety of the ship.

After this first respite, it was decided that they should work in three shifts of thirty minutes each. This they would try to do for ten to twelve hours per day. Hopefully in this fashion they could retain their strength and yet accomplish the task before them.

This arrangement worked well; the survey was completed in just under three shifts.

Luck had not deserted them completely. The best place, when all was considered, to construct or dig out their slip, was right ahead of the bow. Not a moment was lost, they began at once.

The Master headed up one of the shifts, the Mate the next, and Christopher the third. In this order they set about chopping and shoveling enough snow and ice from before the bow to enable them to winch the ship out of the ice's grip.

When Christopher's turn came around, he reported on the ice with his shift to spell the Mate's. He was surprised to see how much had been accomplished. Before returning to the ship and much-needed rest, the Mate explained what the Master wanted them to do. They were to dig a sloping trench the size and shape of the OCTAVIUS's hull and about twice her length, if possible.

The part of the trench that would run right down to her bow was to be the last part dug. There was no point in doing it now, as it would freeze back over before the rest of the trench was completed.

The trench had to be dug in a V shape to accommodate the ship's hull and yet hold her steady. It would do no good to have her careen over on beam's end. There were enough tools of various assortment for every man in each shift to be swinging something, either a pick, a shovel, or operating a drill.

In the hard labor of chopping through arctic pack ice, Christopher was surprised to find himself sweating. The problem here became evident when he stopped for a moment and tried to stand. The sweat froze into his clothing making it stiff and wholly uncomfortable.

Their thirty minutes passed quickly. Before they realized that it had passed, the Master was standing at Christopher's elbow inspecting their work. He explained the plan while Christopher's men were being spelled by his. They would cut the main slip first, all of it, the entire length, twice that of the ship. This would be cut to a depth of four feet below the current top of the pack ice. Then when they had that cut in, they would start to taper it down towards the bow of the ship until such time as they hit water.

Christopher and his crew returned to the ship. As soon as they had quit working, they instantly became very cold, their bodies no longer producing the heat of working bodies. The sweat that hadn't already froze did so now very quickly. They couldn't wait to get aboard and nestle up next to the galley stove which Cooky kept in fine trim. By the time their shift reached the galley, the Mate's group had cleared out to make room for them. The Mate's group retired to their berths for a few minutes of rest before preparing to go back out. Cooky had a steeping hot cup of tea ready for each man as he came off watch.

Christopher quickly pulled his frozen mittens off and held the warmth-giving, hot tin cup between his hands. His hands sapped the heat from the cup, certainly before it could do much in the way of easing his shivering. Numerous articles of clothing were hung all over the galley to both dry and warm them.

Fifteen minutes after they had arrived, just when their limbs started to have feeling again, and they had each downed two cups of hot tea, the Mate came in and asked for them to clear out to their berths so he and his men could catch one last blast of heat before going back out. This also allowed them to dress for the task next to the stove, and hopefully trap some warmth within their clothes. It might just help hold the bitter cold outside at bay.

Christopher had his doubts about whether this worked, but he would certainly try it when his time came. He returned to his berth and spent time bringing his journal up to date. If they get this slip built soon, he thought, and the ship safely hoisted from the water, they should be in good standing until spring.

Life aboard should not be too harsh from that point on. They had plenty of firewood, food, and could melt snow for their freshwater needs. Christopher felt confident that they could weather this storm. He smiled when he thought about trying to describe this to Oteria. How would she understand a world so cold and bleak as this, a barren frozen wasteland of perpetual night, especially when her world was always so warm and beautiful?

During their second shift on the ice, the Master had Christopher's crew drilling a line of holes about a hundred yards from the larboard beam of the ship. He explained that this was necessary because if the pressure from the ice shifting built up too much before they had the ship free, it would serve as an expansion joint.

The going was relatively easy once they got the bits started into the ice. The hardest part was freeing the bit from a hole once it had frozen. The trick they learned was to drill a ways, then stop and remove the bit from the hole to clear it of small particles of ice that would build up and freeze around the bit. In thirty minutes, working with seven braces and bits, they were able to drill between thirty and forty holes.

The Master had his crew doing the same work during their watch, as did the Mate. Each shift was able to drill roughly the same number of holes. By the end of the Mate's watch, they had been able to drill enough holes to create a fair-sized safety line of weakened ice.

Hopefully this would buy them enough time to build the slip and haul the ship out.

After eight hours of work, it was found that all were exhausted. Their clothes were too wet to be dried in the hour's time between their shifts on the ice.

The evening meal was served when they broke off for the night; it seemed funny to call it night. With no sun, there doesn't seem to be any day, only night. Time is being kept by the turning of the master's hourglass. Every hour is marked off by the watch keepers. During the day hours, Sarah and Richard oversaw this task. At night, two men are chosen to stand a four-hour watch. They are relieved by two more men from another shift and so on. Who was to stand watch was done by the drawing of straws, two men per watch, three watches per night. This allowed the balance of the crew twelve hours of rest per night. The men who stood watch at night were excused from working on the ice until they too had rested.

Wednesday, October 27, 1762
Trapped in Ice. Day 2

The work resumed as soon as they had finished with breakfast. They would work all day on the slip in their usual thirty-minute shifts. Today the Mate's crew went first,

Christopher's second and the master's third. Tomorrow Christopher would go first and so on, not one among them could claim to be standing more than his fair share. The wind continued all day, and the cold seemed colder somehow. If only the wind would die down and allow them to complete their task. After that, it could bloody well blow all it liked. They would snuggle up within their heated hull and wait for spring.

They had only been working on this task for one day and already they had less strength than they had yesterday. Christopher wrote this off to strained muscles, but he was sure that it was due in part to the horrible conditions out on the pack ice. The work today was slow and hard, with every swing of the pick or axe, small chunks of razor-sharp ice flew up into faces already red and raw from the arctic wind. Their sweat was freezing the clothing stiff around their bodies, which in turn chaffed around their armpits and shoulders until they felt completely raw.

Added to the discomfort of their bodies, the picks, shovels and axes felt heavier and heavier with each swing. To remove a square foot of ice took one man nearly his entire thirty-minute shift. When the relief did show up, the men could barely make it back to the ship under their own power. As a group, each shift headed back to the ship together, each helping the man next to him to ensure safety.

When they finally did reach safety and the warmth of the galley, the heat from the stove was nearly as painful as it slowly started to penetrate cold brittle skin. The first five to ten minutes in the galley was almost as painful as their time out on the ice! It was not until after that first few minutes that they were finally able to start removing their wraps. That was in and of itself, painful. The sore raw skin from the icy shirts was rubbed more so in getting the clothing off.

Fifteen minutes around the galley stove was all each shift was allowed, as it was time for the next crew to come in and start preparing for their shift on the ice. Preparing for a shift on the ice was the worst ordeal of all. The body had just gotten warm again, the clothes were still damp and cold. The sores were still painful. But all that had to be endured. They went through the motions, pulling on damp cold clothes, and then standing next to the stove in hopes of making the clothes a bit drier before going back out. Then it was thirty minutes of back breaking labor in a climate not fit for beast.

As much as the preparing to go out on the ice was the worst part of their day, coming in for the last time was the most pleasurable. The spirit of each man naturally rose, the body sensed that its day was done, and the final trip back to the ship was the easiest of all. The evening meal was served about a half hour after the last shift was in for the day and tended to be a happy affair.

As Christopher finished writing in his journal, he had doubts about their being able to complete the slip. The task seemed so complex and difficult. However, the Master said that if they were to have a chance at surviving their winter here, the ship must be brought out of the ice. He also heard several of the men saying things like, "I'll not curse the likes of Cape Horn again." He was also having such thoughts.

Thursday, October 28, 1762,
Trapped, Day 3
Snow!

At breakfast this morning they could hear the wind whipping through the rigging. Christopher and his crew were not in the best of spirits as they would be the first to venture out on the pack ice, especially since conditions didn't sound very appealing. As soon as they had finished eating and dressing, they made their way out through the foc'sle hatch only to find that it had started to snow heavily. Since the snow had only started, there was as yet not a lot of it covering the deck, but at the rate it was coming down that would soon change.

Out on the ice they found conditions beyond belief. The wind, strong as ever, was whipping the falling snow around so fiercely that they were in virtual white-out conditions. All of which made working conditions all but impossible.

Half of the shift spent the time clearing snow off the ice. While the other half worked at chipping and breaking chunks of ice out to form the slip. As planned, they were to cut a swath through the top of the ice the width of the ship and twice as long. They had hoped to complete this phase of the project today or tomorrow at the latest. Then they would chop the center of the slip out to fit the keel before digging a slope down to the bow. With all this snow they would require much more time to do the job.

After they had been out in the storm working for about twenty minutes, getting very little done, the Master appeared. He quickly realized how futile working in these conditions were and suspended all work for the duration of the snowstorm. All men were summoned back to the ship with tools in hand.

As soon as they entered the galley to strip out of their gear and warm up, Cooky noticed that Henry, a frail-looking kid from London, had not returned with the rest of them.

Everyone quickly pulled their heavy clothes back on and started out to look for him. To ensure that no one else became lost in the storm, Christopher went to the storage locker and retrieved several long lengths of quarter inch line. Each man had the line tied around his waist with about twenty feet of rope between him and the man on either side. Then, after the final man was secured to the rope, a length of one hundred feet was left behind. The free end was secured to the ship to ensure that everyone got back safely.

They fanned out from the ship in a large horseshoe shape, twenty men all told, each about twenty feet apart. First, they searched before the ship in the area of the slip, no luck there. Then they slowly started to arc around in the lee of the ship in a line nearly five hundred feet long.

Being in this line was a truly strange sensation. Christopher had men twenty feet on either side of him, yet he could not see or hear them. Because of this, they were to tug on the line should they find poor Henry. The problem was that when one would stumble and fall, they jerked the line as they went down. Each time this happened, the men next over would close in, causing the men on down the line to do the same. When they realized that nothing had been found, they would fan back out and continue. Bad as this situation was, there seemed to be no other way and thus they continued.

Facing frostbite and exhaustion, they had nearly given up hope when they started around the stern of the ship to begin searching into the wind and around the larboard side. Suddenly Christopher felt a strong pull on the line coming from his right side. At first, he felt that someone there had just taken a fall, as had happened so much already. The next pull nearly swept him off his feet, either the whole right line had collapsed, or Henry had been found. Christopher jerked on the left side of the line to signal those out that way. As slack in the line allowed, he turned to his right and followed the line, which led to the very stern of the ship. There, curled up into a tight ball to conserve enough heat to survive, was Henry, unconscious but alive. When all had gathered about him so the line could be untied, they scooped Henry up and raced him back aboard the ship.

Henry was laid out on the galley table; his face was almost purple. Quickly, they started to rub on his limbs while Cooky heated a pot of water on the galley stove. After removing Henry s clothes, they took towels soaked in Cooky's hot water and wrapped them around Henry's body. Slowly his color changed from purple to a warm red.

They had worked on Henry for over half an hour when he started to stir. At first, he didn't have the strength or the desire to do more than open his eyes. Christopher didn't think what he saw really registered. Then after another ten to fifteen minutes of constant rubbing and being wrapped in hot towels, Henry suddenly came to his senses and shot up in a sitting position. Finding himself clad only in shorts, he quickly pushed them away and jumped from the table, nearly collapsing as he did so.

"Take it easy lad," the Master warned. "You damn near froze to death out there."

Henry steadied himself against the galley table and pushed their offers to help him away. "Bloody right, I'd say. Couldn't find this bloody ship, Guv'ner. Where the bloody hell did everyone go to? And sudden like?"

"We were recalled to the ship," Christopher offered.

"Didn't ya bloody well think to tell me of it?" Henry was slowly becoming a little more stable now.

"We thought everyone had heard the call to return. George and Liverpool were on the other side of you, and they heard," Christopher tried to reason with him.

"Well, that may well be, Mr. Jamison," Henry nodded and pointed toward Christopher. "But I can assure you that I didn't hear any such call. If'n I had, I sure as hell would have done it, don't ya think?"

"Why'd you go to the rudder?" the Master asked.

Couldn't find the bloody damn ship! When I looked up from me work, the lot of them guys were gone, so's far as I could tell, so I thought I had somehow gotten twisted around in me work. I thought I knew me way back to the ship, only I couldn't find a stick of it, no sir, not one wit of timber did I see. Then I figured I had to find some shelter soon like, or I was gonna freeze real quick. I's found this wind break, but by that time I guess I wasn't thinkin' about what it was, nor did I much care. All that mattered was that it did offer shelter from that bloody awful wind. If I knew it to be the rudder, I sure as hell would have followed the hull around to the gangplank." With that Henry wrapped a hot towel around himself and sulked out of the galley to his berth in the foc'sle. At least he was alive and appeared to be fit. They were lucky just to find him in time to be able to do something for him. Christopher doubted that he could have lasted much longer out there.

As he listened to the wind howling through the rigging, Christopher thought of Eden, it was hard to believe that at a place just four to five thousand miles south of here, a paradise existed where the sun always shone. The gentle breeze was always warm, and the friendliness of the natives made life so pleasurable. Here in this region only night and death existed. A simple thing like what happened to Henry nearly took his life. This could be a very long winter indeed.

Friday, October 29, 1762
Trapped - Day Four
Day of Leisure

They had gone to bed to the sounds of the rigging straining in the blizzard outside. Not one amongst them regretted the extra time and care the Master took to have the timbers reinforced at Eden. When they awoke, the same vibrations from the mast could be felt as though they were charging across angry seas before a gale.

At Breakfast the Master informed them that conditions outside had not improved. Therefore, no one would venture out today. "Rest well men," the Master smiled. "We'll be giving it bloody hell when the weather does break. Hopefully tomorrow. "

Except for mealtimes, Christopher spent this entire day in his berth resting. He could hear and feel the wind starting to abate. They would most likely be back at their labors in the morning. The day of rest had been a godsend. His clothes were now completely dry and the raw skin around his armpits and neck felt so much better.

Saturday, October 30, 1762
Trapped - Day Five
Work Resumes

After breakfast the Master tried to get out on deck, only to find that the hatches were blocked by snow and ice. They were trapped within their own ship! Since time was of the greatest importance, the foc'sle hatch was chopped open far enough to allow a man outside to clear the snow and ice away enough to allow the hatch to swing open. They could get out.

The problem now was that nothing stopped the cold arctic air from blowing right down the companionway. John went to work at once fashioning a new hatch. In the meantime, they used blankets and bedding to block out the frigid cold wind.

More than half of this day was spent on removing snow from the decks and off the slip. The snow was piled alongside the slip in mounds so that once the ship was moved it would offer some protection to the hull from the icy wind.

With the snow removed, the work continued at a more rapid pace. The wind quieted down which made conditions on the ice more humane.

Sabbath, October 31, 1762
Trapped. Day Six
All Saints Day

No service today, as the Master claimed that God would understand if they worked this one Sabbath. The wind died out entirely, while work on the slip progressed smoothly. Each crew working an hour straight in overlapping shifts. By day's end the entire length of the slip was carved out of the ice. All that remained to be done was to chop the V shape wedge out of the middle of the slip and slope it off towards the bow.

Monday, November 1, 1762
Trapped - Day Seven
Slip Finished

The men seemed eager to be on with their labor this morning. Again, they worked in hour-long shifts, but most of them refused to take their breaks and worked straight through. As long as the wind wasn't beating against them, the conditions were almost tolerable.

Maybe they had grown accustomed to the conditions, if that was possible.

By day's end the slip was finished. The only thing that remained was the chopping around the ship and setting the block and tackles into the ice well enough to take on the weight of the ship.

As most of their energy was spent by the time the slip was finished, they returned to the ship for well-deserved rest and a hot meal. They would wait until tomorrow to set the block and tackles and chip the ship free.

Tuesday, November 2, 1762
Trapped - Day Eight
Failure

Half of the crew went with the Master to set the block and tackles out ahead of the slip. If all went well, by the time they had the blocks set, the others would have the ice around the ship cracked deep enough to allow the ship to be pulled free and up onto the ice.

From the start, they were plagued by hardships and trouble. The ice along the hull would not crack. They had to chop and drill for every inch of ice they removed. Not only did the ice break away in small slivers, but they had to chop as close to the ship's sides as possible without hitting it.

Those working around the ship took turns in swinging the picks and axes. In the time it took the others to set the block and tackles, they had managed to chop only half the way down the larboard side. The rest of the crew then joined them. It took more than six hours of constant hard labor to finally create a deep fissure all around the ship's hull.

They had been on the ice working themselves relentlessly for eight-and-a-half hours when they decided to attempt winching the ship out onto the ice. The general fear was that if they waited until tomorrow, it would most likely refreeze, and all the work would have to be done all over.

The lines were checked for frays one last time before they put the strain to them. They slowly and carefully laid into the tackles and kept a close eye on the ropes as they grew taut as bowstrings. Putting everything they had into the task, they heard the popping of hemp strands within the lines as the tremendous burden was laid into the tackles. The ship would not budge. The Master decided that with the amount of ice yet around the hull and the added weight of the cargo, the ship was simply too heavy for the tackles to handle. They would have to off load the cargo but that could wait until they were all rested.

As Christopher finished writing in his journal, he was totally exhausted. Exhausted physically and mentally, nothing seemed to go their way. Everything had to be fought for, every inch a struggle.

He sat on his berth and rethought that a moment. No, that wasn't quite right at all. They had outwitted the pirate. They had managed to find a full load of cargo long after the trading season had ended. They were able to spend nearly two months in Eden. Above all, they were still able to do battle tomorrow.

He suddenly felt like the Israelites after Moses had gone up on the mountain. They had been led out of Egypt, had been guided through the Red Sea, and yet lost their faith so easily. Christopher realized that he had much to be thankful for, and yet he became so discouraged. In truth he was ashamed at his lack of faith.

Wednesday, November 3, 1762
Trapped - Day Nine
Unloading Cargo

After the morning meal, they got right on the task of removing the cargo from the hold. As they carefully brought those precious items out of the hold, Christopher thought back to when Chips and he had packed them there. He took pride in the fact that the cargo had not shifted since they had left China.

One piece at a time, one crate of tea, one piece of furniture, one case of fine china, one crate of wallpaper. As each was brought forth, they were carefully placed under a sailcloth cover on the pack ice.

At eight bells, the usual beginning of the night watch, the Master split the crew into two halves. The first half he sent to their berths for rest. The second half worked on. Then in two hours the first half replaced the second. Through this manner the unloading continued through the night, two hours rest, two hours labor.

Thursday, November 4. 1762
Trapped, Day Ten
Wind

Unloading continued even through the morning meal. Half of the crew was fed, then the other half. The work went on, not that it mattered. One could scarcely get warm in the ship now anyway, with her bowels opened to the elements allowing access to the cargo. They ate a hot pudding of sorts that cooled the instant it hit their tin bowls.

Midday; the wind kicked up again and made their miserable existence even more miserable. Three men always had to be posted out on the pack ice to keep the canvass covering over the cargo. The wind grew in intensity throughout the day. By the time the entire cargo, including the firewood, was off the ship it was gusting to gale force.

Once again, the ship was closed to give it a chance at recovering its lost heat. Again, half of the crew was sent for rest. The other half attacked the ice around the ship's hull. It took more than half the night for the interior of the ship to heat back up.

Friday, November 5, 1762
Trapped-Day Eleven

Christopher was awakened after only an hour's sleep to loud grinding noises. The Master knew straight off what it was and immediately had all hands called out on the pack ice. Time was short.

Again, they put strain into the lines, and again the ship would not budge. In checking fissures around the hull, they found that most had once again frozen closed. About them on sides, they could hear cracks and brakes in the ice happening continually.

They quickly went to work chopping the fissures back open. Every man wielded an ax, shovel, or drill and attacked the ice with renewed purpose. Two hours later they felt that had gained enough on the ice, that the tackles were tried once again.

They held their breath as the lines grew taut, they could not hear the usual straining and popping from the lines due to the calamity happening around them. Suddenly the OCTAVIUS slipped an inch, then two! She was indeed moving;

Every inch took an incredible strain to achieve. Forty minutes after the ship started moving out of the water and onto the pack ice, the lines parted on one of the tackles. Luckily the other two held and the ship did not slide back into the hole they had just brought her out of.

Another set of lines were rigged as quickly as possible. It frustrated Christopher how an object such as a rope can have a mind of its own. When time is of the essence, life and death hanging in the balance, the damnable lines got twisted and knotted. The greatest reason for this was of course the elements. Each line was stiff and hard because of the cold. After much time and effort, the parted lines were replaced and the tackle back in working order. Once again, the ship was inching out onto the ice.

While the Master headed up the winching detail, the Mate headed up the balance of the men. Their job was to move the cargo from where it had been unloaded to a spot next to where the ship should finally come to rest. That way, once the ship was secured, the loading could begin at once.

Shorty after three bells of what would be the evening watch, the ship was finally in the desired position. Chunks of ice were wedged under the hull to brace her into position and hold her steady for the balance of the winter.

Suddenly a sharp cracking noise resounded from abeam of the icy hole that had been the ship's berth only this morning. A ridge of ice rose sharply as a deep crevice opened abreast of the ship's old hole. Amongst the roar of the shifting ice, Christopher heard a shrill scream and saw part of their cargo disappear into the crevice. The large stack of life-giving firewood that had stood between ship and cargo on the ice suddenly toppled over backwards and fell into the icy water of the ship's hole.

Soon as the ice stabilized, they quickly ran over to the crevice with ropes to rescue whoever had fallen into it. They were not to find anything due to the depth of the crevice. They didn't have the luxury of time for a search. The firewood had to be rescued out of water before it became frozen in. If they were to lose that firewood, they would all perish. They would find out later that the lost soul was Ian, the big grumpy Irishman.

The firewood that had not fallen into the hole was quickly gathered up and returned to the ship. The biggest problem before them was how to recover the wood that had fallen into the hole. The true problem was that the hole itself was ten to fifteen feet deep from the top of the pack ice to the frigid water below, with all sides to the hole extremely steep and hazardous. They devised a plan by which they would use several lines run taut over the hole, from which they would suspend a man, hopefully a light man, and lower this fellow to the water so he could scoop out the wood that floated on top.

True to his nature, young Richard volunteered for this task. He was indeed the lightest amongst them and had in past times proved his worth in tasks such as this. Finally, the Master consented to this plan. Richard was fixed into his harness and swung out over the hole. They slowly lowered him down to where he could reach out and haul several pieces of firewood from water. Then with the use of another line, they pulled him back over the pack ice so he could drop his load.

This process was repeated time and time again, but since he could haul only a couple of chunks at a time, the going was very slow. Every third trip he was given a warm dry pair of mittens to protect his hands. The wet mittens were returned to the ship with the retrieved wood, and then tossed on the galley stove to dry.

They had worked for over two hours when the pack ice beneath their feet shifted while they had Richard out over the hole. The lines went suddenly slack and poor Richard dropped in extremely cold ice water. Christopher was one of the first to regain his feet He hauled as fast as he could on the lines and pulled Richard to the ice pack. He quickly undid the ropes and ran Richard to the ship. Once in the galley he was stripped of his wet clothes and in hot towels. In the same manner that had worked so well for Henry, they rubbed Richard's limbs and kept the hot towel coming. Again, the results were great. In no time young Richard was once again in fine spirits.

Saturday, November 6, 1762
Tapped-Day Twelve

Bringing the cargo back aboard took them the entire day, and they had yet to finish. Now, the firewood that remained in the hole would be left there as it had already frozen in. Instead, they have turned their attention to the cargo. Most of that would have to be pried out of the snow and ice to be recovered as well.

The wind seemed to be building in strength. They could barely stand the extreme cold as it sliced through their clothing. Due to the large amount of firewood lost, the Master formulated a plan to conserve what was left.

After the evening meal, the fire would be kept low with just enough embers to allow it to be easily stoked in the morning.

Sabbath, November 7, 1762
Trapped - Day Thirteen

They spent this day mostly within the hull of the ship, as the wind outside was fierce, blowing the loose snow around in such confusion as to make work out on the ice impossible.

Christopher dreamed of Eden again; it wasn't a happy dream. They sailed into the lagoon on a fine beautiful morning. Oteria was standing on the shore, just as she was when they left, clad in that white blouse of his.

As soon as the hook was dropped, they 'lowered the boats and rowed for shore. The problem was that the harder they hauled on the oars, the farther the current took them away from the beach. Christopher screamed out for Oteria, he longed to hold her, to tell her that he would never leave her again. He had waited so long to return to this place only to have this impossible current taking him away from her. He screamed out her name again and again.

"Wake up, Mr. Jamison! Wake up!" It was Richard shaking him. Christopher bolted upright in his berth. It had been a dream, so lifelike, yet only a dream. He nearly cried as the realization of this sunk in.

For the next hour or two, Richard sat with Christopher, offering comfort. Christopher realized how much he cherished this young man. If not for his friendship here in this place, he would hold no hope whatsoever.

Monday, November 8. 1762
Trapped-Day 14

Two weeks have passed since they became trapped in this frozen wasteland. Two weeks Christopher thought, two weeks out of how many? Twenty maybe? That would mean they have already endured a tenth of the winter here. He thought that their situation was not so dire, they had less than one-third of their retrievable cargo yet on the ice.

The day was spent in retrieving that cargo. Since most of it was frozen into the ice, they had to chop it free. Then it was brought aboard to melt the remaining ice off before being stowed below.

By day's end, the cargo was aboard once more. "By day's end," Christopher thought. What a cruel joke, there was no day, he hated not seeing the sun. But soon, it would make little difference. As soon as they recovered all the remaining firewood that could be recovered, they would hole up within the ship for the balance of the winter. But to do so, they would have to recover as much of the firewood as they possibly could, since they had far too little of it now.

Tuesday, November 9, 1765,
Trapped - Day Fifteen

The entire day was spent recovering their precious firewood. They were able to bring quite a lot of it out of the already frozen hole. Instead of swinging Richard out over the hole, they could now climb down onto it and walk on the solid surface, the wood itself had to be chopped from the ice.

All had gone well, until Richard, who was at the time helping haul the freed wood back to the ship, had just returned from the ship and was slowly making his way across the frozen hole. Watching everything that was going on around him, he failed to keep a close eye on the ice in front of himself, stepping into an area that had been chopped open to retrieve wood, and had only partially refrozen. He quickly fell into the frigid water again. Everyone dropped what they were doing and rushed to the boy's aid.

For some reason Richard didn't come right back to the surface, taking nearly thirty seconds before bobbing back into the slushy ice of the hole. Christopher and George grabbed hold of the boy and ran him back aboard. This time the boy didn't spring back as before. He looked pale and remained very sluggish.

The Master decided at this point not to attempt retrieving any more firewood. The risk of wandering around out there in the dark, chopping holes and pulling ice-caked wood that may or may not bum, was not worth the risk.

Wednesday, November 10, 1762
Trapped - Day Sixteen
The Fire Goes Out!

Christopher awoke this morning to bitter coldness. The entire ship was cold beyond belief. He quickly put on his heavy clothes and made his way aft through the 'tween deck in search of the problem. As he made his way along, others had stirred as well, having the same idea as he. As they spoke to each other, the frost of their breath hung heavy in the frigid air. Liverpool reported that the fire had gone out last night. It happened when he tried to put more wood on the fire. Evidently the wood was water-logged and smothered the glowing embers instead of igniting.

Everyone, crew and officers alike, though now there seemed little reason for distinction between the two, gathered in the cold galley. Already frost was gathering on the inside of the hull. More and more, their surroundings began to feel as though they were residing in a cave of ice.

Outside they could hear the wind howling through the rigging. As Christopher sat at the well-worn planks that made up their tables, he could feel the mast vibrating from its top down to the keel. They waited, huddled together, praying and hoping for the Master to have success in relighting the flame.

All day they took turns at doing the same thing, trying to get that bloody water-soaked wood to relight. Christopher even went down into the hold and brought back some of the hand-painted wallpaper and whale oil in hopes of helping build a fire. Numerous times they got the mixture to flame, but only for a moment before it too died out. In the main cabin, the Master had whittled a small pile of wood shavings on the deck. All day, he sat before this pile striking flint against steel without success.

Over on the bench, next to the frosted windows to the rear of the cabin, Sarah sat holding Richard. Rocking back and forth, holding him close to her bosom.

Christopher slowly stepped over to Sarah and Richard. Sarah suddenly looked much older; her normally smooth face was lined with worry. As he stepped next to her, he placed his hand on her shoulder. She looked up as if asking for help, but what could he do?

Christopher then looked down at his dear young friend, Richard's face was a pale bluish color, his eyes appeared swollen and only partially open, the normal sparkle they held was gone.

"Mr. Jamison," Richard stirred, and did appear pleased to see him.

"I'm here my friend, I'm here."

"I wonder," he had to make an effort to speak. Then it only came out in a weak whisper. "I wonder, if you think it is warm in heaven? Warm like it was in Eden?"

"Don't talk like that." Christopher tried to sound firm. "Nobody is going to see heaven anytime soon.

"What do you think it'll be like?" Richard went on, pushing Christopher's statement aside.

"I think heaven will be very much like Eden," Christopher finally replied. In truth, he hoped that it would be. "The bible says that the sky is always clear, and the streets are paved with gold."

"Are there ships in heaven? Ships like this one, so we can sail across blue water under blue, sunny skies?" Richard seemed to have to try harder to speak.

"There are ships and perfect oceans to sail upon until the end of eternity." Christopher assured him. "And fine sailors like Red, Chips, and Ian to man the helm."

"It sounds so nice." Richard smiled faintly then took a more serious look. "Thank you for being my friend and teaching me so much about sailing."

"The pleasure was all mine," Christopher replied through eyes that had started to moist up. He squeezed the boy's hand, then took his leave. The last thing he wanted the boy to see, was him crying.

Richard went to sleep around noon, and for the balance of the day Sarah sat there rocking her son back and forth. Holding him close, trying to warm his body with hers. All the while the temperature within the hull continually dropped, the inside of the hull now had a complete coating of frost.

With nothing to do, and conditions getting worse by the minute, most of the crew took to their berths in hopes of finding some form of comfort there. Christopher did likewise for a time, but the blankets felt as though they had been stored in the pack ice outside. He laid there and shivered for the better part of an hour before he decided to record this day in his journal.

His first order of business to be able to write, was to place his inkwell under his arm to thaw it. As he sat there writing, John came by. He asked if Christopher knew what he found to be the most curious thing about this whole situation? Christopher replied that he didn't know and was informed that John's toes were cold! Not his real toes, but the ones to the foot he had taken off! The toes he no longer had were cold! Then John laughed and asked if Christopher thought one could suffer frostbite on toes, one no longer had?

Thursday, November 11, 1762
Trapped, Day 17-Death

    Christopher found his mind growing sluggish, he wandered about the 'tween deck, going from galley to cabin. Checking, rechecking, and reporting to each on how the other was doing in the attempt to rekindle the fire. He could no longer feel his toes, his ears were causing him pain. Before he could write in his journal, he had to place his hands inside his clothes just to be able to bend his fingers. He had to write in short series as his ink and fingers were freezing quite quickly.
    Sometime this morning young Richard passed away. Sarah had probably known for some time, but when Christopher entered the cabin, he found her still on the window bench rocking back and forth, clutching the cold stiff body of her child. He let her hold him for a time, and then slowly took him from her. He had to bite his lip to keep from crying. Within his arms was someone who had made this voyage a pleasure for him, Richard always

gave so much more than he asked. His small gentle face always alight with an infectious smile. Always a cheerful disposition, always willing to do his part. Now here he was, dead in Christopher's arms. He held the body close to his chest as he carried him to the center of the cabin and laid him near his father on the deck, then covered him with a great pea coat.

The Master had been continually working the flint and steel since yesterday. Now as he drove the flint against the steel, he did so with slow, hopeless strokes. Christopher understood that for the Master there seemed little reason to rekindle that fire.

The Mate had finally talked the Master into allowing him to take over. The Master lifted the coat covering his son. He bent down, picked the body off the deck and held him close. Christopher heard him say how sorry he was. He kissed the boy s forehead and laid him back on the deck, recovering him with the coat.

Death seemed to roam the ship, searching for its next victim, it should not take long to lay claim to someone. Christopher doubted that death was far from any of them now. He sensed that the moment he lifted the boy s body away from Sarah's breast. He wondered if Richard was finally safe and warm in heaven.

The temperature within the ship was unbearable, their breath nearly froze on their lips. A few of the men wandered about aimlessly. Mostly, Christopher thought, to keep from freezing. He looked about himself as best he could in the near total darkness, a small amount of light filtered through the port holes, the only thing that allowed them to see at all. The whole scene within this ice encrusted hull was dark and growing steadily colder.

With the whale oil gone, the lamps were useless. Now, not only did they not have the warmth of a fire to sustain life, but they were also fated to slowly die in near total darkness. Christopher's eyes were accustomed to the darkness enough to allow him to travel about the ship and write in his journal. He wanted so dearly to record all that he could in the event that one day the ship was found here in the ice. Hopefully then family and friends back home would no longer wonder of their fate.

As Christopher was about to leave the main cabin, the Master called out to him. He turned to reply but found no words. Instead he stepped around the coat covering poor Richard and up to the master's desk. The Master looked up slowly from deep red eyes, tears flowed only to freeze to the side of his face. For the first time since Christopher had signed aboard, this man before him, the man he had grown to admire and love as a father, looked so frail and defeated.

"Could you fill in the log?" His eyes showed all the agony of his broken heart. "My hands seem frozen," he said, looking down at his hands in a helpless manner.

"I'd be honored Sire," Christopher quickly replied. It would be his first entry in an official logbook, and it would likely be the last as well.

The Master began to mumble something, Christopher thought it was what he wanted him to write, then from across the cabin Sarah suddenly spoke, the first she had done so this day. "It's getting warmer, warmer I say!" She seemed so full of hope. "I no longer feel so cold! Cooky must have gotten the fire started in the stove!"

The Master looked up into Christopher's face and their eyes met, they both knew that death had found its next claim. The temperature within the ship was dropping, not rising, poor Sarah was freezing to death. Again, the Master started mumbling what he wanted in the log, the only part of which Christopher could catch were the coordinates. These he placed in the log along with a bit about their plight. As in his cabin, he had to warm the ink before he could write.

To thaw the ink well, Christopher had to place it under his shirt and against his body, twice already today his inkwell had frozen to his skin, this one did the same, he now had three patches of flesh torn from beneath his arm.

Before returning to his cabin to continue his writing, Christopher surveyed the main cabin as if for the last time, which he realized was possible. The Master was seated at his desk, slightly hunched over as if in prayer. Sarah laid on the window bench, head resting on her aim, watching the Mate who was sitting before the pile of shavings, striking the flint and steel for all he was worth.

On his way aft, he decided to stop by the galley to check on their progress, all had retired for the balance of the day. The wet wood would not light. They had given up, and rightly so, at least with the wood being so wet. Maybe, if the Lord blessed them with milder conditions tomorrow, and the wood had dried a bit, they might succeed, but not today.

As Christopher sat in his cabin recording his thoughts and feelings, he fully realized the situation. Death was upon them, sweeping about their ship as a stench from a rotten bilge. He could hear a moan or two coming from the foc'sle. John said that his missing foot hurt the worst; odd.

It was strange how clear some things become when one is at death's door. It suddenly occurred to him, that as they slowly froze to death, they were alone. Each one of them was alone. As surely as he could not share in his mates' pain, they could not share in his. Richard died this morning. They lived, he died alone. If he was in the middle of the Pacific Ocean in a small boat alone and dying there, he would not be any more alone than he was right here and now.

He found it odd that they each retired to their berths, little was said. What was there to say? He made his peace with God for his transgressions, especially his lust over Oteria. Even so, he wished that he could see her one last time. He was sure that God understood his weakness for her.

Christopher no longer felt like writing, so he added one smaller paragraph. "If anyone finds this ship and within it, this journal, please see it to my father's hand. My parents will wonder, as will John's wife and children. Please see to it that they know the truth, and whatever comfort they can find in it."

CHAPTER FOURTEEN
BAFFIN BAY-DISCOVERY

Friday, August 11, 1775
Baffin Bay

The HERALD, a whaler out of Greenland had just survived the most terrifying night of their lives. A sudden storm had whipped the enormous body of arctic cold water known as Baffin Bay into a maelstrom. The blinding snow, the crashing waves. The most unnerving of all was the three times they found themselves slammed against the jagged sides of the towering icebergs that dotted this dangerous sea.

As quickly as the storm had come, it was gone. The morning broke over a once again calm frigid sea. As the sun rose in the sky it reflected off the towering white bergs in breathtaking prismatic beauty. Captain Warren scratched his thinning hair in wonder. "How could this place be so calm after a night like that?" he thought aloud as he made his way forward for breakfast. He had made it nearly to the hatch when the lookout sang out, "Sails Ho!"

"Where and away?" Captain Warren called out.

"Broad on the starboard beam," the lookout yelled back in reply. "On the far side of those bergs!"

Another ship in these parts was a rare find indeed, especially after last night. Warren and the rest of his hardy crew moved over to the starboard rail and waited for this stranger to make his appearance. To a man, they had never seen anything like what they now beheld.

The eerie phantom glided out from behind the bergs with a frosty mist about her, her rigging showed her to be a brig. Her yards hung at odd angles to her masts, her sails hung ragged from those yards, and several lines swung slack in their blocks. The stranger had the look of death.

The morning sun reflected off the frosted coating of her timbers, giving her an appearance more of an apparition than real. The water around her showed no signs of a wake, she was being borne by the current.

As the two vessels neared each other, Warren attempted to hail the stranger but to no avail. A quick thinker, Warren instantly realized that if this ship was indeed a derelict, as she appeared to be, he could claim salvage rights and take her in tow, so he quickly ordered the longboat away.

Warren studied the strange vessel as they were rowed to her side. Not finding a proper way of scaling her larboard side, they came about the stem to try the starboard. As they rounded the stern, Warren looked up across the stern at this stranger's weathered nameplate, "OCTAVIUS". Her home port could not be read. He tried to hail her again, again no reply. The hull appeared to be intact. The OCTAVIUS rode deep, but on even keel. The weather had worked her over to be sure, but Warren could not determine from her appearance how long she had been adrift. From her condition, he thought it to be a year or more.

Once on her deck, Warren and his crew found the upper deck deserted, ice and snow covered everything. The ice crackled under their feet as they surveyed the entire deck. In spots the deck timbers were weak and spongy- Warren and "his men realized the danger and walked across the OCTAVIUS's deck very slowly and carefully. This deck had not been touched by man for some time. Many of the lines were rotted about the bits and if not for the ice that held them together, they would surely have fallen into dust.

As Warren made his way toward the foc'sle hatch, several of his crew made it clear that they would stay on the deck. "Nothing good can come of going down there," they warned. The hatch was frozen in place and had to be kicked free. As it slowly opened under protest, a stale musty odor welled up from below and nearly sickened Warren. He took his time, growing accustomed to the foul smell and the darkness before stepping down the companionway.

Each step creaked in protest, but none broke. At the bottom Warren stopped suddenly in total disbelief. All around him, frozen to death in their berths, he counted twenty-eight men. Then another, in a small side cabin toward the aft section of the 'tween deck. Several more of Warren's crew decided to take their leave and returned topside. Warren proceeded aft to the main cabin. As he stepped into the cabin, he quickly stepped back, startled by what he first thought to be living souls, before realizing that they too were quite dead.

To the starboard side at the very end of the cabin was a woman laying upon a bench, head held by one arm. The woman 's face was pleasing to look at, with eyes as clear as if they could still see. He followed her gaze to where a man was hunched over a small pile of wood shavings on the deck. This fellow's hands held a flint and steel. "Too bad the poor bastard didn't succeed," Warren thought. Then he noticed what he thought must surely be the Master, sitting hunched over at the desk. Warren stepped toward the desk, nearly stumbling over a heavy coat laying on the deck. He picked the coat up and found a child frozen to death beneath it. All the dead he had seen looked as though they had died that morning, at least until he looked closely at the Master. A thin greenish mold covered the side of this one's face.

It was the first evidence he had, that they may have died some time before. On the comer of the desk sat a rotting leather-bound journal. Warren recognized it at once as the ship's log. He carefully picked it up, the leather binding had all but rotted and nearly fell off at his touch.

By this time all his crew had deserted him. They were quite anxious to return to the HERALD. Warren knew that he would not be able to salvage this ship. Maybe that was for the best, although he wasn't overly superstitious, nothing good can come of towing a ship filled with death into port. What if they had died of something other than exposure? Being here in this place, he felt certain what had caused their death, but just the same, he would not attempt to salvage their ship.

On his way back through the 'tween deck, something in the small cabin caught his eye. A small leather-bound journal with lots of loose-leaf papers sticking out from the binding. He quickly stepped into the cabin and took the book. As he was turning to leave, he looked over at the dead man on the berth.

The corpse was that of a fair-looking lad of about twenty to twenty-five years of age. The corpse had a death grip on the woolen blankets that covered it, but that was not what caught Warren's eye. Sticking out from under a corner of the blanket was a small carved sculpture of exquisite beauty. Warren reached over and slowly pulled the figurine free from the bed and quickly turned from the cabin.

Once on deck, Warren found that most of his men were already back in the longboat, quite ready to be away from this ghost ship. Having his hands full, he handed the logbook over the rail to those already in the boat. The other book and sculpture he quickly tucked into his coat.

Back on the deck of the HERALD, Warren and his men watched in awed silence as the OCTAVIUS slowly drifted with the current and out of sight. When the ship could no longer be seen, Warren returned to his own main cabin, and then remembered the recovered logbook and sent for it. He was disappointed to find that all that remained of the logbook was four pages. The rest had fallen out and into the sea when transferring ships. The first few pages spoke of the crew and departing England on September 10, 1761. He looked at that date again. Then he turned to the last of the four pages and was relieved to find what was indeed the last entry to be made into the log. This was certain as the bottom half of the page was still blank. Not something that was done unless the log ended there.

>Warren read slowly, almost reverently.
>NOVEMBER 11, 1762, THURSDAY
>"We have now been enclosed in the ice
>Seventeen days, and our approximate
>Position is longitude 160 west, latitude
>75 north. The fire went out yesterday
>And our Master had been trying to
>Rekindle it again, but without success.
>He has handed the steel and flint to the
>Mate. The Master's son died this morning, his wife says she no longer feels the terrible cold. The rest of us seem to have no relief from the agony."

Warren stared in total disbelief at the date and the location given in this entry. ''Could it be?" he questioned. "That entry was made thirteen years ago! And from somewhere in the Arctic Sea!"

When Warren returned to port, he carefully checked out the location given in the OCTAVIUS's logbook. He had already read the journal found in the small cabin and felt a strange kinship with its author. From what he had learned from it, he was not surprised to find that the location given in the logbook placed the OCTAVIUS a point north of Point Barrow when the last entry was made. The OCTAVIUS had become the first ship in history to successfully navigate the Northwest Passage! And she had done so with her entire compliment of crew dead in their berths below deck. She had taken it upon herself to drift with the currents until she was once again trapped in the winter's ice. Then when the thaw came, she would drift some more. Year after year the ship held herself together and slowly completed the trek.

The old man slowly knelt at the well-kept grave of his beloved wife. His heart was weary of struggling along alone. His eyes were swollen and red from crying. He had cried most of the night as he had read the words of his long-lost son.

"We now know what became of our beloved Christopher, Mother," the man sighed. "He did us proud, right to the end." As tears rolled down his weathered face, the old man clawed out a small mound of dirt and placed the small journal and a wooden sculpture of an exotic looking, half-naked maiden into the ground and covered them.

"That's all of him there is, mother. But what there is, will rest with us forever."

June 23, 1767
Eden (soon to be known as Tahiti)

As the British exploration ship DOLPHIN dropped hook in the lagoon, the natives were upon them, offering coconuts and breadfruit for trade. It had been five long years since they had seen a great ship, and they were eager to renew friendships. When Captain Samuel Wallis went ashore, the natives were surprised that they recognized none of these men. And no one was more surprised than their Queen Oteria, who had brought her four-year-old Prince Tristafe, down to the beach in hopes of meeting his father.

FINAL NOTE: On August 11, 1775, the whaler HERALD did discover a ship named OCTAVIUS adrift in Baffin Bay. The last entry in the recovered logbook was as it appears in the story. This is a fictionalized account of the OCTAVIUS's last voyage. The remains of that logbook are stored away in the Archives of the Registrar of Shipping in London, England.

Made in the USA
Monee, IL
24 August 2024